DEFEND
THE
DAWN

ALSO BY BRIGID KEMMERER

Letters to the Lost
More Than We Can Tell
Call It What You Want

—◆—

A Curse So Dark and Lonely
A Heart So Fierce and Broken
A Vow So Bold and Deadly

—◆—

Forging Silver into Stars

—◆—

Defy the Night

—◆—

Storm
Spark
Spirit
Secret
Sacrifice

—◆—

Thicker Than Water

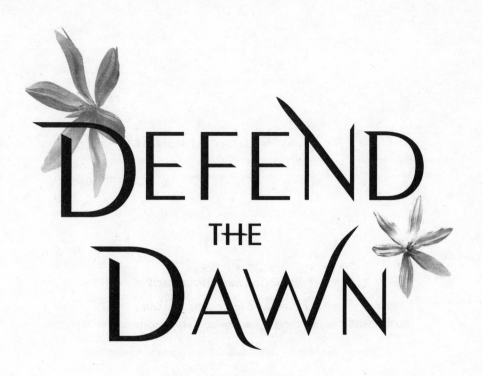

DEFEND THE DAWN

BRIGID KEMMERER

BLOOMSBURY
NEW YORK LONDON OXFORD NEW DELHI SYDNEY

BLOOMSBURY YA
Bloomsbury Publishing Inc., part of Bloomsbury Publishing Plc
1385 Broadway, New York, NY 10018

BLOOMSBURY and the Diana logo are trademarks of Bloomsbury Publishing Plc

First published in the United States of America in September 2022
by Bloomsbury YA

Text copyright © 2022 by Brigid Kemmerer
Map by Virginia Allyn

Bloomsbury books may be purchased for business or promotional use. For information
on bulk purchases please contact Macmillan Corporate and Premium Sales Department at
specialmarkets@macmillan.com

Library of Congress Cataloging-in-Publication Data
available upon request
ISBN 978-1-5476-1007-5 (hardcover) • ISBN 978-1-5476-1008-2 (e-book)
978-1-5476-1195-9 (exclusive edition A) • 978-1-5476-1194-2 (exclusive edition B)

Book design by Jeanette Levy and Yelena Safronova
Typeset by Westchester Publishing Services
Printed and bound in Great Britain by the CPI Group (UK) Ltd, Croydon CR0 4YY
2 4 6 8 10 9 7 5 3 1

To find out more about our authors and books visit www.bloomsbury.com
and sign up for our newsletters.

For Jonathan and Kara

THE KINGDOM

The
Kingdom of Ostriary

TRADER'S LANDING

SUNKEEP

STEEL CITY

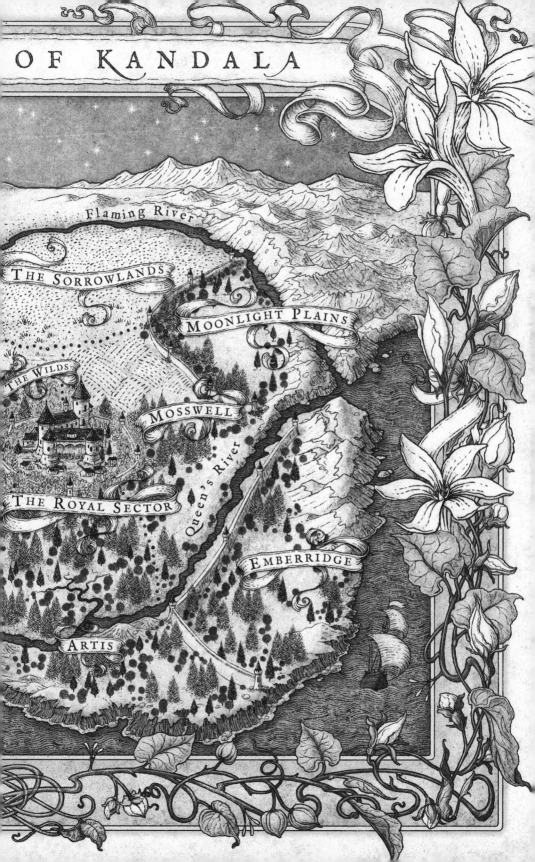

OF KANDALA

Flaming River

THE SORROWLANDS

MOONLIGHT PLAINS

THE WILDS

MOSSWELL

Queen's River

THE ROYAL SECTOR

EMBERRIDGE

ARTIS

THE POLITICAL LEADERS OF KANDALA

NAME	ROLE	SECTOR
King Harristan	King	Royal
Prince Corrick	King's Justice	Royal
Barnard Montague (Deceased)	Consul	Trader's Landing*
Allisander Sallister	Consul	Moonlight Plains
Leander Craft (Deceased)	Consul	Steel City
Jonas Beeching	Consul	Artis
Lissa Marpetta	Consul	Emberridge
Roydan Pelham	Consul	The Sorrowlands
Arella Cherry	Consul	Sunkeep
Jasper Gold	Consul	Mosswell

*Sometimes called "Traitor's Landing" after the former king and queen were assassinated by Consul Montague, leaving Harristan and his younger brother, Corrick, in power.

THE REBELS

NAME	ROLE
Tessa	Apothecary*
Karri	Apothecary
Lochlan	Metalworker

*Now working in service to the king

THE *DAWN CHASER* CREW

NAME	ROLE
Rian Blakemore	Captain
Gwyn Tagas	First Lieutenant
Sablo	Second Lieutenant
Marchon	Navigator and Quartermaster
Dabriel	Cook

THE CURE

The only known cure for the fever is an elixir created from dried Moonflower petals, a plant native only to two sectors: Moonlight Plains and Emberridge. Moonflower petals are strictly rationed among sectors, and quantities are limited.

Consul Sallister has promised to provide enough Moonflower for the population of Kandala for eight weeks.

Many citizens fear that it won't be enough.

DEFEND
THE
DAWN

CHAPTER ONE

The Outlaw

When I was a boy, summer nights in the Wilds always smelled like adventure. Fresh pine boughs. The cloying sweetness of honeysuckle. Someone always had a bonfire going, with plenty of sour ale to pass around. The air was full of lively conversation, or bawdy drinking songs, or men swearing as they lost their last coins on a bet.

Now, summer nights carry the underlying scent of rotting corpses. Most of the fires that burn are funeral pyres. Singing is rare.

Drinking is still common. Maybe more so.

Extra Moonflower petals have been promised, but they've been slow in coming. No one here trusts anyone in the palace. Few people trust the consuls. Even the rebels who are supposedly negotiating for better access to medicine have become suspect.

The rumors—and there are *many*—are outrageous.

When I'm here in the Wilds, I keep my head down and do what I can.

The winding paths through the woods are empty at this time of night, but I cling to the darkness like a ghost. I don't want to run afoul of the night patrol. The pouch at my belt is heavy with my own copper coins, but I have a red mask over my eyes, a hat pulled low over my forehead. In this getup, at this hour, I'd be detained. Worse, I'd be locked in the Hold to await an interrogation. That's the last thing I need.

I step off the trail and slip a few coins from my pouch. The first house is smaller than most, likely only one room inside, but there's a chicken coop and a rabbit hatch out back. I've never seen who lives here, but the animals seem well cared for. I intend to leave a few coppers on the barrel of grain, but then I see a small bundle wrapped up in muslin, next to a misspelled message written in the dust.

THENK You.

I unwrap the muslin to discover a soft pair of biscuits that smell of cheese and garlic.

It's not the first gift I've found, but each time I do, it makes something in my stomach clench. I want to leave it, because I don't need gifts. I don't do this for payment.

But this gift meant something to the person who left it. I don't want to be rude.

I wrap the biscuits back up in the muslin and tuck the bundle into my pack. After I leave a few coins on the barrel, I move on.

The next house has several children, including a new baby. Sometimes I hear it squalling in the middle of the night, and I step lightly so as not to be noticed. I slip coins into the pockets of clothes left to dry on a line. At the next house, I leave the coins on the doorstep. At the next, the coins go onto the windowsill.

At the fifth house, I'm leaving coins beside an ax blade that's been left embedded in a stump, when a figure leaps out of the shadows.

"Aha!" a whispered voice says. "I caught you."

I startle so hard that the coins scatter into the grass. I grab the ax handle and whirl.

I don't know what I'll do if it's the night patrol. An ax won't do much against a crossbow. They aren't supposed to shoot on sight, but I've heard stories of their violence from enough rebels and outlaws to know that what they're *supposed* to do is not always the end result.

Regardless, I stand my ground, the ax ready.

The figure springs back, hands raised. "Whoa!"

It's not the night patrol. It's . . . it's a girl. She's tall, nearly as tall as I am, which makes me think she's older, but her features still have the softness of childhood, and her limbs are lean and willowy. She's in a pale sleeping shift that leaves her arms bare, the hem trailing in the grass. Her blond hair is in a messy braid that reaches past her waist.

"I don't want trouble," I say to her.

"You have an ax." Her voice is low, but she doesn't sound afraid. "You won't be getting any from me."

I ease my grip on the handle and let the ax head hang to the ground. "Then return to where you came from, and I'll be on my way."

Now that I don't have a "weapon," she lowers her hands, but she doesn't turn away. Her eyes narrow as she peers at me, then glances into the darkness at my back. "You're alone."

"I am."

"When coins started showing up, my cousin thought Weston and Tessa were making rounds again. You're not Wes, are you?"

"No." I stare into the shadows, wondering if anyone else is hiding among the trees. My heart hasn't stopped pounding since she appeared out of nowhere.

"Well," she continues in her quiet voice, "rumor says Weston Lark was really the king's brother, anyway. Prince Corrick."

"I've heard those stories."

"One of the rebels caught him," she continues. "In Artis, I think. He was dressed as an outlaw. Mask and all. The king's army had to rescue him."

Rumors about *that* are everywhere. I glance at the sky, which hasn't begun to lighten, but it won't be long. It'll be dawn soon, and I need to get back. I hesitate, considering, then swing the ax into the stump. The noise echoes in the woods, and I wince. The girl's eyes flare, and she inhales sharply, but I drop a few coins on the stump, then turn away to walk.

My shoulders are tight, and I brace for her to send up an alarm— but I forget that people in the Wilds tend to look out for each other. Instead, she jogs through the grass to walk at my side.

"If you're not Weston Lark," she says, "what's your name?"

"It doesn't matter."

"Your mask is red, anyway," she chatters on, heedless. I was thinking she might be fourteen or fifteen, but now I'm thinking she's even younger. "The red makes you look like a fox. I heard Weston's mask was black."

"Go home."

It doesn't work. "Some people think your coins are a trap," she says, striding along beside me. "My uncle calls you—"

"A *trap*!" I swing around to study her. "How could coins left in the middle of the night be a trap?"

"Well, some of the rumors said that Prince Corrick was *pretending* to be Weston Lark so he could trick people into revealing the smugglers." Her eyes are wide and guileless. "So he could execute them."

I snort and keep walking. "That feels like a lot of effort for a man who can execute anyone he likes."

"So you don't think that's true?"

"I have a hard time imagining the brother to the king was secretly dressing as an *outlaw* to catch smugglers."

"Well, he's called Cruel Corrick for a reason. Or do you think the king is the vicious—*ouch!*" She stumbles, then grabs my arm for balance, hopping on one foot.

She's making so much noise that I have half a mind to jerk free and leave her here. But I'm not heartless. I swallow a sigh and look down.

She's barefoot, holding one foot high off the ground. A streak of blood glistens along the pale stretch of her heel, black in the moonlight.

"Is it bad?" she's saying, and there's a hint of a tremor in her voice.

"I can't tell. Sit."

She sits, folding her leg over her opposite knee. Blood drips into the grass below. Something gleams in the wound, either a sharp rock or a bit of steel.

She grimaces. "Ma will kill me."

"You made so much noise, the night patrol might beat her to it." I drop my pack in the grass, then crouch to study her injury. "You should've gone home."

"I wanted to know who you are. My cousin won't believe I caught you."

"You didn't *catch* me. Hold still." I pull the muslin-wrapped biscuits out of my pack and unwind the fabric. I hold out the food to her. "Here."

She frowns, but takes it. I move to pull the debris free, but then think better of it. I give her a level look. "This might hurt. You need to stay quiet."

She clenches her teeth and nods fiercely.

I close my fingers on the offending item and tug it free. She squeals and nearly yanks her ankle out of my grasp, but I keep a tight grip and give her a warning glare. She sucks in a breath and goes still.

Blood is flowing freely down her foot now, but I put a fold of muslin against the wound, then swiftly wrap up her foot, tearing the ends so I can knot it in place.

She blinks tears out of her eyes, but none fall. "What was it? A rock?"

I shake my head. "An arrowhead."

"From the night patrol?"

I shrug. "From someone wearing shoes, most likely."

"Is that supposed to be a joke?"

"You'll have to flush that when you get home," I say. I straighten, then sling the pack over my shoulder. I'll have to find a new route after this. I don't need people sitting in the dark, waiting for me—not even a girl who's barely more than a child. "Be safe," I say. "I have to go."

She scrambles to her feet, limping on her injured one. "But I still don't know your name!"

"Call me whatever you want," I say. "I won't come this way again."

"No!" she calls. "Wait. Please. This is my fault—you don't—" Her voice breaks like she's going to cry. "You don't know how much we all need—"

I turn back and slap a hand over her mouth. "Do you truly *want* to draw the night patrol?"

She shakes her head quickly, mollified. "But your food," she murmurs behind my hand, holding out the biscuits I'd given her.

You don't know how much we all need . . .

I do know how much they all need. The outlaws Wes and Tessa once provided a lot to these people. I've heard so many stories that it makes my head spin. I can't make up for their disappearance with a few coins left here and there. I'm not entirely sure why I keep trying.

"Keep the food." I drop my hand, then fish in my pouch for more coins. "And keep your silence." I hold them out.

She looks at the coins in my palm, then nods quickly and swipes them.

An alarm bell begins ringing in the Royal Sector, and she jumps. I sigh. "Go home."

"You'll come back?" she says.

I give her a stern look. "As long as no one is waiting in the shadows next time."

She beams, and it lights up her face. "I promise."

"What's *your* name?" I say.

"Violet."

"Take care of that foot, Violet."

She nods. "Thank you, Fox."

That makes me smile. I touch the brim of my hat to her, then sprint into the darkness.

CHAPTER TWO

Tessa

There are five men at this table, and most of them want to kill each other. It's making negotiations difficult.

There's another young woman, too, but I don't think either of us are having murderous thoughts. Karri looks overwhelmed by the fact that she's inside the palace. Her brown eyes are wide, and her slender fingers keep fidgeting with the seam of her skirts. A month ago, we would've been whispering about this whole situation, sharing our worries and trying to help each other cope with all that's happened. But now she's in love with one of the leaders of the rebel faction, while I'm involved with the king's brother. That's built a barrier between us that tugs at my heart—but I don't know how to tear it down. Right now, it seems thicker than the wall surrounding the Royal Sector.

Quint probably doesn't want to kill anyone either. The Palace Master is sitting at the opposite end, ostensibly here to keep a record of everything said. His jacket is only half buttoned, a loose lock of red hair drifting across his forehead. He's scratching notes in a leather-bound folio with a fountain pen.

Lochlan, the rebel leader, is seated to my left, and he casts a glare at Quint every few moments. If he had his way, he'd probably kill *everyone*. He already tried once.

"What is he writing?" Lochlan says. "What are you *doing*?"

Quint finishes whatever he was writing, then looks up. "I am here to document your demands," he says equably. "And the resulting response."

"I haven't made any demands yet," Lochlan growls.

Quint isn't easily cowed. I've seen him maintain composure while pieces of the Royal Sector were literally burning to the ground, so a little aggression barely registers. He's also one of the most considerate men I've ever met, and he has a bizarre talent for making people feel at ease during the prickliest of situations.

Quint sets down his pen and turns the paper around so it's more easily visible. "Just now, I was recording the names of those in attendance," he says plainly, without a lick of condescension, "along with the date and location of our meeting. I would gladly have a copy made for you to review, if you would like."

Lochlan glances at the paper, then back up at Quint. His jaw is tight.

"He's just taking notes," Karri says softly, with an apologetic glance at me. She rests a hand on Lochlan's forearm, but he doesn't relax.

Across from Karri is Allisander Sallister, the consul of Moonlight Plains. He should be in prison—or more likely, swinging from the end of a rope—yet he maneuvered his way out of a death sentence when he claimed that no one could handle the harvesting and distribution of Moonflower petals with as much efficiency as the truce with the rebels demanded. The worst part is that he's probably right. It's the only reason he's sitting here. Eight weeks isn't a lot of time to dispense medicine. It's already taken *two* just to get everyone into the same room.

Allisander's expression is a combination of boredom and arrogance. He sighs and pulls a gold pocket watch from under the table to glance at it.

"Do you have somewhere to be, Consul?" says Corrick, seated at one end of the table, directly to my right. His voice is cold, his blue eyes like ice. This is the Prince Corrick I once feared. The one many people in Kandala *still* fear.

He'd light Consul Sallister on fire right this very instant if he could.

The consul glances up. "Many places I'd *rather* be. Surely you could have waited to summon me until the ignorants were fully instructed as to the typical arrangement of a meeting."

Lochlan's chair scrapes back as he begins to rise. "Are you insulting me, you spoiled—"

"You have to ask?" Consul Sallister strokes his goatee. "I suppose I shouldn't be surprised."

"Enough," says King Harristan, and I can't tell if he's talking to Consul Sallister, to Lochlan, or to the guards who've moved away from the door to prevent any trouble. But the king's voice is low, coolly placid. A level command spoken by a man who's used to immediate obedience. His eyes, a darker blue than his brother's, shift to me. "Tessa, you should begin."

"Right," I say. "Of course." I smooth my hands over my skirts to calm my nerves, but the slippery silk does nothing to quell my anxiety. I'm probably leaving handprints on the material.

I wish I were back in the infirmary, calculating dosages with the palace physicians. Weights and measures and vials don't care about diplomacy.

Really, though, if I could wish for anything, I'd wish to be back in the Wilds, sneaking through the darkness with Wes. Picking locks and stealing medicine might have been dangerous—and illegal—but I always felt like I was making a difference.

Here in the palace, trying to convince everyone to work together, I feel like I'm just making a mess. King Harristan and Prince Corrick have been seen as callous and cruel for so long that it's going to be tough to get anyone at this table to agree.

Allisander sighs and peers at his pocket watch again. Harristan clears his throat.

Corrick doesn't glance at me, but he picks up his pen and scratches a few words at the base of his own folio, then casually sets the pen down. The motion draws my eye to the words.

Mind your mettle.

I almost flush. He used to say that to me when we were outlaws: times when we were in danger, or when the sickness was too much to bear. It always helped.

It helps now.

I nod slightly, then look around the table. "Consul Sallister has promised medicine for eight weeks, but beyond that—"

"It should have been two," the consul says.

"It was eight," says Harristan.

"It should have been *two*. I told Corrick that eight was impossible when he made this ridiculous guarantee. Before any of this happened, I said that the spring rains had caused a supply issue—"

"You said there *could be* a supply issue," Corrick says.

"And there is," Allisander says. "If you aren't making payment for eight weeks of medicine, I don't have the guaranteed revenue to pay my workers, so you can't blame them for walking off the fields."

"So there . . . won't be eight weeks of medicine?" Karri says.

"There will be," says the king, and his voice has a note of finality. "Consul Sallister made the promise as witnessed and recorded. If you've stopped paying your laborers, Consul, you can work the fields yourself. Tessa, continue."

I take a deep breath. "I have been sharing my findings with the palace physicians, and we feel that combining Moonflower with roseseed oil to create a longer-lasting elixir may allow the medicine to have a greater effect in a smaller quantity."

"Or more people could die," Consul Sallister says. He sounds like he wouldn't mind.

"Perhaps you could wait in the Hold," Corrick says icily. "I'm certain Quint would be happy to provide a copy of the meeting notes to you as well."

"Tessa," Harristan says evenly, as if neither of them have said a word. "Continue."

"If we were to adjust the dosage this way, the eight weeks of medicine could stretch to *twelve* weeks—"

"Is he right?" says Lochlan. "Would more people die?"

"I don't think so," I say honestly. "When I was delivering medicine in the Wilds, we provided a similar dosage, and we saw it work."

Lochlan is looking at me intently. "So you say."

I don't flinch from his gaze. "You saw it yourself! You know the people trusted us."

"The people trusted *you*." He turns his glare on Corrick. "No one trusts the King's Justice when he's not wearing a mask."

I expect Corrick to snap back, the way he did to Allisander, but he holds Lochlan's gaze. "My goal is to change that." He pauses. "In this, you don't need to trust me. I don't claim to be an apothecary. Tessa is right. I saw her medicine work."

Lochlan doesn't move. It's clear that he doesn't trust anyone.

Quint's pen keeps scratching across the paper, loud in the silence of the room. I wonder if he's only writing down what's said, or if it's more. Quint notices everything. I imagine he's recording every glance, every shift in weight.

"I trust Tessa," Karri says softly.

Lochlan glances at her. In that moment, something in his gaze gentles. After he incited a mob that nearly killed Corrick, and later, led a murderous rebellion into the Royal Sector, I have a hard time finding anything about him likable. But every time he looks at Karri like that, it tugs at my heart and reminds me that he *does* care. Not just about her. About everyone.

So do I.

"So this buys you more time," Lochlan finally says. "Then what? What happens at twelve weeks?"

"If we can prove to others that a lower dose works in the Wilds," I say, "then we can encourage more people among the sectors to use a lower dose. It allows for more medicine to be spread among more people."

"So you're testing your medicine on people too poor to know better," says Lochlan.

"No! I wouldn't classify it that way—"

"Yes," says Allisander.

"We're testing it on him, too," says Corrick. "He just doesn't know it yet."

The consul inhales sharply, his eyes like thunder.

"What?" says Corrick. "Did you think we were tricking the populace while taking a full dose here in the palace?"

"This is absurd!" Consul Sallister cries. "You—you are purchasing full dose allotments and then—"

"Making it last longer," says King Harristan.

Karri smiles. She looks at Lochlan. "See?" she says brightly. "I trust Tessa."

I give her a grateful smile back.

Lochlan doesn't smile. "I don't trust any of them." He pauses. "I can't take this back to the others. They won't trust this either. Give *us* the full dosage. Test your medicine here."

"Trust must go both ways," says Harristan.

"You still haven't said what will happen at the end of the twelve weeks," says Lochlan.

"We are hopeful that the people will see that a lower dosage will allow us to keep more people healthy, and they will be willing to—"

Lochlan snorts. "Don't you see?" He's glaring at me. "Half the people in this sector are sitting on Moonflower petals that they've been hoarding for months. And you're *hopeful* they'll use less in a matter of weeks? Because you say it works on people in the Wilds?" He turns that glare on Allisander. "*You* don't seem very hopeful."

"I don't really care what happens to people in the Wilds," says Allisander. "If you want more medicine than what I'm being forced to provide, buy it." He glances at the rebel's left arm, still splinted and bandaged from the day Corrick broke it in the prison. "Ah. I suppose you can't work in the forges now, can you? So you need to beg? Under this pretense of *helping*—"

Lochlan lunges across the table.

Or he tries to. Two of the guards grab him before he can get a hand on the consul, but not before he knocks over two glasses that send water streaming along the polished wood of the table. Allisander lifts an aggrieved eyebrow and shoves his chair back a few inches, but otherwise makes no effort to stop the mess. An attendant moves away from the wall with a cloth ready.

The guards are wrestling Lochlan back, and he swears. They must twist his injured arm because his voice cuts off with a gasp, and a bloom of sweat breaks out on his forehead.

"Do something," I whisper to Corrick.

His blue eyes meet mine. "Hang them both?"

"*Corrick*," I breathe. I'm not entirely sure he's teasing.

"They're both at fault here," he says pointedly, for all at the table to hear. "We'll never make any headway if the two of you are content to attack each other."

"Fine," Lochlan grinds out. "Let me go."

Karri has risen from her seat, and she glances between Lochlan and me. The guards look to the king.

"Release him," says Harristan. He looks at Allisander. "You will keep your silence, Consul. If you cannot speak in good faith, then you will not speak at all."

"I am speaking in good faith, Your Majesty." Allisander's words are full of contempt. "You can ban me from your meetings and lower my dosages and make all the arrangements you like, but on *this* point, the brute and I agree. The sectors will not accept a hypothesis you've tested on those who have nothing to lose. Those who would be motivated to *lie* if it's a means to more handouts. It is not only the rebels whose trust you need to earn."

Corrick and Harristan exchange a glance. Quint never stops writing.

"The people won't *lie*," says Karri, and there's heat in her voice.

Allisander turns his disdainful glare her way. "You people were willing to burn down the entire sector. I doubt *lying* is beyond anyone's capabilities."

As much as I hate Consul Sallister, he's not entirely wrong. This isn't just about getting the rebels to trust Harristan and Corrick and . . . well, me. *Everyone* needs to.

Lochlan jerks his clothes straight and drops into a chair. "No one is lying. We *also* came here in good faith, remember?"

"Because you narrowly escaped an execution?" Allisander sniffs.

"So did you," Lochlan snaps.

"*Enough*," says Harristan, and there's a pulse of anger in his voice. He takes a thin breath, then clears his throat. Twice.

I watch Corrick's attention zero in on his brother. The king has been hiding a cough for months. At first, I thought it was because he truly needed more medicine than everyone else due to a lingering illness from his childhood. Allisander admitted to cheating the palace of pure Moonflower petals, but that problem was solved weeks ago. His cough should be gone.

It's not.

Quint's pen stops. He looks up, assesses the situation quicker than a heartbeat, and says, "Finn, I believe everyone could do with some refreshments."

A footman moves away from the wall, and the king's cough is covered by the sudden rattle of china and silver.

Corrick is still staring at his brother. A flicker of worry crosses his expression, almost too quick to notice.

I pick up my own pen, then reach over and circle the words he wrote earlier.

Mind your mettle.

It draws his gaze to mine, and he offers a small nod, but the worry in his eyes doesn't vanish. I wish I could rest a hand over his or whisper a reassurance, but neither would be welcome. Everything is so uncertain. I don't want to weaken him.

Finn is setting a cup of tea before each person at the table, along with a small plate featuring a delicate pastry that's been drizzled with chocolate, a wedge of apple beside a tiny pot of honey, and a thinly sliced strawberry that's been dusted with pink sugar.

Karri is staring at the plate, her eyes wide. I remember doing the same thing.

Lochlan is glaring at the food.

Allisander looks bored.

The king has taken a sip of his tea, and it seems to have staved off his cough. I wish he wouldn't hide it. He doesn't want to be seen as weak, I'm sure, but I believe the opposite would be true: it would endear him to the people to see that he's just as vulnerable as they are.

Then again, I understand why he doesn't want that. Harristan and Corrick's parents were assassinated right in front of them, so I can appreciate their worries.

Mine were too.

Karri looks like she's afraid to touch the food, so I give her a smile, then pick up my apple wedge and dip it in the honey. "The apples are the best," I say to her.

She smiles back, then picks up her own piece of fruit.

Lochlan hesitates, but maybe the lure of the decadent food is too much, because he does the same. It's not a concession, but it feels like one.

Out in the hallway, voices echo, but the doors are closed, and we can't make out the words. Even still, it's unusual for anyone's voice to be raised when they near a room where the king is residing. Aside from the guards in here, half a dozen more are on the other side of that door. Maybe more.

Harristan glances down the table at Corrick, who looks to one of the guards, and then to Quint: a bizarre silent communication that always seems to speak volumes in the space of time between heartbeats.

Quint sets his pen to the side and rises from the table. "I will return in a moment." One of the guards joins him by the door.

Karri looks at me. "What's happening?" she whispers.

I don't want to be alarmed, but my heart is kicking in my chest. I was here when the rebels bombed the palace the first time. "I . . . I don't . . ."

Corrick rests a hand over mine. "A palace matter," he says smoothly. "Nothing concerning."

Despite his words, I can feel the tension in his hand.

No one is eating now. Even Consul Sallister looks apprehensive.

Luckily, Quint returns in less than a minute. He leans down to say something softly to the king. Harristan is too well schooled in court politics, so his expression reveals nothing. But his eyes find Corrick's again.

"It seems we may need to postpone our meeting," Quint says evenly. "A matter has arisen requiring the king's attention."

"What matter?" demands Lochlan.

"I'm afraid I'm not at liberty to say—"

"It took two weeks to arrange this meeting. I won't be tricked into waiting longer." He glances around the table. "Especially since I'm pretty sure everyone else in this room will hear what's so important."

Quint inhales sharply, but Harristan lifts a hand. "You're right. Not just everyone in this room. If the ship docked hours ago, rumors have likely already reached the Royal Sector."

"Ship?" says Corrick. "What ship?"

"An emissary," says Harristan, "has just arrived from Ostriary."

I jerk my head around to look at Corrick. Ostriary is the country directly to Kandala's west, sitting on the other side of a wide, dangerous river. Due to the difficulty of travel and the severity of the fevers, there's never been any kind of trade agreement between countries. Weeks ago, I asked Corrick if there were a chance that Ostriary could provide medicine, and he said it would be nearly impossible to find out. At the very least, it would be expensive to even *try*.

He glances at me briefly, and I know he's remembering our conversation. "Ostriary sent an emissary?"

"Not quite," says Quint.

"*They* didn't send an emissary." Harristan runs a hand across the back of his neck, the first sign of strain from him. "Apparently, six years ago, we did."

Chapter Three

Corrick

My world was very sheltered when I was a child, but never so much as Harristan's. As the often ill heir to the throne, he was coddled and protected, with nurses and physicians never far off. Fires were kept roaring if he was in the room, and he was always given the most reliable horses, the least drafty carriages, the most genial tutors and instructors. As the second-born son—as the *healthy* son—I wasn't guarded so closely. I could ride along for hunts through the densely wooded parts of Kandala, galloping behind other nobles on mounts that were far too spirited for royalty. Riding in a carriage? I never bothered. Schooling? Tutors could rap my knuckles. In the training arena, I could spar with anyone I liked, because no weapons master ever had to worry about leaving a bruise.

But I was still protected. Surrounded by guards and advisers who kept my leash very short, even though sometimes I wasn't aware of it.

Harristan knew, though. He was the one who first taught me to sneak out of the palace and lose myself in the Wilds. That's part of why it was so hard to keep my nightly adventures with Tessa a secret.

I'm often surprised he never guessed. He was always more savvy than our parents realized.

He's savvy now, too. I thought he'd want to go immediately to the throne room to greet our new visitors, but he told Quint to make this "emissary" comfortable, and then invited me to his private quarters.

"Do you think it could be true?" I say to him.

He drops into a chair by the table, then looks at the window. "If it's true, he was sent by Father."

"Six years ago, you were seventeen. Do you remember any mention of ships making it to Ostriary?"

I expect him to give me a withering glance, followed by a long-suffering sigh. *I know how old I was, Cory.* But he's silent, considering for a while, a line between his eyebrows as he studies the sunlight. He's unsettled.

"No," he finally says. "Father didn't bring me in on *all* affairs of state."

But he was brought in on most of them. I remember. I didn't start joining them until I was fourteen, and by then, I was desperate to know what kinds of fascinating work was done at those meetings. I quickly learned that they were interminably boring.

Well, until a year later, when assassins burst into the room and our parents were slaughtered right in front of us.

"Allisander remembers that emissaries were discussed, but he doesn't know of anyone being sent to Ostriary," Harristan says. "But his father was consul then. I've sent word to the others, to see if any of them remember Father arranging for such a thing."

"I've heard nothing about this since you took the throne," I say.

"Some of the consuls have changed, but a missing diplomat seems like something that should have come up once or twice."

"I agree." Harristan thinks about this for a while. "And I have no idea who he could have sent. Most shipbuilders consider the Flaming River to be near uncrossable. I don't know that we have many sailors who'd be willing to chance it without a chest full of silver to make it worth their while."

That's true enough. Weeks ago, Tessa asked me directly if Ostriary could be a new resource for the Moonflower. I remember the hope in her eyes, how it cost me something to dash it away. In the Wilds, I was able to be a hero. As Prince Corrick, my hands are often tied by a dozen different knots.

I told her it would be costly—and difficult—to arrange a way for anyone to make the journey to Ostriary. Crossing the river has been done, but it's rare. The northern half has deep rapids and ice floes. The southern half has unexpected rocks beneath the water that have torn so many ships in half that there's a drinking song about how the Flaming River turns longing lovers into widows.

"The emissary docked at Artis," I say. "He didn't come across the Flaming River. He would have had to travel the Queen's River."

"Then you believe he came from Ostriary by way of the *ocean*? That's even harder to believe. And if so, why sail into Artis at all? There are ports in Sunkeep and Trader's Landing. From Ostriary, he'd have to sail halfway around Kandala and up the Queen's River to *reach* Artis."

All true. I think for a while. "Artis holds the closest port to the Royal Sector. Quint said he sailed right into the port and announced himself. That's a rather bold entrance for nefarious purposes."

"I've sent guards to retrieve the logs from his ship," Harristan says. "And his flag. It should be aged if it's been so long. There should be proof that he came from Kandala originally."

He inhales to say more, but instead, he coughs into his elbow, then frowns.

"You're still coughing," I say. "I noticed during the meeting."

"I'm fine."

I rise from my chair. "I'll fetch Tessa. She'll talk some sense into you."

"I'll send her right back out. We have more pressing matters." He coughs again, but lightly, then glares at me when I don't sit back down. "Truly, Corrick. This emissary couldn't have come at a worse time. After the way Allisander conducted himself with the rebels, Lochlan will be returning to the Wilds with stories of how we're planning to use the poor to test wild theories."

"I don't think Lochlan will say anything of the sort," I say.

My brother looks up. "You don't?"

"No. I think it'll be worse." I cross my arms and lean back against the table. "He'll tell everyone that we don't care about their plight, that their efforts were wasted, that we have no plans for real change, only deceit and trickery."

Harristan looks exasperated. "Oh, is *that* all?"

"Of course not. He's probably calling for revolution already."

He sighs and runs a hand through his hair. "We'll be back where we started."

I should disagree—but I can't. He's right.

Tessa has been so hopeful, but nothing about this situation is simple or easy. If it were, we would have solved it long ago. She once implied that my brother could snap his fingers and turn his desires into laws. I wish he could. I wish *I* could. I don't want life in the palace to burn out her hope just like it's done to so many others.

Harristan's expression is grave. I'm sure my own isn't much better.

"Shall we go find out what news this emissary brings?" I say. "Perhaps he has a ship full of Moonflower petals and we can toss Allisander from the palace roof."

I'm joking, but he doesn't laugh. He makes no move to rise either. His gaze falls on the window again.

Anyone else might think he was stalling on purpose. I know better. He's the king, and the world has a way of turning at his whim, but Harristan never uses his station as a means of manipulation. As the silence stretches on, I wonder if there's more to my brother's decision to come *here*, instead of immediately addressing our visitors.

"Do you *not* want to meet with this emissary?" I say quietly.

"I don't trust this," he says.

"Why?"

He shakes his head faintly. "It's too much time. Too . . . unexpected. Why now?" He pauses. "We were attacked once already. Father and Mother were caught unaware, too."

I say nothing. I remember.

A guard raps at the door, and Harristan calls, "Enter."

The door swings wide, and the guardsman there says, "Master Quint requests an audience, Your Majesty."

"Send him in, Thorin."

Harristan's tone is mellow, which shouldn't take me by surprise, but somehow it does. Quint has been a close friend of mine for years, so my brother has always grudgingly tolerated him for my sake, but they've never been friends. I've been present on more than one occasion when Harristan has told Quint in no uncertain terms to *go away*. Quint sometimes comes across as a bit scattered and melodramatic, and many people in the palace find him to be a bit . . . *much*.

I can count on one hand the number of times that my brother has said, "Send him in," without at least demanding to know what the Palace Master could want *now*.

This ship from Ostriary really does have him unsettled.

Quint strides into the room. If he's surprised, it doesn't show. "Captain Rian Blakemore has been shown to the White Room along with his first officer." He flips open the little book of notes that he always carries with him. "A Lieutenant Gwyn Tagas."

Captain Rian Blakemore. It's not a family name I know, and I know everyone of consequence in the Royal Sector. I glance at Harristan to see if the name sounds familiar.

He meets my eyes and shakes his head. To Quint, he says, "Have the guards returned with his ship's logs?"

"No, Your Majesty." Quint snaps his book closed. "Captain Blakemore indicates that he has a small crew as well, all of whom remained with the ship. I've asked the guards to confirm."

"Does he seem forthright?" I say.

"He does, in fact. His initial claims have not changed: he went to Ostriary six years ago as part of a contingent to determine whether relations with the Ostrian court would be a possibility. He is now returning with news of his journey."

"What news?" says Harristan.

Quint clears his throat. "He says he's been instructed to meet with the king alone."

"Absolutely not," I say.

"The guards searched him and found no weapons. He's made no demands. He's been patient and well mannered. Quite cordial, really."

"Consul Barnard never raised his voice," Harristan says, "and he conspired to have our parents killed."

"I'll meet with him first," I say. "What *news* could take six years to deliver?"

"Surely my father didn't expect this journey to take so long," adds Harristan. "What explanation did he offer?"

"Well, King Lucas didn't specifically send Captain Blakemore," says Quint. "He was only a part of the team. Due to instability in the royal court of Ostriary, it has apparently taken him some time to be able to make the return journey."

I exchange a glance with Harristan again. "What does *that* mean?"

"It means he was a young man when he left Kandala. The diplomat King Lucas sent away was his father."

—+—

Despite what Quint said, I expect to find someone older. Between the words *young man* and the fact that he's a captain of a sailing vessel, I presumed I'd be meeting someone close to thirty years of age. But when I stride into the White Room, I discover that Captain Blakemore isn't much older than I am. He's definitely no older than Harristan. He's got thick black hair and light eyes that are more gray than blue. His jaw is sharp and clean-shaven, his skin the deep tan of men who spend their days in the sun. If I didn't know any better, I'd assume the woman waiting with him was the captain. Lieutenant Gwyn Tagas is easily past the age of forty, with weathered skin the color of driftwood, and short, dark hair that's shot through with gray.

They both rise to their feet when I come into the room with Quint, and their eyes take in the six guards that follow us to stand along the wall. I watch to see if the captain or his first officer are startled or alarmed, but they're either *not*, or they're very good at hiding it. They're both dressed as if they came straight off the water, in heavy canvas trousers and broadcloth tunics, though the captain has a loosely buttoned jacket. Nothing about them speaks of wealth—or diplomatic status, for that matter. Then again, they're standing in the nicest room on the top floor of the palace, and neither of them is wide-eyed about the opulence surrounding us. During our failed meeting, Lochlan and Karri looked like they were going to pass out over the presentation of the food.

"Captain Blakemore," says Quint. "May I present the King's Justice, Prince Corrick."

If he's disappointed to be getting me instead of my brother, it doesn't show. He puts a hand to his waist and bows like he's been in the presence of royalty all his life. "Your Highness," he says.

"Captain." I look to the woman who stands just behind him. "Lieutenant Tagas, I presume."

"Yes, Your Highness." She bows as well, although it's not as graceful as Captain Blakemore's. There's a bit of watchful tension around her eyes that doesn't exist in his. Then again, she's not the supposed emissary. Maybe she's used to being watchful.

I extend a hand. "Shall we sit?"

We do, and Quint steps to the side to give orders to an attendant. I'm certain he's calling for food. I'm not hungry, but food has a way of dispelling barriers, so I'll pick at whatever arrives.

"I understand you've had a lengthy journey," I begin. "Master Quint says you've been traveling for six years. You must be hungry."

There's the tiniest barb in my voice, and I see the moment Captain Blakemore hears it, because the side of his mouth turns up. "I sense that our story has already cast some doubts."

"More than a few."

"I'll answer any questions you have," he says. "I understand your caution."

I can see why Quint called him cordial and well mannered. Nothing about this man's demeanor is suspicious. If anything, he's more direct than most of the consuls and courtiers, all of whom load their polished words with dual meanings.

But if he's going to be direct, I will be too.

"Your father was the one sent to Ostriary," I say. "Ordered by my father, King Lucas."

"That's right."

"And where is your father now?"

"Dead." He says this simply, without emotion. "The same as yours."

Quint was approaching the table, but he goes still when he hears this. I'm sure he's wondering how I'm going to take it.

Lieutenant Tagas sighs tightly. "*Rian*," she says under her breath.

"He is," Captain Blakemore says. His eyes don't leave mine, and he lifts a shoulder in a casual shrug. "They are."

I can't decide if I like this man or if I want to push him off the roof of the palace alongside Consul Sallister.

"So you took up his duties?" I say.

"Of course. A son has an obligation to carry on his father's legacy, don't you think?"

He says this just as steadily as everything else he's said, but there's a tiny barb hidden in there, just like the first one I threw at him. He waits to make sure it lands, then continues as if he didn't expect an answer.

"I knew the initial journey took quite a bit of expense," he says. "I may have been young, but I was not ignorant to the importance of my father's mission."

"It seems *I* am a bit ignorant to the importance of your father's mission," I say. "I am unfamiliar with your family name, Captain Blakemore. My brother has no recollection of it."

"Please," he says. "Call me Rian, Your Highness."

That's a clear opening for me to tell him to call me Corrick, but I'm just petty enough to ignore it. "I'll be calling you a prisoner if you don't explain yourself a little better than you're doing."

To my side, I hear Quint sigh very much the way Lieutenant Tagas just did. He won't say a word, but I can imagine his voice. *Honestly, Corrick.*

Rian smiles. "My intention was to be polite, not deceptive. I recognize that the loss of your father *and* mine puts us at a bit of an impasse. I understand that guards have already departed to search my ship. There, you will find my father's log from the initial sailing to Ostriary—as well as my own for the trip here. My crew, admittedly, is entirely comprised of Ostrian citizens, so you will find few answers there, though you are welcome to question them all if you wish."

"I will," I say.

"Good." He nods, then hesitates. "They are good women and men. They'll speak honestly. They shouldn't be harmed if you don't like what they have to say."

My eyebrows go up. "Why would they be harmed?"

"I've caught wind of your *reputation*," he says evenly. "Your

Highness." The words are spoken quietly, but he might as well have lit a cannon.

Quint clears his throat. "I do believe everyone could do with a cup of—"

I lift a hand and he stops short, but I don't look away from Rian. "You've been here all of five minutes. You've caught wind of my reputation?"

"That should tell you just how very impressive it is."

He says *impressive* like he means something else. But he's given me a vulnerability, albeit a small one: he cares about his crew. They care about *him*, based on the way Lieutenant Tagas said his name.

"I still feel as though you're talking in circles," I say. "If you don't want your people harmed, give me plain truths, Rian. If your father was an emissary, if your father was a *member of this court*, then I should know your name. My brother should know your name. We don't."

A light sparks in his eyes. "Ah. Well, allow me to eliminate any confusion. I didn't say my father was an emissary, Your Highness. He wasn't a diplomat or a courtier. As you were a boy yourself, I imagine that's why you don't have any recollection of his presence." He glances around the room. "I imagine you won't find many in your palace who might know him by name."

I frown, then glance at Quint, who looks just as perplexed as I feel. "Then . . . what was he?"

Rian smiles. "A spy."

Chapter Four

Corrick

I send for Harristan. If Captain Blakemore's claims are going to turn to talks of secret spies sent by my father, I feel as though the king should be present.

When my brother appears, he's trailed by his personal guards, followed by two servants bearing a heavy wooden crate with a large padlock, on top of which is a folded length of faded blue-and-purple fabric and several slim leather-bound booklets.

Rian and his lieutenant rise immediately, bowing to Harristan with as much royal deference as they offered me. The servants ease the items onto the table, and I'm surprised when the crate lands lightly. The booklets are placed beside me, revealing the fabric to be a Kandalan flag with tattered edges. Everything smells like the sea, with hints of salt water and something faintly sour.

Harristan's expression is cool and unreadable, and after a moment of tension, Quint leaps to fill the silence.

"Your Majesty," he says, "allow me to introduce Captain Rian Blakemore and his first officer, Lieutenant Gwyn Tagas."

The last syllable has barely left his mouth when Harristan says, "You're not an emissary at all, Captain Blakemore."

I have no idea how he knows, but Harristan never throws tiny barbs. He throws spinning daggers and waits to see if others will catch them or end up impaled.

Rian doesn't flinch. "Ah. Yes. I'm glad to hear that we're all caught up."

"Yet you told the dock agents in Artis that you were. That is how you secured passage to the palace."

"As my father's mission was rather covert, I didn't feel it would be prudent to introduce myself to a dock agent as a *spy*, Your Majesty." He pauses. "I set the record straight with Prince Corrick rather immediately."

"Do you really feel it was *immediate*?" I say.

"I do. And you'll find your proof inside that first log there."

I reach over and lift the cover of one of the booklets. The leather cover is soft and worn, the first page covered with an elegant script. I don't recognize the handwriting.

There's a thick, folded parchment just under the cover as well, and I slip it free. As soon as my fingers touch it, I realize I have everyone's attention, most notably my brother's.

"Read it," he says to me, and from his tone, I can tell that he already has.

I unfold the parchment carefully. The creases are well worn, and there's a dark stain near the bottom. Before I even read the words on the page, my eyes freeze on the signature and court seal. It's my father's, right down to the minuscule initials he used to print inside the slope of the S to prevent forgeries. I've seen it on a hundred different documents I've handled over the years, and my heart jumps to see it now. The date at the top is from six years ago.

I hereby declare Captain Jarvell Blakemore to be an agent of the Kingdom of Kandala, working in the service of His Majesty, Lucas Ramsay Southwell, King of Kandala, acting with full authority of the Crown. Whosoever bears this letter in the name of Captain Blakemore in conjunction with the ring displaying the sigil below shall be presumed to be acting by the grace of His Majesty, the King of Kandala, with the full rights and authority granted under the Crown.

Below my father's signature is the kingdom seal in dark blue wax, which only Harristan and I have, along with a separate seal in a lighter purple that's a bit cracked, but still legible.

I glance up, inhaling to ask for the location of the ring.

But Rian is already holding up his left hand. A gold ring bearing an identical sigil is on his index finger.

Well then.

It's not *proof*, not quite, but it's close. A letter granting the full authority of the Crown carries a lot of power. To my knowledge, Harristan has never offered it to anyone. As his brother, I don't need it. And until now, the only person I've known to be granted such power by my father was Micah Clarke, the former King's Justice. He was killed when our parents were.

I reach for the flag from the top of the chest and unfold it a bit. The edges are frayed and worn, the blues and purples long faded. The steel grommets have gone rusty, and when I run my fingers over the seams, I can feel the effects of exposure to the ocean air.

"We don't have an established relationship with Ostriary," I say. "Why was your father's journey a secret?"

Rian hesitates, and there's a lot of weight in that hesitation. His eyes shift from me to Harristan and back like he's taking measure of our reactions. "You don't have an established relationship *now*, Your Highness. But you once did."

"I have no recollection of any communication with Ostriary," says Harristan. His tone is unyielding.

Rian spreads his hands, but his eyes are equally unyielding. "As I said, we may be at an impasse. I only have my logs and my crew." At his side, Lieutenant Tagas is silent, stony-faced and steadfast in her demeanor.

Everyone is being polite and cordial, but something about this feels like a standoff. I can't tell if that's on our side or his.

"You have quite a bit to review," Quint says. "Perhaps now would be a good time to serve the tea. I'm certain our guests could do with some refreshments."

I look to my brother. He was unnerved before. I wonder if he still is, or if this letter from Father has given him a bit more confidence. There's a part of me that wants to separate Rian from his crewmate, to see what she would say if he weren't in the room.

It's the same part of me that used to force answers out of thieves and rebels.

No one trusts the King's Justice when he's not wearing a mask.

I promised Tessa I would do better. I told Lochlan my goal was to change that.

I hold my tongue. It takes more effort than it probably should.

"Yes," Harristan finally says. He holds out a hand to the table. "Be seated."

We do. While the food is being served, Rian leans over to murmur something to Lieutenant Tagas, and she nods. The sound of dishes and cutlery is just loud enough that I can't catch the words, and I'm sure it's intentional.

"Is there an issue?" I say.

The servants have laid out a dozen pieces of cutlery in front of each person, and I know from Tessa that the rules of palace etiquette can be an unfair maze for the uninitiated. But Rian picks up the correct fork, then holds it between his fingers as he waits for the king to eat first. "No, Your Highness."

"Then share your comment."

"Gwyn worries for the rest of our crew," says Rian. "Have they been allowed to remain with the ship?"

His voice is calm, lacking tension, but it's the second time he's mentioned his crew. Again, I don't know if the tension is on our side or his.

"Yes," says Harristan. "I've sent guards to the shipyard to ensure they're left in peace." He doesn't touch his food, but he takes a sip of tea.

"And so they cannot leave," says Rian.

It's another tiny barb, but Harristan isn't one to be baited. "Yes."

"You still haven't offered much by way of explanation," I say to Rian. "I feel as though our definitions of *immediate* would be in conflict."

He smiles, though there's an edge to it, then stabs his fork into a bit of pork that's been rolled with sliced ginger and a sliver of cheese. "I'm determining where to start. I did not arrive prepared to lecture the king of Kandala on his country's own history."

Harristan sets down his cup and traces a finger around the rim.

"We have that in common, then. I did not arrive to hear a lecture. You say we once had a relationship with Ostriary." His gaze falls on Rian's crewmate. "Perhaps a representative from the country itself can speak for her countrymen. Is this true, Lieutenant?"

"Your Majesty," she says, and now that she's not hissing warnings at her captain, I hear a faint accent to her words. "I am of the understanding that Ostriary once had a trade agreement with Kandala that went sour."

"When?" he says. "It was not during my lifetime."

"In fact," says Rian, "I believe—"

Harristan puts up a hand. "I asked the lieutenant."

For as quiet as she's been, she doesn't back down either. She meets Harristan's gaze evenly. "Before Captain Blakemore's ship docked in Ostriary six years ago, we had not seen a ship from Kandala in over thirty years," she says. "I was only a girl then. I still remember the last ship." She reaches out and taps the tattered flag. "I remember the colors strung from her main sail."

That would be thirty-six years ago, at least. I try to do the math in my head. My grandfather was still ruling then. On the other side of the table, Quint is scribbling notes. He'll be calling for dock records the instant we're done, I'm sure of it. Artis is close, so we'll have them quickly, but if ships sailed out of the other two ports, it'll be a matter of days.

Still, thirty-six years isn't *very* much time. I'm nearly twenty, so I feel like I would remember stories of ships that made it across the river. Surely there would be sailors who would remember.

But then I consider the ring on Rian's finger. The letter we knew nothing about.

Maybe not. Maybe that ship thirty-six years ago was sent under clandestine means, too.

"What happened to that ship?" says Harristan.

Lieutenant Tagas hesitates.

"It was set ablaze," Rian says, and his voice is not without weight. "The entire crew perished."

At that, Quint looks up from his writing.

"There were disagreements," says Lieutenant Tagas. "Between our kingdom and your own. Again, I was young. My mother was a quartermaster on a merchant ship. We were not privy to all of the court gossip. But I remember that ship sailing into our waters, because our naval fleet set upon it so quickly. They shot flaming arrows into the sails. The fire rained down on the sailors below. Anyone who jumped into the water was shot."

Her voice is quiet, and, like Rian's, not without weight. Harristan is staring at her.

"Why?" he says.

"My mother said there was a scandal between our king and yours. But there was talk around the docks about a trade agreement that went sour."

"A trade agreement," says Harristan. "For what?"

She inhales, but Rian lifts a hand. It's a tiny movement, just a bare lifting of his fingers, but she stops.

Rian looks at Harristan, and then at me. "I am sensitive to the fact that this room is not very private."

Harristan glances across the table. "Quint," he says. "Clear the room."

All of the servants exit without any urging. Most of the guards leave, but four of Harristan's personal guards remain. Rocco and Thorin stand along the wall behind the table, close to my brother and me, while Kilbourne and Grier stand closer to our guests.

Quint pulls the door closed behind him when he goes. He'll

learn everything from me within the hour, if he doesn't hear it from Harristan himself. There's nothing that goes on in the palace that Quint doesn't hear about.

The room is very silent once the door clicks shut.

Rian doesn't look away from Harristan. "Do you trust your guards, Your Majesty?"

"I do."

"And do you trust your brother?"

"I do," says Harristan—but the question pricks at my thoughts and lodges there. It takes me a moment to figure out why.

I'm remembering a moment in the Hold with Allisander, when I'd been locked in a cell after being caught as the outlaw Weston. Allisander was threatening me, saying anything to get under my skin, but he poked at my relationship with Harristan. I'd always thought my brother and I were close, but there was something Allisander said that has sat with me for weeks.

Look at the way he left you in prison for an entire day.

Harristan clears his throat, and I've heard him do it often enough that I know he's covering a cough. I blink and focus on the matter at hand.

"Explain the purpose of the trade agreement," I say.

"I need to explain the kingdom of Ostriary first," Rian says. "Most Kandalan maps show the eastern side of Ostriary is over two hundred miles of marshland that leads into dense vegetation. And I'm sure the Flaming River is still considered a challenge to cross." His eyebrows go up.

"Yes," says Harristan. "But you didn't cross it. Not if you docked in Artis."

"No," Rian agrees. "If you sail past the southern point, Ostriary can be approached from the western side."

"The southern point is uninhabited," says Harristan. "We have records of ships that have tried that route. From the south, the western coastline is a bare strip of sand that goes on for hundreds of miles. The northern point is comprised of cliffs. I have dozens of logs that speak of uncrossable current or dense fog that seems never-ending. Even for sailors who can get through the current, it would be impossible to dock."

"I'll challenge your definition of impossible, Your Majesty, because I'd wager that Kandalan sailors are mostly used to the open water in the stretch from Artis to your ports in Sunkeep and Trader's Landing, and a child could navigate that."

"Forgive our subpar sailors," I say flatly. "So you sailed past the southern point to find . . . what? More sand?"

"No. A chain of six islands. Three are separated by less than a mile of water at certain points, and are connected by bridgework. One longer bridge reaches the mainland, but only one."

Harristan sighs. "We have no record of islands, Captain Blakemore."

"I've spent six years in Ostriary, Your Majesty. I've walked the bridges myself." He reaches out and taps the log that belonged to his father. "You can read my father's accounting of the territory."

"The weather patterns that create the fog over the sea have kept the kingdom rather isolated," says Lieutenant Tagas. "And protected."

"Protected from whom?" I say.

"Anyone," she says. "The islands bear a surprising amount of—"

Rian lifts his hand again, and she stops.

"This room is as empty as it's going to get," I say.

He smiles, but the look in his eyes is less jovial and more regarding. "When we left Ostriary, their rulers were unaware that Kandala had a new king in power." He pauses. "Their government is a bit shaky. There were many years of corruption. Political infight-ing. Squabbles over the throne that led to all-out civil war. It's part of the reason it took me six years to return. There are many Ostrian citizens who did not want a trade agreement with Kandala."

"Why?" says Harristan.

"Because your grandfather was seen as conniving and dishon-est, a man who did not honor his agreements. Once your father took the throne, those views did not change."

I go very still. "You are speaking of your former king."

"I was answering a question, Your Highness. There is a reason the first Captain Blakemore was sent as a spy and not as an emissary."

"Maybe you've been in Ostriary for too long," Harristan says. "My father was highly regarded among the people here."

Rian spreads his hands. "Again, you asked why. I can only offer my own observations."

Harristan looks at Lieutenant Tagas. "You're an Ostrian citizen. What are your observations?"

She glances at Rian. "I am a sailor. I did not move in royal cir-cles. But Rian is correct. In years past, the Kandalan king was not seen as an advantageous ally. Rumor said we were sent faulty mate-rials in exchange for our . . ." Her voice trails off for a moment, and she casts a glance at Rian. "Resources," she finishes. "The trade was bad. That's why the final ship was attacked."

"What resources?" I demand.

Rian lifts one shoulder in an unassuming shrug. "I'd rather not say."

He's either fearlessly brazen or just plain impudent. I raise my eyebrows. "You'd rather not *say*? You claim to be an agent of the king, and you'd rather not reveal what you've learned?"

His eyes flick to Harristan. "I wasn't an agent of *this* king."

I draw myself up, ready to . . . to . . . I'm not sure what. Have the guards drag him out of here. Throw him to the ground and demand answers. Hold his feet to the fire, quite literally.

A dark light sparks in his expression, and I can tell he's thinking of the moment he mentioned my reputation. His shoulders are tense, his eyes locked on mine.

He's not afraid. He's ready.

But I think of Tessa, how I promised to be better. My muscles are tight with a need for action.

If I were Weston Lark, I would fight. Demand answers. Something.

But Weston Lark is dead. The King's Justice can't pick a fight over a few barbed comments.

Harristan speaks into my silence. "So you won't say what Ostriary had to offer. What did Kandala?"

"Steel," Rian says easily, as if we weren't just staring each other down like men preparing for a duel. "Ostriary has very little access to iron ore. The mines here are plentiful. There's an entire *sector* named for it."

"Steel City," I say.

He nods. "The inter-island bridges of Ostriary are constructed of Kandalan steel. Faulty steel, in many areas. They are beginning to fail."

"So they need more," I say.

"Yes," says Lieutenant Tagas. "Quite a bit."

Rian gives her a look, and she shrugs. "We do."

"What is your goal here?" I say to him. "Have you become an agent for Ostriary? Is that the reason for all your secrecy?"

"I'd be a fool to say so, wouldn't you think?" he says. "But I have spent six years there, and I can understand their caution. Their country is not without its problems." His eyes don't leave mine. "Neither is yours."

No, I definitely don't like him.

"Fine," says Harristan. "Ostriary needs steel, yet they have nothing to offer. They haven't sent an emissary of their own, just the son of a spy who doesn't bear a clear allegiance to his home country. Regardless of the letter you bear, I have no reason to believe a word you've said. Tell me why I shouldn't commit you to the Hold and send these Ostrian sailors back where they came from."

"Oh," says Rian. "I didn't say Ostriary has *nothing* to offer." He stands.

All four of Harristan's guards immediately step away from the wall. Two of them have hands on their weapons.

Rian freezes. He lifts his hands.

"I'm unarmed," he says to the guards. His voice is quiet. "I have a key to the chest. Allow me to show you."

The tension in the room has doubled.

"Set the key on the table," Harristan says.

Rian frowns, but he pulls a key from his pocket and tosses it onto the table. The key rattles against the wood.

"Rocco," says Harristan. "Open it."

The guard takes the key and draws the chest away, toward the wall. He unlocks the padlock gingerly, as if expecting a trap, but the lock gives way with a *click*, and he lifts the lid.

Whatever he sees makes him gasp—and Rocco is one of the most stoic guards Harristan has. He's not a man to gasp.

"What?" says Harristan. "What is it?"

Rocco turns the chest around. It's packed full of white petals. Easily enough to supply the entire palace for weeks. Maybe even the entire Royal Sector.

"Moonflower," he says, and his voice is hushed.

"Yes," says Rian. "I've heard you might need some?"

CHAPTER FIVE

Tessa

I'm desperately curious about the ship that arrived in Artis, but anyone I can ask about it is busy dealing *with* it. One of the hardest things about knowing Corrick as the prince—instead of Weston Lark, the outlaw—is that he's surrounded by obligations and duties and constraints, just by virtue of his position. There's no secret workshop in the dark hours of the morning anymore. There's the palace, which is full of guards and servants and courtiers, all listening for a bit of gossip about the King's Justice.

So I have to wait. At least *I* don't have any more obligations, so I can get out of this dress.

To my surprise, a message is waiting for me when I return to my quarters. It's been delivered by one of the stewards at the front gates. No seal, just a familiar scrawl.

Tessa,

I wish that had gone better. I don't know if you're allowed to leave the palace, but I was hoping maybe we could meet up as friends again. I'll head for Woolfrey's Confectioners on the chance you have time to come join me. It's been a long time since we could share a chocolate cream. I miss you.

xo,

K

Oh, Karri. I have to press a hand to my chest.

She's right. I wish that had gone better, too.

Woolfrey's Confectioners is a candy shop in Artis near Mistress Solomon's, where Karri and I worked together grinding herbs to create potions and remedies. We used to giggle over a chocolate cream at least once a month, whispering about the frivolous patrons who'd visit Mistress Solomon's shop.

The memories tug at my heart.

Maybe this is a sign. Maybe Karri and I can figure out a way to convince Prince Corrick and Lochlan to find some common ground.

I need to call for a servant to help unlace me from this gown. But if Karri left this message at the front gate, it would have already taken a bit of time to get to me. I don't want her to think I have no intention of showing.

I look down at the silk dress I'm wearing. I can suffer in a corset for a few more hours.

I smooth my skirts, then head for the palace steps, where I ask one of the footmen to call me a carriage.

He gives a slight bow. "Yes, of course, Miss Tessa."

Heat rushes to my cheeks. Weeks ago, I'd never even been *inside* a carriage, and now I can summon one at my whim. "Thank you," I say, but he's already gone, off to attend to the needs of the next courtier.

Since I'm alone, I don't expect anything grand, but I'm still surprised to be escorted to a two-seater open-air buggy with dark purple panels and gold trim. The horse is a large dapple gray in patent leather harness, every buckle and strap shining in the sunlight. The driver tips his hat to me and lowers a wooden step for my convenience.

"To the town square in Artis, miss?"

For an instant, I hesitate. I know how a carriage like this—even a *small* carriage—will be seen in Artis. I know how a young woman in a fancy dress will be seen.

I remember how *I* would have looked at someone like that.

The driver is peering at me. "Miss?"

"I . . . yes." I hesitate, then climb up. The driver clucks to the horse, and we're off, bouncing along the cobblestones.

In the Royal Sector, no one pays me any mind, because carriages like this are common. It's not until we pass through the main gates into the poverty-stricken villages of the Wilds that I become aware of the people who stop to stare. Most of the looks are curious, attention drawn by something shiny and fast.

But some of the looks are hostile. A few heads shake disgustedly. A mother pinches her daughter on the arm for staring, then turns her own glare on me while she shakes out her laundry.

No, no, I want to call. *I'm not one of them. I'm one of you.*

But of course I can't.

The driver misunderstands my silence. "Don't worry, miss," he calls over the sound of the horse's hooves clopping along the path. "No one will trouble you."

"I'm not worried," I say back, but my voice is lost in the wind and the sound of the horse.

Once we make it through the dense forests of the Wilds, the streets of Artis are more crowded, and the buggy has to slow to a walk. There are more horse-drawn vehicles here, hauling wagons of cargo from the docks. It's a warm day, so many children are gathered by the fountain in the center of the town square, splashing each other with water while they shriek with laughter. I garner stares here, too, but nothing quite as hostile as in the Wilds.

We pull up along the front of Woolfrey's, and for the first time, I notice the chips in the pink paint surrounding the doorframe, or the broken bricks forming the walkway. The wood around the window is weathered and aged, and the window is cracked in the corner. Little imperfections I've never noticed before, but suddenly seem glaringly obvious when compared with the brilliant perfection of the Royal Sector.

The driver leaps down to offer me his hand, and I feel a bit foolish taking it. I used to climb the wall surrounding the Royal Sector, and I never gave it a second thought. Now I'm taking a hand to step down from a buggy. Everything from the Royal Sector always seems to be an illusion.

"Shall I tether the horse and wait, miss?" the driver says to me.

"Oh! I—" I break off. I can see Karri's silhouette inside the confectioner's shop. A man nearby sighs heavily, trying to navigate his fully loaded wagon around the buggy that's stopped, obtrusively, quite in the middle of the road. "No," I say. "I'll be fine."

The driver looks dubious. "Are you certain?"

"Yes," I say firmly. I'm capable of walking back. Now that I feel everyone's eyes on me, I almost wish I'd walked *here*.

Karri appears in the doorway of the confectioner's. "Tessa!" she cries, and there's no mistaking the delight in her voice. "You came!"

She strides forward, and I gratefully accept the hug she offers. She's warm and familiar and she smells like the vanilla and brown sugar wafting from the candy shop.

"Of course I came," I say.

She stands back, holding me by the shoulders. "You look so *fine*. I hardly recognized you in the palace."

I flush, more embarrassed than pleased. "I should have changed. I just didn't want to make you wait."

"No! You look beautiful! I just got here anyway."

Oh. I'm an idiot. Because *she* had to walk.

I tug at the bodice of my dress, more uncomfortable now. "I'm just trying to fit in. The palace physicians hardly take me seriously as it is."

Karri hesitates, and for a moment, I think it's going to be uncomfortable between *us*. But she nods decisively. "That's their loss, then. Come inside. The chocolate is fresh." She hooks her arm through mine. "I'm so glad you came. I was . . ." Her voice trails off a bit. "I was so worried."

"I'm still your friend," I say quietly.

"And I'm still yours." She gives my arm a squeeze. I squeeze back and smile.

Some of the tightness in my chest eases. I was right. We can figure out a way to make this work. She and I. Together. We don't need these arrogant men to get in the way of truly *helping* people.

Then she leads me to a table, and Lochlan is sitting there.

I give a small jolt, then drop her arm.

He doesn't look any happier to see me. "You came," he says flatly. "I suppose I'll be buying your drinks, then."

"I—what?"

"He didn't think you would come," Karri says quietly. "He made a wager on it."

Oh. Lovely. I've run face-first into his attitude. "You don't need to pay for me," I say tightly. "Or any of us. I can buy the chocolate creams."

"I'm sure you can."

"Are you going to drive away anyone who offers you something?" I say. "It seemed to be working so well in the palace."

He holds my gaze boldly. "I was just telling Karri that it's all well and good for you two to be friends, but you've changed sides."

"What does that mean?"

He gives me a cool up-and-down glance. "Not much outlaw left, is there?" He gives a pointed look at the doorway leading to the street. "Nice carriage. Too good to walk now?"

"I'm not too good to walk. It took some time for the message to reach me. I didn't want Karri to wait."

He inhales, his eyes darkening, but Karri gives him a solid shove in the shoulder. "Don't argue," she says. "She might not be an outlaw anymore, but Tessa is my *friend*."

"So you've said." He rises from the table and offers me a mocking bow. "Do forgive me, Miss Tessa. Allow me to fetch your confections, ladies."

I open my mouth to protest, but Karri catches my hand. "No," she says. "Let him do it. Maybe a little sugar will change his mood."

I sigh, but I sit while Lochlan heads for the counter.

To my surprise, an awkward silence falls between me and Karri. It's so foreign. We used to sit and chat for hours on end. I still remember the day she realized I was mooning over the outlaw Weston Lark—back before I knew he was Prince Corrick. The memory makes me smile.

Tell me about his hands, she said, and I blushed like a schoolgirl.

"I'm really glad you sent me a note," I say.

That seems to break the tension, because she smiles, too. "Me too." She pauses and flicks her eyes at Lochlan, where he stands by the counter. "He doesn't trust them at all, Tessa. That consul was terrible. It's obvious he doesn't care." She hesitates, and I can hear the fear in her voice. "This morning, Lochlan was worried the meeting was a trap. That you were luring us to the palace. The whole time we were there, he kept waiting for them to drag us to the Hold."

"It's not a trap," I say. "Karri, I would never *lure* you."

"I know. But there are still people who believe that 'Weston Lark' was only a spy to find more criminals to hang."

I frown. "No. He cares. *We* care. The king really does want to figure out a way to make sure there's enough medicine for all of Kandala. But *everyone* has to agree. Not just the elites, and not just the people in the Wilds. *Everyone*. We all have a stake here."

"I know." She hesitates. "Lochlan didn't even think the rumors of the ship from Ostriary were real. He thought it was a ploy to end the meeting until he heard the talk in the streets here."

"It's not a ploy either, Karri! Harristan and Corrick wouldn't do that."

She stares back at me, and her voice has cooled a bit. "It wasn't too long ago that you stood with me in front of the sector gates declaring how much you *hate* them."

The words hit me like a slap. She's right. I did. *She* was the one to chastise me for speaking words of treason.

But that was before I knew who Weston was. That was before I knew everything the king and his brother had at stake.

That was before Corrick and I were captured by the rebels. Before he was *tortured* by them.

Before the rebels set the whole sector on fire as a means to show Harristan how desperate they were.

And here we are.

"You're right." I reach out and put a hand over hers. "This isn't easy for anyone."

For a moment, she's frozen in place, and I worry that we've moved too far apart.

But then she turns her hand to clasp mine. "We'll make it work," she whispers.

I nod fiercely, pressing my fingers into hers.

Lochlan reappears beside the table. "Your chocolate cream, Miss Karri." His bellicose eyes flash my way. "And yours, Miss Tessa."

He's mocking me, baiting me to snap at him. I don't play. "Thank you for your kindness, Master Lochlan."

I could say it primly, but I don't. I say it honestly. Surprise registers in his expression, and he eases into the seat beside Karri. His jaw is tight, but he doesn't say anything else.

"You're suspicious," I say quietly. "I know. I was, too. They have a lot to make up for."

He studies me. "You trust them."

I can't tell if this is an accusation or a question, but I nod. "I do."

"Why?" he says. "*Why?* You know what they've done." He glances at Karri. "You were both in the crowd when he was set to execute the eight of us."

"You saw Consul Sallister," I say. "You see how much power he has. He kept threatening to withhold Moonflower if Prince Corrick didn't do as he said—"

"And that's supposed to be reassuring?" he says. "That the king doesn't have control of his consuls? He's *still* threatening to withhold it. I heard what he said about supply issues and laborers. The king can make him work the fields, but he's still one man."

"You don't understand. They won't—it's not—"

"No." He half rises from his seat, leaning in against the table. "*You* don't understand. This is life or death for us." His eyes glare down at me. "They act like it's a game. The elites think they can convince the fools in the Wilds to take even *less* medicine than they were getting before."

He's looming over me, and I swallow. I don't want to look away from him while he looks so threatening, but we've garnered more than a little attention. Whispers have erupted all around us. The pretty young lady in the fine clothing being dressed down by someone who's probably never had more than a handful of coins in his life.

I'm sure most of them heard what he said, too.

"Lochlan," Karri says quietly. "She's my friend. Leave her alone."

But she doesn't contradict what he said.

Lochlan doesn't move. His eyes don't leave mine. "She might have been your friend before," he says, "but you need to be careful now, Kar."

I know they're worried, but it's hard to find any empathy when he's standing over me like this. I don't want to be afraid of him. If we were back in the palace, I wouldn't be. But we're here in a little confectioner's shop, and I'm thinking of the moment he surged across the table at Consul Sallister.

"Why did you ask me to come here?" I say evenly. "If you didn't want to talk?"

"Karri invited you," he says. "I didn't."

"Then maybe you should let her talk to me," I say, and my voice goes breathy. I can't help it.

I see the moment my fear registers in his eyes, because he jerks back, his eyes wide. "You're afraid of me?" he says. "You're sharing a bed with the King's Justice, and you're afraid of *me*?"

Karri grabs his wrist. "*Lochlan.*"

My cheeks are surely flaming now. "I'm not sharing anything," I growl.

"This is why I can't trust you," he says, his voice very low. "Because I don't trust *him*. The prince is no fool. He convinced you that he was a rebel outlaw in the Wilds because it served his needs as the King's Justice. And now, he's figured out a way to give the people even *less*, and he's convinced you that it's for the benefit of everyone."

His eyes fill my vision, but I refuse to look away. "My medicine works," I say. "It's not a trick, Lochlan. You can watch me measure the elixirs yourself. I can *show* you."

"Maybe he's just tricked you into believing that. Maybe all those people are taking double doses when you aren't looking, just to give you your *proof*." He studies me. "He certainly tricked you into believing you were *helping*. The poor, tortured prince who just couldn't help himself. And you lapped it up, didn't you?"

My chest is tight, and I'm dangerously afraid I might cry.

"I'm telling you to keep your eyes open," he says. "I'm telling you what it looks like from here. If you're not sharing his bed, someone is. He's the brother to the king. As soon as you don't suit his needs, you'll be at the end of the rope, too."

"You're wrong," I whisper, but there's a part of his words that are pricking at my thoughts, sowing doubt in a way I wish I could shove aside.

He must see it in my expression. "Don't you realize," he says dangerously, "that you could disappear tonight and literally *everything* would go right back to the way it was?"

Fear seems to pierce my heart from both directions. "Is that supposed to be a warning or a threat?"

Lochlan smirks. "Maybe you shouldn't have walked out of the palace without guards," he says.

"Maybe she shouldn't have," says a voice behind me, "but I brought more than enough."

My heart kicks to hear Corrick's voice. Lochlan snaps back. I'm suddenly aware of the tense silence in the shop, how we are all the center of attention. I wonder how much everyone heard. I wonder how much *Corrick* heard.

If you're not sharing his bed, someone is. He's the brother to the king.

He must not have heard that part. If he did, I can't imagine Lochlan would still be on his feet.

The people behind the counter are peering between towers of wrapped candies and tiny trinkets, and there's an older woman a few tables over who's openly gawking at the prince—who truly does have half a dozen guards behind him.

Lochlan's eyes have darkened with hatred, but he takes in the guards who have filled the space behind the prince. "The girls were just having fun together," Lochlan says. He pauses, then grinds out, "Your Highness."

Corrick's eyes shift to me. I watch his gaze sweep over my form, taking stock of me. "Exceptional." His voice is rather cordial, almost warm, but I know better. "Are you having fun, Tessa?"

No. Definitely not.

But I can't say that, because no matter what I think of Lochlan, I really don't want to stoke the tension between them. "Karri sent me a note after our meeting," I say. "We were just having a sweet drink." I force a smile onto my face. "Like old times."

Karri looks hesitant again, the way she was in the palace. She glances between me and Corrick and has to clear her throat. "Yes. I did. We were. Your Highness."

Corrick's eyes return to mine, and I give him a tiny nod.

"Very well," he says. "I'll leave you to your friendly chat. Please forgive the interruption." His eyes cool as he looks to Lochlan again, but his voice is just as cordial. "Thank you for the wise recommendation. I'll have the guards remain." He glances at the table. "Perhaps I'll have a drink while I wait."

Karri looks to me, and her hands flutter. She abruptly stands, her chair scraping harshly along the tile floor. "No need, Your Highness. We were just about to leave. You—you can have mine. I haven't even taken a sip."

I stand to stop her. "Karri," I say softly.

She hesitates, then leans over to kiss me on the cheek. "He's still terrifying," she whispers in my ear before drawing back. "And— for what it's worth, I agree with Lochlan."

I don't know what to say to that. I don't have time, anyway. She grabs Lochlan's hand, and they're gone.

CHAPTER SIX

Tessa

I fully expect Corrick to offer me his arm and lead me to his carriage, but he extends a hand toward my seat and gives me an expectant look. "Shall we?"

I don't know what to say. A few of the guards have fallen back to stand along the wall, with one to stand guard outside, while two stand near enough to the table that we're still the center of attention. I don't want to gape at the prince like half the people in the shop, so I clamp my lips shut. I've taken enough etiquette lessons at this point that I can avoid falling all over myself when it comes to royal protocol in public.

I take hold of my skirts and drop into a slight curtsy. "Certainly. Thank you, Your Highness." I ease into the chair.

His expression doesn't change, but a light sparks in his eyes like he's amused. He settles into the chair across from me, then turns the handle of Karri's mug in his direction.

"You look so surprised," he says.

"I *am* surprised."

Mistress Woolfrey bustles over hurriedly. She's a tall, portly woman with light brown skin and fuzzy braids wrapped on top of her head. I've always liked her, so I smile, but like everyone else here, she's only got eyes for Prince Corrick right now. Some of the people are terrified of him—but others are in awe. The king and his brother might not be well liked, but they are very definitely well respected, even if it's a respect born of fear. Stories about the King's Justice sitting down in a common shop will feed the rumor mill for *days*.

I'll admit that once you get past his reputation, Prince Corrick isn't difficult to look at. Vibrant blue eyes sit well in his face, which is full of angles, with just a sprinkling of freckles to steal some of his severity—though a narrow scar over his eyebrow adds it right back. It's late enough in the day that a shadow of beard growth has slightly darkened his jaw, too. The silver buttons on his brocade jacket glisten in the light, and the jeweled hilt of an ornate dagger is revealed at his waist. I've learned that he spends a number of hours training with the man-at-arms at the palace, so he's no stranger to physical exertion, but his hands are clean, with long, elegant fingers, his palms smooth and free of calluses. He looks so out of place among the laborers and dockworkers who have stopped in for a sweet treat after a hard day at work.

"Your Highness," the shop owner says in a rush, dropping into a curtsy herself. "Allow me to have one of the girls make you a fresh drink."

"No need," he says.

"Oh, I *insist*," she continues effusively, already reaching for the mug.

His eyes flick up. "I insist that you not."

His voice isn't forceful, but Corrick never needs to be. He has a cool confidence that always seems unflappable. An expectation that things will go his way. The king is no different.

Mistress Woolfrey's hands go still, and she jerks them back against her body. Her mouth works like she wants to say something, but she isn't sure *what*.

"We'll alert you if we need anything," Corrick adds.

"Ah . . . yes. Of course." She bobs another quick curtsy, then returns behind the counter. Conversation in the shop resumes quietly.

Corrick picks up a spoon and stirs at his chocolate cream like he's completely unbothered. "Why so surprised?" he says easily, as if we weren't interrupted.

"This is hardly the place anyone would expect to find the King's Justice," I say, keeping my voice low. "You're giving everyone enough gossip for a *week*."

"Just a week?" He lifts the mug and takes a sip. His eyebrows go up. "That *is* rather good. Perhaps the King's Justice should make this more of a habit."

"I'm not sure Mistress Woolfrey would survive the shock." I haven't touched my own drink. "Why didn't you want her to make you a new one?"

"Because I felt rather certain the one she made for your friend Karri wouldn't be poisoned."

He says this as equably as everything else he's said, but it makes me hesitate before reaching for my own cup. I know the *good* side of Corrick, the man who wants to help his people. I forget that everyone else still sees him as Cruel Corrick, one of the most terrifying men in all of Kandala.

"Right," I say weakly. Now I'm worried about the cup Lochlan placed in front of *me*. I let go of the handle.

"Here," says Corrick, and there's a gentle note in his voice that no one will hear beyond this table. He slides his cup toward me.

I meet his eyes and see the warmth there. The kindness. The awareness.

This is what he never allows anyone to see.

This is what people like Lochlan *need* to see.

"Thank you," I say, and I'm not quiet about it at all. I take a sip. It's *divine*.

"Lochlan was right, you know," Corrick says. "You shouldn't be leaving the palace without protection."

"I'm no one of importance," I say.

"I beg to differ. He's lucky I didn't have one of the guards put an arrow in his back for standing over you like that."

I choke on my next sip. "Well. That would have made for an interesting second meeting." I ease the cup onto the table, but as I lift my eyes, a slight movement beyond Corrick catches my attention. A man and woman are sitting near the window, but the man is glaring at the prince. He's older, with thinning hair and a thick gray beard, but his arms are heavily muscled. His shirt bears sweat stains and a few threadbare spots along his shoulders. His skin is sun-darkened and weathered like a dockworker.

His hand is in a tight fist on his knee.

Corrick takes a lazy sip. "You look concerned."

"There's a man over there." I keep my voice very low. "He's glaring at you."

"Ah."

I glance at the guards to see if they've noticed. I can't tell. But at least they look *alert*. When I look at the dockworker again, he catches my gaze and startles. He deliberately unclenches his hand, turning to look out the window instead.

I drag my eyes back to Corrick's. "Aren't *you* concerned?"

He lifts a shoulder in a shrug. "When I found the note in your chambers, yes, I was concerned. When the porters told me you'd left *alone*, yes, I was concerned." He gives me a look. "One man glaring at me is a matter of course, Tessa."

"You didn't need to worry. I was fine. I knew you were busy with other things."

"People know you're important to the king." His voice is practical, but a bit of that gentle warmth slips in. "That you're important to *me*." His hand brushes over mine.

It's uncommon for him to touch me in public. A blush heats my cheeks. "Well."

He smiles, and I feel that warmth all the way down to my toes. I've been at court long enough to know that a true smile from the prince is rare.

When he was Weston Lark, he smiled often. Every time I earn a smile from Corrick, it's both a reminder of who he truly is—and who he can no longer be.

The glaring dockworker is looking at him again, and it robs some of my warmth. I clear my throat. "What happened with . . ." I hesitate, but we're close enough to the docks in Artis that people here have surely heard about the boat arriving from Ostriary. "What happened with the ship?" I say. "Can you tell me?"

"Not here. But that's part of why I came to fetch you."

"Really!" My eyebrows go up. "What—"

A roar of rage cuts me off. The dockworker explodes from his seat as he launches himself at the prince. Light glints on a blade, and I suck in a breath.

I don't know if Corrick sees my reaction or if he hears the man coming, but he sweeps out of his seat in one smooth movement, pushing me toward the guards before I even realize he's tugged me out of my chair. The man slams into him, and they crash to the ground together. They skid into the table, and the drinks wobble before tipping over, spilling to the floor. The mugs shatter on impact. Chocolate splatters my skirts.

"We'd be better off without them!" the man is shouting. He lifts a dagger, and my heart stops. "Finish the revolution! Kill him! Kill the—"

Corrick punches him right in the throat. The man's words break off with a gurgling sound, but he swings that dagger anyway. The guards will never be fast enough.

They don't need to be. Corrick blocks, then flips the man onto his back. The blade goes skittering across the floor. I don't even see the prince draw his own dagger, but it's there, against the man's throat, just as the guards move in, crossbows aimed and ready. One restrains the man's companion, because she squeals when her arm is twisted back. One of the other guards draws back the bolt on a crossbow, aiming for the man's head.

I inhale sharply. One of the girls behind the counter lets out a cry.

"No," says Corrick, and his voice is just as quiet and even as when he told Mistress Woolfrey that he didn't need a fresh drink.

The guard with the crossbow hesitates, looking up, waiting for an order.

Corrick's blade is still against that man's throat. The man's breathing shudders—but then his eyes narrow, and he spits in Corrick's face.

A line of blood appears around the blade, trickling toward the floor. "I've cut men's tongues off for less," Corrick says, his voice as low and vicious as I've ever heard it.

I'm frozen in place. So is everyone else in the shop. I wait for Corrick to let him up, to order the guards to take him out of here, but he doesn't move.

That line of blood darkens. Thickens. The blade has gone deeper.

The man hisses a breath, then chokes on a sob, rebellion shifting into fear. "Please," he gasps. "Please."

I'm thinking the same word in my head. *Please, Corrick. Please.* I have to bite my tongue so I don't say it out loud.

Corrick leans close. Blood still flows. "So you beg when it's *your* life in question."

A tear leaks out of the man's eye, finding the blood to trail down his neck.

My stomach is tight, and I don't know what to do. No matter who Corrick is to *me*, he's the King's Justice to everyone else. I can't interfere.

But I can't watch him kill someone. I can't.

My fingernails press into my palms.

An eternal moment later, Corrick says, "Take him to the Hold. He can stand trial like the others."

Then he wipes his blade on the man's shirt and tucks it back into its sheath.

My heart is pounding so hard, refusing to settle. I thought I was about to witness an execution. Based on the tense silence of the shop, so did everyone else—including the man the guards are dragging to his feet.

Everyone is still staring at Prince Corrick with a mixture of horror and fascination, as if he'll say, "Just kidding," and cut the man's throat anyway.

When the prince turns to look at me, his eyes search mine for a moment, and I have no doubt he can read the panic that hasn't fully melted away.

The guards are leading the man out of the shop. One of the others has begun questioning the woman, who's wringing her hands, casting terrified glances at Corrick.

He ignores them all and offers me his arm. "It seems we no longer have a drink to share. I do require your services at the palace. Shall we?"

I have to shake myself. "Ah . . . yes. Of course." I rest a still-trembling hand on his arm. He's so good at hiding every emotion, but I don't have anywhere near as much practice.

He begins to lead me to the door, but he pauses before we cross the threshold to look to the counter. "Mistress Woolfrey," he says.

Her face goes pale, and I'm sure she's ready for him to levy an accusation that she might have been involved. When she speaks, her voice is breathy and shaking. "Yes—yes, Your Highness."

He withdraws a handful of coins and holds them out to her. "The drinks were very good. The guards will assist in cleaning up the mess, but I'd ask that you have an accounting of any damages prepared. I'll send a steward to cover any costs."

She startles, her eyes widening as he hands over enough silver that he's probably covering her costs for a *month*. "Your Highness. It's . . . it's nothing."

"All the same." He gives her a nod. "For the trouble then. You have my thanks."

Then he leads me through the door, and we climb into his waiting carriage.

—◆—

I drew a lot of attention on the way to the confectioner's, but that's nothing compared to the looks we get on the way back, sitting in the prince's burgundy carriage, trailed by half a dozen guards. My heart is still rattling around in my chest, leaving my fingers to tremble along my skirts. I have my eyes fixed on the window, so I see every glare we get.

I've cut men's tongues off for less.

Every time I want to forget who he was, the world seems determined to remind me. I want to ask if that's true, or if he only said it for effect.

But I'm afraid I already know the answer.

Corrick sits on the opposite seat of the carriage, and there's a part of me that wants to ease to his side, to hide in the circle of his arms for the short journey back to the palace. Another part of me wants to run away from everything that just happened.

I can't do either. Everything about our relationship is massively complicated now. When I first moved into the palace, it all seemed simple. Easy. Corrick and I could go for walks, or play games, or have a late dinner on the terrace. He could steal kisses in the moonlight, and I could taste his breath and remember what it was like to be in the Wilds, just the two of us against the dawn.

But then I learned that nothing about his life is simple. I'm an apothecary working in service for the king, and he's second in line for the throne. I'm a girl from the Wilds, and he's the King's Justice. Any courtship would be watched. Studied. Judged. At dinner one night, I overheard a woman telling her companion that it was adorable how the prince allowed his little mistress to dabble in medicine.

Lochlan himself already proved it: *If you're not sharing his bed, someone is. He's the brother to the king.*

Our work to make enough medicine for everyone in Kandala is far too important to sully it with rumors that I'm only in the palace at the prince's whim. Our late night walks ended. So did our stolen kisses and private dinners.

It's left me feeling adrift. Uncertain.

And I resent this doubt in my abilities. That just because I'm from the Wilds, my theories and research and medicine are somehow seen as lesser, just because I wasn't trained in the Royal Sector. That the only reason I might be in the palace at all would be for Corrick, not because I truly have something to *offer*.

Maybe we weren't helping *all* of Kandala when we were delivering medicine as outlaws, but at least I felt like I was helping some.

So I sit here, and Corrick sits there, and I content myself with watching the passing terrain, longing for his touch. When I finally tear my eyes away from the window, I expect to find his gaze on the blur of greenery as well, but he's watching me.

"Don't worry," he says. "The carriage can withstand a few bolts from a crossbow."

Well, I wasn't worried about that until *now*. "You think someone is going to shoot at us?"

"No, but I didn't expect someone to leap at me with a dagger in a candy shop either."

"Are you frightened?" I try to be as even-keeled as he sounds, but my voice is hollow.

Any dry humor fades from his voice. "I've been attacked before. I know how to defend myself. The guards did their job, and they did it well."

I smooth my hands along my skirts, then frown. He could have been killed. He could've been the killer. How does he go through every day like this?

I wonder if he's regretting the way he told the guards to take the man to the Hold. I imagine the King's Justice from a month ago might have let that blade go another inch, just to send a message. I don't want to think so—but again, I'm afraid of the answer, so I don't ask the question.

Corrick is studying me now, and his voice turns very careful. "I know Karri is your friend, but I don't trust Lochlan." He pauses. "You shouldn't either."

I glance at the window again, because I don't want to meet his eyes. "Lochlan told her the same thing about *me*—in regards to *you*."

"He was very displeased with the way the meeting progressed. It could have been a trap."

"It wasn't a trap."

"He wouldn't even have to coerce Karri. She wouldn't have to know. He just needed to get you there." The prince's eyes narrow. "As much as I hate him, he's not a fool. He could have drugged your drink, made you feel a bit woozy so they'd have to help you outside—"

"Corrick." I bring my gaze back to his. "It wasn't a trap. He's right to be anxious. It's life or death for them. You remember."

"It's life or death for us, too." Corrick's eyes don't leave mine, and his tone is unyielding. "He used you against me once before."

When we were captured together, and Lochlan figured out that Weston Lark was truly Prince Corrick. They nearly beat him to death. I don't want to think about that.

I don't want to think about Lochlan using Karri against me either.

"That was different," I say.

"Was it? How?"

He's not challenging me, not really, but my skin feels hot and prickly. I don't know how the whole day has gone so wrong. I scowl and frown.

After a moment, he says, "Are *you* frightened?"

I swallow, and my throat feels thick. I can't look at him, but I nod.

"The guards will take the man to the Hold. He'll stand trial. You weren't his target."

I don't know how to respond, so I keep my gaze trained on the window.

"Or," he says quietly, "are you frightened of me?"

I don't answer, and he makes an aggravated noise and runs a hand over the back of his neck.

"I'm sorry," I say.

"Lord, Tessa, I don't want you to be *sorry*." He pauses. "He was going to kill me. That was his goal."

"I know. I heard him. I just—" I break off and hold my breath. Sometimes, I think about my position and what I've accomplished. I'm helping the king find a better path to medicine for the people.

But when I think about everything they've done wrong, I question whether I'm on the right side.

"I wasn't going to kill him," Corrick says. "But I had to make him think it. I had to make them *all* think it."

I hate that he made *me* think it. "Why?" I whisper.

"Because the King's Justice can't go soft overnight. The people are already emboldened. No one would have *dared* to attack me in public a few weeks ago." He makes an aggravated sound again. "This was so much easier as outlaws."

I want to disagree with him, but I can't. It *was* easier. "No one trusts anyone now."

He sits back against the cushions. "Welcome to life at court."

I scowl. My fingers have ceased their trembling, but my insides feel tight and unhappy. "What happened with the ship from Ostriary? Did you really need me for something, or was that to get me out of the shop?"

"Oh. Yes. I want you to look at some flower petals and tell me if they're truly Moonflower."

"The palace physicians weren't sure?"

"They are, but after they didn't detect the difference in the petals Allisander was supplying to the palace, I still can't decide if they're incompetent or traitors."

"Where did they come from?"

"Captain Rian Blakemore arrived with a chest full of them."

"The emissary?"

"The *spy*. His father was supposedly sent by my parents years ago. He says he has two dozen crates of Moonflower on his ship—and the means to get more. He claims that the king of Ostriary would like to begin trade negotiations, because they are lacking in resources for iron and steel. Kandala, of course, has quite a bit."

There's a note in his voice I can't quite parse out. "You don't believe him."

"I'm not sure yet. But Harristan has invited him to dine with us." He pulls a jeweled pocket watch out of his jacket and glances at the face. "We should arrive in time for you to prepare."

My eyebrows go up. "I'm to join you?"

"I've surprised you again?"

"A little."

"Quint will attend, too. Captain Blakemore has made more than a few references to my *reputation*, so Harristan felt it would do well to have you attend to keep the conversation a bit more . . ."

"Honest?"

Corrick smiles. "Social."

"Will Harristan be bringing someone as well?"

"No." He seems startled. "Haven't you noticed? My brother never invites a companion."

I hesitate. I haven't been at court very long, but I've spent enough time in the palace that I've become accustomed to the usual players. Some of the consuls are married, like Roydan Pelham, an older man who's rather devoted to his wife, while others seem to rotate through courtiers as regularly as I wash my face.

Until this moment, I hadn't considered that Harristan never has someone at his side. I haven't even seen him engage in so much as a casual flirtation.

Though honestly, the thought of Harristan doing *anything* in a casual manner is almost laughable.

When the sector was under attack from the rebels, Harristan and I slipped through the woods of the Wilds together. He'd once told me that it was easy to love your king when everyone is well fed and healthy, but not so much when everyone is sick and hungry. Harristan is always stoic and reserved, but I remember seeing his composure crack, just a little, when I told him that *he* could be loved.

Corrick watches me work through this in my head. "He doesn't trust anyone, Tessa. Too many people have tried to take advantage of us." He pauses, and his voice drops, even though we're alone.

"And it would be difficult to keep his lingering illness a secret. I don't think he'd allow anyone to get close enough."

That makes me sad. I can't chase Lochlan's comments out of my head, so I find myself asking, "What about you? Any frequent companions for the King's Justice?"

I'm trying to keep my tone light, but he holds my gaze, and I know he hears the true question there. "Ah, Tessa." There's something simultaneously wicked and warm in his eyes. "No one dared, until you."

CHAPTER SEVEN

Corrick

Dinner in the palace is often a grand affair, served in the vast dining hall behind the salon, with dozens of courtiers and attendants and diplomats creating a cacophony of sound that often becomes exhausting before anyone eats their fill. I don't mind it much, but Harristan hates being so widely accessible, so I'm not surprised when I hear that we're dining in the Pearl Room.

It's an interesting choice, because the room is very fine, but not *too* fine. The walls are a faint gray, with a dark blue artful swirl that stretches from corner to corner and seems to faintly glisten. As you get closer, you can see a tiny line of real pearls embedded in the design. The table is a block of white marble, topped with a floral arrangement of vibrant blue lilies that exactly match the floral pattern on the seat cushions. Servants stand ready to pour glasses of wine and stronger things. A side table full of delicacies sits beneath the window, which overlooks the rear gardens of the palace. Stonehammer's Arch is visible, an arc of brightly flaming torches that hang suspended over a pond.

To my surprise, Tessa and I are the first to arrive. Harristan hasn't yet appeared. Neither has Captain Blakemore, for that matter.

Tessa stands at my side, resplendent in deep green velvet that clings to every curve, a gown that allows a generous expanse of neckline. Her hair has been curled and fixed to hang down her back, with shining green and silver hairpins in place to tie a bit back from her face. She looks warm and elegant, and every inch of bare skin reminds me of her vulnerability.

When I saw Lochlan looming over her, I really did want to have a guard shoot him with a crossbow.

I don't know who I'm fooling. I wanted to do it myself.

After seeing her fear in the carriage, I'm glad I didn't. I wish I could go back and erase the worry from her gaze.

Are you frightened of me?

She said nothing. But that said everything.

I hate this forced distance between us. I should make an official declaration of courtship. Our time together is always too public, too politically charged. Any private moments are too brief, limited to shadowed walks behind the palace, or quiet games of chess before breakfast. But I worry that anything more would weaken our efforts. Everything is already so precarious.

I think of that man in the candy shop. If Tessa and I were openly involved, she'd be *more* of a target.

Then again, if we were openly involved, I'd drag her into my chambers and we wouldn't leave for a week.

I need to stop thinking like this.

"Wine?" I say to her.

She shakes her head and presses a hand to her abdomen. "If I start drinking wine, I'll never remember the correct fork."

I smile and lean in to speak low, then risk brushing a finger along her chin. "In that dress, no one will be looking at your cutlery."

She flushes, but she gives me a rueful look. "Fine. Maybe one glass." I gesture for a servant, and Tessa adds, "Mind your mettle, Corrick."

My smile widens. "Mind yours."

She takes the glass she's offered, but the slight smile drops from her face. "Are the consuls attending this dinner?"

I turn to see two consuls approaching: Roydan Pelham, of the Sorrowlands, and Arella Cherry, of Sunkeep. They haven't been in the palace very much since the rebels attacked, and I rather doubt they've been invited to dinner. Months ago, I had speculated about them being involved with the rebellion. They've been cleared of any involvement, but that doesn't make their prior behavior any less suspect. Their sectors both border Trader's Landing, which lacks a consul, so they've shared management of the area, but I've told Harristan that needs to change. They've had too many secret meetings, too many opportunities for plotting.

They might not have been involved in the last rebellion, but it doesn't mean they aren't plotting their own.

I sometimes find the thought a bit disappointing. Arella often challenges me, but I know it's done out of a desire to make things better. And Roydan is the only consul who ever showed us a glimmer of kindness after our parents died.

Arella has a hand on Roydan's arm, though I'm sure it's more for his benefit than for hers. He's three times her age, and he walks with a trembling step.

"Consuls," I say.

Arella offers a brief curtsy, and Roydan gives me a nod. He's too old to bow.

"Your Highness," Roydan says. He gives Tessa a kind smile. "Miss Cade."

His warmth tugs at me. I just can't imagine him doing something nefarious.

"Consuls," Tessa says, her tone a bit shy. I can tell she's deliberating whether she should move away and give us some privacy, but I want to keep this conversation social, so I rest a hand over hers.

"I didn't know you were joining us for dinner," I say to the others.

"We're not," Roydan says. "Arella and I will eat in the salon. I was hoping to catch a minute of your time, Corrick. I don't want to be a bother."

"You're not a bother."

He pats me on the shoulder as if I'm ten years old and I've been a good boy. "Harristan asked me if I remembered sending warships to Ostriary. He was concerned about this new captain."

My eyebrows go up. "I am, too. Do you?"

"I do. Just a bit—though I don't remember many of them reaching Ostriary." He gives Tessa a smile. "That said, I'm an old man and my memory isn't what it used to be." He pauses. "But I do remember there were squabbles between Steel City and Trader's Landing. Arella and I have been reviewing the shipping logs, because it seems there have been some inaccuracies going back for decades. Maybe even a century. And it does look as though we were sending tons of steel on a fairly regular basis to half a dozen unfamiliar cities. Not just steel either. Explosives and lumber. Arella and I have been trying to piece it together for weeks, and we'd started to think they were code names for secret destinations, because we couldn't find those on any maps we have. But then Harristan mentioned that this man claims there are islands on the western side of Ostriary."

"Yes," I say. "He does."

"These shipping records stop," Roydan says. "Thirty or forty years ago. There's no further mention of the cities—but I thought perhaps they could refer to the islands this sea captain mentions." He pauses, then reaches into his coat to withdraw a folded piece of parchment. "I wrote down the names of the cities for you."

I unfold the paper and look down at Roydan's shaky handwriting.

IRIS
KAISA
ROSHAN
ESTAR
SILVESSE
FAIRDE

"Do you know how many islands he mentioned?" Roydan says.

Six. This could be a coincidence—or it could be evidence to support the captain's story. But I don't want to feed a rumor mill. "I don't quite recall," I lie. "Why did the shipments stop?"

"I don't know." He gives a little shrug. "And there's been no one in Trader's Landing to ask since . . . well." His gaze turns a little sad, and he pats me on the shoulder again.

Since our parents were killed by the consul from Trader's Landing.

I blink away emotion before it can form. I look at Arella because I can't be icy with Roydan. "Why were you investigating shipping logs to begin with?"

"The longer Trader's Landing goes without a consul, the more opportunity for corruption," she says coolly. Her brown eyes don't flinch from mine. "For example, the explosives used on the palace came right out of that sector."

I can't tell if she's making an accusation or a declaration. "So I've heard. Do you know anything about it, Arella?"

"I know desperate people will take drastic measures to survive."

"Now, now." Roydan pats her hand. "The prince has business to attend to."

Anyone else, and she'd smack his hand away. Like me, she has a fondness for Roydan, so she sighs. "We should head for the salon before it becomes too crowded."

But she doesn't move, and I know she's expecting an invitation to join our meal. There's no disguising the curiosity in her eyes. I'm sure everyone is desperate to meet the emissary from Ostriary.

But if she's not going to be forthcoming, I'm not going to be either.

"Don't let me delay you," I say.

She accepts the defeat and offers another brief curtsy, and they turn away.

I drain half my glass of wine.

Tessa is gazing up at me. "Is that true? Was Kandala sending steel to Ostriary?"

I fold up the parchment and tuck it into my jacket. "Steel and explosives. I can't tell if that's friendly or hostile."

"Maybe both." She takes a sip of wine, then slowly lowers her glass. "Now Consul Sallister is here."

I frown and turn to follow her gaze. She's right. Allisander has slipped into the room. He has a girl on his arm, a young woman I've not seen at court before. Much like my brother, he rarely has a companion at his side, but Allisander's issue isn't one of trust. Or . . . not the same kind. He always worries someone is after his money.

They're certainly not after his charming disposition.

I hope he'll avoid me, but I'm never that lucky. He makes a beeline right for us, and I try not to sigh.

"Corrick!" he says. "I'd like to introduce Laurel Pepperleaf, the daughter of one of my barons. I've insisted that we join you for dinner."

I inwardly sigh. I'd rather have Roydan and Arella.

I haven't met Laurel Pepperleaf, but I know *of* her. She's the daughter of Landon Pepperleaf, one of the wealthiest landowners in Allisander's sector. She's prettier than he deserves, with long, shining blond hair, and lips painted a glossy red. Her dress is yellow satin, with diamonds lining every seam. It's both expensive and provocative, and I'm intrigued enough to meet her eyes, wondering if she's with Allisander for her own reasons, or for his. "Laurel," I say. "A pleasure."

She offers a slight curtsy. "Your Highness," she says. Her eyes meet mine boldly, but there's no disrespect there. "The pleasure is mine."

"This is Tessa Cade," I say, because Allisander would fall over dead before he'd acknowledge the girl on *my* arm. "The king has asked her to act as adviser regarding the Moonflower elixir dosages."

"I've heard about your research, Miss Cade," Laurel says. "I find it rather intriguing, especially as our production has been cut by half."

"Oh!" Tessa says in surprise. "I do, too. I'm sorry—did you say your production has been cut by *half*?"

"Yes," says Allisander. "As I've said, we are having our own challenges from both weather conditions and labor shortages, while you keep promising more medicine for *free*."

"Which is why I would love to hear more about your theories," Laurel says. "I specifically asked Consul Sallister to make an introduction while I was at court."

"Did you." I look right at Allisander and take a sip of my wine.

He gives me a level look right back. "And here we are, making an introduction." He takes a sip of his own.

The door to the room swings open, and I expect my brother, but instead, I get Quint. He strides through to join us. Allisander looks like he wants to snarl at him, so I head that off at the pass. There was a time when the consul could have chased Quint out of a room by virtue of his position, but right now, Allisander is living on borrowed time. I don't care if I irritate him.

"Quint," I say. "Join us." I seize a glass of wine from an approaching servant and offer it to my friend. "Have you met Laurel Pepperleaf?"

"I have, in fact." He takes the glass, then nods to Tessa and to Laurel. "I'm glad you both could join us. The king should arrive shortly."

Allisander's lip curls. "And these boatmen will be joining us, too?"

He sounds like he expects them to drift up to the palace gates on a crudely tied raft. "The emissary?" I say. "Yes. Captain Blakemore and a few members of his crew."

"I understand they have their own supply of Moonflower. Surely you don't believe these claims, Corrick. There were thieves all over Kandala. These petals could be from anywhere. This *captain* could have loaded a ship in Sunkeep, sailed for a day, and turned up in Artis with the exact same story."

"Tessa examined the petals," I say. "They're legitimate." I pause. "And I rather doubt they came from Moonlight Plains. You were supplanting yours with a faulty supply, were you not?"

He inhales sharply, ready to bluster, but Laurel says, "My father has taken a much greater interest in our sector's exports. I don't believe you will be finding many more *faulty* shipments, Your Highness."

"I'm glad to hear it," I say.

Allisander is scowling. He turns to Laurel. "We should find you some refreshments." He doesn't wait for a response, but he just shifts as if to guide her away toward the table.

She's hardly gone for a second before Quint drops his voice to say, "Baron Pepperleaf has apparently made some remarks that he would like to be considered for consul if Allisander were removed from power."

"Well, now I understand why she's making a point to seem like she has him in hand."

Tessa looks at me. "Has their production really been cut in half?"

I wince. "You heard him during the meeting with Lochlan. We can demand all we want, but if there really is a supply issue, there's not much to be done about it. I can't control the weather. What am I going to do, threaten to throw his remaining workers in the Hold?"

"Then having a new consul would be a good thing, right? He could fix things? If he's opposed to what Allisander was doing?"

"It could be," I say. She looks so hopeful that I hate to be pragmatic in the face of it. "If he truly is opposed."

"What does that mean?"

"It means I find it hard to believe that Allisander's wealthiest baron had no idea what was going on."

Her mouth forms a line. "So . . . you think he's just saying what you want to hear while Allisander is in trouble."

"Yes. And his daughter appearing at court with so much enthusiasm for your findings is a bit much. You've seen what happens when people believe I'm courting another. It's just one more avenue for deceit." I roll my eyes and take a sip from my glass.

Tessa says nothing to that. I glance over to discover that she looks wounded, and now she's truly frowning.

Lord. "Tessa—I didn't mean—"

"No! No, I know." Her eyes have gone a bit glassy, but she blinks it away. She huffs a breath, then downs half her glass of wine. "It's fine. I keep forgetting that there's a reason you and your brother are so . . . cynical."

"Again. Welcome to life at court."

"Thanks. I hate it here."

I frown. I don't know if there's a kernel of honesty in there or not, but I'm not sure my heart could take the truth right now. I tap my glass against hers. "Cheers."

"Honestly. The two of you." Quint sighs, looking at Tessa. "Don't let them make *you* cynical, my dear."

"How do *you* avoid it?" she says.

"Because I've already seen the changes you have brought to the palace."

"Well, I nearly witnessed an assassination this afternoon, so I'm not sure I'm doing much."

The guards swing the doors open. Again, I expect my brother. Instead, Captain Blakemore walks in, Lieutenant Tagas at his side, along with two other men who must be members of his crew. They're both older than he is, by at least ten years. I half expected them to return in the seaworn clothes they were wearing during our first meeting, but they've clearly been given leave to return to the ship to prepare. Their attire isn't Kandalan, but it's not altogether foreign either. Rian is freshly shaved, his hair combed back, his clothes clean and more elegant than I expected. His jacket is leather instead of cloth, and shorter than the current style in Kandala, with buttons situated diagonally across his chest. His boots are buckled instead of laced. He's quite obviously the youngest of the group—and just as obviously the one in command.

"Oh," says Tessa, and there's a note of intrigue in her voice that I absolutely cannot ignore.

I look at her and raise my eyebrows. "*Oh?*"

She hesitates. Her voice drops. "The sea captain isn't what I expected."

"Hmm." I drain my glass. A servant immediately hands me another.

"Your Highness," Captain Blakemore says when he reaches us. "A pleasure to see you again. And Master Quint." He nods to the Palace Master, then bows to Tessa with perfect courtly manners. "An even greater pleasure to meet your lovely companion."

It's a throwaway comment, something I've said to a hundred courtiers over the years, but Tessa is so earnest that she takes it to heart. She blushes and takes hold of her skirts to curtsy in return. "I'm Tessa Cade."

"Miss Cade." His eyebrows go up. "The apothecary, then."

"Yes." She looks surprised—and a bit delighted—that he knows who she is.

His smile warms. "Around the docks, I heard some fascinating stories about an outlaw named Tessa sneaking into the palace to bring news of a better cure."

"Well," she says. "You know how rumors are. I just want to help people."

"I do know how rumors are." His eyes flick to me before returning to hers. There's less flirtation and more genuine intrigue in his expression now. "Hopefully we'll be seated near each other. I'm eager to learn the truth."

She'll be seated with me.

I almost say it. I almost *growl* it. The words sit on the tip of my tongue, hot and possessive. But every syllable would sound petty and chauvinistic, and I swallow my words with another sip of wine.

"I'm eager to hear about Ostriary," Tessa says. "Weeks ago, I was asking Corrick if it could potentially be a resource for Moonflower petals."

"I'm hopeful I can help that come to pass," he says.

"We'll see," I say.

He finally looks back at me. "I suppose we will, Your Highness."

Quint must sense the tension between us, because he says, "Captain Blakemore, I don't believe we've met the other members of your crew."

"Of course," Rian continues smoothly, as if there's no strain at all. "This is Sablo, my second lieutenant." He indicates a heavily freckled man who's well over six feet tall, thickly muscled, with a bald head, pink cheeks, and a dense red beard that's neatly trimmed. "And Marchon, my navigator and quartermaster," Rian says, indicating the other man, who's as narrow and swarthy as Sablo is broad and pale. His hair is longer, slicked back and knotted at the back of his neck.

"Your Highness," says Marchon, and his deep voice carries a rasp, and the same slight accent as Gwyn's. "We are grateful for the invitation to dine with you this evening."

Sablo gives me a nod.

"Sablo doesn't speak," Rian adds.

My eyebrows go up. "By choice?"

"No," says Rian, and there's a protective note to his voice that reminds me of how readily he spoke up for his people earlier.

"A pleasure to meet you both," I say, but I take in Sablo's size and wonder if he's more than just a sailor. He carries himself with a certain stillness that speaks to military training. So does Marchon, now that I'm looking at them. He's not as big as Sablo, but there's a breadth to his shoulders that suggests strength. They could be body-guards—or assassins. Surely the guards searched them for weap-ons before they came in here.

I cast a glance at the wall, where the guard captain has only sta-tioned four guards. There will be more once Harristan arrives, but not too many to overwhelm the room, since this is supposed to be a casual dinner.

I stop these thoughts in their tracks.

Maybe Tessa and Quint are right. Maybe I am too cynical.

Across the room, Allisander is looking at the sailors with a curled lip. I don't know if he's more annoyed that they might have access to Moonflower—and might cut into his profits—or if he's such a snob that he finds them beneath him. Knowing Allisander, it's prob-ably both.

But I look back at Rian, because Roydan gave me an idea.

"Captain," I say. "One of our consuls has found some aged ship-ping logs from a southern sector that may confirm part of your story."

His eyebrows raise. "That's good news."

"I hope so." I pause. "You said there were five islands on the western side of what we know to be Ostriary."

He regards me carefully, as if he suspects a trap. "There *are* islands. But I said there were six of them."

"Name them."

He looks startled by the command, but he holds out his left hand, palm down, then rotates his wrist so his fingers are pointing to the left. He taps the back of his hand. "If you imagine this to be the main island—Fairde—each finger is roughly where the others sit." He ticks off each one, starting with his thumb. "Iris, Kaisa, Roshan, Estar, and Silvesse."

Beside me, Tessa lets out a breath, and I know she recognizes the names from the list as clearly as I do. But I study Rian carefully. There's no hint of guile in his expression.

I don't know what this means—but it *is* meaningful.

His eyes narrow slightly. "Did I pass your test, Your Highness?"

A herald bangs his halberd near the main door. "His Royal Majesty, King Harristan."

Everyone turns to face the door, to greet my brother.

But I lean close to Rian. "Not yet."

CHAPTER EIGHT

Tessa

Somehow, I do end up seated across from Captain Blakemore, but it doesn't allow for much conversation. Harristan has been grilling the sea captain and his lieutenant on Ostriary and their infrastructure. It's probably for the best anyway. I've been smarting a bit since Corrick told me that Laurel's interest in my methods might be a farce to help put her father into power. It makes me glad I'm not seated next to *her*.

At the opposite end of the table, Quint has Allisander and Laurel engrossed in conversation about the demand for Kandalan silk coming out of Trader's Landing, and it's so detailed yet innocuous that I highly suspect that he's been charged with keeping the consul occupied for as long as possible. Sablo sits beside Captain Blakemore, and he's easily as imposing as Rocco, my favorite member of the king's personal guard. Sablo is listening to every word that's said, watching Corrick and Harristan as if he doesn't trust them. To *his*

left, Marchon the quartermaster looks bored by Allisander's blus-
tering with Quint, but he's just a bit too far for me to engage in casual
conversation.

So I sip politely at my soup spoon and wonder how something
that should be so *simple*—providing more medicine to sick people—
could get so wound up in political negotiation and palace intrigue.

I want to pull on my homespun skirts and climb over the wall
so badly that my feet almost twitch with the need to run.

"You look a bit sad, Miss Cade."

I glance up to find Captain Blakemore studying me, and there's
a warmth in his gray eyes that's tough to look away from. I expected
someone older and stuffy, not a younger man with sun-kissed skin,
black hair that gleams, and a set of shoulders that whisper of
strength.

"Not sad," I say. "I just don't have much to offer when it comes
to the demand for silk"—my eyes flick to the end of the table—"or
the supply of steel."

"I don't have much interest in silk either," he says with a small
smile. "But when it comes to steel, I know Ostriary needs it. Badly.
After the war, many cargo ships were damaged. The country is trying to rebuild, but without ships and bridges, transporting goods
has become a massive challenge."

"And you want to help?"

"I do."

Corrick would hear that with a skeptical ear, just like his doubt
over Laurel's enthusiasm for my work. That means I probably
should, too. But unlike Laurel, whose father is just one more man
volleying for power in Kandala, Captain Blakemore has nothing to
gain here. He's not making demands, and he's not backing anyone
into a corner with empty promises and imperious threats.

I know there are political levers at work. He's asking for steel on behalf of Ostriary, and offering Moonflower petals in return. But somehow he's made it simpler than that. He's asking for *help*—and he's offering it in return.

"I want to help, too," I say.

"I know. As I said, I heard stories around the docks. Anyone who could break into the palace with a plan to *heal* people instead of harming them must be very brave indeed. Especially considering the harsh penalties for breaking the law here in Kandala."

"I don't know about brave," I say, but I can't stop the warmth that floods my cheeks. "Just determined."

"They're pretty much the same, don't you think?" He takes a spoonful of his own soup, and it robs the sentiment of too much weight. "I was young when my father was sent to Ostriary, but from what I recall, the punishments issued by the Crown were never quite as severe as they are now."

"Kandala was a different place six years ago," Corrick says, and I'm startled to realize we've drawn his attention.

"In a lot of ways, it seems." The captain takes another spoonful. His eyes return to mine. "Do you think the actions of the King's Justice have been an effective means of keeping the peace?"

Beside me, Corrick goes still. He knows how I felt about the King's Justice, well before I ever knew that the benevolent outlaw Weston Lark was the same prince who was executing thieves for smuggling and treason.

I hate the prince, I often said to him as Wes—followed by *I hate you*, once I knew he was Corrick.

The room has gone very quiet, as if the question, spoken gently, drew everyone's attention just by virtue of the weight behind it. Even Allisander is watching me, waiting to hear what I'll say.

My mouth is frozen, my thoughts spinning.

"I'd like to hear your thoughts," says Harristan, and his voice isn't harsh. One of my favorite things about Harristan is that when he asks me for my thoughts, he really wants them. But he's still the king, and he never has to be harsh to make my pulse jump. I set down my spoon and smooth my hands over my skirts.

"I think the King's Justice was doing the very best he could," I say, "during a very challenging time."

Under the table, Corrick's hand finds mine, steady and warm. He gives it a squeeze.

Captain Blakemore offers a wan smile and takes another spoonful of soup. "I didn't intend for my question to make you uncomfortable." He pauses. "Or to put you at risk. Forgive me, Miss Cade."

I'm not at risk, but maybe it would be impolitic to say so. This conversation is like walking a tightrope.

"You haven't been here, Captain," Corrick says. "You haven't seen the desperation for medicine, or what people were willing to do to get it."

"I see that the people within this sector's walls seem rather healthy, while those outside are not." Captain Blakemore doesn't look away. His tone is just as unruffled as when he was speaking to me. "I see that I have brought you *medicine*, something you claim to dearly need, and you treat me with suspicion and hostility."

Corrick draws himself up. "You've returned to Kandala for less than a day and you're being openly critical of your king? You certainly don't do much to demonstrate loyalty to your home country."

"Do you want *loyalty* or do you want *obeisance*, Your Highness?" The prince looks right back at him. "For a man who seems to want to protect his crew," Corrick says, "you couldn't go wrong with either."

The captain goes very still. "Don't threaten my crew."

The words are spoken quietly, slowly, with emphasis on each syllable. They crack through the room like a bolt of lightning.

Corrick's jaw is tight, and I know that there's a part of him that wants to have this man dragged to the Hold. It's the same part that made me think he would have cut that man's throat in the candy shop.

My own chest is in a vise grip, and I want to say something to undo this. It's like the moment I sat in the confectioner's with Karri: there are too many sides at work, too many people to keep happy.

But it's Laurel who speaks up.

"Your arrival comes at an interesting time, Captain Blakemore. Our sector is being forced to provide medicine to the people of Kandala, and here you appear, ready to negotiate the cost for another country."

The captain hasn't looked away from Corrick. "You have to *force* your sectors to provide medicine? When people are dying?"

The censure in his voice is impossible to ignore.

"There is no proof that you have more Moonflower," says Allisander. "You want our steel, and a great deal of it. What proof do we have that *you* will arrive with the medicine you're offering?"

"It's a worthwhile question," says the king.

Captain Blakemore spreads his hands. "I have no proof other than what I've already given. But I do have a ship. You're welcome to return to Ostriary with me to complete the negotiations with their king yourself."

"You can't possibly think the king of Kandala would board a ship based on nothing more than your promises," says Corrick.

"Then come yourself." The captain casts a darkly amused look at Corrick. "If you're interested, I highly suggest you leave my crew unharmed. You know your own sailors can't make it."

"Who says your crew needs their captain?" says Corrick.

"Corrick," I whisper.

"I won't sail for anyone else," says Marchon, and it's probably the first thing he's said since sitting at this table.

"Nor will I," says Lieutenant Tagas.

Sablo slaps the table and then his chest. He nods his agreement.

Captain Blakemore smiles, and his eyes brighten with something akin to true delight. "Now *that*," he says, "is loyalty."

"It's impressive," says Harristan. His voice is cool and low, undercutting all the tension in the room. "It speaks to your character."

Even Corrick looks over in surprise.

The captain could gloat, and I half expect him to. But the smile on his face eases, and his expression is as earnest as it was when he was only speaking to me. "Thank you, Your Majesty."

Corrick looks like a coiled spring waiting to release, but this seems to unspool some of his anger.

"I've sailed a lot of ships," Marchon says. "Under a lot of captains." He nods at Captain Blakemore. "When war first broke out among the islands, Cap's the only one who stayed near the shoreline, picking up survivors. He didn't care which side they were fighting for. If they were broken and bleeding, he'd pick 'em up."

A raw note in his voice makes me wonder if Marchon was one of the broken and bleeding. I glance at Sablo, the man who doesn't speak.

By choice? Corrick asked.

No, the captain said.

Captain Blakemore watches my eyes flick between the members of his crew. "We all have a story, Miss Cade. You'd do the same, I'm sure."

"Yes," I say. "I would."

His eyes flick to Corrick, but he says nothing.

Servants stride into the room with loaded trays, bringing the distraction of the next course. Soup bowls are cleared, and fresh plates are delivered to the table. Light conversation resumes, spurred by Quint, who looks to Marchon and says, "Quartermaster *and* navigator, you say? Tell me, do you ever sleep?"

At my side, the prince is silent, his movements tight and precise. Corrick is too schooled in courtly politics, at hiding every emotion when the need arises. I want to reach out and rest a hand over his, to offer him a glance or a word or *something* to steal the rest of his tension. When we were outlaws in the Wilds, it was so easy to support each other.

Here in the palace, it always seems impossible.

Especially since we're sitting directly in front of Captain Blakemore, and it's very obvious that Corrick doesn't trust one word that comes out of his mouth.

"Was your offer genuine?" says Harristan.

The captain takes a sip from his wineglass. "Which offer?"

"To return to Ostriary to handle negotiations with their king directly."

"It was."

Allisander stares from the opposite end of the table. "You cannot be serious. The consuls would never stand for it."

Captain Blakemore glances between them. "The consuls rule the king? Have I been gone so long?"

"No," says Harristan. He clears his throat, then drinks half a glass of wine.

I watch the movement and wonder if he's covering a cough. He should call for tea, but I know he won't.

Allisander says, "You haven't replaced Leander Craft. Steel City stands without a consul. You never replaced the head of Trader's Landing after King Lucas died. You invite the rebel leaders to nego- tiate with this untested apothecary, all while your sectors languish, and now you will *leave Kandala—*"

"Enough," says Harristan. "You are here by virtue of what you can offer your country, Consul, and you've already indicated you won't be able to offer as much as you promised."

I wonder if Laurel Pepperleaf will add a comment, but she takes a sip from her own glass. Happy to watch Allisander hang himself, I suppose.

Maybe *some* of Corrick's cynicism is rubbing off on me.

Captain Blakemore looks across the table at me, and there's something conspiratorial in his gaze. His voice drops. "Rebel lead- ers, Miss Cade?"

I wince. "Apparently you haven't heard *all* the gossip."

"I wasn't intending to go myself," Harristan says. He looks at his brother. "I was referring to Captain Blakemore's offer to Corrick."

At that, the prince startles. So does the captain. It's a tiny move- ment of surprise, but it's the first hint that he seems to be thrown off-balance by Corrick as well.

He recovers quickly. "As you like. I believe Ostriary would be very eager to hear your terms."

"You said the government is a bit shaky," says Corrick.

"Not as much now as they were. The old king passed away a few years ago. He had three sons and two daughters, all illegitimate. Several half-siblings, many nieces and nephews." He pauses, and his voice slows, growing heavy with emotion. "As I said, battles for the throne turned into civil war. Island against island. For *years*."

I study him. Those gray eyes are faraway for a moment, and he downs his glass of wine.

"You're upset," I say quietly.

He blinks, then looks at me. "No." He pauses. "Well. Perhaps. War is . . . war. My father died in those battles."

I frown. "I'm sorry, Captain Blakemore."

His expression flickers, as if I've surprised him. "Thank you, Miss Cade."

Corrick might think all of this is pretense, but the captain's grief feels genuine to me. "Please," I say softly. "Call me Tessa."

He gives me a nod, then a small smile. "Then you must call me Rian."

Harristan speaks through the emotion with casual efficiency. "Who won?" he says.

"Galen Redstone won the throne," Rian says. "If you can even call it *winning*. He was an illegitimate son, and his primary rival was a man named Oren Crane, the king's half-brother."

"His uncle?" I say.

"Yes," Rian says, "but I don't believe they knew much of each other before the conflict. Power changed hands many times over the course of months."

"And what happened to Oren Crane?" says Harristan. "Was he killed?"

"No. But he made enough enemies that his allies began to fall, one by one, until he had no choice but to yield. Now, the country has stabilized under this new leadership, and focus has shifted to rebuilding instead of fighting. Which is why I'm here now."

"So you're close with this *new* king," says Corrick.

"Close? No. But I spent enough time on their shores that I've earned their trust. I truly do have an interest in helping them rebuild. I knew of the conflict with Kandala's former kings, but I have my father's ship and his seal. I offered to sail here to act in good faith." He holds Corrick's eyes. "It would be my pleasure to escort the King's Justice and act as liaison with Ostriary's court as well."

"I don't need you to act as liaison," Corrick says.

Rian smiles. "I suppose I'll just sail the ship then."

"What about the fevers?" I say. "Do you worry about carrying disease to Ostriary?"

He hesitates, looking around the table. "Rumor says that it's not contagious. That there's no rhyme or reason to who is affected. Is that true?"

"Yes," I admit.

He considers this. "Ostriary is desperate enough for steel that I'm willing to risk contagion, at least on a small scale. If it becomes an issue, we have more than enough Moonflower to go around."

"What are your terms?" says Harristan. "What do you require, to bring this to pass?"

"My *terms*?" Rian sits back in the chair, and he glances between the king and the prince. "Do you expect me to ask for chests full of silver? Do you have many to spare?"

"Don't play with me."

"I'm not playing. I'm not doing this for myself. We need steel.

You need Moonflower petals." He casts a dark glance at the end of the table. "Since apparently your own countrymen are reluctant to provide them."

"*'We* need steel,'" Harristan repeats. "Your father may have been loyal to Kandala, but you've clearly changed allegiance."

Rian hesitates, then frowns. "It's not a matter of allegiance. I spent a quarter of my life there, Your Majesty. There was no escaping the fighting. I was forced to pick a side, just like everyone else." He pauses. "I want both countries to have what they need, and I don't see any reason why you can't come to terms with the new king himself. He seems to be a reasonable man. He *also* wants to rebuild." He glances down at Allisander and Laurel again. "He doesn't want to take advantage of suffering people to line his own pockets."

My heart is a steady thrum in my chest. Maybe it is naive, but I believe him. I believe every word. And it's not just the strength of his conviction. It's the loyalty of his crew. The way Marchon looked to him when he said the words *broken and bleeding.* The way they all declared that they wouldn't sail for anyone else. He just turned down silver, when surely he has the leverage to demand it. It's the first time I've heard someone speak of hope and promise without caveats and conditions.

Maybe that's what gives me the courage to look at Corrick and say, "You should go."

He hasn't looked away from the captain. "Oh, I should, should I?"

"Yes. Because I want to go with you."

He snaps his head around like I told him I want to leap off the roof. "Tessa!"

"I do!" I say. "Consul Sallister clearly has no desire to give us enough medicine. If Ostriary has Moonflower, this could help all of Kandala, Corrick. This could buy us more time to protect more people while we deliver a better cure. This could be the very key to finding a way out of this sickness."

The table falls silent, and I realize my voice has grown loud, impassioned. Across the table, Captain Blakemore is regarding me with raised eyebrows.

"Forgive the prince's pet apothecary, Captain," Allisander says from his end of the table. "She understands little of politics and negotiation."

"On the contrary," says Captain Blakemore. His eyes don't leave mine. "I sense that Miss Cade understands quite a bit."

"Finding more medicine shouldn't be a matter of *negotiation*," I say hotly.

"No," Corrick agrees. "It shouldn't." His jaw is tight, and I can't tell if it's anger at Allisander or concern over what the captain is offering. Likely both.

"Your Majesty," says Laurel. "Surely you have considered that this could be a trick or a ruse."

"Why would I need to trick you?" says Captain Blakemore. "Ostriary has more than enough Moonflower to offer as fair trade. Put us back on the ship and I'll fetch more to prove it." He glances at the end of the table again. "But it would take me several weeks. Possibly a month or more. From these conversations, I sense you're rather desperate."

"We are," I say. "Besides," I add determinedly, thinking of the way the prince fetched me from the confectioner's, "who else are you going to trust to inspect their supply?"

Corrick hesitates, and I know I've got him.

But then I glance across the table sheepishly. "Ah . . . if I'm invited." If I call him Rian, I think Corrick might actually catch on fire, so I say, "Captain Blakemore."

He smiles, and a light of true amusement flickers in his eyes. He's no fool himself. "I would be honored, Miss Cade."

"If we accept your offer," says Harristan, "I will assemble a team of sailors to accompany you."

At that, Rian looks up. "No."

Harristan's eyebrows go up.

"As you are amenable to *terms*," Rian continues, "I'll place one restriction: no sailors, no navigators. One ship: mine. You've already indicated a worry about contagion—and Ostriary's king is still dealing with a strained court. Their people are recovering from war. If you are able to reach a point of accord with their king, I will happily teach your shipmen to navigate the open sea beyond the southern point. But until then, I will not be responsible for bringing the naval forces of a potential rival into the waters of Ostriary."

Harristan says nothing for a long moment . . . but then he coughs.

I glance over in alarm. So does everyone else at the table.

It's only one cough, brief and brought under control readily. Harristan casts a briefly annoyed glance at Corrick, who looks ready to spring out of his chair.

The captain watches all of this, then spreads his hands. "I understand your hesitation," he says. "If you would prefer that I return with a letter, or a request, it would be my pleasure."

Harristan considers, then glances at Corrick. "We'll discuss your offer, Captain Blakemore." He pauses. "If not sailors, I will send guards with my people. You cannot expect less than that."

Rian nods. "Understood."

"If Miss Cade will be in attendance, I would like to sail as well," Laurel says from the end of the table.

"You can't be *serious*," Allisander says in a rush.

"I am," she says. "I would like to be privy to these negotiations, to ensure fair trade is maintained."

"Captain," says Marchon, and the quartermaster's raspy voice draws the attention of everyone at the table. "The *Dawn Chaser* is not a passenger ferry. We have limited quarters and staff."

"Indeed," says Rian. He looks at Harristan. "I'll limit your number to six. Including guards."

"Twelve," says the king.

"Six." When Harristan frowns, the captain adds, "This is not a negotiation. I'm thinking of the safety of my crew *and* your people, Your Majesty."

He's so resolute. So principled. It's a bit fascinating when compared to the king, who's been forced to negotiate and cajole to maintain control. When compared to Corrick, who's been forced to *kill* to maintain control.

Then again, Captain Blakemore has a ship and a small crew. Harristan and Corrick have a whole country overrun by illness and desperation.

"I'll step aside in favor of more guards." I glance at Corrick. "Or . . . whatever you think you'll need."

His eyes are ice blue, but they thaw when he looks at me. "I haven't agreed to go at all, yet."

Rian glances between the two of us. "I'll await your decision, Your Highness," he says. He gives me another smile. "Miss Cade, I certainly hope you make the cut."

CHAPTER NINE

Corrick

By midnight, dinner is long gone, and the sky is very dark outside my brother's window, clouds obscuring the stars. It's too hot during the daytime for a fire, so the hearth sits cold, and a warm breeze eases through the room to ruffle the papers on Harristan's desk.

I'm sprawled in his desk chair. We've received early reports from the docks at Artis that confirm ships departed for "exploratory journeys" over thirty years ago—that never returned. After dinner, Harristan sought out Roydan himself, asking more pointed questions that seemed to strain the old man's memories. Roydan said he does remember many lively debates about the price of iron coming out of Steel City. He said that Barnard Montague, the former consul of Trader's Landing, used to rant about not getting a cut of the profits when steel had to pass through his sector.

We can't ask Barnard directly because he was implicated in the assassination that killed our parents—and he died in the attack.

I should be working through all of these details, trying to draw parallels. Trying to figure out all the points of risk and reward. I should be planning. Strategizing. Working through the risk of traveling to a relatively unknown country, and whether it's worth the potential reward of bringing more medicine back to Kandala.

Instead, I keep replaying the moments when Captain Blakemore quite obviously captured Tessa's attention. She's so clever. So brave. So empathetic.

Unfortunately, he seems to be the same. I saw the way his crew looked at him when he referred to the war. There's no way to fake that kind of loyalty.

We need steel. You need Moonflower petals. Since apparently your own countrymen are reluctant to provide them.

It's a harsh contrast to the moment I was holding a dagger to that man's throat in the candy shop. Or when I had to dash Tessa's hopes about Laurel Pepperleaf's interest in her findings.

Thanks, she said. *I hate it here.*

Me too.

Jealousy isn't an emotion that lodges in my brain very often. I'm the brother to the king, so I rarely want for anything. I've spent years shoving away fear and anger and disappointment to where they can't be seen. With jealousy, I have no practice.

The emotion isn't about Captain Blakemore anyway. Not truly. I barely know him.

It's about everything I can't be for Tessa.

"Corrick," says Harristan.

His voice calls me back, and I look over. "What?"

"I asked if you *trust* him."

"I'm not sure. There's a part of me that *wants* to."

I think of the man who strode into the palace this afternoon. He's charming. Appropriately deferential yet also unwavering in his commitment to his crew and his mission. His story is solid, right down to the flag from his ship and the ring on his finger. His people have caused no trouble, and Harristan was right: their loyalty *is* impressive. It does speak to Captain Blakemore's character—especially when he's asked for nothing more than a chance to establish trade between countries. No coins, no jewels, not even a better ship or a bigger crew—and he certainly could have asked for all of it.

"Are you truly unsure," Harristan says, "or are you worried that he's caught Tessa's eye?"

That's so on point that I frown and look over. "Do you really think he's caught her eye?"

He sighs and runs a hand down his face. "Cory."

I give an aggravated sigh myself. "Fine. I don't *distrust* him." I pause. "I'm sure it's also occurred to you that if *he* made it here unscathed and unnoticed, this new king could have a whole naval force just waiting to see what we say."

"Yes. I've considered it. I didn't stop a revolution just to get embroiled in a war."

A war we wouldn't win. Not right now. Harristan doesn't need me to tell him that.

"If you send me," I say, "it will further complicate matters with the rebels. Tessa can remain here, I suppose, but they already don't trust us. I'm sure they'll believe that any Moonflower we receive from Ostriary will go right into the Royal Sector."

"I considered that, too." He's watching me now, gauging my reaction. "Which is why I believe you should bring Tessa, seeing as she's willing to go." My heart kicks, but then my brother adds, "Along with the rebel Lochlan."

"What?" I demand. "*Why?*"

"Because Captain Blakemore has limited our number to six, and that will allow for three guards. Laurel Pepperleaf will demand to go as well, but I will refuse. I want to send a message to her father that I will not pander to their sector any longer. If there are other avenues for medicine, we have a duty to explore them, and I will not risk Moonlight Plains interfering in the negotiations when they're already threatening to halve their production. We will see what Ostriary has to offer, and we will negotiate accordingly. Half the consuls were ready to overthrow the throne, Corrick. This is a delicate balance from all sides."

"No—I *know* that. But what does that have to do with Lochlan?"

"He doesn't represent a sector from a position of authority. For us to extend an invitation to one of the rebels instead of someone in a position of privilege, it will be seen as an extension of trust, and I believe it will go far to convince the people of the Wilds *and* the wealthy sectors that we are considering the needs of all our citizens."

I study him. "And it'll get him out of the way so he can't plan any attacks while I'm gone."

Harristan gives me a sly smile. "That, too."

I don't smile back. He keeps hiding a cough. The consuls can't be trusted. We were under attack a few short weeks ago.

I don't want to leave him alone.

But if Ostriary has medicine, I don't think we should wait. I don't think we *can* wait.

My life, as always, seems torn between poor options.

A hand raps at the door, and we both look up in surprise. It's after midnight. I wonder if it's Quint. He's the only person in the palace who sleeps less than I do—and the only one who might be looking for either of us at this hour.

But a guard calls out, "Your Majesty, Guardsman Rocco has requested an audience."

That *is* a surprise. I raise my eyebrows and look at Harristan. Rocco was at the king's side for most of the day. "Hasn't Rocco been off duty for hours?"

"Yes." Harristan frowns, but he calls, "Send him in."

The guardsman strides through the doors to stand at attention, but he's no longer in his palace livery and armor. I don't think I've ever seen him in ordinary clothes, but he's no less imposing in calf-skin pants and a buttoned jerkin.

"Your Majesty," he says. His eyes flick to me. "Your Highness. Forgive me for interrupting. I know the hour is late."

"Forgiven," I say easily, because I'm more curious than annoyed.

Rocco looks to my brother. "I would have sent a message through the guard captain, but I thought it best if I spoke with you directly."

"Go ahead, Erik."

I blink, startled. "Is that your first name?"

"It is."

"I don't believe I've ever heard it." I don't know why this is star-tling, whether it's Harristan's casual *use* of it, or the fact that I never considered it. Maybe both. The man saved my life. I feel like I should have known.

Maybe I look poleaxed, because the guardsman gives me an ironic nod and adds, "A pleasure to meet you, Your Highness."

His tone is so dry that it almost makes me smile. I don't know any of Harristan's guards *well*, but I've liked Rocco since the day the palace was attacked. I should probably like him best for saving my life, but that's not it. It's that he was willing to obey my order to break Allisander's fingers to prevent the consul from overthrowing Harristan.

Then again, maybe that says more about *me* than the guardsman.

Harristan gives me a withering glance. "Go ahead, *Rocco*," he says.

"I understand you will be selecting guards to sail to Ostriary," he says. "Captain Huxley presumes you will not choose from among your personal guard, but I would like to volunteer."

"Why?" says Harristan.

"Captain Blakemore is not allowing any sailors from Kandala on board his ship." Rocco glances at me. "But I believe the risk to the King's Justice is rather great."

"So you believe members from the king's personal guard should go?" I say. "Right now, the risk to Harristan is far greater."

"I don't disagree. But a sailor loyal to Kandala should be on board. Someone with the experience to know the route followed, the way the ship is sailed." He hesitates. "Someone who could bring the ship back if something were to happen to Captain Blakemore."

"I can't simply dress up a sailor as a guardsman," Harristan says.

"No, Your Majesty," Rocco agrees. "But . . . you could send a guardsman who knows his way around a ship. I grew up around the docks in Sunkeep. My brother and his wife still sail the trade route along the coast of Sunkeep and Steel City. I joined them when I took a week's leave last spring."

Interesting. Harristan and I exchange a glance.

"So you'll be a sailor and a spy," I say.

"A guard," he says, a bit ruefully. "I'll keep you alive, Your Highness—and I'll be able to ensure your safe passage, regardless of what happens to Captain Blakemore." The weight of those words sink in as he looks to Harristan. "I wanted to make this offer before you made any announcements so there would be no later changes that might invite questions."

I watch my brother turn this around in his head, examining it from all angles, looking for points of weakness. When he settles on one, it's not something I considered.

"This is a good suggestion," Harristan says. "You didn't want to discuss this with the guard captain?"

The guardsman hesitates. "Captain Huxley still has not determined how the rebels were able to gain access to the palace during the initial revolt. I've already seen how quickly Rian Blakemore and his crew have heard rumors around the Royal Sector—rather specific rumors about you, Your Highness, and Miss Tessa, as well. If I made my skills known to Captain Huxley, I worried that there would be no way to keep them secret."

He has my full attention now. "Are you saying you think the guard captain is a security risk?"

Rocco glances between me and my brother. He might be in the king's personal guard, which carries some benefits, but he's not an officer. Making an unfounded claim against the guard captain could put him out of a job, and he looks like he's just realized he's cornered himself.

"Go ahead," says Harristan. "Answer freely."

Rocco hesitates again, but then he nods, and I realize that he might not trust the guard captain, but he must trust my brother. "Captain Huxley has been known to accept a bit of coin for gossip about the royal family. If someone started asking questions, I think he's likely to look the other way if a bit of silver crossed his palm."

"Are there any other guards with your skills?" says Harristan.

"Not that I know of—but again, I didn't want to inquire and invite questions."

Harristan nods. "Very well. I'll accept your offer. I'll be sending three guards. Choose the two who you feel would make the best match for this assignment, and bring me their names when you're on duty tomorrow. Anyone but Thorin. Don't go through the guard captain. I'll tell him I made the selection myself."

Rocco's eyes widen in surprise. "Yes, Your Majesty."

"You're dismissed," Harristan says.

Once he's gone, I say, "The guard captain will choke when you don't involve him in the decision."

"Rocco has earned the chance to choose his own team." He pauses. "And I trust him to bring guards who will be loyal."

I study him. "I don't like that he doesn't trust Captain Huxley." It makes me not want to leave, but I don't say that. "Why did you tell him not to choose Thorin? He probably would have been his first choice."

"Because you're leaving." For the first time I see the worry in his eyes that I already feel in my gut. "I need someone I can trust, too, Cory."

―⊢―

It's late enough when I leave my brother's room that I expect Quint to be asleep, but when I stride down the hallway to his chambers, I find him up and waiting with a half-finished bottle of wine and a quarter-finished book.

His door was slightly ajar when I arrived, but I push it closed behind me. Quint slips a piece of paper into the book to mark his place, then adds it to the pile of books and papers on his desk. Servants tend his rooms just the same as everywhere else in the palace, so my friend's quarters aren't *messy*, but there's definitely a good dose of clutter, as if one thing drew his attention before something else claimed it.

I remove his abandoned jacket from the other chair, toss it onto the foot of his bed, then drop into the chair myself. He doesn't ask if I want a glass of wine; he simply takes one look at me and pours.

"It's late," he says. "I wasn't expecting you."

I raise an eyebrow. "I'm never asleep at this hour."

"At dinner, you looked ready to take Captain Blakemore's head off. I fully expected you to be spending the evening making Tessa forget that a ship even sailed into port."

I frown and take a gulp of wine. I probably should be. But I was worried that every petty and jealous thought would find its way out of my head. She's asleep by now anyway.

Probably.

I wish I could stop thinking of that moment in the carriage when she was afraid—and some of her fear was of *me*.

This is too complicated. I shove the thoughts away and focus on more immediate matters.

"I was discussing Blakemore's offer with Harristan," I say.

"Are you going to go?"

"Yes."

His eyebrows go up. Maybe he wasn't expecting such a definite answer so quickly.

"Tessa was right," I say with a sigh. "And as much as I hate it, he seems earnest enough. If they're willing to provide medicine in exchange for steel, we have an obligation to do what we can to provide for our people." I tell him about Harristan's suggestions for Lochlan to attend—and Rocco's clandestine offer.

"I don't like this uncertainty among the palace guards," Quint says. "Especially *now*."

"I agree," I say. I think about the day that Tessa snuck into the palace. She followed some girls right into the servant's entrance, and even though I had the guard dismissed who overlooked it, this is the first time I examine that moment from a new angle. Could the guard have been prepared—or bribed—to allow a rebel into the palace?

But Tessa herself did it on a whim. She wasn't an assassin.

Did someone else slip into the palace that day?

It's been too long. There's no way to know.

I sigh. "Any kind of instability among the guards puts Harristan at risk. I wonder if there are others who feel similarly about Captain Huxley." I pause, thinking. "I wonder if he's the only one."

Quint reaches for one of his little folios and makes a note on the page. "Many of the guardsmen linger with the kitchen girls. I'll find a reason to be in the kitchens and see what I can find out." He sets down his fountain pen to look back at me. "You're not as severe as you used to be. I wonder if that's emboldened some dissenters."

I grunt noncommittally. As much as I want to disagree, a man leapt at me with a knife in the middle of a candy store this afternoon. My chest is tight with indecision. I hated being Cruel Corrick, but I hate the idea that *not* being Cruel Corrick will bring about more problems.

Especially if I'm about to leave.

Tessa once asked me why I couldn't just step out of my role and lose myself into the Wilds as Weston Lark if I hated the palace life so much.

I couldn't leave my brother.

That's what I told her.

And now I'm doing exactly that. Rebels got into the palace a few weeks ago, and we narrowly escaped. Would Harristan be able to escape again, if he were alone? I might have Lochlan with me, but that doesn't mean there aren't a hundred others who could build an explosive.

I wish I could go to Tessa, but I'm terrified of admitting weakness just now, as if putting voice to my fears would make them more real. I'd give anything to don a mask and climb down a rope and find her in the workshop, the way I used to. Now, everything is just as dangerous, and somehow ten times more complicated.

And Weston Lark is dead anyway. I frown and run a hand back through my hair.

"Corrick."

Quint's quiet voice snaps me out of my reverie, and I realize it's the second time that's happened this evening. "What?"

"As much as I adore being audience to your silent angst, I should remind you that it *is* late."

He's right, and I'm being rude. I sigh, drain my wineglass, and stand.

But then I stop. Quint wasn't sleeping. He was reading. His door was open.

There was an empty wineglass waiting.

"You never chase me out of your quarters," I muse.

"I'm hardly chasing you."

"Quint." I feign a gasp. "Are you *waiting* on someone?"

He gives me a look. "Don't invent drama for me when your own is too much to bear."

He's probably right, but now I've found a thread to pull, and I want it all to unravel. "Who is it?" I say.

"No one. Truly."

He'd fool anyone else in this palace, including my brother, but I know Quint far too well. I lean in. "You're *lying*."

He sighs. "You have far more important things to worry about—"

"Please tell me it's Captain Blakemore, because that would solve the *vast* majority of my problems."

"I rather doubt it would."

"As your friend," I add conspiratorially, "I *do* feel an obligation to warn you that I didn't get the impression that he would be interested in—"

"*Corrick.*"

I stop.

"Honestly." He gives me a withering glance. "It's not Captain Blakemore, and it's nowhere near as salacious as what you're imagining. But that's all you're getting out of me this evening."

"Fine." I smile, and for a moment, I'm grateful that he's given me *something* to draw my attention away from matters that seem so impossible. "Enjoy your visit."

I say *visit* like I mean something else entirely, but Quint doesn't take the bait. He picks up the book he was reading when I walked in. "Have a pleasant evening, Your Highness."

"Yes, of course, Master Quint." My smile turns into a grin. "I'll leave the door open when I go."

But at the door I hesitate. A moment of distraction isn't enough to bury all my worries.

Quint looks up. He knows me as well as I know him, because any teasing disappears from his voice. "I truly wasn't chasing you out. Sit if you need to sit. A game of chess perhaps?"

I consider it for a moment, but he clearly *was* waiting for someone, so I shake my head. "You're right. I should retire."

But I still don't move. Quint waits.

"He's never had to do this alone," I say quietly.

He looks at me steadily. "Neither have you."

The thought is jarring. But . . . of course he's right. I've been thinking of all the risks to Harristan. I hadn't considered that we'll be apart for the first time since our parents died. I hadn't considered that I'll be boarding a boat to negotiate the price of steel with a king I've never met in a kingdom I know little about.

I have to force worries out of my head, or I'll stride right back down the corridor to tell Harristan I've changed my mind.

But I look back at my friend, one of the few people in this palace I truly trust. "Take care of him, Quint."

He nods. "You have my word."

CHAPTER TEN

The Outlaw

It's late and I'm tired.

I trudge the empty paths of the Wilds with a heavy step. The sky above is an inky black, clouds obscuring any stars, keeping the woods dark and full of ominous shadows. A misting rain fills the air. The moon is so faint it might be a memory.

I'm leaving coins with less care this morning. A handful here, a tiny stack there. I don't look for messages in the dust or touch any waiting gifts. I just want to do what I can before there's any chance I'll be missed.

I dip a hand in my pouch for a handful of coins, then move to drop them beside the ax blade at the fifth house.

"Don't be mad, Fox," says a soft voice.

My heart trips and stumbles, but there's a part of me that isn't surprised. I sigh and turn. "You gave your word, Violet."

"I know, I know." She uncurls from the shadows, shivering in her sleeping shift. Her eyes are wild and guileless. "I started to think maybe I imagined it. You know? Like maybe it was a dream. I had to make sure you were real."

"I'm real." I glance at her feet, bare in the grass. A bandage is still tied tightly in place, but it's not the same torn muslin I used. "How's the foot?"

"Good!" she whispers, and there's a gleeful note in her voice, as if she's relieved I'm not angry at her. "I told my mother it happened in the stable."

I nod and drop the coins on the stump beside the ax, then turn away to move on.

She swishes through the long grass to walk beside me.

I sigh and keep walking. Maybe if I say nothing, she'll grow bored and go home.

I'm not that lucky. "Where do you go next?" she says.

"Right back where I came from if you insist on following."

"My cousin doesn't think you're from the Wilds. You've got too many coins. That's why you wear the mask, right? Why did you pick red? Are you—"

"*Violet.*" I round on her.

Her eyes stare back at me, wide and innocent. "What?"

"Go home."

"But I want to help you."

"You can't." I glance down. "And even if you could, you're in bare feet. You'll end up with something worse than an arrowhead."

"I'm always in bare feet. I walked my toes through my last pair of boots, and Mama says there'll need to be snow on the ground before she'll find coins for a new pair."

Oh.

Despite what I'm doing, I'd somehow forgotten just how very desperate some of these people are.

I reach into my pouch and pull out another few coppers. "Here," I say brusquely. "That should be enough for boots to last until then."

"Oh!" She takes them and slips them into a pocket of her sleeping shift. "Thank you, Fox. But I'll give them to Toby. He lives next door. His da broke his arm, so he can't work at the mill. Mama has been baking them extra bread." Her voice drops. "Toby's mother died last winter."

I'm not sure what to say. I want to give her another handful of coins, but there's a part of me that wonders if she'll just give them to another neighbor.

She glances at the path, and her eyebrows flicker into a frown. "Don't you have more coins to leave?"

"I do." I turn and start walking again.

She strides along beside me. "Maybe people will see us and think we're Wes and Tessa!"

She sounds like this would be the ideal scenario. "The whole point is *not* to be seen," I say.

"But *I* saw you."

"Trust me, I'm regretting it al—"

A shout erupts somewhere ahead of us on the path, and I swear, then duck into the foliage, dragging Violet with me. She squeals at the suddenness of it, and I slap my hand over her mouth.

"Quiet," I snap in her ear, my voice low and rough.

She nods quickly behind my hand. Her breathing is quick, and she's all but straining against my grip, trying to see the path. Footsteps are definitely heading this way.

"I hate going out all this way," a man is saying. "That rebel meeting isn't supposed to be until the end of the week."

Rebel meeting. I'm frozen in place.

"I know," grunts another one. "But I saw the coins on a step. That thief is out *tonight*."

I bristle. I'm not a thief. Violet cranes her head around to look at me. My heart is pounding in my chest, begging for action.

I glance down. My clothes are all shades of black and brown, invisible in the faint moonlight, but her sleeping shift is pale and might as well be a beacon in the darkness.

"Take off your mask," she whispers behind my hand.

My eyes snap to hers. "What?"

"Take off your mask. Say you were taking your sick sister to find a physician."

"I—*what*?"

She gives me an exasperated look, like *I'm* the crazy one, then flops against my shoulder dramatically, her head lolling back, her eyes half open. She goes limp so quickly that I barely catch her before she tumbles into the undergrowth.

Well, damn.

"Look!" a man calls, and I swear inwardly. "What's that up there?"

I'm frozen in place. I can't take this mask off. I *can't*.

Or . . . maybe I *can*. It's the middle of the night, and there's little moonlight. I couldn't name a single officer in the night patrol, and I rarely have cause to be in the Wilds. The chance of anyone here recognizing me at this hour is low.

But not nonexistent.

Violet hisses, "Move, Fox."

I reach up and jerk the mask over my head, scrubbing my hand through my hair to muss it up, then shove the silken red fabric down into my pouch. I stand, dragging her with me, trying to awkwardly scoop her into my arms.

She doesn't help at *all*. I'd be impressed by her commitment to the act if I weren't so irritated.

"Who's there!" another man shouts, and I hear the click of a crossbow bolt being loaded.

This could go very badly. I take a slow breath so I can strip any tension from my voice. "Is that the night patrol?" I call. "I need to get my sister to the physician." I try to add a plaintive tone to my words, but I wasn't prepared to perform on demand, and I likely just sound aggravated. "She can't wake."

Violet somehow goes even more limp, and she nearly slips through my arms. I adjust my grip, then pick her up fully. She's even thinner than I thought.

Then I can't think at all because two crossbows are pointed right at me.

I've envisioned this outcome a dozen times, but my imagination didn't prepare me for the bolt of fear that pierces my chest. I almost can't breathe around it. For an instant, my thoughts spin, because it's obvious that they don't recognize anything about me—and just as obvious that they'd pull those triggers without thinking twice about it. I'm alone and it's dark and there'd be no one around to care. No one would even notice. Not for *hours*.

"Please," I say. I have to clear my throat, because my breathing has gone ragged. "My . . . my sister."

Violet lets out a low, painful moan.

One of the men lowers his crossbow, and he leans in. "What's wrong with her?"

She didn't have the sense to listen when a masked outlaw told her to go home.

"I don't know," I say. "I found her like this." I think better of it, then tack on, "Sir."

In my arms, Violet begins making retching sounds, and it's so realistic that I almost fall for it myself. But the man springs back.

I hold her toward the other man with the crossbow. "She can't stop vomiting, sir. Can you help me carry her?"

He stumbles back a step, too.

"Oh no, Will," she moans. A hand flops onto her stomach. "It's going to come out the other end."

If she somehow makes *that* happen, I am absolutely dropping her.

But the first patrolman grabs the other's arm and jerks him back another step. "Get her to the physician, then," he snaps. "Be quick about it. You're not supposed to be out after midnight."

"Yes," I say quickly, nodding like a fool. "Yes, sir. Thank you, sir."

He glances at Violet and curls his lip when she groans again— but then he turns away, striding through the darkness.

I keep walking, sticking to the main path. Violet hangs limply in my arms and doesn't make a sound aside from plaintive moans.

Eventually, they're long out of sight and I'm out of breath from carrying her for so long. For as thin as she is, she's certainly not tiny. The next time she lets out a sound, I say, "That's quite enough. They're gone."

She all but *springs* out of my arms and grins at me. "I was rather good, wasn't I?"

"Good enough," I allow. I shove my hand into my pouch to find the mask.

"I saved your *life*, Fox!"

I give her a look. "You endangered it by following me."

She scowls. I ignore it and untie the knot in the red silk so I can put the mask back on.

As I do, though, I realize she's studying me.

Maybe it's not as dark as I thought.

I set my jaw and turn away, glaring into the woods. I've taken too many chances tonight. "Forget what you saw."

"I don't *want* to," she says dreamily. "You're more handsome than I imagined."

That's so unexpected that it startles a smile out of me. She's barely more than a child, but I don't want to hurt her feelings, so I say, "I'm honored, but my heart longs for another, Violet."

"Truly?" She sighs. "Is it very serious?"

That actually makes me laugh. "Quite." I tie the knot in place, then turn back. "Who's Will?"

"My cousin." She pauses. "What's *your* name?"

"Fox is fine." I glance down the path, then up at the sky. "What's the rebel meeting they were talking about? Do you know?"

She shakes her head—then nods. "Mama says the Benefactors have a new leader. But it's not one of the consuls."

Interesting. "Do you know where the meeting is?"

"No—but most gatherings take place in the commons. Do you know it?"

I do, but I shake my head. "It's not important. Will you be able to get home safely?"

She nods. I fish another handful of coins out of my pouch and hold them out to her. "For *boots* this time."

She inhales sharply, but I narrow my eyes, and she nods.

"Yes, Fox." She sighs.

When she takes the coins, I study her in the darkness. "I might not be able to come around very much for a while."

Her eyes flash wide. "What? Why? Because of me? Did I—"

"No. Not because of you." I hesitate. She's already seen my face, and hopefully I won't come to regret that. I can't afford to give her much more information. "I will return as soon as I can, but for now, I have duties that will . . . that will keep me away for a matter of days. Possibly weeks."

Possibly forever. But I don't say that.

Her lips part. "But . . . but we *need* you."

I flinch, then glance in the direction of the Royal Sector. "I know. But right now, there are others who need me more."

CHAPTER ELEVEN

Tessa

I'm always surprised how quickly things can happen when people have money in hand. When I worked for Mistress Solomon, I remember she once had to wait four weeks to have a shipment of creams sent to a buyer in Sunkeep, just because she wasn't willing to pay a wagoner to make a special trip. I thought for sure the creams would go rancid from sitting out in the summer heat, but Mistress Solomon sent them anyway, saying it wasn't her fault that the buyer wasn't willing to pay a premium for a faster delivery.

But in the Royal Sector, it seems like all someone has to do is make a decision, and they can have whatever they want at their door in a few hours. For the king, it's sometimes a matter of *minutes*. After meeting him, I never considered Harristan to be a frivolous man, but there are times that he requests something offhandedly, completely oblivious to the time and effort it must take to fulfill his wishes. He'll call for tea, and it'll appear more quickly than it's possible to boil water. He'll order an assessment of steel shipments across Kandala over the last fifty years, and advisers will have stacks of paperwork to review within an hour.

The king agreed to this mission to Ostriary, and the traveling party was arranged and outfitted within a few days. My trunks were packed before I was even aware that I was going. I don't know many of the details, because Harristan and Corrick have been tied up for much of the week, but it's clear that I'm to be included. Eagerness keeps making my heart skip.

But now it's dusk on the third day since the ship arrived, and I've hardly laid eyes on Corrick since the dinner with Captain Blakemore. The prince's tension was so potent at the table. It's obvious he doesn't like the other man, but it's hard to argue with a supply of Moonflower petals when people are still dying and rebels are still calling for revolution. I know Corrick has been embroiled in planning with the king, but it's left me with a lot of time to stare at the ceiling and replay the conversations over and over again. I keep remembering Rian's voice when he said, *You have to force your sectors to provide medicine?*

The captain is so principled. His people are so loyal.

Kandala's people are terrified of Prince Corrick. In the candy shop, for a spare moment, *I* was terrified of Prince Corrick. I wonder what that says about *his* character.

And my own.

I often wonder what my parents would think of where I am now. I know they would have supported the way I was stealing medicine to distribute among the Wilds. They were doing it first, after all. But then I ended up in the palace. I ended up working for the prince, and sometimes I wonder if I'm helping anyone at all.

I don't like the direction of these thoughts. They always seem to travel in directions I don't want to explore.

But I do think my parents would be proud of what I'm doing now. I'm going to *Ostriary*. To help negotiate for *medicine*. I once stood in the shadows with Corrick and told him we should start a revolution—and later, I helped the king stop one. But since then, I've been stuck in stuffy rooms, working with physicians or trying to negotiate with Lochlan. Everything is so . . . so *slow*. So ineffective. I've missed my nightly runs with Wes so much that I sometimes wake in the middle of the night and worry that I'm going to be late to the workshop, before remembering that I'm in the palace—and Wes doesn't exist.

A knock sounds at my door, and my heart leaps. Maybe he's finally found some time to see me. As usual, my future feels so uncertain. I need to look into Corrick's blue eyes and hear the warmth in his voice. I need to erase the memory of the man on the floor of the candy shop, Corrick's dagger stealing blood from his throat. I need to remember why we're doing this together—why I trust him at all.

But a guard calls out, "His Royal Majesty, King Harristan."

WHAT.

I have to slap a hand over my mouth to keep from saying it out loud. The king never visits me personally. If he wants to see me, he sends a summons.

I all but choke on my breath and call out, "Come—come in!" I barely have a chance to get to my feet before the door swings wide, and then the king is in my room.

"Your Majesty," I say, offering a curtsy.

The door swings shut behind him, and I can't help but stare. We've always had a bit of an odd relationship. Even though we hiked through the Wilds together and faced down the rebels side by side, I sometimes forget all of that when he's here in the palace being . . . the *king*. He's Corrick's brother, but he's still the most imposing man I know. I don't think I've been alone with Harristan since . . . well, *ever*.

Harristan doesn't seem to notice—or care—because he wastes absolutely no time. "The winds have turned," he says without pre-amble. "Captain Blakemore worries that a storm is brewing, and at this time of year, it could last for days. My advisers concur." He pauses. "Rather than waiting to see how the storm manifests, you will be leaving this evening."

I stare at him. *This evening*. I wish I could read something in his voice. I twist my hands together. "Yes, Your Majesty."

"I will expect you to ensure everyone from Kandala continues to receive the correct measure of Moonflower elixir each day," he says. "Quint is arranging for your apothecary tools to be on board the ship, along with a supply of Moonflower from the palace stores." He pauses, and a new weight enters his voice. "I am entrusting you with this, Tessa."

I take a deep breath, but nod. "Yes, of course."

"We are all hopeful that Captain Blakemore has access to med-icine that works equally as well, but we've been tricked before."

"I understand."

"The materials will be kept locked in your room. You will not allow anyone else to prepare the medicine. Is this understood?"

There. I hear it in his voice. The fear.

I nod quickly. "Yes. I understand."

"I will have four weeks of medicine provided. You will attend with Prince Corrick, of course, along with Lochlan Cresswell."

My eyebrows shoot straight up. "You're sending *Lochlan*?"

"Yes. If we are sending a contingent from Kandala to determine a better source for the Moonflower, I felt it could be beneficial to send representatives of *all* my people."

Wow. I don't know what to say. I'm staring at him like he told me the sky is green.

"Do you disagree with my choice?" he says.

"No. I . . . I'm surprised."

"I'm hopeful that it will go far to gain trust with the rebels. Three guards will be joining you. Rocco and Kilbourne, of my personal guard, as well as Silas of the palace guard." He hesitates. "If you have any concerns about the medicine, about the captain, about anything at all, you are to bring them to Corrick himself, or to Rocco. No one else. Not even the other guards. Am I understood?"

I study him, trying to figure this out. There's more to all of this than he's saying.

He's not offering more information, so I swallow and nod. "Yes, Your Majesty."

Harristan studies me back, and *his* scrutiny is intimidating. Sometimes, when I'm in his presence, I simultaneously want to yell at him to *do something*, while I also just want to give him a hug.

Because he's the king, I can't do either.

Harristan's voice drops, just a bit, until there's no danger of him being overheard outside this door.

"In reviewing records and shipping logs, we've been able to corroborate some of Captain Blakemore's story," he says. "But this is not a journey without risk, Tessa. Captain Blakemore appears to be very forthright in his desire to help both Ostriary and Kandala, but this could still be a means to separate me from my brother, to an end that no one has foreseen."

Sending Prince Corrick is such a risk, but I know why the king wouldn't send someone else.

Harristan doesn't *trust* anyone else.

The king is always stoic, even in the moments when he should be vulnerable. I remember Corrick sitting in the carriage telling me why Harristan never has a companion by his side, and it's a bit heartbreaking. If anyone needs a little gentle care, the king should probably be at the top of the list. I think about the royal brothers' lot in life often, and I wonder if they would have ruled entirely differently if, after their parents were killed, the consuls had found the patience to show them a moment of grace, instead of bickering over the throne and who could volley for most power.

"I have one more request for you," the king says. "And this is a request I would like to keep between us." He pauses. "Just us. Not even my brother."

I hesitate. "Am I allowed to ask what it is before I agree to that?"

"I would like for you to prepare a month's worth of elixir," he says. "For me alone."

I frown. "You distrust your physicians?" I say quietly.

"I'm worried the disloyalty in the palace runs deeper than any of us realize. There are very few people I trust, Tessa. Three of you are climbing aboard a ship tonight."

Now I understand why Harristan wants to keep this a secret. If Corrick knew his brother was this worried, he wouldn't go.

I frown. "I can't make medicine that would last for a month. It wouldn't be effective." Storm clouds fill his eyes, so I rush on, "You once said you spent a lot of time with the palace physicians. If I put together the pieces, maybe you could mix everything together yourself each day?"

He's studying me, but for a bare instant, a flicker of fear and uncertainty crosses his features.

"It wouldn't be difficult," I say. "I can create vials with most of the mixture, but you'd have to grind the Moonflower yourself, then add the powder. I can separate petals so you wouldn't have to weigh them. Do you have somewhere to hide everything?"

"Yes. I'll send Quint to fetch whatever you can prepare."

Quint. I'm sure Corrick will miss his friend, but I'm glad the Palace Master will be here to look out for Harristan. I nod briskly. "I'll do it right now. I'll label everything."

He nods and takes a step back, and that flicker of fear and uncertainty crosses his features again. I almost reach out to squeeze his hand.

But then it all smooths out, and he's the forbidding king once again.

"Farewell, Tessa," he says.

I curtsy again. "Farewell," I say, and the word carries so much more weight than it should. "Your Majesty."

Without another word, he opens the door, and the king disappears into the hallway.

I've lived in Artis all my life, so I'm familiar with the docks on both sides of the Queen's River. My parents used to travel by ferry across the river once a week to tend to workers at both harbors. I remember gaping up at some of the larger ships that would transport wealthy citizens up and down the river, or the massive cargo vessels that were always stacked high with crates of goods from all over Kandala. Flags and sails are always snapping in the wind, workers calling out instructions from every direction. Dozens of shops line the streets around the harbors, so it's a bustling, busy area, especially in the summertime.

The fever sickness always runs rampant along the river, and I've never been able to determine whether it's from the close quarters shared by the workers, or if it has more to do with the constant contact with other illnesses that might make boatmen more susceptible to the fever. My father used to say that everyone at the harbor would end up with a fever and a cough eventually.

It's late when my carriage draws up to the docks, but more people are about than I expect. Oil lamps line the crowded walkways, and someone has installed a few electric spotlights to point at the pier where the wealthiest vessels have been moored.

When I step down from my carriage, I spot the ship at once, because there's no mistaking a vessel that has a full contingent of royal guards surrounding the gangway, awaiting the arrival of the King's Justice. Harristan is bidding his brother farewell at the palace in some kind of brief public ceremony, but I was sent ahead to ensure the medicinal supplies are as they should be. I don't mind, because it gives me a chance to look up at the ship without all the guards and fanfare that Prince Corrick will bring with him. Clouds hang heavy in the sky, so the sails are wide and gray in the filtered moonlight, fluttering in the wind. The name *Dawn Chaser* has been painted in swirling white script along the hull. It's not as big as many of the other ships, but it's much larger than I expected after Captain Blakemore refused to take any more than six people.

Then again, the captain is clearly worried, too. That's why he didn't want any sailors or navigators on board. This journey is requiring trust on both sides.

I intend to wait with the carriage, but Rocco and Kilbourne are off to the side of the guards, standing at attention, waiting like the others. They're in palace livery stitched with blue and purple, with a few weapons at hand, but unlike the other guards, they wear no armor.

I think of the king telling me that I can only bring concerns to Rocco, not any of the other guards. He must trust the others to some extent if he's sending them on this trip—but the warning still gives me pause.

When I approach, Rocco glances at me and gives me a nod. "Miss Tessa."

"Rocco," I say. "I'm really glad you're coming." I mean it, too. Most of the palace guards are formal with me, but Rocco has always been kind, and a bit more open. He and Thorin saved all of our lives when the palace was under attack, and that's created a bond among us all that seems to transcend rank and title.

Rocco nods to the man standing beside him. "Kilbourne will be with us as well. Guardsman Silas is already on board."

Kilbourne isn't as tall as Rocco, but he's easily as broad across the shoulders. He's a bit older, too, probably close to thirty, with short blond hair and ruddy cheeks.

"Kilbourne," I say. "I'm glad to make your acquaintance."

"As am I, Miss Tessa." He smiles. "I'm honored to be chosen for the journey."

There's an interesting weight to the way he says that, and I'm trying to puzzle it out, when Rocco says dryly, "He means it's good pay. Kilbourne's wife is expecting their first child."

Well, that's charming. "Congratulations!"

His smile widens, and his cheeks redden further. "I didn't want to leave her, but Sara all but shoved me out the door. I want to buy her a house before the baby comes."

He looks as aloof and indomitable as the rest of the king's personal guard, but when he talks about his wife and future baby, his eyes sparkle, and I can hear the affection in his tone. Not just affection: excitement.

"When is she due?" I ask.

"Late autumn, we think."

"And she's feeling well?"

His eyes soften even more, and he nods. "Very well, thank you."

I like him. I'm glad he's coming. There's something very calming about his presence that has already eased my nerves.

"No armor?" I say to them.

"It's traveling with us by chest," says Rocco. "We'll have it once we arrive in Ostriary."

A male voice speaks from behind me. "If an armored guardsman goes overboard, he turns into an anchor."

I turn to find Captain Blakemore striding down the gangway leading to his ship. His dark hair is a bit windblown, and his eyes are in shadow, but despite all the guards, he looks more relaxed here than he did at dinner. He's clearly at home on his ship. His jacket is unbuttoned, revealing a short dagger belted at his waist.

"Miss Cade," he says, then offers me a bow.

As I curtsy in return, my cheeks warm in spite of myself. I don't think I'll ever get used to anyone treating *me* with courtly manners, especially outside the palace. "Captain Blakemore."

"The guardsmen won't be going overboard," Rocco says, and there's a note in his voice that somehow makes it sound like a warning.

"I rather hope *no one* will be going overboard," the captain says brightly. He offers me his arm. "Miss Cade, would you like to come aboard?"

"I have things that I need to keep with me." I pause. "I can wait for a porter."

"As you like. But I hate to leave you in the rain when some of the others have already selected their rooms."

Oh.

I'm not sure what to say or do.

Captain Blakemore's eyes search mine. "Ah, forgive me. Will you be sharing quarters with Prince Corrick? If you'd like for him to be present to choose, I can offer—"

"Oh! No. I—we—he's—I—" I break off and flush again, because I wasn't expecting a question like that—and I'm definitely not ready with an answer. I can't imagine Corrick would expect us to room together. "I'm here as an apothecary. I will have my own quarters, Captain."

He watches the emotions play out on my face, then straightens. "Of course, Miss Cade. I apologize. My assumption was too bold." He pauses. "Once again, I sense that I have asked a question that might . . . put you at risk."

"No! I'm not—he's not—" I break off. His expression is so earnest. It makes all my stammering feel foolish.

Rocco saves me. "Miss Cade has earned the king's favor," he says. "And his protection."

Again, the words carry a hint of warning, and the captain's eyes spark with intrigue. "Noted."

I'm not sure what to say to *that* either. A lick of wind carries across the dark water to swirl between us, ruffling his hair and swirling my skirts. A few drops of rain nip at my cheeks.

"There's a storm coming," I say. "Is it safe to leave at night?"

"The winds will put us well ahead of it." He smiles. "Water is water, Miss Cade. Tonight won't be our only night at sea."

"Oh. Yes, of course." Wind whips between us again, stronger this time, and I shiver as more rain strikes my cheeks.

Behind me, Rocco says something too quiet for me to hear, but a moment later, I realize Kilbourne is pulling my apothecary trunk from the carriage.

"I can ensure your things reach your quarters," he says. He nods to the captain.

I open my mouth, then close it. "Well, I—I suppose we can get out of the rain."

The captain offers his arm again. After a moment, I take it.

The gangway isn't very long, and as we draw close to the top, I see lanterns have been hung along the main deck, and figures in shadows are tying ropes and moving crates. I recognize Lieutenant Tagas and the others who were at dinner, but there are a few people I haven't seen before. They're calling orders and directions to each other, and there's a sense of hurried preparation. No animosity, just a lively camaraderie. These are sailors who are used to working together. No, it's more than that. These are sailors who *like* working together. It's very different from the wary tension among the guards on the dock. The same wary tension that clings to the palace.

That knot of worry in my belly eases, just a bit.

The main deck is broad, with three masts supporting heavy sails, two of which are already unfurled. The largest mast is in the middle, nearly thirty feet high, with a crossbeam and crow's nest at the top. The ropes lashing the ship to the dock strain and creak as the wind catches the sails. At the front of the ship, there's a raised area leading to the prow, which is empty, but the back half—the *aft*, I think—has a set of doors that must lead into the officers' quarters. Ropes and chains and rigging seem to be everywhere, and two men are lugging crates toward an open panel on the deck that must lead to a ladder. The boat shifts in the wind, and the younger one slips on the newly wet deck. The crate drops, cracking onto the planks. Wood creaks and splinters, but the crate stays together—barely.

The older man swears loudly, then growls, "I told you to have these in the hold an *hour* ago."

"And I told *you* that—"

Captain Blakemore gives a short, sharp whistle through his teeth. "Gentlemen."

They startle, then look over. The older one looks a bit mollified. "Sorry, Captain." His Ostrian accent is thicker than the people who joined us at dinner. He gives me a nod. "Miss." But then he turns a glare on the other man and grabs hold of the crate. "Try not to break my foot this time, Brock."

Brock takes hold of the other side and snorts derisively. "Once these crates are loaded, I have a mind to break your face."

All right, maybe not *everyone* likes working together.

The captain looks at me, and his eyes are bright, but his voice is sedate. "Forgive my crew. They can be a bit rough-spoken."

I notice that he has a hint of their accent, too. I didn't hear it at dinner. I wonder if it's stronger now that he's back among his ship-mates. Something else he picked up in his six years in Ostriary, I suppose. "I grew up around the docks," I say, waving off his concern. "I'm no stranger to the mouth of a sailor."

The ship rocks hard against the dock, and my fingers dig into Captain Blakemore's arm until I catch my balance. But then a second gust tilts the deck in the opposite direction, and I stumble forward, right into his chest.

He catches me easily, keeping me upright, seeming to have no trouble with the motion of the ship. I inhale sharply, because it puts us very close. His eyes are so dark in the shadowed moonlight.

At my back, Kilbourne clears his throat.

I struggle to right myself. "I'm sorry. It's windy." Another gust tugs at my skirts, and I nearly do it again. I wish I'd had the good sense to wear trousers. "What—ah, what were we saying?"

The captain smiles. "You were saying that you're no stranger to the mouth of a sailor."

In a second I'm going to have to throw *myself* overboard. "I *meant*—"

"I know what you meant." He's still smiling, but his gaze has turned a bit appraising. "So you're familiar with a ship then."

"Oh! No. Well, a little. I was raised here in Artis. My father was an apothecary, though. We used to treat the dockworkers." I shiver. "I've seen it all. Sun poisoning, the Rose Rash in the winter, the Saltwater Cough in the summer months, the rope burns from the—"

The ship sways, nearly knocking me right into his chest again. Even Kilbourne staggers sideways with my trunk.

"Sorry," I say again. "I'm sure I'll find my sea legs in no time."

Captain Blakemore catches my arm, but this time he glances at the sky, then frowns. The easygoing look vanishes from his eyes.

The two men from earlier are emerging from below the deck, and the captain looks to them. "Brock, check that rigging." He looks across the deck, then whistles. "Gwyn!" he calls. "Drop that main sail. I want to shove off as soon as the prince is on board." Without missing a beat, he looks back at me. "Come, Miss Cade. Let's get you under cover."

CHAPTER TWELVE

Corrick

For all the memories I have of my brother sneaking out of the palace as a boy, I don't have any recent ones. The king can go where he likes, do what he likes, see who he likes. There's never any need to *sneak* anywhere.

But tonight, he's in the back corner of my carriage, wrapped in a cloak. I'm so keyed up about the journey that I almost shout for a guard before I recognize him.

"Don't make a fuss," he says quietly.

My heart is pounding so hard that I can't speak for a moment. I've stopped short in the doorway to the carriage, and a porter behind me says, "Your Highness?"

I force air into my lungs. "Yes. We should be on our way." I give my brother a look as I climb into the carriage, then tug the door closed behind me. "You're lucky I didn't pull a weapon," I murmur.

Outside, rain begins to patter on the roof of the carriage, and the driver clucks to the horses. As we begin rattling over cobblestones, I wait for Harristan to talk, but he says nothing, so I say nothing. The carriage bounces along forever, until I finally say, "What are you doing?"

"I wanted to see you off."

"You just did that."

And he did. It wasn't very grand, as we're leaving earlier than expected, but he said his goodbyes in the salon in front of the few courtiers in attendance. He said something appropriately regal and clasped my hand, but I was barely listening because my thoughts were screaming at me about the fact that any of this was happening.

"No, Cory," he says, and his voice is low and quiet. "I didn't."

The sentimentality of that strikes me. I can't believe he did this. I can't believe he's *here*.

In truth, I can't even remember the last time we shared a carriage together. Surely before our parents died. Once he was crowned king, the security risk was always too great to chance putting us both in the same vehicle. I should probably call for a stop right this instant.

I don't.

"None of your guards are with me," I say, and my voice is rough. "How did you get in here?"

"I told Quint he needed to use his skills of secrecy for *my* purposes this time."

My eyebrows go up. Quint is just full of surprises this week.

Then again, maybe it's not a surprise. They aren't friends, not even close, but Quint would never deny the king anything.

"How will you get back?" I say. "Or are you planning to stow away altogether? I'm sure I have a trunk strapped to the carriage."

"I thought about it."

He's teasing, but there's a note of truth in there.

I hate that there's a tiny part of my brain that wishes this were a possibility.

Maybe he does, too, because a sad light glimmers in his eyes when he says, "I'll offer the driver a few coins for a return trip to the palace."

I smile. "You'll give him a heart attack."

"I suppose I could walk."

I imagine him strolling up to the palace gates like an ordinary citizen. He would never. *Could* never. The gossip mill wouldn't stop churning for weeks.

But I can play this game. "It's a cloudy night," I say. "Watch out for cutpurses."

Harristan grins, his smile bright in the shadows. It reminds me of all the times we went tearing through the sectors as boys, when no one knew who we were. He's so severe as the stoic king that I sometimes forget he knows how to smile like that.

The rain picks up, rattling hard on the roof. It's not a long carriage ride to the docks. But my brother holds my eyes, and his smile fades. "Are you afraid?"

He's the only person who would ask me that so directly—and also the only person who'd get a wholly honest answer. "A little." I pause. "Are you?"

"A little." He hesitates, then coughs faintly.

"We don't need to leave today." I pause. "We could wait."

"Do you want to wait?" he says.

It's a genuine question. I could say *yes*, and he'd call this whole thing to a stop.

But we've discussed this with our advisers and some of the top sailors from Artis, most of whom agreed that leaving ahead

of the storm would provide strong winds for a quick journey—
and less risk.

Delaying now could look fearful and indecisive. That doesn't seem
like a good way to begin trade relations with the new Ostrian king.

"No," I say. The ground under the carriage has changed as we
draw close to the docks. Between the heavy clouds and the weather,
it's hard to make out much detail through the tiny window of the
carriage, but I can make out the letters curving along the hull.
The Dawn Chaser.

Lord. Even the name of his *ship* seems over the top.

My eyes scan the docks. I don't see Tessa, but I know she left
ahead of us. I have no idea whether Lochlan is on board yet. There's
a part of me that thinks Harristan should have just locked him in
the Hold and *told* everyone he was on the ship. Maybe we still could.
I bite at the edge of my thumbnail.

"Cory."

I look at my brother. "What."

"Do you want to wait?" He says each word with quiet emphasis.

His eyes are searching mine, and I search his right back. I keep
thinking of what Quint said, how this is the first time Harristan
and I will be doing any of this alone. The enormity of that tightens
my chest. We've never been alone. Not when we were boys, sneaking into the Wilds with a few pieces of silver in our pockets, not
when our parents were killed, not when rebels stormed the palace
and we ran for our lives.

"Harristan," I say. "Do *you* want me to wait?"

He says nothing, and the carriage draws to a stop. Suddenly,
there's no rattle of hooves on cobblestones, and the air between us
is silent.

A porter begins to swing the door open. "Your Highness—"

"Not yet." I reach out and snap the door closed. My voice drops until it's barely louder than a whisper, and I repeat the question. "Do you? Do you want me to wait?"

He inhales deeply—then coughs.

I frown.

He lifts a hand, then takes a slow breath. "I'm fine."

I clench my jaw. I hate this.

"We have an opportunity to do something good, Cory," he says. "Father was so well regarded." He pauses. "I don't want fear and anger to be my legacy. I want to be . . . better."

He sounds . . . *hopeful.* I don't remember the last time I heard my brother sound hopeful.

"I do too," I say.

He nods, then extends a hand.

I reach out and clasp it. Harristan isn't one for affection, but his grip is tight and sure. For one brief second, my throat tightens, and I'm not sure I'm going to be able to climb out of this carriage.

But then he blinks and lets go, then reaches out to ruffle my hair, ending with a light shove, the way he did when we were boys. I scoff and bat his hand away, then reach for the latch on the door.

"Corrick," he says quietly, before my hand pulls the latch.

I turn. "What?"

He says nothing for a moment, and in that breath of silence, I feel the weight of his emotion.

"Come home safe, little brother."

I give him a nod. "I promise. Be here when I get back."

Then I open the door and slip into the falling rain alone.

Porters and footmen carry umbrellas, but the wind is such that I've got rain in my boots and down my collar by the time I make it to the line of guards who've assembled for my departure. I'm still tangled up with emotion about my brother, full of doubts and worries about the trip, and then Rocco informs me that Tessa is already on board with Kilbourne and Silas. "Captain Blakemore sought to get Miss Tessa out of the weather," Rocco says.

I'll bet he did.

"Excellent news," I say flatly. I glance around at the guards standing at attention in the rain. "What about Lochlan?"

"On board as well," he says. "He'll be watched by Guardsman Silas until we determine he's not a threat to you, Your Highness."

"Well chosen," I say, but I'm not entirely sure about that. Of all the guards Rocco could have chosen, I wouldn't have considered Silas. He's younger than I am, and I doubt he's ever been charged with anything more important than babysitting empty carriages. He's hardly been a member of the guard for six months. But his family owns a number of iron mines in Trader's Landing, and they have a bustling shipping business.

Meaning this guard will know iron and steel—and will likely know ships as well. That will be an asset right up to the moment when I need an experienced guard.

I glance at the gangway, then pull my pocket watch free. Water droplets immediately speckle the face. Men and women are shouting orders on the deck, and the rain steadily beats down. I didn't expect—or *want*—fanfare, but I did expect *someone* from the *Dawn Chaser* to escort us aboard.

Or maybe I'm just irritated because this means Tessa is on board with the captain, while I'm standing down here getting rain in my boots, and the king of Kandala is hiding in a darkened carriage, waiting for me to go.

The thought feels petulant, and I hate it. Surely they're busy preparing to leave in this weather.

From above, a woman on deck shouts, "Captain! I think he's down there now."

I glance at Rocco. "Have I kept them waiting?"

He inhales to answer, but before he can, Captain Blakemore all but slides down the gangway, springing agilely off the end to land right in front of us.

"Your Highness," he says a bit breathlessly. "The ship is ready to depart." The ship's sails snap in the wind, and he glances at the sky. "If you'd still like to outrun this storm, we shouldn't wait much longer."

"Do forgive us for the delay," I say, but I'm pretty sure my eyes say, *I'm about to push you off the dock.*

That spark of challenge lights in his gaze. "Forgiven, Your Highness."

His eyes say, *Go ahead and try.*

But he glances at Rocco, then steps back and extends a hand. "Shall we?"

My feet almost refuse to move. I don't want to.

But of course I'm being foolish. I force myself to step onto the gangway. My heart gives a jolt when my foot meets the wood, the world seeming to tilt. I have to take a deep breath to clear my head. *I'm leaving my brother.*

Captain Blakemore steps onto the gangway just behind me. Rocco will follow us both. Somewhere at the top of this ramp is Tessa, whose presence fills me with warmth—but also Lochlan, who will surely be a problem at some point. We only have a small handful of guards, all of whom are outnumbered by the shadowed workers on the ship deck.

Harristan's voice breaks through the sound of raindrops slamming the deck. "Captain."

Captain Blakemore turns in surprise. So do I. A ripple of alarm runs through the guards waiting on the dock, and many of them shift to flank the king.

Harristan ignores them all and steps onto the gangway. Rocco quickly steps aside to yield passage. My brother strides right up to Rian, and there's fire in his eyes.

"I expect Prince Corrick to return unharmed," he says, and there's a note in his voice I don't think I've ever heard before. The promise of vengeance hangs in every syllable.

Captain Blakemore doesn't back down, but he matches Harristan's intensity when he says, "Understood, Your Majesty."

The rain pours down among us, but my brother doesn't move.

Harristan needs to see confidence in my expression, so I clap him on the shoulder. "I have no doubt Captain Blakemore and I will be old friends by the time we return."

Rian smiles slyly. "I'm *so* glad to hear it, Your Highness."

I cut him a glance. "Do you want him to let me get on the boat or not?"

Harristan sighs as if he's tired of us both, but then he stifles a cough.

I frown. "Your carriage is waiting," I say, as if this was entirely planned, and there's no surprise to my brother being out on the docks. "Get out of the rain. We shouldn't delay."

My brother nods, then takes a step back. "Farewell, Cory."

Somehow this is harder than it was in the carriage.

Without warning, a dozen random memories flash in my thoughts. The time he spilled tea down the front of his jacket just before a meeting with the consuls, so I shrugged out of mine before anyone would catch him in a state of disarray. The time we snuck into the Wilds and a fortune-teller tried to trick me out of the few coins I carried, but Harristan saw through his ruse and snatched my money back out of the man's palm. The time when he couldn't catch his breath in the training arena, and his opponent, Allisander himself, took advantage of the moment to chase my brother into the dirt. I was only ten or eleven, but I climbed the fence and tackled Allisander myself. The weapons master had to haul me off him.

The moment Harristan dove to cover me when our parents were assassinated.

My throat threatens to tighten, so I blink the memories away.

"Farewell," I say, and my brother steps onto the dock.

"Follow me, Your Highness," Captain Blakemore says, before my heart can start pounding at the thought that *this is it*. He doesn't even wait to see if I follow; he simply heads toward the top of the ramp. "Miss Cade insisted on allowing you to select your choice of quarters first."

If anything could send a bolt of warmth to the center of my chest, it's the mention of Tessa. I'm not alone here. Not really.

I shove wet hair back from my face and stride forward, Rocco at my side.

I expect Prince Corrick to return unharmed.

My brother's words, his vehemence, add to that bolt of warmth in my chest.

But then I consider what Rian said in response.

Understood, Your Majesty.

Not an assurance. Not a promise.

An understanding.

I glance at Rocco. "Stay sharp," I say quietly.

"Yes, Your Highness." He glances at the sea captain striding ahead of us. "You have my word."

Chapter Thirteen

Tessa

I've only been on the boat for half an hour, but my stomach is already threatening to empty itself all over the floorboards of my room. Or possibly Corrick's room. He can decide when he arrives. We're not even at sea yet, but I'm ready to tear apart my apothecary kit, because I could chew through an entire twist of ginger root. I definitely wish I'd waited for Corrick on the docks. It might have been raining, but at least it was *stable*. I press my hands to my abdomen and wonder what's keeping him. I saw the flicker of worry in Captain Blakemore's eyes when he looked at the sky.

Rapid footsteps cross the floorboards overhead, stepping with purpose. I try not to wonder if the storm is worse than they expected, if we're too late to leave safely. A large porthole sits on the opposite side of the room, heavy glass crossed by steel bars, and rain has been steadily beating at the window since I walked in. I've been trying not to look through it because all I can see are the gas lamps on the dock shifting up and down.

When Captain Blakemore showed me to this room, he said, "We've given you all the rear quarters since you're not used to being at sea. The going should be a bit smoother here." He then pointed at the ceiling and said something about the officers' stations and navigational rooms being above us, but by that point, I was trying to keep from stumbling into him again.

It's bad enough that it happened once.

I wonder if Kilbourne will say something to Corrick. I remember the flare of intrigue in the captain's eyes when he asked if I would be sharing quarters with the prince. It feels like the kind of detail a guardsman wouldn't leave unremarked.

A knock raps at the door, and Kilbourne calls, "Miss Tessa. An audience has been—"

My heart leaps. Oh thank goodness. He's here. I don't even wait for Kilbourne to finish his announcement before I stride to the door and throw it open.

I stop short. It's not Corrick. It's Lochlan. His eyes are hard and his jaw is set.

My heart's leap turns into a stumble.

I haven't seen Lochlan since he caused a scene in the candy shop, and I was doubtful when I learned he'd be on this journey. A willowy young man in palace livery stands behind him, but it's very obvious that he's been charged with keeping Lochlan out of trouble. He looks more like a student than a guard.

He also looks just as green as I feel.

Lochlan doesn't waste time on any pleasantries. He pulls a small woven pouch out of a pocket and holds it out. "Here," he says, and while his voice is gruff, it's not unkind.

"What is it?"

"It's from Karri. For the seasickness." He gives me a quick

up-and-down glance. "Peppermint candies. And some ginger caramels. She made them both this morning when she learned we were
leaving so soon." He pauses. "You look like you could use some."

"Oh." That tempers some of my wariness. I reach out and take
the bag just as the boat gives another surge. I have to grab hold
of the doorframe so I don't crash into Lochlan, too.

My mouth is already watering, and I shove a hand into the bag
for one of the caramels. "Thank you," I say, as I slip one into my
mouth. "Don't you need them?"

"She made some for me, too," he says. "But I always catch some
summer work on the fishing trawlers. I don't get seasick." He glances
at my hand clutching the wood. "It'll be better once we pull away
from the dock. They've got the sails up, so we're fighting the ropes."

There's no belligerence in his voice, and I'm reminded of the
way he spoke gently to Karri. I've only ever known him as a rebel
who tortured Corrick and tried to burn down the palace, but
there has to be another side to him that he's reluctant to show.
Karri is too smart, too discerning. She wouldn't be with a man
like him otherwise.

"Be careful," I say. "You might trick me into thinking you're
kind, Lochlan."

"I am kind," he says simply. The boat sways, and he compen-
sates, then throws a glare at the ceiling. "Figures we'd be made to
wait on that stupid, spoiled—"

"I suggest you not finish that sentence," says Kilbourne, and all
the warmth that existed in his tone earlier is gone now.

"What are you going to do?" says Lochlan. "Throw me overboard? Don't think I don't know why I was *invited*."

"You were invited as an extension of *trust*," I say.

Surprise lights in his expression, and he gives a brief, derisive laugh. Any flickers of kindness have vanished. "The sad thing is that you really believe that. Karri loves you, so I'm going to have to assume you're just naive, because anything else would be insulting."

"Oh, good," I say. "I'm glad you're not going to get *insulting*."

He takes a looming step toward me, and my heart thumps.

He must see the fear in my expression because he stops. "Again," he says, "you're scared of *me*, when you should be scared of *him*. You probably think he brought you for some reason other than keeping him warm at night." My cheeks flame, but he's not done. "Somehow you're smart enough to make the Moonflower work better, but you're too stupid to figure out that the King's Justice is a dirty liar who should be chained to the rudder—"

Kilbourne shoves him into the opposite wall so hard that the doors rattle. The movement is so quick and so violent that I give a little yip and press my hands to my abdomen. He might be good-natured, but he's still a guardsman. Even Silas looks startled, but he catches up more quickly than I do. He puts a hand against Lochlan's shoulder to pin him there, then glances at Kilbourne as if to ask if they're taking it further.

Lochlan doesn't fight him; he just looks at me. "Do you see?"

"I gave you fair warning," Kilbourne says.

Footsteps echo from the opposite direction, and I turn to see Captain Blakemore approaching, followed by Corrick and Rocco.

The captain's steps slow as he sizes up the situation. The hallway is narrow, but he waits for Corrick to draw abreast. "Your Highness. Are your people going to be a problem?"

Corrick's eyes flick from me to Lochlan. "It doesn't look like my people were the ones *causing* the problem. Silas, see that he returns to his quarters."

Lochlan draws himself up like he's going to retort, but then he lets out a breath and shakes his head. He looks at me. "Just wait. You'll see." He pauses, then throws a look of pure hatred Corrick's way. "And when it happens," he says to me, "be sure to tell Karri I loved her." Then he shoves past the prince and the captain and slips into a room just a bit down the hall.

Corrick looks at me. His hair is damp, his clothes shining where rain soaked into the shoulders of his jacket. His eyes, as usual, are piercing. "Did he hurt you?"

"No," I say. I realize my fingers are still clutched around the candies that Karri sent. "He wasn't doing anything wrong." As I say the words, I can't decide if they're true. Too much happened in a short span of time. "He brought me medicine from Karri."

"Are you unwell, Miss Cade?" says Captain Blakemore.

"I just need to get used to the motion of the boat," I say. There's too much tension in the hallway, and I want to undo it. I just have no idea how. "Corrick, I . . . I didn't know which room you'd want."

"Any room will do," he says. His eyes haven't left mine. "Captain, you have my thanks." Then, without hesitation, he takes my hand, leads me into the room at my back, and closes us inside.

—◆—

Before I learned the truth about Weston Lark, I never saw the prince up close—if I ever saw him at all. But the few times I *did* see Prince Corrick, I remember that he always looked distant and aloof, his eyes cold and unforgiving. The perfect King's Justice. The perfect executioner.

The night he caught me sneaking into the palace was the first time I knew him for who he truly was, and I'll never forget the look of panic and fear and uncertainty that was etched into his features for one brief second, before going cold and hard and unreadable, the truest mask he ever wears.

Those are the same eyes looking at me right now. "Are you sure?" he says to me, and there's a demand in his tone, a demand backed by concern. "I saw the guard shove him away. You weren't hurt?"

"No," I say. "He didn't hurt me. He was just . . . just mouthing off. Kilbourne shouldn't have hit him." The first small caramel has dissolved, and my stomach already feels better. I take one of the peppermints next.

Corrick watches my action, but he says nothing. I wish I could read his expression.

I hold out the bag. "Would you like one?"

He hesitates, then shakes his head. "No. Thank you."

The cabin is dim, lit only by an oil lantern hung suspended along the wall. It's light enough for me to see his tension, the tight set of his shoulders.

I should have waited on the dock.

After a moment, this candy settles my stomach enough for me to take a deep breath, and maybe that eases the tension in the room, because Corrick sighs, too. He runs a hand back through his damp hair, then begins roughly jerking at the buttons of his jacket. Once it's loose, he shrugs free to toss it over the back of a chair.

"So you'd like this room?" I say to him.

His eyes snap to mine. "What?"

"Captain Blakemore asked me which room I'd like, and I told him I ought to wait for you to choose yours first."

His eyes narrow the tiniest bit. "Did he."

Much like his eyes, I can't read his voice at all. "You're the King's Justice. I only thought it appropriate—"

"Lord, Tessa. I don't care which room I have."

He's so uneasy. The worst part is that I don't know what worries him the most. Leaving his brother? Going to Ostriary? Lochlan? Captain Blakemore?

The ship sways, and my stomach dips, and once again, I stumble. Corrick lightly catches my waist.

"We must be shoving off," he says.

"Why is everyone else so sure-footed?" I say, aggrieved.

"Oh, I'm not," he says. "I grabbed hold of you for balance."

He's teasing, but his voice is too grave for it to be funny. I swat him on the arm anyway, and he half smiles, but he doesn't let go of me. A hand lifts to stroke a stray lock of hair back from my cheek.

"I'm so glad you're here," he says softly. In his tone, I hear a dozen things unsaid: his longing, his hope . . . his fear. It reminds me of that moment with Harristan in my quarters.

Corrick quietly adds, "Harristan snuck into my carriage for the drive here."

My eyebrows go up. "He did?"

Corrick nods.

I want to be surprised, but . . . I'm really not. I'm touched. One of my favorite things about the brothers is their endearing closeness. I wish they would allow others to see it. It's the most humanizing thing about them.

"He confronted Captain Blakemore and demanded my safe return," Corrick says. "I thought the guards might have a fit."

That makes me smile, but it's fleeting, because I can hear the worry in his voice. "Harristan is afraid."

I expect Corrick to say something bold, like, *The king fears nothing.*

He doesn't. "We all are, Tessa."

I want to touch him, but I hesitate, because I'm so used to guarding my emotions when I'm with him in public. But we're alone. We're out of the palace. What he's risking—what they're *both* risking—is profound. I wonder what the king said to him before watching his brother climb onto a ship to an unknown country. I wonder if I can ask.

Maybe I don't have to. The emotion is right there in his gaze.

I reach out and put a hand to his cheek.

He takes a breath, then closes his eyes. His hands are still on my waist, but he's not steadying me anymore—he's *holding* me, which is altogether different. Something about it reminds me of our days in the workshop, when we were listening to the sector alarms blare and we were worried about the night patrol.

I sigh and lean into his strength. "I'm glad you're here, too."

His eyes open to find mine, and his hands shift, his thumbs skirting along my abdomen. It's such a tiny movement, but my heart kicks.

I'm not sure if I make a sound or take a breath or if there's just a spark in the air, but Corrick's blue eyes seem to darken a shade, and then his mouth is on mine.

At first he's slow, controlled, gauging my response. After weeks of chaste walks and courtly manners and light kisses at sundown, I nearly melt right into his arms. When I yield to his touch, he grows more sure, his lips chasing mine, and I feel the bare edge of his teeth, then the brush of his tongue. He tastes like peppermint—or maybe *I* taste like peppermint, sharp and sweet. He pulls me closer, until I'm all but flush against him, and a bolt of warmth shoots through my belly. The only time he's ever kissed me like this was in the Wilds. In the workshop. He keeps so much of himself hidden that

I somehow forgot he could be like this, all wildfire attraction and unbound passion.

His hand shifts higher, growing more daring, until his thumb brushes across the bodice of my dress, lighting a fire in my belly and stealing every clear thought from my head. I shiver and make a tiny sound, and that's all the encouragement he needs to tug the laces a bit looser. His mouth finds my neck, and his fingers slip past the laces of my bodice to trace the swell of skin.

I inhale sharply. "Oh," I whisper, because I can't think of any other words. I'm sure someone will be knocking at the door for the prince at any moment, but right now, I don't care. Butterflies scatter in my abdomen. "*Oh.*"

He smiles at my reaction, lifting his head to kiss me again. His arm snakes around my back to pull me even closer, and this time we're clutched so tightly that I can feel *everything*. The boat sways again, and I press against him, and it's *his* turn to make a low sound in his throat.

"I've wanted to be alone with you for so long," he says, and there's no disguising the intense longing in his voice. I don't know if he means the time we've been together in the palace, where watching eyes and listening ears were everywhere, or if he means the time we spent together in the Wilds as Wes and Tessa, when he was so afraid of discovery that he'd never let me catch a glimpse of him without his mask.

Either way, it doesn't matter. He kisses me again, his fingers slipping under my corset in a way that makes me whimper into his mouth.

"Hush," he whispers, and a wicked light sparks in his eyes like we're co-conspirators. "We shouldn't give Rocco and Kilbourne *too* much to think about."

My cheeks burn fiercely—but my thoughts have stalled on his comment, tempering some of my flames. A part of me doesn't want him to stop. I crave the strength of his hands and the warmth of his mouth. I want him to keep going until every last stitch of fabric is on the floor.

But another part of me knows he's only being so free because we *are* out of the palace, where Prince Corrick would never be caught bedding a . . . a commoner.

We shouldn't give Rocco and Kilbourne too much to think about.

The words seem to have a lot of different meanings, and I'm sure he means to protect me from the listening ears of the guards.

But just now, on the tail of Lochlan's comments about Corrick's reasons for bringing me along, it's enough to chase all my warmth away. Because there's a part of that sentence that sounds like he's protecting *himself*.

Corrick notices immediately, because he's drawn back to look at me. "Tessa?"

"I—just—we should—" I'm choking on my words because my thoughts—to say nothing of my *body*—weren't ready for such an abrupt change in direction. I have to take a deep breath to steady myself. I tug at the laces of my corset, pulling it tight again. "You're right. We shouldn't give the guards reasons to gossip." My cheeks feel hot, and I already know I'm going to have trouble looking Rocco in the eyes. "We've been in here too long. Surely it's inappropriate—"

"Tessa." His hands fall on mine, forcing them still.

For a moment, I let him. My eyes are on the collar of his shirt, on the smooth column of his neck. His fingers are warm against my own.

He ducks his head, his eyes seeking mine. "Talk to me," he says. Quietly. Gently. No command in his tone.

I pull my hands free and fuss with the laces, dodging his gaze. I don't know what to say. My emotions are all tied up in knots, my stomach churning again. This time, it has nothing to do with the rocking of the ship. All my thoughts are crashing into each other, and I hate—*hate*—that Lochlan put these doubts in my mind.

But now they exist, and they cling to the inside of my head and refuse to let go.

"Lochlan thinks you brought him along just so you can make sure he falls overboard," I say. "Please tell me that's not true."

Corrick blinks and draws back. It takes him a moment to answer. "I wouldn't shed a tear if it happened. That shouldn't be a surprise."

It's *not* a surprise. But it's also not the answer I want to hear. "Is that why you brought him? Are you and Harristan getting rid of him?"

I don't know what's making me demand answers on *this*, of all things. There's no love lost between me and Lochlan either. But despite all his promises, I know everything Corrick has done. The King's Justice was feared throughout Kandala for a reason.

And maybe the thought of asking questions about *myself* is too frightening to bear.

Corrick's eyes have locked down so quickly that it's like I've been thrust into a room with a stranger. "I could have put a rope around his neck on the docks, Tessa." His voice is cold and flat when he says it. "I could've had the guards put an arrow in his chest in that candy shop. I could have had him chained to a post and set on fire during the—"

"Stop it!" I say sharply. "Stop!"

"As I've said in the past, I bring nightmares to life. If I wanted him dead, I didn't need to drag him aboard a ship. Trust me, I'd rather have another guard with us."

My heart keeps clipping along, and I'm completely flushed for an entirely different reason from five minutes ago. I don't know how he can shut down his emotions so quickly. Right now, it's a talent I wish I shared. "Any of those things would have been public," I say. "On a ship, you could claim he *fell*, or that he was killed—"

"Do you mean to accuse me of something?"

His voice is low and dangerous, and for a brief second, I remember Captain Blakemore's voice on the dock when he worried that he might be putting me at risk.

I hate the path all my thoughts have chosen to follow. I have to swallow and square my shoulders, and I knot my corset tightly. "No," I say. "I hope you find this cabin acceptable. I'll . . . I'll retire to my own." I turn for the door.

Corrick catches my arm, and I gasp, expecting him to grab me, but he doesn't. His fingers are gentle, which shouldn't be startling, but it *is*. When he hears my indrawn breath, he lets me go instantly. Something fractures in his gaze. "Tessa. Please. Stop. Tell me what just happened."

"You said you've waited so long."

He frowns, but he nods.

"*I* didn't make you wait," I say.

He's frozen in place for the longest time, his jaw tight as he regards me. He's the brother to the king. He can't make promises or declarations. I *know* he can't.

My cheeks are hot again, but I hold his gaze. "I don't deserve to be treated like a secret, Corrick."

A muscle in his jaw twitches. I wish he would say something. I wish he would *do* something.

"Forgive me," he finally says, and his voice is as proper and courtly as I've ever heard it. "That wasn't my intent."

I know, I want to say, but I don't know. Just like with the man in the candy shop, or with Lochlan's presence on this ship, I *don't* know. Not for sure.

So I curtsy just as formally, as if I weren't just drowning in the taste of his mouth. "Thank you, Your Highness."

That hits him like a dart. I can almost see the impact. He takes a step back and gives me a nod. "I bid you a pleasant evening, Miss Cade."

That hits *me* like a dagger. My throat swells and my eyes blur, and I have to turn on my heel and stride for the door.

Just as I open it, I hear his voice, soft and beseeching. "Tessa."

But the door is already open, Rocco and Kilbourne both standing at attention in the hall.

I don't look at either of them. I allow the door to fall closed behind me, and I step across the corridor to close myself alone in the last remaining room.

CHAPTER FOURTEEN

Corrick

I honestly hadn't thought things could get worse.

I want to go after her, but I don't know what would undo this. A profession of love? A plea for forgiveness? Offering the kingdom on a string?

I'm not even sure she'd want any of that. It's not even my kingdom to offer. It's my brother's. And right now, Kandala is no prize. I might as well offer her a hornet's nest.

I wish I knew what Lochlan said to her. Right this instant, I want to do everything I said I would do to him.

Her words to me keep echoing in my thoughts.

I *didn't make you wait.*

No. She didn't.

The worst part is that she didn't say the words with censure. She said them with . . . with *understanding*. She knows who I am. She knows my role. She knows that any promises come with the weight of the crown behind them.

She also knows who I've spent the last four years being. The King's Justice. One of the most feared men in the entire country.

She didn't say it, but she didn't have to. I heard it in her voice when she asked about my intentions for Lochlan. When I took hold of her arm, she almost flinched.

I need to focus. I have duties here. An obligation to my king and my country. I shouldn't have marched into this room and started . . . *that.*

But as I walked onto the ship, I kept thinking about the way Captain Blakemore invited her aboard ahead of my arrival, or the way he told her to call him by his given name at dinner. I kept thinking of his words about loyalty and honor and duty, and how his comments made my efforts to protect Kandala feel misguided and ineffective.

I kept hearing her voice from the moment he appeared in the dining room. *Oh.*

It's far too similar to the way she said the very same word when my fingers found the lacing to her—

I force these thoughts to an abrupt halt. They're going nowhere good.

I drop onto the side of the narrow bed and run my hands over my face. I wasn't prepared to replace lust and desire with anger and frustration, and my body hasn't fully caught up with my thoughts yet. The room feels too hot. Too small. I could step onto a battlefield and wage war this very second. I tug at my shirtsleeves to free the cuffs, then roughly shove them back.

The boat rocks and sways, but less than it did along the docks. We must be fully into the Queen's River now.

This is happening. I'm leaving. I'm leaving Kandala.

I'm leaving my brother.

I have too many emotions, and they're all colliding. I shove myself to my feet and stride for the door. I have no idea what I'm going to do, but I need to do something or I'm going to throw *myself* overboard.

But as my hand reaches for the door handle, I hesitate. I've hardly been on the ship for half an hour, but I don't need anyone to think I'm upset—especially not my own guards. I've been King's Justice for four years. I know how to swallow my temper. Close quarters never keep secrets well. If my guards start whispering about a spat between me and Tessa, it'll be all over the ship in a matter of hours, and that's the last thing I need.

I take a step back and run my hands across my face again. There's a tiny mirror in the corner, over the empty washbasin, but my eyes still look like thunder, so I glance away. I unroll my sleeves and refasten the cuffs.

I wish I had Quint. Or Harristan.

My chest tightens unexpectedly, but I lock this emotion away with the others. I walk to the small, barred porthole and stare out into the blackness. The bars remind me of a prison cell. Only a few tiny lights along the shore glow in the gloom. I count to ten. To one hundred.

And then I do it again.

Eventually, my temper cools. I'm no longer inhaling fire.

A knock sounds at my door, and I whip my head around. My heart kicks. Maybe she's come back. Maybe I have a chance to fix this.

I grab the handle and jerk the door open.

It's not Tessa. It's Kilbourne. There are two men behind him, both lugging heavy trunks that glisten with rainwater.

"Your Highness," the guard says. "Your trunks have been brought down."

I stare at him. I'm trying to decide if he looks like he knows what happened between me and Tessa.

Maybe I *can't* swallow all that emotion.

While I'm deliberating, one of the men blows a lock of hair out of his eyes and says, "They sure are getting lighter, Your Highness," and the other man makes a sound like he's trying to stifle a laugh.

My eyes narrow, and I'm tempted to make these men hold them for a solid hour, but it feels petty. I know how loyal Rian's crew is. I don't want to turn them *all* against me.

"Forgive me," I say. "Just set them inside."

They do. They're not gentle about it either. With hardly a glance at me, the men leave the trunks, then head back into the hallway. One of them wipes sweat or rain—or both—from his brow as he goes.

I'm irritated, and I probably don't have any right to be. They aren't here as my servants.

"Where are the other guards?" I say to Kilbourne.

"Silas is setting our room to order. Rocco is walking the ship." Kilbourne casts a glance at the empty hallway, then drops his voice. "The captain promised a thorough tour once we're ahead of the storm, but Rocco doesn't want to wait that long."

Interesting. Probably smart. I glance across the hallway at the two closed doors. I wonder which one is Tessa's. "Miss Cade is comfortable?"

He hesitates. "As far as I can tell." He studies me, and in that moment, I can tell he noticed Tessa's sudden departure from my quarters.

He has the good sense not to mention it, which I can appreciate.

"What did Lochlan say to her?" I ask.

Kilbourne draws a slow breath.

I've been on this ship for less than an hour, and I'm already exhausted. "Just tell me."

"He said the king placed him on the ship for the purpose of making him disappear. He said you were a liar who deserved to be tied to the rudder." He hesitates. "He said you brought Miss Tessa along for . . . ah, companionship."

My jaw is tight.

"In the bedroom," he adds.

I give him a look. "Thank you, Kilbourne. I made the connection."

"Yes, Your Highness."

I sigh and close myself back into my quarters. No wonder she started demanding to know my intentions—especially when I did nothing to put her fears to rest. Instead, I probably stoked them.

I need action, but I'm not in the right frame of mind to go find it. I really would wring Lochlan's neck. I crouch beside the first chest and unlatch it. The clothes on top are a bit damp from where rain has snuck past the leather stitching of the trunk, and I sigh, then move to hang them from hooks in the wardrobe. I could call for someone to do this for me, but now that my hands are buried in the fabric, I'm reminded of the scents of the palace, so different from the scent of seawater and fish that seems to cling to everything on board the *Dawn Chaser*. I'm sure Geoffrey, my valet, chose each piece carefully, because everything is practical for a journey by sea, with a few more regal pieces, surely intended for once we reach Ostriary.

But then, at the bottom of the chest, I find a worn leather riding jacket that's jarring with familiarity, though I'm sure I haven't seen it in years. My brows flicker into a frown, because I can't imagine what inspired Geoffrey to add it to my trunks. It's fine leather, with detailed stitching, a belted waist, and buckles across the chest, but I have little use for riding attire on a ship. Honestly, I'm rather certain this used to be Harristan's, anyway—

I freeze, struck by a memory. I was fourteen, so Harristan was eighteen. It was late autumn, and our parents were still alive. We were visiting the consul of Trader's Landing. My parents wanted Harristan to travel by carriage, because the colder air always seemed to make his breathing worse, but by then he'd reached an age where he could refuse. He'd ridden beside me through miles of leaf-strewn trails—and he'd paid the price. By the time we reached the consul's estate, Harristan couldn't speak a full sentence without gasping halfway through.

He recovered quickly once we were inside, but after hours at tea and luncheon and afternoon gossip in front of a fireplace, I grew bored with all the royal protocol. I left my brother and my parents and slipped into the dimness of the stables. I heard the low rumble of voices in the tack room, but I didn't think much of it, until I realized what the stablehands were doing: mocking my brother.

"I'm going—" A feigned wheeze. "—to—" Another. "—I'm—" The boy launched into exaggerated coughing.

"What's that, Your Highness?" another laughed. "You're going to *what*?"

I didn't think. I just tackled one of them. I wasn't even sure which one. My fist was swinging before I was aware of who I was hitting.

The stables were mostly deserted, and I'm sure they didn't expect the younger prince to come strolling through. They definitely didn't realize who I was at first, because the boy was older and bigger and shoved me into the dirt before one of the others grabbed his arm and stopped him. They all stared at me in panic, and I remember thinking that they were either going to finish me off—or run away.

I probably would have tackled them again, but Harristan appeared in the doorway to the tack room.

He looked from me, with my lip already swelling, to the stablehands, and his gaze had darkened. Tension clung to the room for the longest moment, and I felt the other boys weighing their fate.

"Cory," Harristan finally said. "Mother sent me to find you. Consul Montague is preparing for dinner." He glanced at the stablehands. "Let's allow them to get back to work before Father comes looking."

The implications of that were clear. I got to my feet, and the boys scattered, finding duties *quickly*.

I wiped a hand across my jaw, and I was surprised to find blood on my knuckles. Harristan sighed, then pulled a handkerchief to wipe the blood off my mouth. "You can't fight *all* my battles, little brother."

I wanted to brush off his tending, but I knew from experience that Mother would be furious if she found evidence of brawling on my shirt. "You heard them?"

He shrugged and rolled his eyes. "You think I don't hear it from our own servants?" He didn't wait for an answer; he just unfastened his jacket. "Here. Put this on. You've ripped your shirt. Mother will come undone."

I put on his jacket and buttoned it closed.

His jacket. *This* jacket.

I'd forgotten all about that moment.

Now, my fingers stroke across the lapels. Geoffrey wouldn't have packed this.

Which means my brother did.

I think of the way he slipped into my carriage tonight. I dig at the pockets, in case Harristan has slipped a note into one of them, but there's nothing.

I sit on the edge of the bed again and inhale deeply. The jacket smells of oiled leather and sweet hay, with just the tiniest undercurrent of equine sweat. I sigh and lay back on the bed, feeling the motion of the ship beneath me, listening to the rattle of rain against the porthole window. I pull the jacket to my chest and close my eyes.

You can't fight all my battles, little brother.

That changed later, when he named me as King's Justice. I've fought plenty of his battles, to the detriment of myself.

I'm sure I'll fight plenty more. I don't want to disappoint him.

I don't want to disappoint Tessa.

As usual, those two choices seem to be in opposition.

But just now, I can lie here and stare up at the ceiling, inhaling the faint scents of home, and I can put off my worries for a few minutes.

◆

I don't mean to sleep, but I do. When I wake, I'm in the same position as before, lying on the bed, staring into darkness, the boat rocking beneath me. For an instant, I have a moment of disoriented panic, because I can't remember where I am. But awareness snaps into place quickly, and I sit up sharply, causing my brother's jacket to pool in my lap. The oil lantern has burned out, and the room is cold. I have no idea what time it is, and it's too dark to see my pocket watch.

It's too dark to see *anything.*

I do have the jacket, so I slip my arms into the sleeves and ease across the room in the darkness, shifting slowly with my hands out.

My shins slam right into a chest anyway, and I bite back a swear, then catch myself against the wall.

At least it helps me find the door.

I tug at the handle, then blink in the sudden light. Two lanterns hang in the corridor. Rocco was sitting cross-legged in the center of the aisle, but he's on his feet before I've swung the door all the way open. An array of playing cards were laid out on the wooden boards, but they scatter a bit from his movement.

"Your Highness," he says in surprise.

"Forgive me," I say. "I've ruined your game."

"It's no trouble."

My thoughts are still a bit wild and tumultuous, and I simultaneously feel wide awake and in desperate need for more sleep. It's a feeling I remember well from my early morning runs with Tessa. I tug my watch free and glance at the face.

Half past three in the morning.

Sounds about right.

I look back at Rocco, then rub at my eyes. "You drew the night watch?"

"Kilbourne will relieve me at dawn." His eyes flick down my form, and I realize that, aside from the jacket, I'm wearing the exact same clothes I wore when I boarded the ship—right down to my boots.

That makes me feel like a fool.

Doubly so when I glance across the hallway and see Tessa's closed door.

I look back at Rocco, who's studying me as if he's wondering whether he would be within rights to suggest I go back to sleep. It's quite possible I look hungover.

I wish I were. "Kilbourne said you walked the ship earlier," I say.

"I did."

I rub at my eyes again. "Give me ten minutes, Rocco. Then I'd like to hear what you've learned."

"I . . . yes. Of course."

I hesitate before turning back for my room. "And one of your lanterns, if you please."

Once I close myself back in my quarters, I take less than ten minutes to feel more human. I didn't expect indoor plumbing, but I'm pleased to find a private water closet, complete with a pitcher and basin for washing. I exchange my shirt for something less rumpled, hoping it will help me feel a bit less rumpled myself, but it doesn't. I want to shove my brother's jacket back down in the chest, because it really has no place here . . . but something about its presence is reassuring. It's cold anyway. I buckle it into place.

I make my way back to the door and tug at the next chest, wondering what I'll find. It's very heavy, and I remember one of Blakemore's men making a comment about how they weren't getting much lighter. I snap the latches and flip the lid open.

Bottles glisten in the light. Wine and whiskey and rum and brandy—a whole assortment of liquors from the palace. There's an opener, too.

Quint, I love you.

I am absolutely certain that he meant for me to use them to impress dignitaries in Ostriary, or possibly to gift them right to King Galen Redstone himself, but right now, I don't care. I seize the brandy, tug the cork free, then drink right from the bottle.

Lord, Tessa.

I plug the bottle and go for the door again. Rocco has put the cards away, and he's standing at attention in the dimmer hallway.

I tug a trunk in front of the door to prop it open, then gesture to the little table and chairs that are bolted to the floor. "Come in. Sit."

He takes in the bottle in my hand, then steps across the threshold. He's tall enough that he has to duck through the door a bit. "We can wait for dawn, Your Highness. If you'd rather."

"I wouldn't." There aren't any glasses in my quarters, but there are four wooden cups stacked in a little sleeve that's also bolted to the table. I set two on the table and pour, then drop into a chair.

Rocco assesses this, then eases into the chair across from me. "The *Dawn Chaser* is well outfitted," he says. "The king had guards search the ship when Captain Blakemore first made his claim, and his logs seem to be in order. There are enough provisions on board for a crew of this size. The sailors seem competent, if a bit rough around the edges. Most of them seem quick and sharp. They're loyal to their captain."

"Do you trust him?"

"No."

My eyebrows go up, and Rocco shrugs. "He kept our numbers low. It seems reasonable, but the ship is easily large enough to carry a dozen more people. The lowest decks are mostly empty. As it stands, if it came to a fight, we are outnumbered two to one. More so, if you consider that Miss Cade may not be fit to fight. To say nothing of the rebel." He grimaces. "Who knows which side *he'd* fight for, if it came down to it."

"Whatever side ended with me at the bottom of the ocean." I pick up my cup and drain it in one swallow. "What else?"

"This supposedly isn't a gunship, but there are cannons tethered on the middle deck. We questioned Captain Blakemore, and—"

"Cannons!"

"Yes. A dozen. It's been explained that the cannons have been with the ship since his father first sailed from Kandala, and it would be costly to remove them, so they've been tethered in the stern."

"Could that be true?"

"Yes." He pushes his cup toward me. "It could also be a lie, Your Highness."

"I poured that for you."

"I know."

There's a part of me that wishes I hadn't touched the first one— and another part that wants to drain the whole bottle. "So we're on a ship that's *not* a gunship, but *could be* a gunship if the need arises."

"Yes." Rocco sits back in his chair. "Do you have anything to write with? I'll show you how it's laid out."

I check beneath the bottles of liquor and find a box of fountain pens and a new leather folio with a stack of crisp parchment.

Rocco sketches quickly. "They've given us the rooms at the stern, saying they're the better quarters because they're larger and provide a smoother ride. That *could* be true—or it could be that we've got a short corridor and it would be easy to confine us, if the need arose. It gives us a bit of an advantage, too: a single man can guard the hallway. Short of a frontal assault, there's no real way to take a guard unawares. But to get above or belowdecks—to *escape*—we'd need to head for the center of the ship. Aside from the captain and his first officer, the crew quarters are at the bow, with full access to everything: the galley, the gun decks, the hold."

"Where's the captain?"

I expect Rocco to make another mark on his drawing, but he

points at the ceiling. "Captain Blakemore and Lieutenant Tagas have sleeping quarters directly above us, along with his stateroom."

I glance up at the heavy beams and wonder how soundproof they are. I take a breath, studying his diagram. "Where are the cannons?"

"One deck below." He makes another line. "The firing bays are latched closed, and the cannons are tethered here." Another mark. "And here."

"Do they have an armory?"

"Yes. Double locked. But the guards who searched the ship reported that it was fully stocked."

"With what?"

"I don't know. That's all their report said. *Fully stocked.* They were searching for contraband, not weapons, so I'm sure they didn't think to make a full accounting." He pauses. "I inquired when I walked the ship, but the crewman didn't have a key. There really *is* a storm at our backs. They couldn't fake that."

"I'll have to ask for a tour myself." I run a hand across my face, and before I can think better of it, I drain the other cup. My voice has already gone a bit husky from the first one. "What are the chances I just walked into a kidnapping, Rocco?"

"The captain's story seems solid, and he certainly has the proof: his ring, his logs, the flag. If this is a kidnapping, it's a secret kept from the crew. I don't feel a sense of malice."

I don't either—but one of Rocco's very first statements was that he doesn't trust the captain. The crew doesn't need to know about a kidnapping if they'll act when Captain Blakemore commands it.

"But . . . ?" I prompt.

"I'm assessing who of the crew is critical to sail, and who's not. If it comes to it, Kilbourne is set to take out Sablo and Marchon.

Silas has a mark on Tagas, while I have one on Blakemore—though Tagas might be our better bet to keep the boat afloat. She's got a daughter among the crew, so we'd have leverage, and if we take out the captain, we're going to need leverage against someone with rank."

His voice is surprisingly ruthless. Practical. I so rarely hear that note in anyone's voice but my own.

I study him, and for some reason I'm reminded of the way Harristan called him Erik when he wasn't in palace livery. It's a level of familiarity that's unsettling, because I was never really *aware* of it. Rocco and the others must have had conversations like this with my brother all the time. My domain has always been the Hold: The smugglers and their earned punishments. The prisoners, the guards, and the night patrol. Since he's the king, my brother's domain has always been . . . all of Kandala.

I consider Rocco's tone, and I realize Harristan must have had similar conversations about *me*, in the days after Tessa's arrival at the palace. I wonder how long it took for him to question what secrets I kept, if it was his conversation with Tessa, or if it was Allisander spreading lies about his own wrongdoings.

"How long was my brother suspicious of me?" I ask Rocco now.

It's an abrupt shift in the conversation, but he takes it in stride. "Only these last few months."

He says it so easily, so casually, as if nothing about the time frame should be a surprise. But the words hit me so hard it almost knocks me out of my chair.

"For *months*?" I demand, and now he has the grace to look startled.

"Yes, Your Highness. I thought you knew."

No. I didn't know. My brain tries to skim through months of memories, every minute I would sit with my brother, evaluating the consuls, discussing the smugglers we caught, deliberating over the best way to maintain order and control in the streets of Kandala. All the times I sat in his room and listened to his breathing, worrying he was going to fall prey to the fevers. I think of every minute I spent trying not to destroy myself for *his* sake, and he was busy suspecting *me*.

I think about this jacket, the way my brother tucked it at the bottom of my chest.

"Did you have conversations like this with him?" I say. "About me?"

Rocco says nothing.

"Answer me," I say.

"I will not betray the king's confidence."

"Which one of you had a mark on *me*?"

Again, he says nothing.

"Did he have suspicions about this journey, too?" I say sourly. "Did he worry that I might somehow be plotting with Captain Blakemore? Is that why you're here?"

Rocco's eyes hold mine, unflinching. "My orders," he says evenly, "as stated by the king, are to ensure you return to Kandala unharmed."

That could mean a lot of things. I wish I could stride across the hallway to Tessa. But of course I can't.

I let out a long breath. My anger, my agitation, is not with Rocco. And if I'm going to survive this journey, I need him on my side.

"Fine," I say. "Advise." It's what my brother always says, when he wants his guards to formulate a plan. I don't know if I've ever said it.

Rocco doesn't hesitate, but then I'm sure he's heard it a thousand times. "For now, I recommend that you do your best to enjoy the journey. Do not allow our suspicions to come to light. The longer they believe we are willing passengers, the more we can learn. They'll lower their guard. Let Lochlan be the troublemaker, since he seems so willing. It won't be a distraction for us, but it will be for them." He pauses. "I would not share your doubts with Miss Tessa either."

I frown and imagine Tessa in her own quarters. *I don't deserve to be treated like a secret, Corrick.*

It takes everything I have not to wince. I may have fallen in love with Tessa Cade, but as usual, I'm reminded that she didn't fall in love with Prince Corrick, the King's Justice.

She fell in love with the outlaw Weston Lark.

She fell in love with a man who doesn't exist.

I want to pour another glass of brandy. "Rocco," I say, "you don't need to worry about that."

CHAPTER FIFTEEN

Tessa

When I sit up in bed and find a purplish dawn sky through my porthole, I have a moment of disorientation. I know where I am, but I'm startled that I slept so well. I hardly even remember falling asleep. The ship's rocking, which at first was nauseating, was somehow calming after the tumultuous moments with Corrick.

But now it's morning, and he never came to my door. I expected him to apologize. Or . . . at the very least, to make amends.

He didn't. And now it's morning.

My mouth still burns with the feel of his kiss.

Maybe I *am* naive.

The prince boarded the ship like a tornado, sweeping me into his quarters with no hesitation, taking me into his arms like a famished man set before a feast. I could see every ounce of emotion in his eyes, just like King Harristan in those few moments when he asked me to prepare his medicine. This journey means something to them both. Corrick's eyes were wild, but his hands were warm and sure. Eager. Desperate. Wanting.

And then it all fell apart. I don't know if that's my fault—or if it's his.

I scrub my hands over my face. At least I have a job to do.

After taking care of human needs, I dig through one of the trunks that was delivered last night. If it's windy, I don't want skirts, so I'm pleased to discover trousers and boots and vests along with more formal attire. Once I dress and rebraid my hair, I dig through my apothecary kit to find the individual bags of Moonflower. It doesn't take long to grind petals and make six vials, though the rocking of the ship makes me spill more than I'd like. I'll have to be more careful when I make the evening doses.

I take one vial for myself, then plug the rest and arrange them in a small velvet bag that I tuck inside my vest. Once complete, I make my way to the door and find Kilbourne in the hallway.

The guard doesn't look surprised to see me. "Miss Tessa," he says, then offers me a smile. "Good morning."

"Good morning," I say. "Do you know what time it is?"

"Half past six," he says without looking at a timepiece. "Rocco just retired."

I wonder if they have a strict schedule already worked out. I hadn't anticipated them standing guard through the night, but maybe I should've.

I feel antsy and uncertain, but I definitely don't want to lock myself back in my quarters, waiting for a conversation that clearly isn't coming. "I'm going to head up to the main deck," I say. "I need some fresh air."

"Should I wake His Highness?"

"No!" I say too quickly. I have to clear my throat. "No. Thank you."

"I can call for Silas to accompany you."

I think of the guardsman who's probably younger than I am. "No, I'll be fine."

For an instant, I expect Kilbourne to refuse. While I'm certainly not a prisoner, there's no secret that everyone from Kandala has suspicions about this endeavor. I'm not entirely sure how much freedom I have here, and the last thing I want is a shadow in the form of a guardsman everywhere I go. But there must be some level of understanding that the guards can't be everywhere at once, because he nods. "I'll alert the prince as to your whereabouts when he wakes."

That might be the best I'm going to get. "Thank you." I hesitate, my hand on the bag of elixirs. I want to leave it with him, so everyone can take their dose when they awaken, but the king was very clear that no one was to tamper with my medicine—including the guards. I pull one vial free. "This is your morning dose," I say to him. "If you wouldn't mind making sure everyone knows I have their doses prepared once they wake."

"Yes, Miss Tessa."

I nod, then tuck the bag back into the inner pocket of my vest.

It's early, but I see no one else as I head for the staircase. When I climb out into the fresh air, the wind catches tendrils of my hair and the laces of my vest. The deck dips and sways with the current, only slightly less tumultuous than yesterday. We're miles from shore, so I can just make out the largest buildings, the occasional gleam of lights from the cities lucky enough to have electricity. The sails billow and snap overhead, and the wind roars in my ears.

I gaze up at the stars, barely visible at this hour, and see that the storm is still behind us, a solid line of deep purple clouds looming in the distance. But we seem to be outrunning the weather, because the morning sky ahead is clear all the way down to the pink horizon. The bare edge of the sun gleams over the southern stretch of Artis that borders the east side of the Queen's River.

"Miss Cade," calls a male voice, but it's faint in the wind, and I turn.

"Up here," he calls again, and I look straight up, at the miles of ropes and broadcloth that make up the rigging and sails. For an instant, the sway of the ship makes it dizzying, and I put a hand out for the mast, but then I see him. Captain Blakemore, at least thirty feet above me, one foot on a stretch of rope, the other braced against the main mast.

"Good morning, Captain," I yell up to him.

The sky is still too dim for me to see much, but I catch the sudden gleam of his smile. "The rigging's just a bit fouled," he calls, tugging at the ropes. "I'll be down in a moment. There's coffee in my stateroom if you'd like some. Don't mind the mess."

Coffee. It's very rare and ridiculously expensive in Kandala, because the plants only grow well in the southern parts of Sunkeep. It's the least populous sector, leaving few people to work the fields. Most harvesters and field hands find better money in Emberridge and Moonlight Plains anyway, where the Moonflower grows. I don't know anyone outside the palace who's even *tried* it. I once asked Corrick, and he made a face and said it tastes like a hot mouthful of dirt. They don't serve it in the palace unless someone requests it.

But here it is on a sailing ship, being offered as easily as a glass of water. That's almost as shocking as the casual way the captain told me to help myself to his stateroom. It's so different from

Corrick, who reveals so little that every admission feels like I've stolen something. I'm so intrigued by this unexpected trust that I weave across the swaying ship to make my way toward the doors at the back of the deck. There are three, and I hesitate for one second before Captain Blakemore calls, "Starboard side." That doesn't make things better, but he quickly adds, "The one to your left." I turn the knob.

His stateroom is larger than I expected. A massive round table sits in the center of the room, with books and maps spread everywhere: navigational maps and country maps and river maps and star maps. Some are pinned down, while others are held in place by books and ledgers. On the one windowless wall is a massive clock, its ticking loud in the enclosed space. Below that are three long swords, sheathed and held in place by small wooden pegs, followed by two spears, bolted similarly. A few more pegs sit empty, but fading on the wall tells me that weapons are *usually* there. I wonder where they are.

A small coal stove sits in the corner, filling the room with warmth, and there's a cast-iron pot situated in a little slot on top. Windows fill the three other walls, so I can look out behind the ship, then off to the west—*starboard*, I remind myself—and then out across the main deck. Wind whistles through the window hinges, rattling the door a bit. I don't want to touch the coffee, or anything else for that matter, but I let my eyes linger on the maps.

I've never seen a detailed map for a country other than my own, and here in front of me is a map that shows Kandala and the islands of Ostriary—along with two more land masses set farther to the north and west. My eyes are wide as I trace the borders of the islands, each much larger than I assumed, stretching westward, all connected by the bridges Captain Blakemore mentioned. All together, the land mass is almost as large as Kandala. I wonder if Corrick has seen this.

I consider the way I left his quarters last night, to say nothing of the way he never came after me, and I rather doubt I'm going to have the chance to ask him anytime soon.

Motion on the deck catches my eye, and I glance up to see the captain climbing down the rigging, quick and sure on the ropes as the ship tips from side to side. He's still ten feet above the deck when he springs to the boards like we're on solid ground. His dark hair is windblown, his cheeks a bit flushed from the cool morning air. His jacket is loose, revealing a maroon shirt that's unbuttoned at his neck, leaving his sun-kissed collarbones bare. A short blade hangs belted at his waist, with a longer one buckled to his thigh. I don't think I've seen him wear a weapon before.

Then he's at the door and his eyes meet mine, and I realize I was staring.

I'm no stranger to the mouth of a sailor.

The words pop back into my thoughts, and I feel myself redden. As the captain pulls the latch and comes across the threshold, I snap my gaze back to the maps.

"I've never seen a full map of Ostriary," I say. I have to clear my throat. I'm probably talking too fast. "When you mentioned the islands, I didn't realize they'd be so big."

"Much like the sectors of Kandala, they're all different in their own way." He steps up beside me, smelling of sea, wind, and sunshine. He points, naming each, and I remember the way he related them to his palm and fingertips: Fairde, the largest in the center, followed by Iris, Kaisa, Roshan, Estar, and Silvesse. His finger settles on Kaisa. "Here is where the Moonflower grows. It's the northern-most island, and one of the most populated. Two bridges to Fairde, though both were destroyed in the war."

"Is that the capital city?"

"Fairde is, yes." He points to the southeastern shoreline. "There was a citadel here: Tarrumor. The royal residence was once called the Palace of the Sun, because the center courtyard was paved with gold, every window made of stained glass in reds and yellows. Quite spectacular, really."

"What is it called now?"

"Nothing." He hesitates, and his voice takes on that hollow note. "The palace still stands, but much of the citadel is in ruins. Without the bridges, it's difficult to rebuild swiftly."

I put a hand over his. I know he wasn't born in Ostriary, but as he said to Corrick, he spent a quarter of his life there. He lost his father there. And that was during a time the country was being torn apart by war. "I'm sorry," I say softly.

He glances up in surprise, and I withdraw my hand.

"I didn't mean to be so forward," I say.

"You're not being forward. You're being kind." He studies me a little too intently, so I swallow and look back at the map.

He follows my lead, and his finger shifts to the southern space of ocean between the countries. "The winds here can be very strong, easily fifty knots on a calm day, and the currents coming from Silvesse Run—which you know as the Flaming River—flow fast into the ocean. It's the toughest part to navigate, especially compared to what you'll discover once we come out of the Queen's River. Off the southern point of Sunkeep, the water is so clear and smooth that you could swim alongside the ship for miles. But here—" He points to a spot in the ocean where there's a small square drawn on the map. "This is the hardest part. On Kandalan maps, it's Bedlam's Berth. In Ostriary, it's Chaos Isle. The winds can be intense, and storms come up quick. The water gets shallow unexpectedly, so you can find yourself on a sandbar if you're not careful. Between the wind and the currents, this is where many ships turn back—or wreck."

"And you have no trouble?"

"I won't say it's not a challenge." He shrugs, but there's no arrogance to it. "Calm seas don't make sharp sailors, Miss Cade. I've done it before. I can manage it again."

I just watched him climb a thirty-foot mast in the wind when the sun had barely crested the horizon, so I believe him. "You really can just call me Tessa," I say.

The side of his mouth turns up. Half a smile, but half not. "If I did that, I'm worried Prince Corrick might try to put a knife in my back."

Mention of Corrick makes my temper sit up and pay attention. "He'd better not," I say hotly. "He's not in charge of my name, Captain Blakemore."

"He's not in charge of mine either." His smile turns a bit more genuine. "You really can just call me Rian."

He says it so equably that it eases some of my anger. "Oh," I say. "Forgive me." I hesitate. "Rian."

I expect him to call me *Tessa*, but he doesn't. "Why are you awake so early?" he says. "I usually have the deck to myself at this hour."

"Oh—I'm an early riser." After his comment about Corrick, it feels dangerous to say anything about the doubts that kept me awake for many hours last night.

Rian smiles. "I'll look forward to your company, then." He glances down to see no drink in front of me. "No coffee?"

He says it so casually that it almost startles a laugh out of me. "Coffee is *quite* the delicacy in Kandala, so I couldn't quite tell if you were being serious."

He blinks as if he's appalled. "I never joke about coffee." He moves away to take two heavy ceramic cups from a low cabinet. "And it's not a delicacy in Ostriary. I have barrels of it." He takes a small cloth and lifts the cast-iron pot from the stove, then pours. "Here." He extends the first to me.

I take it, inhaling the steam. It *does* smell a bit like dirt, but in an earthy way. It's not a bad scent. The color is a deep brown, darker than any tea I've ever seen.

I venture a sip, then make a face before I can help myself. "Ah—forgive me."

Rian notices, and he smiles. "It's definitely an acquired taste by itself." He finds a few stoppered bottles. "Here. Cream is a bit hard to come by on a ship, and we usually make do with powdered milk. But we do have sugar." He gives me a wry glance. "Gwyn was able to stock the galley when we weren't being interrogated by the Crown."

I wince and take the bottles he offers. "You have to admit—you did show up with quite the story."

"I knew we would be doubted," he says. "I'm sure we still are."

That sounds like a prompt. I stir the milk and sugar into my coffee, and I keep my eyes on the cup. "I won't be a source of gossip about the royal family," I say.

"I don't expect you to be. I don't *need* you to be. Secrets never last long on a ship. You don't think I noticed the way that man

Lochlan was looming over you in the hallway? The way he faltered once the prince arrived?"

He's so forthright that I forget that I don't have to look for prompts and hints, the way I would with anyone in the palace. Heat rises to my cheeks, but I say nothing.

Rian speaks into my silence. "When I asked His Highness if his people were going to be a problem, he immediately said it wasn't *his* people who were causing trouble. That's very telling."

"Why?"

"Because Lochlan *is* one of his people, is he not?"

I frown. He's not wrong. It makes me think of everything Lochlan said last night. He might be boorish and aggressive, but the rebel leader showed hints of kindness, too. *Tell Karri I loved her.*

When I asked Corrick about whether he intended for Lochlan to fall overboard, he said, *I wouldn't shed a tear if it happened.*

Right this instant, they're both being so pigheaded that I don't feel compelled to defend either of them. But it still stings a bit to hear the captain's criticism of my countrymen.

I've been silent too long. The room is warm, and while the windows don't make the space seem small, there's a bit of intimacy here that I didn't expect.

Rian is studying me. "Have I made you uncomfortable?"

"Oh. No." I take a hurried sip of coffee, prepared for it to be terrible.

Heavy warmth swells over my tongue, and my eyebrows go up. It's not like dirt at all. It's a rich, milky sweetness with hints of cinnamon. I think I like it better than the chocolate creams I used to share with Karri.

Rian smiles at my reaction. "What do you think?"

"I think you've spoiled me for tea forever," I say.

"I'm glad to hear it." He takes a sip of his own. "I have to check the rest of the rigging if you'd like to walk with me. But you're welcome to stay out of the wind if you'd rather."

I imagine all the ways Corrick would spin this into a trick or a trap or a manipulation, the way he brushed off Laurel Pepperleaf's praise of my skills.

But then I consider the way the captain sent me into his stateroom without hesitation. The way he talked about wanting Ostriary to rebuild, or the way he wants to make sure Kandala gets the medicine we so desperately need. The way he so openly professes a desire to help everyone—not just whoever might line his pockets.

The way he's offering to leave me here, among his private belongings, while he attends to his duties—without one single moment of hesitation.

The hell with your cynicism, Corrick.

"I'd love to walk," I say.

CHAPTER SIXTEEN

Tessa

Rian seems to check every knot, every chain, every bolt, every plank. He could tell me he knows every stitch of every sail, and I'd believe him. As we stop at each mast, he stares up at the complicated assortment of ropes and chains and netting, then hands me his cup while he climbs to sort out some tangle or check some issue he's spotted. I keep listening to his breathing, looking for any signs of the fever sickness of Kandala, but I hear nothing. No cough, no signs of fever.

When he climbs down from the second mast, I say, "Your crew was in Kandala for a few days. Has anyone shown signs of illness?"

"None at all." He glances at me. "Are you concerned?"

"I was surprised when you were the only one on deck. I didn't realize the captain himself would be checking each sail."

He shrugs and takes his cup. "Usually Sablo does it, but they all worked late into the night to get ahead of this storm. We run a lean crew, so I'd rather they take extra sleep where they can find it."

That must mean he took the morning duties *for* them.

No wonder Rian's crew is so loyal.

It rattles around in my head with the way he asked about whether Lochlan is one of Corrick's people, too.

"I can help," I say as we walk to the next mast. "Wherever you need." I hesitate, wondering if this offer is out of place. "I mean— I'm not a sailor. But if you're shorthanded."

He looks startled, but he grins. "Sure." He nods toward the last mast. "Climb on up and check those ropes for me."

"All right." I hold out my cup.

He loses the smile, and for a heartbeat of time, I expect him to say, *I was joking*, because he very clearly was.

But he takes the cup, and he says, "Look for signs of fraying, or anywhere it might be fouled. The sails—"

"Fouled?" I say.

"*Tangled.* The sails should each hang straight from the beam." He points.

"Right." I nod. Then, just as I saw him do on the other masts, I hook my fingers in the ropes, put my foot on the first rung, and begin to climb.

"It's very high," he warns.

"I'm not afraid of heights. I thought you heard the rumors about Tessa Cade scaling the walls of the Royal Sector."

That grin is back. "I did indeed. Go ahead then."

I begin to climb—but I quickly learn that this is very different from scaling a wall on solid ground. When I'm fifteen feet up, the wind is blasting at my cheeks, pulling tendrils free of my braid.

The boat dips without warning, my foot slips off a rung, and the world spins. I catch myself in the netting, clutching tight. My breath is a wild rush in my lungs, my heart slamming in my chest, and I expect Rian to call me back down.

Instead, he calls, "Take a minute. Get your bearings. Look at the horizon."

His voice is steady. Patient. Unworried. I do as he says, and it helps.

My foot finds the next rung, and I keep climbing. I'm slower now, less confident. This seems higher than the sector walls ever did. If I let go, it seems that I would fall upward and lose myself in the morning sky.

By the time I'm two-thirds of the way there, I chance a glance down, and somehow there's only water below me. I suck in a sharp breath. It must be an optical illusion caused by the sway of the ship— but everything seems so far. The ship rights itself for a moment, then tips again in the wind. I cling to the rigging and the mast and close my eyes, but that's worse. I dip and sway and grip tight. For a minute. An hour. I have no idea.

"Come now, Miss Cade, you can't be tired already."

His voice is right in front of me, and I gasp. My eyes snap open to find Rian right there on the opposite side of the rigging, his fingers hooked in the same web of ropes. He's not clinging for dear life like I am. He looks like he could stay up here all day.

"It's possible I was too bold," I say, and he smiles.

"No," he says. "Just bold enough."

My fingers refuse to unclench. "If you could have meals sent up, I'll just stay up here for the rest of our journey."

He laughs. "That wouldn't make for a very good story." He looks up. "You've only got another ten feet."

I take a deep breath and look up.

He's right. It really only is about ten feet.

"Either way," he adds, "you have to climb up or climb down. Ten feet won't matter if you fall."

I huff a startled laugh. "Well. That's reassuring."

"I thought so, too."

But in a way, it *is* reassuring. I take a deep breath and fix my eyes on the individual strands, then move my hand up to the next stretch. And then another. And another. A minute later, my hand grasps the crossbeam that holds the sails, and I'm gasping, partly terrified, partly amazed. I still can't make myself look away from the solid objects right in front of me. Just a stretch of wood. Just a few ropes.

It takes me a minute to realize I actually came up here with a *job* to do, and I trace my eyes over the lines. I feel a bit foolish, because Rian is obviously going to do the same thing, but my heart is pounding from the opportunity to do something wild and dangerous again. Wes and I spent so much time hiding from the night patrol and scurrying down darkened roads, while these last few weeks have been interminable palace meetings and measuring dosages with physicians and charting efficacy rates.

Wes.

I thought of Wes. Not Corrick.

Without warning, the memory makes my eyes sting. Of course Corrick can't slink through the shadows and steal Moonflower from the Royal Sector anymore. The rumors are already wild enough. He could never go back. I don't even know if he'd want to.

I blink away the emotion and study each individual rope. At first, they all look the same, but then I realize the second one from the end has a bit of a twist in the line.

"There!" I call, pointing. "I think that one is—"

I break off with a gasp when I realize Rian is right in front of me again, on the opposite side of the ropes.

He's staring up at the line, too. "That one is all right. Just the wind." He pauses and turns back to me, only a few inches of space between us. His eyes are lighter than Corrick's, a blue so faded they're gray. He studies me. "Good catch. I'm impressed."

I feel my cheeks warm. "Thank you."

"You're welcome." He pauses, and wind whips between us. "Look out from the ropes. The view is worth it. I promise."

I hold my breath and cast my gaze to the left—and he's right. The sea stretches out in all directions, the sky a fading purple overhead. Below us, the main sails billow out, hiding much of the deck from view. From up here, it's like I've climbed a ladder to the heavens.

"It's like flying," I say.

"When I was a boy, I thought the same." His smile turns a little sad. "My father used to say that if I wasn't careful, I'd catch the right gust of wind and find myself in the clouds."

He misses him. I can hear it in his voice. I wonder how long the former captain Blakemore has been dead, and how long Rian has had to play emissary—or spy.

Before I can ask, he has a question of his own. "Will Lochlan be a problem, Miss Cade?"

I look across the web of ropes and shake my head. "He hates Corrick—" I catch myself and wince, wondering if I need to be more formal now. "He hates *Prince* Corrick, but I don't think he'll be a problem for the ship." I hesitate. "He said he used to take summer work around the docks. He might be willing to help, too. If you're shorthanded."

"No—I meant, will he be a problem for *you*."

Oh.

"I don't know," I say quietly. I inhale to say more, but my tongue stops on an explanation. I'm not entirely sure what I'd say anyway.

Lochlan took me and Corrick prisoner. He marched us through the mud to a waiting mob that wanted to kill the King's Justice.

But Lochlan had no other options. As horrible as he was, I understood why he did it.

I swallow, and my throat feels tight.

Rian's eyes search mine, and I know he's trying to puzzle that out, to determine what kind of conflict we've brought aboard his ship.

"And the prince himself?" Rian says, and his voice is very careful.

I didn't make you wait.

The words I said to Corrick burn in my heart, and warmth climbs up my cheeks again. "The prince wants the best for Kandala," I say. "He won't cause any problems. He's eager to find a new supply of Moonflower."

Rian rubs a hand across his jaw. "Again," he says gently, "I meant for *you*."

The wind whispers between us now, a brief lull in the sweeping gusts, and we're almost close enough to share breath. I wasn't prepared for these kinds of questions, especially not at the top of a mast.

"We're flying," Rian says. "No one can hear your words up here. Speak freely."

"I'd speak freely on the decks," I say.

"Would you?"

My chest feels hot and tight, and I don't know what to say. "Of course."

But there's really no *of course* about it.

"I saw the way people jumped when the king spoke at dinner," Rian says. "I see the way you look to the prince before you say a word." He hesitates. "I've told you before, I don't mean to say things that will put you at risk."

"I'm not at risk!" I snap, and then I scowl because I hate that he brought out my temper—when he's not the one who deserves it. At the same time, I wonder if what he's saying is true. Do I look like I'm deferring to Corrick and Harristan? Do I look like I'm at risk?

The memory of Corrick holding a dagger to that man's throat in the candy shop is seared into my brain as clearly as the time I found him in the rubble of the Hold after one of the first rebel attacks. He'd cut two prisoners' throats, then. I keep thinking of Lochlan's warnings in the hallway. They feel a little too accurate all of a sudden.

Or the way Karri leaned in to whisper in the candy shop. *He's still terrifying.*

Rian studies me for a long moment. "Around the docks, there are dozens of rumors about a girl named Tessa who used to work with a man named Wes to steal Moonflower to help the people. That she was one of the bravest outlaws the people had ever known. That she risked her life to sneak into the palace to bring news of better medicine."

That wasn't why I snuck in, but it's a better story than saying I hoped to assassinate the king after I thought "Wes" had been killed by Prince Corrick.

"Their doses were too high," I say. "We're trying to convince people that more could be done with less. No one trusts the Crown yet."

"But they trust you." He pauses. "Even though *Wes and Tessa* disappeared from the Wilds."

He says that like he knows the truth—but the prince has never directly confirmed his involvement. Everything happened so quickly that night, and certainly no one could prove it. I don't know what to say.

"They *do* trust you," Rian says. "Not just the people either. Prince Corrick brought you along to ensure the Moonflower in Ostriary is the same as what you have in Kandala. The guardsman said you've earned the king's favor and protection, too. I sense that's not a small thing."

"No," I say softly. "It's not a small thing."

His eyes search my face. "What I heard about you is vastly different from rumors about the King's Justice." He pauses. "Surely you can understand my confusion about the company you keep, and whether you're at risk—or whether you're at his side by your own choosing. Did Prince Corrick really hang bodies along the gates of the Royal Sector? To prevent thieving?"

There's no disguising the judgment in his voice.

I can't even deny it. I wish I could. I'll never forget the bodies, the daggers protruding from the eye sockets, the Moonflower blossoms planted on the corpses that hung in the summer sun. Sometimes I smell something rotten, and it triggers memories of the stench, the buzzing of the flies, the guards mocking me for staring in horror. It triggers memories of my panic and grief, to see my friend's body displayed in such a way.

Corrick, I think. *Corrick did that.*

The corpse I saw wasn't Wes. Not really. And the man he hung in his place truly was a criminal. Sometimes I have to remind myself of that.

But he wants to be better. He wants to *do* better. In the candy shop, he could have executed that man right there, but he didn't. He had him arrested and taken to the Hold.

Though I don't know what he did with him after that.

"I've upset you," Rian says.

"No." But maybe he has. "Corrick was trying to maintain order." My voice is rough. "The sectors—the consuls—" I break off with a frustrated sound. "You don't know what it was like. Everyone had a different idea of what was *right*."

"Sometimes what's *right* isn't debatable, or a matter of opinion. Clearly *you* didn't think what they were doing was right."

He doesn't say it like a question. He says it like he knows. He says it like he *agrees*.

"No," I say, and my voice is so quiet it's nearly pulled away with the wind. "I didn't."

"It's hard to take from people who feel like they have nothing to lose," he says. "I saw what happened during the war in Ostriary."

That's right. He survived a war. We merely postponed a revolution.

"We aren't far from war in Kandala," I say.

"I know," he says. "I'm hoping we can prevent that."

We. He's talking about the Ostrian court allying with Kandala, trading steel for Moonflower petals.

But for a flicker of time, with his eyes so close, it sounds like he's talking about *us*. Rian and me.

The wind steals my breath, and the ship dips and tilts, and my fingers tighten on the ropes. I close my eyes and swallow.

Rian rests his fingers over mine, his grip warm and secure. "Easy," he says. "You won't fall."

"Oi, Captain!" a woman's voice calls from below, and my eyes snap open.

Another man yells, "Is she stuck? Or do you reckon he tied her up there?"

Someone else laughs.

Rian smiles. "My crew is awake."

I flush, realizing just how closely we were suspended together. "I suppose we should get down."

He nods, but he makes no move to descend. "I'm usually the first one on deck, Miss Cade." He pauses. "If you'd like to help me check the rigging tomorrow."

I take a deep breath and look into his eyes. "Of course, Captain Blakemore. I'm happy to help."

CHAPTER SEVENTEEN

Corrick

W hen I wake for the second time, light streams through the window over my bed. I can't see the sun from the porthole, but the sky is bright, the shore so distant it could be an illusion. Waves glisten in the sunlight, the ship rocking along. I rub at my eyes and hope that my middle-of-the-night conversation with Rocco was all a dream, that I've slept straight through.

But it wasn't.

How long was my brother suspicious of me?

Only these last few months.

Months. And Harristan never said a word.

I shouldn't be so upset about it. Honestly, he should have been suspicious of me for *years*.

He left me in the Hold for an entire day. It makes me wonder if he's put me on this ship to get me out of the way as efficiently as he did with Lochlan.

But he snuck into my carriage before I left. He all but threatened the captain.

He sent this jacket. I slide a finger along the lapel.

I wish I could talk to my brother. My throat threatens to tighten, but I breathe through it. I'm being ridiculous. I'm not a little boy.

I want to talk to Tessa—but the irony is that I've closed that door, too.

My joints are sore from a poor night of sleep. Or maybe I truly am hungover this time. I should just go pick a fight with Lochlan and get it over with. Or that captain. Surely he's around here somewhere. That might be more satisfying.

Perhaps I'm just hungry.

All of these options require leaving my quarters. I find my pocket watch and discover it's past midmorning. Very late for me. I should have asked one of the guards to wake me.

I wash my face, then take a good look in the mirror and realize I should spare a few minutes to shave, too. It's my first morning on board the ship. No sense looking how I feel.

I consider leaving that jacket in the trunk, but something about it keeps calling to me, so I buckle it into place again. By the time I emerge from my quarters, I'm buttoned up and presentable, my tumultuous thoughts locked away. The King's Justice, Cruel Corrick, ready to face the decisions of the day.

Kilbourne is down the hallway a bit, near the staircase, but he heads my way when he sees me. "Your Highness."

"Kilbourne." I have no doubt that the guards have discussed every second of what has transpired over the last twelve hours, but they're too well disciplined to mention any of it to my face. Even still, as Kilbourne strides toward me, I remember my early morning conversation with Rocco.

Which one of you had a mark on me?

I wonder if it was Rocco himself.

These thoughts all war with each other as Kilbourne draws close and stands at attention. "I can give you the morning's accounting," he says.

"Go ahead."

"Silas is above board with Lochlan and Tessa. Rocco retired at six. He will relieve one of us at midday, unless you'd rather I call for him sooner."

Lochlan. I remember the way he was looming over Tessa in the hallway. "Lochlan and Tessa are above board together?"

"I don't know. I've been stationed in the hallway."

Because I was sleeping. I scowl. I'm hungry and irritated, and I feel like I've completely lost control of everything in my life that matters.

And I'm in the middle of the Queen's River, hurtling toward . . . who knows what.

"Miss Tessa awoke before Lochlan," Kilbourne continues. "I was able to see a bit of the main deck from the stairwell. She was climbing the rigging with Captain Blakemore early this morning, but now it seems most of the crew is awake. I don't think she's in danger from Lochlan."

"Wait—did you say she was climbing the rigging?"

"Yes, Your Highness." He pauses. "They seemed to be in good spirits."

I scowl. I want to storm onto the deck and demand answers, but I know that will only reinforce the illusion that I'm bothered by any of this.

What did Rocco say last night? *Do your best to enjoy the journey. The longer they believe we are willing passengers, the more we can learn.*

Fine. Kandala is most important. I can lock away my feelings. I've been doing it for years.

I tug my jacket straight and look at Kilbourne. I keep my voice light, as though I don't have a care in the world. "Surely there's a kitchen on this ship. Do you know the way?"

"I do."

"Good. Have you eaten? I'm famished."

—◆—

The kitchen is at the front of the ship, directly opposite our cabins and one deck lower. There's an undercurrent of smoked fish and sour ale in the air as we approach, but above all that is the sweet warm scent of something baking. When we step through the doorway, I discover the "kitchen" to be not much more than a set of ovens built into one wall, and a wide stove set into the other. No windows, so the space is overly warm, and sweat finds my brow almost immediately. Pots and pans and utensils are hung everywhere there's room, including over the tables and benches bolted to the floor.

A middle-aged woman is pulling a pan full of tiny loaves out of one of the ovens, a stern expression on her face. A young girl sits nearby, chopping root vegetables at one of the tables. She can't be more than seven years old, but she wields the knife with the precision of a surgeon. When her eyes fall on me and my guard, the knife goes still for a moment, but then she returns to her task without saying a word. A tiny line forms between her eyebrows, the shadow of a frown on her lips.

Splendid. I don't know what I've done to aggravate a *child*, but somehow I've accomplished it.

The woman sets the pan on a flour-speckled counter in front of her, then bobs a half-hearted curtsy. "Your Highness." She swipes at a sweat-damp forehead and barely glances at me. "Looking for some breakfast, I assume?"

She sounds annoyed, too, and I frown.

No one talks to me like this in Kandala. I'm not offended, not really, but it rattles my foundation. I don't know how to move forward. They can't *all* be angry that I'm not fawning all over their captain. We might need Moonflower, but he's the one who came to *us* looking for steel.

"Yes, in fact." I pause, wondering how soon Rocco will be awake and ready to eat. "For my guards as well."

"I cleaned up from breakfast two hours ago. I'm on to lunch now."

"Lunch, then."

"It'll be ready in an hour." She pulls eggs from a cabinet and begins cracking them into a bowl. The little girl scowls at me and chops her vegetables with renewed vigor.

"Are you truly angry that I did not arrive on time for breakfast?"

"Angry?" She laughs, but there's no humor to it. More like she can't imagine my audacity. "I have six extra people to feed. I'm *busy*." She starts whisking the eggs briskly.

I try to imagine Harristan being treated this way. I can't even fathom it.

Then again, I can't see my brother downing shots of brandy at three in the morning because he'd been spurned by a girl. Harristan would have been on time for breakfast.

I could seek the captain and complain, and he'd probably make her prepare me breakfast, but that wouldn't endear me to anyone on the crew. It doesn't seem like a good idea to alienate the cook. I'm also certain he'd have a quip that would make me feel inadequate. No, thank you.

"What's your name?" I ask the woman.

"Dabriel," she says. She nods at the girl. "This here is Anya. She doesn't like strangers."

She says *strangers* as if we boarded the ship like pirates. The girl glances at me with shadowed eyes but says nothing. Her hands are swiftly slicing through the vegetables, but I see a dozen scars lining her tiny forearms. Straight, clean lines that had to come from a blade.

"Your daughter?" I say.

"Not mine. Gwyn's."

Gwyn's. So this girl is Lieutenant Tagas's daughter, the one Rocco said we could use as leverage. For a moment, I'm struck by the brutal practicality of his suggestion. I thought he meant a younger member of the crew. I hadn't realized he meant a *child*.

As King's Justice, I've been forced to do a lot of terrible things, but I've never harmed a child. I'm sure there are rumors of me boiling children alive, but truly, I don't have much interaction with children in any way at all. Some of it is due to my vicious reputation, and some is due to my brother's cool aloofness, but either way, children rarely grace our halls.

It was very different in the Wilds, when I could lose myself in the persona of Weston Lark. I knew dozens of families. Easily a hundred children.

I helped dig graves for some of them, when the medicine wasn't enough.

Maybe Anya can sense my sudden disquiet, because the girl

looks up, her dark eyes evaluating me. I shouldn't be kind, in case Rocco's warnings come to pass, but regret has already started eating at my gut.

"Are those for lunch?" I say to her.

She hesitates, then shakes her head.

Then the vegetables she's chopping are obviously for dinner, but I say, "Ah, so you must be preparing a meal for the fish, then. You throw them overboard? Get the fish nice and fat?"

She looks at me like she can't decide if I'm crazy or stupid. Dabriel glances over, and it's clear she probably thinks I'm both.

Anya shakes her head again.

"You feed them to the seagulls, then? I really don't think seagulls like carrots."

A tiny smile begins to peek through. "They're for *dinner*," she whispers.

"We're having seagulls for dinner?" I say, feigning horror.

That brings out the full smile. "No! The carrots."

"Oh. Just carrots for dinner then."

"Not *just* carrots. I have potatoes, too." She spreads her hands as if I can't see the neatly sliced vegetables on the table. "And Dabriel does the fish."

"Oh. *You're* the head cook. I should have known." I nod appraisingly. "You're very good with a knife. So obvious now. I should have asked *you* for breakfast."

She giggles, then holds up a piece of carrot. "Here."

"My guard is very hungry, too. Could you slice it in half?"

She laughs, full out, then holds out a second piece.

I take them both, then give her a nod. "You have my deepest gratitude, Miss Anya. I promise not to be late for breakfast tomorrow."

She grins, but I turn away to extend a hand to Kilbourne, offering our "breakfast." This time *he* is the one who's looking at me as if I'm crazy.

"Close your mouth, Kilbourne," I say.

He snaps his mouth shut, then takes one piece of carrot.

"Take them both," I say to him as we turn for the doorway. "It's my fault you didn't get to eat."

"Your Highness," Dabriel calls from behind me.

I turn, and I'm glad I have quick reflexes, because she's tossing an apple at me—and then a warm roll from the pan. "For your guard, too," she says, and she tosses a second set. Kilbourne snatches them out of the air.

"My thanks," he says to her.

"Mine, too," I add.

"Just don't make a habit of it." She doesn't smile.

But I do. It's a tiny win, and rather meaningless, really, but for the first time aboard this ship, I feel like I've done something right.

CHAPTER EIGHTEEN

Tessa

Once the ship woke up, the deck became a flurry of activity. In the quiet of dawn, with wind billowing the sails and nothing but the rush of water below us, it was hard to imagine there'd be much to do. But once Rian's crew got to work, I started to wonder how they have time to *sleep*. Torn sails have to be mended, and rigging repaired from what the captain identified this morning. The sail beams have to be adjusted for the changing winds and the river currents, and I quickly learned that every rope seems interconnected: if they loosen one, it requires tightening somewhere else.

I was serious in my offer to help, but it's obvious that this crew is close-knit and used to working together. There doesn't seem to be a place to fit, especially with so much to be done. When Rian called for Gwyn and Marchon in his stateroom, it was clear they had important things to discuss, and I didn't want to be in the way. Through the windows, I could see them going over maps and jotting notes—and I'm sure they were also discussing the newcomers on board. I didn't miss their eyes glancing my way every so often.

I watch the crew, listening for coughs or rough voices, wondering if anyone has any complaints about chills or exhaustion. They weren't in Kandala for *very* long, but I'm still worried that the fever sickness might break out on this ship—and I'm pleased to hear nothing of concern.

Brock and Tor are the men who were bickering on the deck last night, but it seems they don't hate each other; they just love to argue. They spent the morning stripping rust from chains and setting the fishing nets, and then, once those were tossed overboard, they worked with others to drag the haul onto the deck. By then, Lochlan had come up, and I'd tensed, wondering if he'd start picking at me again, but he barely even met my eyes. He took the medicine I offered, then saw the other men at work and set to join them.

I guess he didn't have a hard time finding a place to fit at all.

Then fish were being gutted and nets were being repaired and the decks were being washed. The whole time, I don't see Corrick or any guards aside from Silas, who's taken a position at the front of the ship, probably so he can keep an eye on everything at once. By the time morning gives way to midday, the waves have gotten rougher, occasionally splashing over the side, forcing me to stand near the mast because I'm terrified I'll go over the railing. I'm wondering if I would be better served to return to my quarters.

But then one of the men shouts, another swears, and a flurry of activity erupts near where they were gutting the fish. They're all on their feet, tension thick in the air. At first, I can't tell what's happening, but Lochlan shoves Brock square in the chest.

The other man draws himself up, but he doesn't fight back. He's talking, but I can't hear what he's saying. There's a fish knife clutched in one of his fists.

Lochlan shoves him again. Brock's teeth are clenched, and his fingers adjust on that knife.

My heart leaps into my throat. All I can think about is Rian asking Corrick if his people are going to cause trouble, and we haven't even been on the ship for a full *day.* "Hey!" I call, striding across the deck, praying I'm not going to lose my footing. "Silas!"

But Silas has seen the impending brawl and is starting forward himself. I'm distantly aware of booted feet behind me, but I don't realize it's Captain Blakemore until he puts a hand on my arm, drawing me to a stop.

"Slow," he says. "Don't make it bigger than it is."

"They're going to fight—"

"No one fights on my ship. Not like this." He lets out a whistle, and half the men startle, then exchange glances. Many of them take a step back from where Brock and Lochlan are glaring at each other. Even Silas hesitates, his hand on a weapon.

"Brock," Tor hisses. "Brock, it's the captain."

It's like Rian's presence is magical, because Brock blinks slowly, then looks up. The tense readiness eases out of his frame. "Sorry, Cap." He jerks his head at Lochlan. "We were just fooling around. I didn't know he'd be so sensitive."

Lochlan inhales, his fists primed like he's ready to surge forward. I expect Brock to retaliate, but he doesn't. He takes a step back, out of the way, and I see the rebel preparing to go after him.

"Lochlan." Rian's voice is low and lacking in force, but there's something in his tone that demands attention. A confidence. A sureness.

It's effective, because Lochlan sets his jaw and looks up. I don't know if he expects a rebuke or a punishment, but his eyes are belligerent, the way he looks at Corrick. "What?"

"I saw you hauling lines with the crew." He pauses, looking at Lochlan's wrist, which is still bandaged from when it was broken. "Your arm doesn't give you any trouble?"

The question must be unexpected, because Lochlan blinks. "I do all right. I don't mind the work."

"Well, I appreciate the extra hands. I'll make sure you're compensated for your time." Rian looks at the others. "The rest of you better finish with the fish or you'll have Dabriel up here next."

I only met the cook for a minute this morning, but the threat of her temper must be unifying, because the men grunt and edge around Lochlan and return to their positions, even Brock. Their tension seems forgotten.

Lochlan stands in their midst, but the belligerence has slid out of his expression. He glances from the men to the captain like he's not sure how to proceed.

Tor looks up at him. "Come on, man. I'll tell you about the time Brock was trying to convince a pretty girl to dance, and he nearly shat himself. Right there on the dance floor. Cleared the whole place out."

Brock picks up a knife and sighs with the weariness of someone who's heard an embarrassing story one too many times. "You're in front of a lady, Tor."

"It was your own fault. I told you it weren't safe to drink that spiced rum on Iris." Tor glances at me and grimaces. "Sorry, Miss Cade."

Lochlan sits down next to Tor a little uncertainly, but he picks up a fish and takes a knife when another crewman hands one over.

He looks up at Rian. "Thank you, Captain." He hesitates. "Sorry for the trouble."

I freeze. I don't think I've ever heard a genuine apology out of Lochlan's mouth.

But Rian just says, "No trouble." His voice is easy. Genuinely appreciative.

I almost want to stare at him. I think I *am* staring at him.

He finally turns away from his crew. "Miss Cade. I'm glad to find you still on the deck. I was wondering if you would—" He must catch my expression, because he breaks off. "What?"

"I—that—just—" I can't form a coherent question. "I thought they were going to start stabbing each other. How did you stop that?"

He shrugs it off. "That was just a little bit of pride."

I study him, considering the times I've seen Corrick and Lochlan face off. The prince is the one who first broke his wrist, but now doesn't seem the time to volunteer that information.

I lower my voice. "I've never seen Lochlan back down. I thought you'd have to . . ." I rack my brains for a punishment I've heard of on a ship. "I don't know. Chain him to the bow."

He laughs a little, but not like anything is really funny. "And you ask why I worried about putting you in harm's way."

"What?"

"I imagine your King's Justice very well would have chained him to the bow. He probably would have done worse. And for what? Getting upset over a few careless words?" His eyes flick to his crew. Lochlan is laughing at something Tor has said now. "We're one day out of port. If I start hanging men overboard, it would make for a very uncomfortable journey. For my people *and* yours."

I think of the way his men went back to their tasks so readily.

The way he said *no one fights on my ship*. Even I was ready to break up the fight with force, calling for Silas automatically, but Rian defused the entire situation with a few words.

It's not just that his people are loyal. They *trust* him.

Like this morning on the ropes, I'm in danger of blushing at him. I look away, just as the boat dips and sways, and my breath catches. I put out a hand automatically, catching his arm. It's warm and sturdy, and again, I remember falling against him last night, in the rain.

Then I remember what he started to say. I have to clear my throat. "What . . . ah, what were you wondering?"

"Yes, Captain." Corrick speaks from off to my right. "What *were* you wondering?"

Of course.

I turn and look at the prince. Last night, Corrick's eyes were a little wild, every emotion plain on his face. Today, he's locked down, as severe as ever. He's wearing a hip-length leather jacket that's such a deep brown that it's almost black. Every button and buckle is in place, his vivid blue eyes sharp and expressionless. I think of the way he took me in his arms, and I want to shiver. *That* Corrick is nowhere to be found.

I don't know what to say to him. Too much time has passed now. Do I owe him an apology? Does he owe me one?

His expression doesn't change, but I see the tiny movement of his eyes as he takes in my hand on Rian's arm. I unclench my fingers from the captain's sleeve.

"Sablo cut his arm on a bit of rigging," Rian is saying. "He's refusing any stitching, but as we have an apothecary on board, I said I would ask you to look at it." He pauses and glances at Corrick. "With your permission, Your Highness."

"If Tessa is willing," Corrick says.

"Of course," I say. *Sablo.* I remember the large, red-bearded man from dinner. He couldn't speak. I didn't realize until now that I haven't seen him on the main deck this morning.

"He always takes the night watch," Rian says. "But he should be awake by now. We can head below." He regards Corrick coolly. "You're welcome to join us."

The prince regards him coolly right back. "Am I?"

"Let's see to Sablo," I say brightly, before the two of *them* can start a fight. "I'll have to go to my room to get my bag."

"I'll escort you," Corrick says. "Surely the captain would like to offer his officer a bit of warning. And Miss Cade can give me the details of her morning."

Miss Cade would like to go back to sitting by the mast.

Rian's eyes shift to mine, seeking acquiescence.

I hesitate, then nod. "Maybe we can return here," I say. "Or your stateroom, Rian—ah, *Captain*. For the sunlight. If it needs stitching."

"Certainly."

Corrick offers me his arm, and I don't want to take it. For him, it's probably nothing. Courtly manners.

But for me, it feels personal. Intimate.

So much changed between us overnight—and unlike stitching up an arm, I don't know how to fix it. I gingerly rest my fingertips on his sleeve, and it reminds me of my first day in the palace, when he was my worst nightmare and my greatest ally all rolled into one man.

When we turn away, I sense the eyes of the crew on us, but I can't focus on any of that. I'm focused on the prince at my side, whose emotions are all a mystery.

Well, most of them. His emotions about the captain aren't a mystery *at all.*

We're barely down the steps and out of earshot when I whisper, "He just stopped a fight, and I thought you were going to start one."

"Good morning to you, too, Miss Cade." Corrick isn't whispering at all. "It sounds as though *you* are about to start one."

I scowl. "Of course not." I try to make my voice as cool as his, but I just sound like I'm mocking him. "Good morning, Your Highness."

"And by *he*, do you refer to Rian?" He pauses dramatically. "Ah, do forgive me. *Captain Blakemore.*"

My cheeks are flaming entirely against my will. I let go of his arm.

"What fight did he stop?" Corrick asks. Some of the chill has slipped out of his voice, and genuine curiosity has slid in to replace it.

"Lochlan had a bit of an altercation."

Corrick's eyes flick skyward. "You don't say."

"It sounds like a crewman started it."

"See? I won't need to throw him overboard. The captain will end up doing it for me."

I frown and say nothing.

"I'm kidding," he says.

"Well, forgive me for not being sure." We reach my door, and I push through.

Corrick follows me in, letting the door fall shut behind him, closing Kilbourne in the hallway—and us into this room. He leans back against the door and folds his arms, looking as darkly dangerous as ever.

I ignore him.

He doesn't return the favor. "Kilbourne told me you were climbing the masts with the captain this morning."

"I was." I find my apothecary kit by the end of my bed, and I take a moment to eat one of Karri's peppermints. The bag is all I really came here for, but Corrick doesn't move away from the door.

I set my shoulders and look at him. "The captain was checking the sails, and I was wondering how difficult it was. Do you find that hard to believe?"

"That you were curious, or that you were fearless?"

"Both."

"I watched you stop a revolution." His eyes hold mine. "I don't find either option hard to believe."

Something in his tone makes me shiver.

"You don't like him," I say. "I don't understand why."

"It doesn't matter if I like him. I'm not sure I can *trust* him."

"You don't trust anyone," I scoff.

Those words hit him in a way I don't expect, and I'm not entirely sure how I can tell, but they do. Maybe it's a little flinch in his eyes, like he's taken a blow he wasn't ready for.

"I didn't mean that as an offense, Your Highness."

I say it lightly, but a muscle twitches in his jaw, and I regret calling him that. He says nothing.

With a start, I realize that maybe I've found myself on the list of people he doesn't trust.

I pat my bag. "We should go up."

He straightens, drawing the door open, ever the gentlemen. "After you, Miss Cade."

I move to stride past him, but the prince catches my arm,

drawing me to a stop. My breath stops and my heart kicks, but his hand is gentle, warm against my sleeve.

"Wait," he says quietly. "Please, Tessa."

He said it last night, too, and I didn't listen. I was too flushed. Too embarrassed. Too angry.

Today, I stop, and I look up. The prince's eyes burn into mine, but his voice is low, even and formal. "We allowed Lochlan to come because Harristan believed it would be seen as a gesture of goodwill—and would also prevent him from organizing another rebellion in my absence." He pauses. "So Lochlan is right that our invitation was not wholly altruistic. But I did *not* bring him with the intention of killing him conveniently. Last night, I was apprehensive about the trip, about the captain's motives, about my brother and his . . . Well." He frowns and runs a hand back through his hair. "I saw Lochlan looming over you in the hallway, and my temper got the best of me. Forgive me. Please."

It's a good speech—and I believe every word. The apology is profound, because I know he means it.

But I can't stop thinking of Rian's voice in the wind this morning. *Lochlan is one of his people, is he not?*

Or the way Lochlan backed right down when he was allowed a moment of dignity, instead of rebelling against dark threats and armed guards. Even Kilbourne slammed him into the wall last night.

My thoughts don't know where to settle, because I've found Lochlan pretty frightening myself. But I know what it's like to be backed into a corner. Choices never seem like *choices* when the world only offers us bad ones. I once told the king that I would have been lighting the fires of revolution right alongside Lochlan if I hadn't found myself in the palace with Corrick. We stopped a war—but the feelings of disdain and scorn are still alive and well. On *both* sides.

"You need to find a way to get along with him," I say.

"I've been perfectly cordial to the captain."

"I'm talking about *Lochlan*."

"Why." Corrick doesn't even say it like a question.

"Because you dragged him onto a ship to get him out of the way. It's no better than locking him in the Hold, Corrick. If you want to fix things in Kandala, you and your brother can't keep putting your opponents in *prison*."

He stares back at me, but I tug my arm free before he can say anything else. I have a patient to treat, and I need to get away from the intensity in his gaze. When we stand in the shadows, he reminds me too much of Weston Lark, who was *kind* and *good* and would never hurt a soul.

As usual, I need to remind myself that Wes *was* a part of the man in front of me. That *goodness* is inside him.

But it's just a part.

Sometimes I worry that it's not quite enough.

Chapter Nineteen

Corrick

When I was in the palace, it was never *easy* to be the King's Justice, but I could count the minutes of my day, knowing eventually the clock hands would crawl toward the early morning hours when I could escape into the Wilds with Tessa.

Even once the ruse was over—because Tessa was in the palace and we were working toward a new solution—I could reassure myself that we were bringing about change. That things would be different. That we would work *together* to make things better.

But as the days passed, true change began to feel slow and ineffective. Potentially impossible. Like that meeting that ended with Lochlan diving across a table at Consul Sallister. At least in the Wilds I could see medicine making a difference. As King's Justice, I only saw my failures.

Now I'm on this ship, and with every censorious glance Tessa throws my way, I feel like more of a monster than I ever was.

She wants me to get along with Lochlan. He's out on the deck, gutting fish with other men from the crew. The low sound of their voices hardly carries over the wind, but I can tell he's found a place among them. There's a part of me that envies the simplicity of it.

When I walk across the deck with Tessa, he stops talking, and his eyes follow me. He leans toward the man beside him, saying something too low for me to hear, then uses his knife to rip a fish in half.

No subtlety there. He wants me to have a reaction.

I ignore him.

The captain is in his stateroom with Gwyn and Sablo, but when Tessa and I enter with Kilbourne at our backs, it's obvious that the room isn't quite large enough to fit six people. The work table takes up a good deal of room, and the burning stove blocks a whole corner. I wouldn't mind taking a look at the maps, but I can't get close to the table. Tessa takes a stool to sit in front of Sablo, who's holding a bandaged arm to his chest. He looks a bit alarmed at the sudden crowd.

Tessa glances up at the rest of us, but it feels more pointed when her eyes find me. "Maybe you all could give us some privacy."

Fine. But I'm not being evicted by myself.

"Captain," I say. "I understand you've offered my guardsman a tour of the ship. I wouldn't mind the same." I pause. "If you have the time."

He surprises me by saying, "Sure." He extends a hand toward the door. "After you."

We step out into the wind, the sails snapping overhead. The blue sky stretches on ahead for miles, but gray clouds still crowd the sky behind us. I've been on the deck three times now, but both times I was focused on what was in front of me: Tessa. Now, I inhale the sea air and look beyond the masts. The scent of fish is thick in the air, but it's not overpowering thanks to the wind. I've sailed the Queen's River before, but never quite like this. Our parents only boarded the finest ships, wide vessels with servants and attendants and liveried officers. The *Dawn Chaser* is a decent ship, but it's not built for royalty. When we were boys, Harristan and I were always cloistered away, kept out of the wind, far from any railings. My brother never really took to travel by sea, so once he was king, he never asked for it. Our journeys to other sectors are almost always by land.

But now, feeling the wind bite at my cheeks and tug at my clothes, I find myself wishing I'd done this more often. There's a part of me that wants to lean over the railing just because I *can*.

The thought feels juvenile, and I shove it away.

Lochlan would probably take a chance to pitch me overboard anyway.

When I glance over, I find Rian studying me.

"First time at sea, Your Highness?"

I can't tell if the question is meant to be condescending, but he sounds forthright, so I am, too.

"No," I say. "Not really. But it's been ages." I step past him, toward the railing, because the lure is just too great. Beneath us, the water rushes past alarmingly fast, waves slapping at the hull. It's a bit dizzying, but I like it.

"We're making good time," Rian says. "It was a boon to get ahead of the storm. Good winds should have us in the ocean south of Sunkeep by tomorrow night. The following day at the latest."

That *is* good time, and I wonder if it's too good.

Once we pass Port Karenin, I'll be truly on my own.

I have to tamp down the lick of fear that loops around my spine, and I straighten, moving away from the railing. The captain extends a hand, and we walk, heading toward the bow of the ship.

"I heard Lochlan started a fight already," I say.

"Not a fight," he says. "Just a bit of wounded pride between men." He pauses, and one of those tiny barbs finds his voice. "You understand, I'm sure."

"You really don't like me, do you?"

He smiles, but it's more cunning than it is friendly. "Do I give that impression? I believe the king was assured we'd be old friends by the time you return."

"Don't be contemptuous, Captain. It doesn't suit you."

His smile widens. "I wouldn't dream of it."

Another barb, but I don't take the bait. A gust of cold wind sweeps across the deck, tugging at my jacket, and I tuck my hands in my pockets. "You're judging me by rumor and opinion," I say.

"Perhaps I am," he says equably.

We've reached the bow of his ship, and from here, I see nothing but open water and distant ships, the wind in my face and the sky stretching on forever.

"Was death truly the penalty for stealing Moonflower?" he says.

"Yes," I say. "It was well known throughout Kandala."

"And as King's Justice, you were in charge of determining the method of punishment?"

"I was."

"These punishments," he says. "They were public?"

"Sometimes," I say. I hear him trying to trap me, so I turn and look at him. "You were not here in the beginning, when people were quite literally fighting to the death over access to medicine. My brother had an entire country to consider. He ordered me to take action, and so I did."

"I see."

I wait for him to say something else, but he doesn't. We head along the opposite railing, toward where the men are gutting fish. They keep their eyes on their task, but they've fallen silent. I'm sure the lure of gossip, even on board a ship, is too great to ignore.

Luckily the wind will carry my words away, especially if I keep my voice low. "That's it?" I say. "*I see?*"

"Yes," he says. "Now I can claim to be judging you by fact."

Maybe I liked it better when he was being contemptuous. "I've spent four years being hated by everyone," I say. "Please don't think I'll be very affected by your opinion of me."

"Of course not." He glances my way. "I'm just here to sail the ship, Your Highness."

He's not quite mocking me, but it's close. "I do admit to being surprised by your boldness. You're the one who came begging for steel."

"Only because you couldn't manage to reach Ostriary to beg for Moonflower."

I bristle. Every time I have a conversation with this man, I can't find my footing. I'm both furious at his impertinence and intrigued by his mettle. "Have I wronged you in some way I'm unaware of, Captain?"

"Not me directly, no. But I was sent to Kandala to see if the new Ostrian king would be able to negotiate for steel so the kingdom can be rebuilt. I expected to find King Lucas, a ruler who was known for fair dealings throughout Kandala. Instead, I'm bringing back a man who put citizens to death after they'd been left desperate, with no means for survival."

"You weren't *here*," I say roughly. "You don't know the circumstances. My father might have been known for *fair dealings*, but he never had to deal with widespread illness. His consuls had an equitable balance of trade between sectors. But once the Moonflower was determined to cure the fever sickness, it caused a massive shift in which sectors had money and power—and which ones did not. Suddenly his consuls—*our* consuls, Captain—held leverage over the throne, while ordinary citizens were quite literally killing each other over medicine. We had terrible choices to make, and we made them."

"So the choice was to anger your consuls or execute your people?"

"The choice was to restore order by whatever means possible. People were already dying, Captain. The penalties had to be harsh or they wouldn't have made a difference."

He's quiet for a moment, but hostility crackles in the air between us.

"If I locked you in your quarters without food," Rian finally says, "and if I said you'd be put to death if you tried to escape, how long do you think it would take before you'd risk it anyway?"

My jaw is so tight. I don't have an answer.

Or rather, I *do*, but I don't like it.

I don't think it would take very long at all.

"And which is the greater crime?" he says. "Is it the imprisonment? Or the punishment?"

"You've made your point."

"Or does the crime matter?" he continues. "Since the same person is responsible for—"

"*I said you've made your point.*"

I say the words sharply. Most of the men were pretending to ignore me, but my raised voice is enough to draw attention. Even Lochlan is glaring now. Kilbourne must sense trouble, because the guardsman has drawn closer.

"Come along," says the captain, as if the tension between us isn't as thick as the scent of fish guts and seawater. "I promised you a tour, Your Highness." Without waiting, he keeps walking, but he calls back over his shoulder. "Brock, if you can't get through that lot, Gwyn and I will help in a bit."

I follow him. "I sense you'll be recruiting my guards, next."

"If they want to work, I wouldn't turn away the extra hands."

"Is that why you had Tessa climbing the masts this morning? You needed extra hands?"

"She volunteered."

"And you thought it was a good idea? Sending my apothecary to the top of the main mast?"

"I thought it would be a poor idea to suggest she couldn't do it." He pauses. "Jealous?"

That really does startle a laugh out of me. "No."

But . . . maybe. Not just of the time with Tessa. I've spent weeks locked in the palace, surrounded by advisers and courtiers and royal demands. I stare up at the miles of rope and sails and rigging that hang suspended above us, and I can't help the swell of intrigue.

If he weren't being such an ass, I'd admit it.

Instead, I focus on the matter at hand. I want to review the maps in his stateroom, but that's going to have to wait until Tessa is done. "For now," I say, "I'd appreciate seeing the lower decks."

"Where would you like to start?"

"Rocco said you have cannons on board. I'd like to see your gun deck."

If he's surprised, it doesn't show. "Right this way."

Once we're on the steps to the lower levels, I say, "In case there was any uncertainty, I don't like you much either."

"Truly? You've been incredibly subtle."

"I'm going to knock you down the stairs."

He stops and turns, his eyes in shadow now. "Do not pick a fight with me."

He says it evenly. Coolly. The same way he said, *Don't threaten my crew* when we were sitting at dinner.

I stare back at him, and there's something about his quiet composure that makes me want to throw the first punch. I'm sure he can read it in my gaze, because he doesn't move, and he doesn't look away.

Just a bit of wounded pride between men.

Yes. I definitely understand.

But I need him to get us to Ostriary. I'm not failing in this mission over something as frivolous as *pride*.

"I certainly wouldn't pick a fight by announcing my first move," I say, and there isn't an ounce of tension in my voice. I glance past him as if I'm bored with this delay. "Lead the way, Captain."

The gun deck is exactly as Rocco described: wide and dusty, with the cannons tethered together at opposite ends of the ship. The gun bays are sealed shut, making it very dark down here, but Rian brought a lantern, and he leads me around the space. A large section sits at the front of the ship, with a padlocked door behind the cannons. That must be the armory Rocco mentioned.

"You indicated that it was too costly to remove them?" I say to him.

Rian nods. "They were quite literally built into the ship." He points to the deck above us. "We'd have to pull apart two decks to get them out. Even then, we'd need a crane. But here, I can offer you more proof about this ship's origins." He moves closer to one of the cannons, holding the lantern close to the end.

For a moment, I'm not sure what he's showing me, but then I see it. The forge mark hammered into the steel at the back of the cannon.

STEEL CITY METAL WORKS

The cannons were forged in Kandala—and if the ship was built around them, that means the ship most likely was, too.

"This mark appears in other spots, too," Rian says. "Inside the ovens in the galley, on some of the chains along the main mast, on a few of the steel beams along the hull. But this is the most convincing, because there's truly no way for me to bring these cannons aboard."

I brush my fingers along the letters. It *is* pretty convincing.

I look up, gesturing to the padlocked door. "And your armory? Rocco said your crewman didn't have a key."

"I don't either."

I don't believe that for an instant. He's the captain of the ship. "Surely we can hate each other without having *lies* between us," I say.

He smiles, and this time it's a bit more genuine. "Yes, we can, but this isn't a lie. I don't carry the key on me, and I will not be retrieving it for your purposes."

"You allowed the palace guards to search the armory," I say. "They reported it was *well stocked*."

"And you don't trust the palace guards?"

No, but I'm not going to admit that. Just the words send a chill down my spine. We already suspected something was amiss with the palace guards, but until this moment, I hadn't considered that this journey might be part of it.

I shake off the worry before it can manifest in my voice. "Personally," I say smoothly, "I'd like a little more insight as to what's inside."

"No."

It's so uncommon for me to run headfirst into a flat refusal that I'm more intrigued than irritated. "*No*? Why?"

"For the same reason I refused to have sailors on board or ships sailing behind. I'm not giving you or your people access to a room full of weapons that can be used against my crew."

I stare at him in the flickering lantern light, listening to the splash of water against the hull.

"My guards have weapons," I say.

"I expected them to have weapons."

"Then we don't need yours."

"Exactly. The contents of the armory are unnecessary all around."

His voice is so calm, so reasonable, that it's making my demands feel *un*reasonable. I can't tell if he's hiding something or if his worries are genuine. I wish I had Rocco at my back right now. Kilbourne will defend me without hesitation, but I've learned that Rocco is a good partner from an offensive angle.

But it bothers me that Rian is refusing to open the door to what must be a simple room.

"I demand that you open the door to your armory, Captain Blakemore. That is an order. I am here by the authority of the king."

He holds up his left hand, and his ring, the one bearing my father's seal, catches the light. "So am I."

Fury swells in me, hot and sudden. "My father is dead. Any power granted by that order is rescinded."

"No, it's not. The order is very clear that it's backed by the Crown, not the man wearing it. King Harristan took no action to rescind my authority. I still bear the ring. I still carry the letter."

My heart is pounding. I'm thrown, scrambling, trying to find my footing again. Was this an oversight? Did Harristan forget?

I clearly did.

"Turn back," I say. "Return to Artis. We can resolve this with Harristan right now."

"I will not sail directly into a storm because you're in a pique over a locked door," he says, and his voice is grudgingly tolerant, as if I'm a toddler throwing a tantrum. "If you wish to dock in Sunkeep and send word to your brother, so be it. I will continue on to Ostriary and inform their king that you were belligerent and obstinate, and you delayed negotiations because I wouldn't give you a key to a room you *truly* have no need to access."

My fingernails are biting into my palms. My pulse pounds in my ears now. I'm afraid to move, because I really *might* throw a punch.

"Captain!" a voice calls from above. "Marchon needs you at the helm."

Rian takes a step back. "We'll be nearing Port Karenin in a day or so," he says. "Inform me of your decision then." He pauses, then holds out the lantern to my guard. "I'll leave you with the light, Your Highness."

I hate him.

The instant I have the thought, I remember how many times Tessa thought those exact same words about me.

"Captain," I call, when he's nearly to the stairs.

For an instant, I don't think he'll stop, but he does. "Yes?"

"You've gotten the wrong impression of me," I say.

"I don't think I have."

"Oh, I know what the people say of me. I know the stories you've heard, and I see the way your crew looks at me. Rumor may claim that I'm cruel and thoughtless, and my *reputation* may paint me as impatient and forceful, but you won't be the first to learn that it's a misstep to underestimate me." I take the lantern from Kilbourne and take a step toward him. "So make no mistake. When I pick a fight, you'll know it."

CHAPTER TWENTY

Tessa

I was glad when Corrick left with the captain, because the tension in Rian's stateroom had been thick enough to choke the air out of the room. I caught a few glimpses of the two young men walking the deck, and their mannerisms seemed amiable, but I know Corrick well enough to recognize when he's unsettled.

So far it's been the entire duration of his time on board this ship.

When Corrick and Rian disappear down the steps to go below, Gwyn sighs and says, "If those two went at it under the sails, I wouldn't know which one to put money on."

Sablo huffs a quiet laugh, then hisses as I use my tweezers to pluck another rope fiber out of his wrist. His wound is a rope burn that runs down the length of his forearm, but he's got a dozen rope splinters embedded in the skin. The burn is deep enough by his hand that it's drawn blood, so it's nothing I can stitch, but I can tell it's painful.

I give him a commiserating glance. "Sorry." He's a big man, nearly as big as Rocco, so I thought he'd be intimidating, but he's not. I glance between him and Gwyn. "So I'm not the only one who can tell they don't like each other?"

"Rian doesn't have a lot of tolerance for rulers who mistreat their people," she says.

"I don't either," I say, plucking at another rope fiber. "Prince Corrick isn't the sum of all the stories told about him."

"Surely not," she says easily, which startles me. "He got on the ship, and that took most of us by surprise."

Sablo makes a sound that sounds like *hmph*, then rubs the fingers of his free hand together, then makes a flicking motion.

Gwyn smiles. "He says he should have put money on *that*."

I look up from the wound. "You would have bet on Prince Corrick?"

He nods vigorously, and I raise my eyebrows.

"Sablo likes the underdog," Gwyn adds.

"Aha," I say, smiling. "Well, don't let *him* hear you call him the underdog."

Sablo blows a breath through his teeth and draws a finger across his neck like he's slitting someone's throat.

I think he's teasing, but I frown. I remember a night when Corrick had to do exactly that, because Consul Sallister was threatening to withhold medicine from the whole country.

But of course I can't say that. I don't know how to defend Corrick without revealing everything I know.

I don't know if he deserves it anyway.

I try to turn the conversation in another direction. They're casual with the captain's name, so I am, too. "Rian said that the citadel in Ostriary was destroyed in the war," I say. "Where does the king live now?"

"Galen Redstone still lives on Fairde," Gwyn says. "Tarramor was blown to bits, but the king was able to hold the palace. The walls are gone, so you can see the palace from the sea. One by one, he claimed the other islands. There are still pockets of rebellion, mostly led by men who couldn't take the throne, but most of those have been snuffed out. The king built his campaign on promises to rebuild, to restore Ostriary to what it once was. He might not have had the *strongest* claim to the throne, but he had the most compelling promises. There's been too much damage, too much bloodshed. The people are tired."

Sablo grunts and hits his chest with his uninjured arm, and Gwyn smiles, a little sadly. "Yes," she says. "*We* are tired."

I look at Sablo. "Were you injured in the war? Is that why you can't speak?"

Storm clouds shift through his eyes, but he nods. He looks to Gwyn and gestures from her to me.

She draws a slow breath, and they exchange a glance. I can see her weighing what to say. "At dinner, Rian mentioned Oren Crane, one of the old king's half-brothers. He's one of the few who keeps rebellion brewing. Oren's a skilled sailor, and he has a fleet of ships that still linger in the waters of Ostriary. Hidden allies on all the islands. He was close to the old court, too, which helped his claim. He's clever—but vicious. Not the kind of man you want to cross."

I look at Sablo. "Did you cross him?"

Those clouds haven't left his eyes. He scowls.

"Sablo was a supply runner," Gwyn says. "He'd pilot the ships from island to island. He's well known at each port, so sometimes he's paid to carry . . . information."

I glance between the two of them. "So you were a spy."

He taps a finger to his forehead, and Gwyn says, "Not really a spy. More . . . an untraceable way to send a message. No need to write anything down. Sablo's mind is as sharp as cut glass."

He smiles darkly and nods.

"But then he got a message about Oren," Gwyn continues. "About where he was planning to hide his ships. Sablo knew he could sell this information to Galen Redstone's people, and indeed they came knocking—"

Sablo makes a cutting motion with his hand, sharp and decisive through the air.

"I know, I know," she continues. "You're no snitch." Her eyes shift back to me. "He refused to sell his knowledge to Redstone—or anyone, for that matter. But Oren caught wind that someone was working against him. He grew suspicious, and he wouldn't take a chance."

My hands have gone still on my tweezers. "He thought you betrayed him."

"He had him beaten near to death," she says. "Then they cut his tongue off."

Those storm clouds in Sablo's eyes have turned into a tornado.

"It was a message," Gwyn says. "Like I said, Oren's a vicious man."

"I'm sorry," I say softly.

Sablo shakes his head.

"Rian found him," Gwyn says. "Facedown in the sand. The captain could have left him, but he didn't. There was nothing in it for

him, but you heard him at dinner. Rian's not the type to leave someone hurting." She shrugs. "So here we are."

So here they are.

"Were you there?" I ask.

She shakes her head, then says, "No. Anya and I joined up later."
She shrugs, then glances away. "We've all got a bit of a story. You'll
likely hear 'em all before we're done."

"I hope so," I say, and I mean it.

"What about you?" she says.

I glance up. "What about me?"

"What's *your* story? There must be more than just the prince's
apothecary."

Heat finds my cheeks. Her voice isn't suggestive, but again, I'm
reminded of Lochlan's threats in the hallway last night. "I'm not the
type to leave someone hurting either. I'm glad Prince Corrick sees
the benefit in that."

"Me too," she says. "That's why I think there's more to your
prince than what he seems."

I look at her in surprise. "You do?"

"Well, your king must be very desperate," she says, "to send the
two of you off so quickly."

I hesitate, then nod. "He is. We are."

"It took courage to climb on the *Dawn Chaser*," she says. "Rian's
not blind to that."

I glance at the window. The prince and the captain disappeared
down the steps, but they haven't emerged. "It took courage to sail
here to ask for help." I pause, feeling warmth on my cheeks again,
because that sounds more personal than I intended. "You're truly
not worried about bringing the fever sickness back to Ostriary?"

She shakes her head. "You're all well. We've got more than enough Moonflower to go around."

I suppose that's true.

I flick my gaze toward the map on the table. "Rian said we wouldn't have trouble until we reach the southern point of Ostriary. Are the waters there very rough?"

"They can be." She moves toward the table and taps her fingers on the map. "It's not even the sailing that's the hard part. There are dozens of hidden coves along here, and the fog is dense at this time of year."

I frown. "You mean we might hit something?"

Sablo snorts, then lifts a hand to his head in a gesture I can't make out. I look to Gwyn.

"Pirates," she says.

"Pirates!"

She nods, like it's common, then shrugs. "Like I said, Crane keeps the rebellion brewing. There are just enough men still loyal to him to cause trouble. He's still got half a dozen ships in the water, and he's a clever bastard. The *Dawn Chaser* is a small ship, so they probably won't pay us any notice, but you never know."

I don't know what expression is on my face, but it must look worrisome, because she smiles. "Don't worry. Crane hasn't been able to put a hand on Rian yet. Trust me, he's tried. Cap's pretty clever himself."

—◆—

The rest of the day passes surprisingly quickly, but I can't stop myself from turning over the stories that Gwyn told me about pirates in the waters surrounding Ostriary. I should probably tell

Corrick—unless he already knows. I deliberated over it earlier, chewing on my anxiety, wondering if Corrick and Rian would bring their tension back to the stateroom. But Rian eventually returned to the main deck to join Marchon at the helm, while the prince remained scarce.

Good. I certainly have no desire to go chasing after him.

As soon as I have the thought, sadness hits me in the gut. A wedge has formed between us so fast. I hate it. Is it his fault? Is it mine?

Either way, I can't sit and dwell on it, because I'm going to make myself crazy. I eventually ask for more tasks. I'm shown a burn that needs a measure of salve, followed by a small cut that looks a bit infected. Later, Sablo gives me a needle and thread and a pile of fishing nets that need repairing. He shows me how to weave the strands together, his large hands deftly forming an even pattern that's loose enough to flow freely, and tight enough to trap fish. Later, lunch is served on the deck, a light fare of warm rolls, soft cheese, and fried fish.

Still no Corrick.

I frown and stay with my nets, sitting on a bench along the ship's railing. I was so eager for this journey, for the chance to do some-thing *bigger*, but it seems I'll be spending the entire trip with my stomach tied up in knots.

By the time the sun begins to slip below the horizon, the sky is lit up with shades of pink to our west, the storm an ever-present line of purple clouds to our north—though it seems more distant. Gwyn rings a bell for the crew to fetch their dinner, but I have a small pile of nets left to repair, so I don't move.

Brock spies me across the deck before he goes down the steps, and he lets out a whistle. "Come along, miss. Tor always grabs seconds before anyone else."

I smile. "I'll be down in a minute."

The deck empties, but not everyone goes below. To my surprise, Lochlan remains. I'm determined to ignore him, but he heads right for me.

I hate that my first thought is to wonder if one of the guards is still up here. It feels rude to look for them, so I keep my eyes on the nets.

Lochlan stops a short distance away. He's quiet for a moment, then says, "Aren't you eating?"

"I will," I say.

He fidgets, shifting his weight, which makes me look up.

"I should apologize," he says.

"Well, that's almost enough to make me fall over the railing," I say.

"Not for what I said about the prince," he says quickly.

"Of course not."

"But I shouldn't have been so crass. Karri would never forgive me." He pauses, running his hand across his jaw. "I am sorry, Tessa."

He sounds genuine, so I nod. "Thank you," I say.

"I'm not . . . I'm not worried about him tossing me overboard anymore."

My eyebrows go up. Maybe Corrick *has* built a bit of trust with the rebel somehow.

But then Lochlan adds, "I don't think the captain would allow it, you know? He's a good man."

I'm struck by the confidence in his tone. So much so that my hands go still. "I think so, too."

He nods. "I thought this whole thing was a little crazy at first. Just a trick to put me on the bottom of the ocean. But now . . . now I'm more worried that the prince will ruin our chance to get more medicine. That he'll spit in the face of the Ostrian king and we'll go home empty-handed."

"Prince Corrick has more political savvy than *that*," I say.

"Well. Maybe." He screws up his face, then glances at the stairwell. "Do you want me to bring you some food back?"

I blink in surprise—and for a fraction of a second, I realize it *shouldn't* be a surprise. He brought me Karri's candies last night. *I am kind*, he said.

Maybe he is, and I just never looked beyond the obvious.

"No, thank you," I say. "I'll be down in a moment."

He nods, then turns away.

Without warning, the main deck is suddenly as empty as it was this morning, when I first woke. Wind tugs at my braids and lifts the nets around my boots, but I don't mind the quiet twilight, where the only sounds are suddenly the sounds of the ship: waves slapping the hull, the creak of wooden beams, the faint jingle of chains attached to the rigging.

When a man emerges from the stairwell a few minutes later, his features are in silhouette, so I assume it's a member of the crew. But then I recognize the line of his jaw and the familiarity of his movements. *Corrick.*

I keep my eyes on the nets. I can't decide if I want him to come over here—or if I want him to keep his distance. The needle slips over and under, closing gaps.

I stay so focused on my task that I don't realize he's approached until he's right in front of me. I hardly look up past his boots, but I can tell he has a plate in one hand, a wooden cup in the other.

"You aren't eating?" he says.

His voice is quiet, but not tentative. I can't read anything from his tone.

"I wanted to finish this first."

The sun sinks a little lower in the sky, lengthening the shadows between us.

After a moment, Corrick steps to the side, then drops to sit on the bench beside me.

"You must be hungry," he says, and his voice is low. "I'm happy to share, Miss Cade."

In the dark, he always reminds me of Wes, and without warning, my throat tightens. "You don't have to do that."

"I know. Here." He selects a berry from the plate, then lifts it to my mouth.

It feels too intimate, and there's too much unsaid between us. For a heartbeat of time, I'm not sure what to do.

That berry hovers in front of my lips, and I say, "Are you sure you want your fingers near my teeth?"

Light glints in his eyes. "I'll risk it."

I take the berry, careful not to touch his fingers. Sweetness explodes on my tongue. I really *am* hungry. "I have a needle in my hands, too."

"I'm not worried. You once had a chance to poison me, and you didn't do it." He holds up another berry.

I take this one more readily. "I punched you below the belt, though."

He winces. "I think I've blocked that memory."

Another berry. This time his fingers brush my lips, and it's the tiniest movement, but warmth shoots to my cheeks.

I swallow hard. My voice goes a bit breathy as I say, "I need to finish the nets."

"You really don't."

"I said I would. I'd like to keep my word."

His eyes narrow. "To whom? Rian?" He says it like he already expects the answer.

"No. To Sablo. He's the one who showed me how. Rian has been busy all afternoon." I pause. "Maybe you'd know if you weren't hiding in your quarters all day."

"Hiding?" Corrick's eyebrows go up. "Is that what you think I've been doing?"

"Well, you went on a 'tour' of the ship and never reappeared, so—"

"I've been trying to avoid conflict, Tessa." He lifts another berry, but he doesn't offer this one to me. He pops it into his own mouth. His voice is still low, but a conspiratorial note has entered his tone. "I've been in conversation with Rocco and Kilbourne. The captain has a locked room on the ship that he won't allow us to access."

"Why?"

"He says it's full of weapons he doesn't want us to have."

I frown. "I don't understand."

"He says he doesn't want us to have access to weapons that would allow us to overtake the ship."

"Why would you want to overtake the ship?"

"Exactly," Corrick says. "It feels like overkill. I don't like it. I don't *trust* it. Rian has offered to dock at Port Karenin to allow us to disembark."

I think about this for a minute. "So he's keeping these weapons locked up because he doesn't trust *you*, and you're thinking about abandoning this mission because you don't trust *him*."

"Do *you* trust him?"

I consider the conversation I just had with Lochlan. "The captain has been nothing but kind—"

"No. Tessa." Corrick leans close. "I know you hate me right now, but on this, I truly need your judgment. Please."

That hits me like an arrow. "I don't hate you." I swallow and glance over at the deck. More of the crew is emerging from below, their hands full of plates and cups. "I don't think the captain is trying to trick anyone at all. I've heard a bit of what's happened in Ostriary, and I believe he's truly worried for his crew."

His blue eyes hold mine. "Tell me."

I keep my voice low and tell him about Sablo, how he wouldn't sell information to King Galen, but he was punished by Oren Crane anyway. "Gwyn said the captain rescued him," I say. "You remember what Marchon said when we were in the palace, how he would look for survivors and pick them up, regardless of what side they were on." I hesitate, thinking of Rian's voice when we were suspended on the rigging, fifty feet above the swirling river currents.

Surely you can understand my confusion about the company you keep, and whether you're at risk—or whether you're at his side by your own choosing.

"Rian is very protective," I say.

"Protective," Corrick echoes.

I can feel heat climbing my throat, and I stab the needle through the last bit of netting.

He studies me, then says, "Have you met Anya? Gwyn's daughter?"

I frown. "The little girl?" I say. "I met her in the galley."

"She has scars up and down her arms." He nods at some of the crewmen. "Many of them seem battle worn."

"Well, he did say they were just at war, and Gwyn said he doesn't approve of rulers mistreating their people. Maybe they've *all* run afoul of this Oren Crane. What did Rocco say?"

"Nothing of consequence. Here." He lifts another berry.

I turn my face away. "Wait. You spent the afternoon with your guards and they said *nothing of consequence*?"

"Well." He shrugs, then eats the berry himself. "Nothing I'm able to share."

I scowl, then knot off my last line of repair to the nets. "Of course not, Your Highness."

He frowns. "You're angry with me again."

"Last night, you climbed onto the ship and acted like you'd finally been given leave to touch me. Today, you've hardly spoken to me, and now you're trying to charm me into sharing secrets."

He blinks, startled, and then he shifts closer. "I am not trying to—"

"Honestly, Corrick. If you're not going to be forthright with me, just leave me alone. I'll bring your evening dose to your quarters after dinner."

"Tessa." He leans close, but I'm done with this. I try to shove him away, but he catches my wrist.

His grip isn't tight, but it's secure, and my breath stutters.

A male voice speaks up. "Let her go."

For a moment, I think it's Rian, but it's not. It's *Lochlan*. Brock is by his side, along with a few other members of the crew.

Corrick goes still. Any emotion in his eyes vanishes.

But he doesn't let go of my wrist. His grip is too tight for me to break his hold.

I stare across at him. *Cruel Corrick.* That's what people in the Wilds used to call him.

That's what *I* used to call him.

My breathing is tight and shallow. I don't know what to do. He's stronger than I am; I can feel the strength in his grip.

"Let her go." Gwyn's voice.

Rocco has drawn up from the shadows to stand near the prince.

"Now, Your Highness." I don't see the captain, but I hear his voice. I remember his comment from this morning. *No one fights on my ship.*

I guess we're going to see in a moment.

But then Corrick speaks, his voice smooth and unaffected. "Miss Cade, perhaps you've forgotten that you have a needle in your hand."

My eyes flick to my hand, to the needle that's still clutched between my knuckles, almost invisible in the gathering darkness.

Corrick sets his plate aside, then reaches up to pluck the thin strip of metal from my fingers. He lets go of my wrist, and his eyes hold mine. "I didn't want you to hurt yourself."

I swallow hard. I don't know what to say.

He offers the needle on his palm. "If you want to strike at me, at the very least I urge you to do it bare-handed."

I take the needle, rolling it sheepishly between my fingers. He was right. It could have gone right through my palm.

We still have a bit of a crowd, but some of the tension has dissipated. "Is that offer open to all of us?" says Lochlan.

Corrick ignores him. "I'll leave the food," he says. "I know you're hungry." He stands. "Rocco, I'll return to my quarters. Stay with Miss Cade."

My heart is beating so fast. "Corrick," I whisper.

His eyes finally meet mine. "I know people expect the worst of me," he says quietly. "I didn't realize you were among them."

I shake my head, but he's already turned away.

The crewmen yield a path, and the gathering darkness swallows him up.

CHAPTER TWENTY-ONE

The Outlaw

Tonight, I'm not wearing a mask.

I shouldn't be doing this at all, truly. Tensions in the Royal Sector are high now that Prince Corrick has boarded a ship to Ostriary. The guards and sentries around the palace have tripled. The sector gates stay locked; the wall remains heavily patrolled.

But out here in the Wilds, the security is a bit more lax. The extra guards and patrol officers had to come from somewhere.

It doesn't matter. I'm not slipping through the shadows. No chance for Violet to find me in the darkness. I'm not an outlaw at all this evening. It's earlier than usual, well before midnight, and I'm just a man on his way to the gathering.

I stoop, picking up a handful of dirt, rubbing it between my palms as I walk, then flipping my hands to make sure I get some in my knuckles. I wipe my hands on my trousers, then run a hand across the back of my neck and over the neckline of my shirt.

Another handful of dirt, another dusting of my palms, and I rake my fingers through my hair.

Voices are a low rumble in the distance, and I catch a few notes of a lyre on the wind. There will probably be a bonfire. Maybe dancers or a fortune-teller. Definitely ale.

My heart is beating a little too hard, and I try to slow my pace. This is farther than I usually go, and there's still a scrap of a chance that I could be recognized.

I need to shove these worries away.

I slink through the trees as the music and voices grow louder, until suddenly I'm not alone. The forest gives way to a bit of a clearing, and people are everywhere. The bonfire is huge, surrounded by logs and stumps and even mats made from woven grass. An older woman on a stump picks out a tune on her lyre, while a young girl twirls in circles by her knees, slightly crushed flowers tucked into her braids. Some older men with thick beards are passing around a tankard of ale, and one laughs, then glances my way when I step between the trees.

I nearly stumble. My heart gives a stutter. For a moment, I expect everyone to turn, to look at me. I wait for a shout, for a pointed finger.

Honestly, I wait for an arrow to appear in my chest.

But the man glances back at his companions. Nothing happens. No one pays me any mind. Just another worker looking for a bit of gossip and a bit of food now that the day is done. No different from a dozen others.

I run a hand across the back of my neck again, and this time, I find it a bit damp. There's a series of stalls at the edge of the clearing, near the road, selling food and ale, and I make my way across.

The first one doesn't have a line, so I step to the counter, and the man working there gives me a pleasant nod. "What'll you have?" he says.

"What are my choices?"

"I had some roasted chicken legs, but they went quick," he says. A fire flickers in the grill behind him, and sweat threads his hair at the temples, turning the blond streaks brown. A few days of beard growth clings to his jaw. "All I've got left is some honeyed cheese on nut bread, or some dried venison and jam."

"The first, if you please," I say.

He smirks. "*If you please*," he repeats, then laughs under his breath, though not unkindly. "Putting on a few airs, are you?"

I inwardly wince. Playing this role used to be as easy as slipping into a pair of worn shoes, but it's been so long. I've almost forgotten how to do this. I force a bashful smile on my face. "More than a few, I suppose. I nearly forgot I wasn't in the Royal Sector anymore."

He laughs and cuts a slab of nut bread, tops it with a slab of cheese, then sets it on a grill over the small fire behind him. "You work in the sector?"

"Just a delivery. We brought a horse down from Moonlight Plains. Some girl needed a perfect dapple gray." I scoff, then roll my eyes. I always say I work with horses because it comes the most naturally, and it's unlikely to be questioned. "Like they don't have enough nags of their own in there. I swear I heard her say she wanted to have the animal shod in gold."

He grins, then slides the bread off the grill and onto a fold of wax paper. He drizzles honey over the cheese, then wraps it up. The smell is heavenly, and my mouth is already watering. I'd forgotten how generous the portions are in the Wilds, and they sell them for almost nothing, really. I'm wishing I could give him a handful of silver without giving myself away, when he says, "So you're only down here for the night then?"

His voice is a little lower, and I can't quite figure out his tone, but he extends the wrapped food.

"Yes. I heard there was some kind of gossip about outlaws, so I wanted to see what I could hear." I reach to take the food, and his fingers brush mine.

The motion is gentle, but very deliberate. My eyes snap to his.

"What's your name?" he says.

I stare back at him. I'm so utterly flummoxed that I'm not sure what to say. I came here for information, but I was so completely unprepared for . . . for *flirtation*. No one flirts with me. No one ever dares. Aside from Violet making eyes at me a few nights ago, I can't remember the last time anyone has said one single thing about my appearance. Nothing to indicate attraction, surely. But here's this man with sleeves shoved back and sweat in his hair and firelight in his eyes, holding my gaze like it's the most natural thing in the world.

My thoughts have completely stalled.

"I didn't mean to shock you." His smile widens. "My name is Maxon."

I inhale to say I'm not shocked—even though I am, and it's quite obvious that I am—but I choke on my breath, then cough hard. I turn away and cover my mouth with my forearm, but I cough again. When I inhale, it's like breathing through a wet rag, and I try to talk myself out of the initial surge of panic that swells anytime I can't breathe.

It's almost impossible. No one here knows me. No one here cares about me. If I can't catch my breath, I'll die in the middle of the Wilds and they'll throw my body on the pyre with everyone else.

Lord. I was so *foolish*. I should run out of here, back to where I came from.

Then again, *running* would probably kill me quicker. I cough again, and my eyes water.

"Here." Maxon touches my arm. His eyes are full of concern now, and I realize he's pushing a cup of tea across the counter at me. "Here, drink this."

I don't know what it is, but right now I don't care. I lift the cup to my lips.

The water isn't very warm, and the tea is bitter. I almost choke on *that*. But then I get a swallow down, followed by another, and breathing suddenly isn't *quite* so difficult.

I take a final swallow, then realize why the tea is bitter, and I look at Maxon in surprise. "You gave me Moonflower."

He hesitates, then nods. "I had some for tonight." He pauses. "And you clearly needed it."

I glance down at the empty cup, then back at him. "But *you* need it."

"I don't have a cough right now," he says. "I can skip a day or two." His eyes search mine, and he shrugs. "It's all right. You'd do the same, I'm sure."

I'm not sure about anything at all right now. I can't think of anyone I know personally who would offer their own dose to me without expectation of something in return—and this man handed me the cup as a matter of course. It's a casual generosity that's so unfamiliar that it's more shocking than the flirtation.

That smile finds Maxon's face again, but this time it's a bit more hesitant. "Maybe I've earned your name now?"

I look back at him. He gave me his dose of medicine. Possibly his *only* dose of medicine. There's a part of me that wants to give him my real name, in addition to every coin in my pocket.

But of course I *can't*.

Something about his kindness reminds me of young Violet in the woods, the way she was so clever in helping me hide from the night patrol.

I finally return Maxon's smile. "Fox," I say.

He grins. "Fox? That's it?"

"That's it." I take the wrapped bread and cheese, then pull a handful of coins from my pocket. I give him a nod. "You have my deepest gratitude, Maxon."

"So formal again, Fox," he teases—then breaks off as the coins rattle into his palm. "Wait! This is—this is too *much*." His fingers close around the money, and he's trying to pass the coins back to me.

I turn away without taking them. "Surely you'd do the same, right?"

Then I unwrap an end of the bread, take a bite of honeyed cheese, and lose myself among the crowd.

More people gather than I expect. I don't carry a pocket watch into the Wilds, but when I was a boy, we had an astronomer who taught me to tell time by the placement of the moon, and it's nearing midnight now. I'm tired, yet anxious. Unsettled. I thought this was supposed to be a casual gathering, but there are hundreds of people here. More musicians have joined the first, and some people are dancing, keeping the mood lively and festive. The endless steins of ale don't hurt. But I keep to myself and wait, though I've been considering giving up for the better part of an hour. A mob once attacked "Weston Lark" when they discovered he was the King's Justice. I don't want the same to happen to me.

The music finally goes silent, and the dancers fall still, and the bonfire has begun to dwindle. Many people take a seat on the stumps and logs—though others stand, whether against trees or leaning against each other. I pull a little more deeply into the shadows and press my back against a tree. The food stalls have long since stopped selling food, but the smell of roasted meat and sweet breads carries through the clearing. My square of nut bread is long gone. A hush falls over the crowd, and I spot movement among the trees. Someone important is coming.

"I'm surprised you're still here."

I jump a mile, but it's Maxon. I clear my throat and try to tell my heart to stop hammering. "I wanted to see what all the fuss was about."

"I heard some of the washerwomen talking. Apparently one of the consuls is coming."

I whip my head around. "What?"

He misunderstands my surprise, because he nods. "I know. It's not Beeching, though."

He's talking about Jonas Beeching, the consul of Artis. I wouldn't expect him to be at a gathering in the Wilds. He's hardly been seen in the Royal Sector at all since the rebels killed his lover during their siege on the palace.

Honestly, I wouldn't expect any of the others either.

"Who is it?" I say.

"I guess we'll have to wait and see." He pauses. "The washer-women said this one was involved with the Benefactors."

Allisander. Or Lissa Marpetta. I pull back farther into the shadows. Lissa hasn't left her sector in weeks. Not since she was accused of helping Allisander to stage a coup in the palace. I'm torn between running like hell, or standing right here to find out what she's up to.

"Fox," Maxon says quietly, shifting closer, but my thoughts are all tangled up and I don't realize he's talking to *me* until his hand falls on my arm.

No one ever touches me, and it takes me by surprise. I jerk my gaze over to meet his.

He's holding out the handful of coins. "Take it back," he says. "It's too much."

"It's not," I say. "I insist."

He frowns a little, like he's trying to figure me out, but then a murmur runs through the crowd, and motion from the trees catches my eye.

A tall woman with deep brown skin is striding into the clearing, her hair bound back tightly, her clothing very fine, but understated.

"Arella," I whisper.

Then I notice the man at her side, and I go absolutely still.

"You know her?" says Maxon. "She's not the one with the horse, is she?"

I have no idea what he's talking about. I can't stop staring at the man walking along beside Arella Cherry.

It's Christopher Huxley, the captain of the palace guard.

They're followed by Laurel Pepperleaf, daughter of the most powerful baron in Allisander's sector.

I don't know what to do. Consul Cherry and Captain Huxley are not friends. Laurel Pepperleaf has no business here at all. I don't know that I've ever seen any of them exchange words. My heart is pounding so hard that my lungs can't keep up. Breath rattles into my chest, and I'm worried I'm going to start coughing again.

"Fox?" says Maxon.

"Thank you for coming," Arella says loudly, her voice carrying effortlessly over the crowd. "There are so many more of you than I expected."

"The Benefactors cheated us," a man calls from the other side. "Who's to say you aren't going to do the same?"

"I'm not offering medicine," Arella calls back.

"Then what do you have?" a woman says. "We need medicine, and they still haven't given us enough. They took Lochlan away."

"No one is telling us anything!" another man shouts. The din is growing, and Arella raises her arms, but the shouts continue.

"If you don't have medicine," someone calls, "then what do you have?"

"Information," she says. "Please! There are patrols in the woods—"

Another shout cuts her off. "What good is information going to do if we're dying—"

"Information on the king!" Captain Huxley shouts, and his voice is even louder. "On how he's *tricking* you."

"He's telling you to take less medicine!" Laurel Pepperleaf calls, adding her voice to the fray, but she's nearly drowned out by the people. "Only because he knows there will never be enough to go around!"

"Lochlan went to get more medicine!" someone else shouts. "When Lochlan returns, you'll see!"

"That ship is a farce," calls Arella. "It'll never reach Ostriary. The king is getting the prince and Lochlan out of the *way*."

"Fox," Maxon murmurs.

"We have proof!" Arella continues. "Shipping logs that prove how he's been lying to you all."

My thoughts are still too twisted up. I can't make sense of this. "They're lying," I say. "They're lying."

"How?" he says. "How do you know?"

His voice is so earnest, reminding me of the way he gave me his medicine. Some of these people are too trusting, too desperate. They'll believe anything they hear—especially if it reeks of scandal.

I think of Violet with her romantic ideals of Weston and Tessa.

"Say something," Maxon urges. "Do you want me to get their attention? What do you know? Did you hear something in the Royal Sector?"

"No!" I almost shout it, and I tamp my voice down to a whisper. "No, don't say anything." The absolute last thing I need is for anyone from the palace to notice me in the crowd. "I need to get out of here."

Then someone else cries, "The night patrol!"

Screaming erupts, and people leap up from the logs and stumps, tearing into the woods.

"No!" calls Captain Huxley. "You're doing nothing wrong! I'll call them—"

But his voice is drowned out by the melee. These people have already been besieged by the night patrol over stolen medicine. They're not going to wait around to see what happens.

I'm not either. "We need to run."

Maxon grabs my hand and tugs. "Come on. I know a way."

At first, I follow, but we're heading south, and I need to go north. I need to get to safety. But I quickly realize that Maxon *does* know a way, because the path seems densely packed with underbrush, but he's quick and sure-footed and we dart under branches and over fallen trees. I'm wheezing hard, but I will my lungs to *work*, to go just a bit farther.

A whistle splits the night, and wood cracks. Maxon cries out.

"A crossbow," I gasp. "Run. Just run."

We run. Another whistle and crack, but we keep going. His hand is still tugging at mine, like we're friends, like we're more, like we're not strangers who just met an hour ago.

But after a while, the cracks stop, fading into the distance, and we slow, gasping for breath, eventually drawing to a stop. We've run in a bit of a loop, turning north at some point, but we're well away from what just happened. My thoughts are tumbling over and over, replaying what I heard in the clearing, while also considering how very close I came to taking a shot right through the back.

I'm still breathing hard, but Maxon isn't. "Are you all right?" he's saying. "Fox, are you all right?"

"I will be." I cough once, then try to slow my breathing. "You likely saved my life."

"Hardly."

"You did," I say. "I'm in your debt. Believe it or not, that's no small thing, Maxon."

"Well." He smiles, and it's a bit shy. "I'll be looking forward to figuring out what *that* means."

That makes me smile in spite of myself. "Not what you're imagining, I'm quite sure."

He blushes, and it's endearing. Charming. I can't think of a single time in my life that I've ever made someone blush.

"Come on," he says. "We need to get out of the woods."

He grabs hold of my hand again.

I let him.

A whistle blazes through the woods, and the point of an arrow bursts through the center of Maxon's chest.

Then another. And a third, all in rapid succession.

His eyes flare with panic, and his mouth opens, but no sound comes out.

I'm staring. Not breathing. I'm struck by the worst kind of déjà vu as my world centers on those arrow points. The blood beginning to seep around them. A shout comes from somewhere distant, but I can't move.

Maxon's eyes go dull. He falls to the ground. His hand tugs free of mine.

Another whistle, and my ear explodes with pain. For a terrifying moment, I think this is it, that I've been shot in the head and my final thoughts will be nothing but terror and confusion. But no, my hand slaps to my head and comes away with blood. The arrow only clipped me, probably because Maxon's falling body tugged me sideways.

I stop thinking. I run.

More arrows fly, but I duck and dodge and weave between trees. I know how hard it is to hit a moving target.

Pain explodes in my leg, and I nearly go sprawling. It's the side of my leg, so I haven't been impaled, but every step brings a sharp tug of fire through the muscle. My thoughts feel fuzzy, and I can't tell if it's from blood loss or if I simply can't breathe. I don't often run for long distances, but fear is making for a good motivator.

Somewhere in the distance, a man gives a sharp whistle, then yells, "Sergeant! Let that one go. We've got enough to drag back to the Hold already."

I keep running anyway, worried it's a trap, that the instant I stop, a bolt will strike me right between the shoulder blades. I keep seeing Maxon's face, the sudden shock and panic as he realized he was going to die.

It feels like I run forever, but eventually my legs refuse to work anymore. My breathing is ragged and uneven, a thin whistle of air into lungs that don't want to work. I grab hold of a tree trunk and try to hold myself upright, then do my best to orient myself and find my bearings.

At first, nothing looks familiar. Farmhouses, a few distant buildings. I'm still in the Wilds, but I don't know what part. I'm not even sure what sector.

But then I recognize a wagon. A front porch. A barn door with a flower painted on the side.

Violet's barn.

Would she help me? Could I trust her? I'm not sure. I do know I can't run much farther. When I try to walk, my leg insists on limping.

I glance down. The entire side of my trousers are soaked in blood.

I touch a hand to my ear and flinch. The flesh feels torn. My neck is sticky, too.

I swear. There will be no hiding this.

I limp through the grass, gasping with each step.

When I make it to the stump with the ax, I'm debating whether to hide in the barn until sunrise, or whether I should risk tapping at the door.

I don't need to make a decision. Violet pops up out of the shadows like she waits for me every night.

"You came!" she cries. "I've been sleeping in the barn at night. Mama thinks I'm a bit addled, but I don't care. I knew you'd come back eventually. You can't—" Her eyes fall on my neck and she breaks off, coming closer. "Fox," she whispers. Her gaze skips lower. "*Fox.*"

"Violet," I say, and my breath is so thin that the word is barely audible. "I need your help. Can you hide me?"

"Of course! I'm good at hiding. I hid from *you* that first night we met—"

"Violet."

"Right. Yes. Oh, there's blood everywhere. Here, put your arm around my shoulders."

She's as lean as a willow, and I rather doubt she could support my weight, but she tugs at my arm and half drags me toward the barn. "I do the morning chores, so no one will come in until the afternoon, when Will mucks the stalls."

"Good," I say. My thoughts are spinning. "I need you to go to the Royal Sector. I need you to carry a message."

"To the Royal Sector!" she exclaims.

"Violet, please. Listen."

"I'm listening."

I think of the dozens of obstacles she'll face when she gets to the palace. There are footmen and doormen and guards everywhere— guards who may not be loyal to the king, if Captain Huxley was in the woods with Arella Cherry. I don't know what to make of any of this, and my thoughts refuse to organize.

They tried to kill me once. Is this a second attempt?

Are they trying to kill Corrick?

A sob nearly forms in my chest, but I swallow it down.

"You will go to the palace steps," I say to her, and her eyes flare wide, but she bites her lip to keep from exclaiming. "There is a footman there named Gryff. You will tell him that you have a private message for Master Quint. You will tell *no one else*. Do not stop pestering him until he fetches Quint. Do you understand me?"

"Yes," she whispers, nodding quickly. "Gryff the footman. Master Quint."

I wince and stumble on my leg. Sweat slips down my back. "You are only to talk to Gryff and to Quint. No guards, no other servants."

"Gryff. Quint." She nods again.

"You will tell Quint that Sullivan was injured, and needs his assistance. But only he is to come."

"Sullivan." We ease through the barn doors. "Is that your real name?"

"No. But he'll know what it means." I let out a breath and ease against the wall of the barn, then drop to sit in the straw.

"How will I get through the sector gates?" Violet says. "It's the middle of the night."

Damn. I hadn't considered that.

I swallow and reach under my shirt, to where my signet ring hangs on a chain. I tug it over my head. I don't want to involve guards, but I'm going to have to. Then I pull the rest of my silver coins out of my pocket.

Violet's eyes get even wider. "Fox," she breathes.

"Keep the ring under your clothes," I say, holding out the chain with the ring and the coins. "Try to bribe the guard at the gate first. Tell him you want to leave a plea at the palace steps but your mother would be upset, so you have to do it in the middle of the night."

She nods. "Then why do I need the ring?"

"If he won't take a bribe, you'll need it to prove you need access to the palace. But still, my message stands. You have a message for Quint alone. Only use the name Sullivan."

"I don't understand. Why would the ring get me through the gates?"

I wince and shift my weight. I'm going to need bandages, too, before she goes. "Because I'm the king, Violet. And that ring proves it."

CHAPTER TWENTY-TWO

Corrick

This time, when I awake before sunrise, I stay up. According to my pocket watch, it's not quite six, but if everyone on this boat is going to hate me, it feels like the only time to avoid a deck full of censorious glares.

It's early enough that Rocco is still outside my door, cards in an array on the floor before him. I don't startle him this time, but he begins to rise immediately.

I wave him back down. "Stay," I say to him. "I hoped to get some fresh air."

He stands anyway. "One of us should accompany you. I'll fetch Kilbourne."

"If you must."

I don't wait.

The sea is rougher this morning, and I need to grab the railing as I ascend. A few stars still twinkle in the sky when I climb above,

the moon hanging at a distance. The sails throw shadows everywhere, and I spy a lone figure at the helm, but whoever it is, I ignore
them and head for the front.

Knowing my luck, it's probably Captain Blakemore.

When I step around the forward mast, I see that this end of the
ship isn't deserted either. Little Anya sits on the forecastle, just out
of the wind, bouncing a tiny ball inside a low-walled box. She looks
up in surprise when she spots me, drawing in a sharp breath. For
an instant, I'm reminded of the way Tessa almost flinched when I
caught her arm, and something inside me clenches tight.

I hate the way everyone sees me. I'm used to it in Kandala, but
I can lose myself in the palace, where no one would dare to send a
glare my way.

Here on this ship, the condemnation seems inescapable.

But recognition lights in Anya's eyes, and instead of cringing
away, her features brighten. "Do you want to play with me?"

Not really, but I'm not going to shun the only person who doesn't
look like they want to pitch me overboard.

"Sure." I drop to sit across from her. Inside the box are half a
dozen tiny wooden shapes in addition to the ball she was bouncing. "What are we playing?"

"Knucklebones," she says.

"You'll have to teach me." From the corner of my eye, I notice
that Rocco has come onto the deck as well, but he's keeping his distance. Maybe he can gape at me like Kilbourne was.

"We take turns," she says. "I bounce the ball and take a bone—"

"These are *bones*?" I say, feigning horror.

"No, silly. They're pretend. Now, watch. I bounce it again, then
try to take two, and then three, and if I miss, it's your turn—"

"Oh," I say, suddenly understanding. "I know this game. It's jacks."

"No, it's *knucklebones*."

"Well, it's *jacks* in Kandala. I'll warn you: I'm very good."

Her smile widens, and she leans in, taunting. "Not as good as me."

"Go ahead, then. Prove it."

To my surprise, she is very good. She's quick and sharp and doesn't miss until she goes for her fourth set. I quickly see the reason for the box: the rock and sway of the boat would send the ball all over the deck.

But every time she reaches for the jacks—the knucklebones, I suppose—the sleeve of her shirt draws back, and I see those scars across each forearm. They're not very long, in varying directions, and very straight. Definitely caused by a blade.

I frown, thinking of the cook's warning yesterday, or the way a shadow fell across her features before she recognized me. *Anya doesn't like strangers.*

I think about the fact that Sablo is missing a tongue, or the way Tessa told me about the gutted citadel and the pirates in Ostriary.

I think about that locked room that Rian refuses to open.

There is a part of me that wants to get off this ship at Port Karenin.

There's another part of me that wants to wait around and find answers.

When I bounce the ball, I realize that it's harder than it looks on board a ship. I fail on my second set.

Anya grins. "I told you!"

"You did indeed." I hand her the ball and try not to think about the fact that Rocco suggested that we could use this child as leverage, if necessary.

"Are you really a prince?" Anya says.

"Yes."

"Why isn't there a princess?"

"Ah, most likely because I don't have any sisters."

For some reason she finds this *hilarious*, and she giggles so hard that she only catches one of the wooden trinkets. "No, why don't you have a *wife*."

"A *wife*? Miss Anya, you are rather forward." I take the ball, bounce it, and make it to three this time.

She takes the ball, but before she bounces it, she peers up at me. "Why is your name *Your highness*?"

That makes me smile. "It's not. My name is Corrick."

Her face screws up. "Then why—"

"Anya." Gwyn speaks from behind me. "Leave the man in peace. Dabriel is ready to start the breakfast rolls anyway."

Anya gasps, then springs to her feet, taking the box with her. Her voice calls out behind her as she clatters down the stairs. "Goodbye, Your Highness Corrick!"

I uncurl from the deck more sedately to face Rian's lieutenant. I'm not entirely sure what she thinks of me, but I know what the *captain* thinks of me, and I remember how Gwyn told me to let Tessa go last night. I wonder if she was alarmed to find me sitting with her daughter.

The better part of me wants to say something reassuring, an encouraging statement like, *What a bright child, Lieutenant. You must be so proud.*

But the worst part of me is feeling tense and prickly and

judged, so I say, "Don't worry. She was clever enough to keep out of my reach."

I'm expecting her to dig back at me, the way Rian would, but her expression doesn't flicker. "I wasn't worried."

"You certainly seemed worried about Miss Cade last night."

She snorts. "I wasn't worried about her either. I didn't want a bunch of hotheaded sailors to get in the middle of a lovers' quarrel."

We're not lovers.

The words stall on my tongue. Putting voice to things like that always seems to make them more official. More finite.

Maybe Tessa would want me to say it, though.

But by the time I've reasoned all this out, the moment has passed, and wind is whipping across the water, battering the sails overhead. I slip my hands into my jacket pockets and regard Lieutenant Tagas.

"You don't hate me like your captain?" I say.

"There aren't too many people I hate," she says. "You're not on the list." She hesitates. "The war in Ostriary was brutal and vicious, Your Highness. I know you and Rian don't see eye to eye, but he's seen a lot of terrible people do a lot of terrible things. So have I."

I think of those scars on her daughter's arms. Most people probably wouldn't comment on it, but I'm just agitated enough to push. "Like what happened to Anya?"

She freezes, and a flare of rage fills her eyes. "Oren Crane is a bad man."

"He did that to her?"

"Yes."

"Why?"

Her gaze holds mine. "To punish me for getting away from him."

I frown.

"It was war," she adds, as if that explains everything.

Maybe it does, and maybe it doesn't. I keep thinking about the moment Rian challenged me, when he implied that Harristan and I were putting people in a situation where they had no choice but to risk their lives. There are certainly people in Kandala who would refer to us as bad men, too. But we didn't have any good choices either. At least we weren't torturing children to make a point.

Though Rocco did say we could use Anya for leverage.

I thought he meant an adult at the time, but I didn't confront him once I knew the truth.

I don't like the path of these thoughts.

I've been quiet too long, and Gwyn says, "I didn't come over here to talk about Anya. I'm trying to make sure you and Rian make it to Ostriary without one of you going overboard. I don't think either of you should throw away a chance to make things better over a pissing match."

A pissing match! I bristle. "Did you offer Captain Blakemore this same lecture?"

"I did."

Oh. For some reason that's not the answer I was expecting, and I wonder if it's true.

But I remember her sitting in that first meeting, how she didn't quite chastise him for his attitude, but almost.

"He told me what he said to you," she says. "About locking someone in a room—then threatening death if they tried to escape."

"Splendid. Perhaps we should form a quorum regarding the governing practices of Kandala, and you can all pass judgment." Despite my words, I'm still stinging from the analogy. I don't want it to show on my face, so I look out across the water. The sun is beginning to peek above the horizon, and I can see the mouth of the river widening where it dumps into the sea, the land on either side giving way.

We're close to Port Karenin. I'll have to make a decision.

I don't trust Captain Blakemore any more than I did when I got on board this ship. But I don't like the thought of disembarking. Everything about it seems fearful.

"I'm not trying to pass judgment," Gwyn says. "As I said to Rian, you didn't lock anyone in a room."

She's wrong on that. I've locked plenty of people in cells.

They can think what they want of our tactics. We kept as many people alive as we could.

"Why would you defend me?" I say. "You don't know me at all."

"I know Ostriary needs steel," she says. "I know the royal court of Ostriary is barely in place, and the war was very hard-won. I told your girl Tessa about Oren Crane and the other rebels who are waiting for a chance to take control. People are tired and want to be done. If Rian can bring you back to arrange a deal, it would go a long way toward maintaining peace."

Your girl Tessa. I know I should be focusing on the rest of what she's saying, but my thoughts have caught and stalled on those words in particular.

I frown. "So you've been sent to keep the peace between me and him."

She lets out a breath. "Maybe I'm being impolitic. But I'm a sailor first, not a courtier. I don't think it would serve anyone well for you to disembark at Port Karenin."

There's a note in her tone that gives me pause, and I study her, trying to figure it out. She and Rian have both talked about peace, and fair trade, and how both countries are eager to be at peace and have what they need. But since the moment I set foot on the *Dawn Chaser*, I've felt a deep, unsettling suspicion, and I can't seem to shake it.

I'm just not sure where the greatest risk lies.

"I'll take it under advisement," I say.

She gives me a nod as if she's not surprised by my answer. "Thank you for hearing me out." She hesitates, then gives a nod toward the captain's stateroom. "He'll be out here checking the rigging before long."

"Is that a warning?"

She smiles, and the skin around her eyes crinkles. "I just thought you should know. Maybe you could be the one to climb with him today."

"I would absolutely try my hardest not to push him off."

She genuinely laughs at that, which takes me by surprise—and makes me smile.

"I've got to get back to the helm," she says. "Let me know your decision by breakfast so we can adjust course."

"I will."

When she moves away, I'm not alone for long. Rocco draws close.

He says nothing, but I know he's waiting for me to state whether there's any cause for concern. I rest my hands on the railing and say, "She doesn't want me to get off the ship in Port Karenin."

"I truly don't think the captain does either." He doesn't nod at the horizon, but his eyes are fixed on the water ahead of us. "Do you see those ships far in the distance?"

I stare out at the sea. It takes me a moment, because they're *so* far that I wouldn't have noticed them at all if he hadn't pointed them out. "Yes."

"I'd need a spyglass to see if I could tell much detail, but it's unusual to see two ships of that size sailing together."

I frown. "Are you concerned?"

"We're nearing the southern end of the river. Again, I'd need a spyglass and a sextant to be sure, but they seem far enough that they could be well into the ocean."

"And you don't think they're Kandalan ships?"

"I don't know. We'll need to get closer to know for sure. They could be ships waiting for Captain Blakemore—or they could be ships waiting for *you*."

I keep my fingers on the railing so I give no indication of what we're discussing. My heart has begun a deep thrum in my chest. "Advise."

"The captain offered to let you leave the ship. That suggests this isn't a kidnapping—at least not on his end."

"So did Lieutenant Tagas. She asked me to alert her if I've made the decision to change course." I hesitate. "Are we overthinking this?"

"I would feel better if he were more forthright about the contents of the locked room." He pauses. "He can keep the key hidden, but what's the risk of allowing you to *see* the weapons?"

"I agree."

"And what's to stop us from breaking in?"

I whip my head around.

"It's a simple lock." Rocco shrugs. "They truly are shorthanded. There are one or two watchmen overnight, but during the afternoon, most of the crew is either sleeping or gutting fish." He pauses.

"Of your guards, there are generally only two of us on duty at once."

While the other is presumably sleeping.

"Do you think you could break the lock?" I say, my voice low. My heart keeps hammering along, torn between relief that the captain probably is as forthright as he seems—and terror that somehow this ship will be overtaken and I'll be captured by someone worse.

"Breaking it wouldn't be a problem," Rocco says. "Leaving evidence would be." He glances at me. "He'd know it was done by your order—if not done by you yourself."

I have no idea how Captain Blakemore would react if I broke into that room, but I have no doubt he'd take it personally. That's not a story I need carried to the king of Ostriary either. Rian can say whatever he wants about my *reputation*, but my actions in the Royal Sector were to enforce laws that were well known. Breaking into a locked room on this ship would be a lot harder to explain away—and it certainly wouldn't demonstrate that the king of Kandala and his brother were prepared to negotiate in good faith.

I stare out at the water, at the two distant ships, at the sun that's beginning to burn a path into dawn.

I wish I could talk to Tessa.

I remember her face when I caught her wrist, when that needle was clutched so precariously against her palm.

I remember Lochlan at my back. *Let her go.*

As usual, everyone already expects the worst of me. It's part of the reason I expect the worst of everyone else.

At the opening to the deck, a head appears, peeking above. It's Tessa, early as usual. She's looking the other way, so she doesn't see me. My gut clenches, and I'm tempted to call for a return to port just so I can get off this ship and go back to the way things were.

But if I've learned anything, there's no going back. I can't undo my mistakes with Tessa. I can't fix the fever sickness, and I can't reverse everything Harristan and I have done wrong along the way.

I can't undo the assassination of my parents.

All I can do is move forward.

I look at Rocco. "Tell Lieutenant Tagas to stay the course. We'll continue on to Ostriary."

"And what of the ships?"

Tessa finally turns and spots me. Her mouth is a line, and I can't read her expression. Experience tells me she's every bit as conflicted as I feel. She's probably thinking about leaping off the ladder and returning to her room.

But she doesn't.

I sigh. "Let's wait and see."

CHAPTER TWENTY-THREE

Tessa

I didn't realize he'd be up here.

Sometimes I think back to my moments with Karri when we worked for Mistress Solomon, when I'd sigh over thoughts of Weston Lark. She used to warn me about how outlaws were just looking to string girls along.

In a way, I guess she was right. He *was* tricking me.

For a moment, I wonder if Corrick is going to remain by the railing with Rocco, to avoid any uncomfortable conflict after last night.

I should know better. Corrick's whole life is conflict.

He strides across the short span of deck, then extends a hand to me. "Miss Cade. I trust you've put your needles away?"

I ignore his hand and step onto the deck on my own. "I'm sure I can find another one."

It's the type of sharp banter I've grown accustomed to exchanging with him—whether we're working in accord or not. I expect the usual flare of challenge to light in his eyes, but . . . it doesn't. He meets my gaze and holds it.

"Why are you so angry with me?" he says.

His voice isn't loud, but Corrick never is. What he lacks in volume, he makes up for with intensity. The question nearly hits me like a fist.

"You know my reputation," he continues. "You *knew* my reputation. Better than anyone, in fact." He pauses. "You know what I've done. From both sides." Another pause. "It's discouraging to think that you would allow a few insults from Lochlan to sway your opinion of me so dramatically. I thought your character was a bit more resilient than that. Perhaps I was wrong."

No, wait. *Those* words hit me like a fist.

"It's not just Lochlan," I say, and I have to will strength into my voice.

"Then what?" he says.

Wind carries off the sea to tug at our clothes and hair. I study him, those vibrant blue eyes that I know so well, and I refuse to look away. "It's discouraging to think that *you* would climb onto a ship that's out of the public eye and see it as an opportunity to get under my skirts."

I expect him to flinch, but he doesn't. "Is that truly what you think?"

"It's exactly what you did, Corrick."

"I'll grant you that the *action* is true." He takes a step closer to me. "Yet not the motivation."

He's so close that I can feel his warmth. My emotions are all tangled up.

He takes advantage of my indecision to move a step closer. When he speaks, his voice is low and sure. "I'm going to say something that could sound very arrogant, and very cruel," he says. "So before I do, I want to make sure you understand that I am speaking them as . . . as a *truth*. As a statement of fact." He brushes a lock of hair out of my eyes. "Not a means to cause harm."

I swallow, but he waits until I nod. I have to brace myself. "Go ahead."

He leans in to whisper, so there's no chance of our words being overheard by anyone but the wind and sky. "You've known me for a long time. There have been many nights between us. Many times we were alone. Out of the public eye, as you say."

His voice is low and husky and familiar, and I shiver even as my cheeks catch on fire.

Then he adds, "If all I wanted was to *get under your skirts*, I could have had you, ready and willing, at any moment of my choosing."

I jerk back so sharply that I almost lose my balance. I'm flushed, gasping with sudden fury. My fingernails are curled into my palms so hard that I'm in danger of drawing blood.

I can't decide if I hate him, or if I just hate that he's *right*.

"I warned you," he says.

"So gallant," I say, seething.

"Gallant?" His eyebrows go up. "Do forgive me if my ideas of *gallantry* do not align with your own. Would you rather I had made better use of our table in the workshop? I seem to recall you throwing yourself at me on more than one occasion."

I must be so red I could be a beacon. There's a good chance I'm going to punch him in the crotch *again*, or possibly draw that dagger that's belted to his hip. Or maybe I'll just smack him square in the face. All three. All at once. Rocco's going to have to drag me off him.

But Rian speaks from behind me. "Problems, Miss Cade?"

"No," I grind out.

"Miss Cade was having a difficult time remembering the intricacies of our past interactions," says Corrick. "I simply offered a reminder."

"Did she want one?"

"I rather doubt it's any of your business," Corrick says, and his voice has gone a bit dry, "but she quite clearly offered me an invitation." He says it like he's implying something else.

That's it. I swing a fist.

Rian steps in front of Corrick, deflecting my strike a bit, but I wasn't expecting it, and I catch the captain in the shoulder. "I'm sorry," I gasp.

He takes hold of my wrist gently, but his voice is firm. "Don't hit him."

"I don't need you to defend me," says Corrick, and that's probably true. Rocco has moved closer, and it's clear he's paying close attention to this interaction.

"I'm not defending you," says Rian.

"No one fights on your ship," I say hollowly. "Again, I'm sorry."

"I wasn't worried about the fighting. I wasn't sure what the response would be if you'd landed that punch."

That thought sends a chill up my spine. I take a step back, and I have to rub at my arms to shake off the shiver.

Corrick watches the motion. "Your concerns are misplaced, Captain. Tessa has struck me before. I've never retaliated." He pauses. "Perhaps a reminder of *that* is in order as well, Miss Cade."

Also true.

I don't know how we got here. It's like Weston Lark and Prince Corrick have split into two different people again, as if the friendly, roguish outlaw really is a man who was killed by the cruel prince in front of me.

But they're not, and it takes more effort to remember that than it should. I have to take a deep breath. "He's right," I say to Rian. "He wouldn't hurt me." I sound like I need to convince myself, and I hate it. I turn a glare on Corrick. "Maybe I shouldn't have tried to hit you." My cheeks redden again, completely against my will. "But you shouldn't have said . . . *that*."

Rian looks between the two of us. "What did he say?"

"That is a private matter between us, Captain," Corrick says. "Surely you have duties that we're preventing you from completing."

"I'm completing them right now. Gwyn told me you don't want to dock in Port Karenin anymore."

"I'm not having you return to Ostriary with stories of how the king's brother was intractable and obstinate."

Rian folds his arms. "You think he won't figure it out on his own?"

"I got on the ship with you," Corrick says. "Rather quickly, in fact, and at no small expense. I'm continuing the journey, despite your refusal to be forthright with me about what you might have on board this vessel. My people have caused no trouble, and you've made great use of my apothecary for your own needs, finding no objection from me." Corrick takes a step forward, and the air crackles with animosity. "I am not a pretentious man, Captain. I should hope that's rather obvious. But I am the King's Justice, and I am second in line to the throne of Kandala. You may not agree with our laws, and you may not agree with my judgments, but I have brought no harm to your ship or your crew. I am not a criminal, and I am rather done being treated as one."

Rian stares back at him, and I wonder if this tension is finally going to snap and one of them is going to throw a punch.

But Rian sighs and uncrosses his arms. "Fine."

Corrick's eyebrows go up. "Fine?"

"Yes. Fine. You're not a criminal. You boarded the ship to do right by your people. You agreed to my terms. You haven't caused harm." Rian runs a hand through his hair, and I can't tell if he's exasperated—or just exhausted by this whole conversation. I know I am. "You were right," he continues. "I do have duties that require my attention." He takes a very deliberate pause. "Your Highness." He offers me a nod. "Miss Cade."

Then he turns away.

Whoa. I let out a breath through my teeth.

But Corrick's not done. He turns that belligerent gaze on me. "You can be angry at my words, and you can take issue with my actions. Hate me if you like, but you know I'm right. I have *never* harmed you, and I've never taken advantage of you. When you snuck into the palace, I did everything I could to keep you safe— including offering you the opportunity to leave. I put a bag of silver in your hands, Tessa. A dagger right off my belt."

All true. I swallow. "Corrick . . ."

"I'm not done. Any distance between us at court was because I respect your work and I value your intelligence, and I did not want to give anyone cause to doubt the integrity of either." His voice is so low, but so intense, lending weight to every single word. Every *syllable.* "I resent that a man with questionable motives has instilled such . . . *misgivings* in you."

"Oh, stop being so cynical!" I snap. "Rian doesn't have questionable motives."

That draws him up short, but I'm not entirely sure why. Corrick stares back at me, but he says nothing.

After a moment, the tension is just too great. I can't take it. "What?" I demand.

"I wasn't talking about Rian," he says slowly. "I was talking about Lochlan."

Oh. I take a step back.

"Our captain has instilled misgivings?" Corrick says. "I shouldn't be surprised, but I do feel as though I need an explanation."

I'm unsure how to proceed again.

Corrick's eyes narrow. "Maybe I don't need an explanation. Maybe I've already seen the effects. He arrives at court with an attitude full of censure for how Kandala has fared—for how we've maintained order—and you agree with every word he says."

"But why is that a surprise?" I demand. "Of course I agree with him! When you were Wes, *you* would have agreed—"

"But you know the truth, Tessa. We pored over maps, and I told you that it's not as simple as taking every petal of Moonflower Kandala has to offer. If it were, we wouldn't be locked in tense meetings with the rebels. We wouldn't have faced a revolution at all." He looks truly angry now. "If it were *simple*, I would not be on this ship."

"I know."

"I don't think you do. I think you've realized that Wes never existed, *could* never exist, and you'll never have our adventures back. I think you've met a man who could offer more than endless debates in stuffy conference rooms, and you've leapt at a new chance to make a difference, because *my* way was too slow and boring."

"Please stop. That's not it at all—"

"Oh, it's not? Because I realize that it may seem appealing to follow a man with clear ideals, but you haven't been to Ostriary yet. You haven't dealt with their king, and you haven't seen what awaits us there. You accuse me of being cynical, but you stood right there and said that Rian doesn't have questionable motives. Maybe I should find Lochlan and befriend him, because on this, we would agree: you *are* naive—"

"Don't you dare," I snap. "Just because I know more about medicine than I do about ruling a country doesn't mean I'm some clueless idiot. Just because you believe the worst of *everyone* doesn't mean that there aren't *good* people in this world."

"It's kept me alive, Tessa. It's kept my brother alive. And now I'm trying to keep *you* alive. You question *my* motives, but you don't question the captain's. I would ask why he claimed the political climate of Ostriary was stable when we were seated at dinner—yet now tells stories of pirates who may lie in wait. I would question why he feels the need to keep a room on this ship locked away. It's no surprise to me that we've been on the ship for a matter of two days, and he's already worked to sow discord between us."

"He's not the one sowing discord," I say.

Corrick grits his teeth. "I would question which kingdom truly has his loyalty, because right now, it's rather clear it's not Kandala."

"Your Highness." Rocco has stepped close, and his voice is low, but urgent enough to cut through Corrick's tirade. He gives a deliberate glance past us, at the main deck, where more members of Rian's crew have begun to appear. No one is directly staring at us, but it's clear we're the center of attention. Again.

I sigh and take a step back. Close quarters don't keep secrets well at *all*.

I stare up at Corrick, whose jaw is tight. I hate that he's right about so much of it.

But not *all* of it. I take a long breath, then tuck a loose tendril of hair behind my ear.

An unintelligible shout rings out near the rear of the ship, and it takes a moment for me to realize it's Sablo, standing at the helm. When I step around Corrick to look, I see that he's got a spyglass in his hands, and he's calling for the captain. Rian joins him, taking the spyglass himself.

I see two ships in the distance, but they're too far to see too much detail. At my side, Corrick has gone very still. I look at him, wondering if he's seen.

As soon as I meet his eyes, despite everything between us, I can tell that he has, and something about the ships is important.

His gaze shifts to the captain again.

"Are we in danger?" I whisper.

"I don't know," he says. "Rocco spotted them, too."

"Would Harristan have sent them?"

"If he did, he made no mention of it." He pauses, and I can tell he's truly considering this. "Even if my brother did decide to break his word, there's absolutely no strategic advantage to keeping that knowledge from me." He turns to look directly at the helm, then raises his voice to call, "Is there a problem, Captain?"

Rian slowly lowers the spyglass. He's quiet for a moment, then calls back, "No problem. Sablo spotted some brigantines on the horizon."

Corrick looks back at me. His voice is a little mocking as he says, "Do you think he's telling the truth?"

"I do," I say, but for the first time, I'm not sure.

"Maybe you could find out for sure," Corrick says.

"How am I supposed to do that?"

"Well, I'm not the only one who enjoys spending time with you." I bristle, but his voice isn't arrogant anymore. It's evenly assessing. "Not just Captain Blakemore either. It seems everyone is willing to share a bit of information with the apothecary. Even Lochlan." He pauses. "It's exactly what stopped the rebels in the woods. It's what stopped the revolution. People like you. People *trust* you."

I open my mouth again, but his eyes bore into mine. "Like it or not, the captain is hiding something on board," he says. "And now we've got two ships in a place they're not supposed to be." He pauses. "It's time to think about your own loyalties, Miss Cade. You said you're not naive. Prove it."

Chapter Twenty-Four

Harristan

Hours pass. I spend some of them sleeping, and most of that is against my will. The first time I wake, I'm jolted by a barn cat that climbs into my lap. I inhale sharply and look around in a panic, but the barn is still dark, moonlight shining through the windows by the doors.

I shift my leg, and the movement is weak, pain throbbing through the muscle. When I lift a hand to my head, I discover that the blood has crusted to my ear and in my hair, but I can't tell how bad the injury is.

I blink and remember Maxon, the kindness in his eyes. He was a complete stranger, but he gave me medicine just because I needed it. He tried to lead me away from the night patrol.

And then they killed him. They killed him before I could do anything about it.

I don't know how Corrick did this for years. Only now do I

realize how very much my brother risked. How much guilt he must have carried.

I wish my brother were here.

The thought slips into my brain so quickly that my chest tightens and warmth rushes to my eyes. But I didn't cry over my parents, and I certainly won't cry over this.

I can imagine Corrick here in the barn, rolling his eyes at me.

Lord, Harristan, next time just take me with you.

Yes, Cory. Next time.

I sleep again, waking when a rooster crows. Hens are clucking on the other side of the barn. The cat is sound asleep in my lap, a warm weight across my throbbing thigh. Morning sunlight is beaming through the window now.

Morning.

A swell of panic fills my belly. Violet has been gone for too long. Something must have happened.

Was she captured? Delayed? What if one of the guards threw her into the Hold? Am I to sit here waiting for discovery?

And I gave her my ring. I have no way to prove myself now. I'm injured and half soaked in blood. Even if Violet's family found me and believed me—which is doubtful—I rather doubt the night patrol would.

They shot Maxon. They shot him, and he didn't even do anything wrong.

You'd do the same, I'm sure.

The words seem to have two meanings now. I clench my eyes closed and try to breathe.

I press my hands into the ground and shift my weight, and the cat uncurls, annoyed, but I ignore the animal and try to get my legs underneath me. I can stand, but I feel lightheaded, dizzy. My trousers are tacky with blood, and I can see through the tear in my pants that the injury is still seeping.

I draw a ragged breath and swear.

Well, I can't just stand here. I limp into a stall with a cow and attend to human needs. I'm not quite thirsty enough to share the animal's water trough, but it's close. Violet's family has a draft horse, but when I limp to his stall, I discover that he's old and sway-backed, and most likely broke for harness, not for riding.

I'm so dizzy that I'm not sure I could stay on top of a horse anyway.

I wish for clothes, but there are none in the barn. I could try to walk toward the Royal Sector, but I gave Violet all of my money, so I don't even have coins to pay for a ride in a wagon.

I have no idea which is worse: staying here, waiting for discovery, or heading out in the sunlight and praying that no one recognizes me.

I think of Captain Huxley standing with Arella and Laurel.

If you don't have medicine, then what do you have?

Information on the king. On how he's tricking *you.*

I'm not tricking anyone. This is more treason and betrayal—and as much as I hate to admit it, I'm a bit shocked it's coming from Arella Cherry.

Corrick is gone. If I can't trust my guards, I have no one.

Quint.

But if Arella is working against me, maybe I can't trust Quint either. Maybe Quint is the one who had Violet locked up, and he's just now gathering guards and consuls to come take *me* into custody, to parade me back to the palace in chains for doing the exact same thing Corrick was doing.

A chill crawls up my spine, and I make my way back to the wall of the barn, then slide back to sitting. The deepest, darkest part of me wants to run and hide, to lose myself somewhere. No one would ever know.

But that would mean abandoning my throne.

Abandoning my people.

If anyone deserves to escape this role, it's my brother.

Without warning, I hear hoofbeats, and I freeze. It's more than one horse, so it can't be Quint alone.

I struggle to my feet again, then brace a hand against the wall when I begin to slip sideways. My heart stutters in my chest, then bolts, pounding so hard that I feel it in my head. I wish I had a weapon. I don't know how long or how well I can fight, because the weapons master always goes too easy on me. It makes him nervous when my breathing gets strained.

But I rather doubt I'll last long. Running as far as I did last night just about killed me.

Then, without warning, the barn doors are rolling open, the sun so bright that I have to blink it away. Figures fill the doorway. I recognize Violet first, because she bursts forward. "Fox!" she cries. "You're still here!"

"Still here," I say. My eyes are on the men following her. They step out of the sunlight slowly, and I'm frozen in place. Quint is there, his expression tense when his eyes land on me. I'm not sure it's a relief, because he didn't come alone, as I requested. He's backed by two guards, Thorin and Saeth, and they look as fierce and foreboding as ever.

I keep thinking of Captain Huxley's words in the clearing last night—or Rocco's warnings to me and Corrick before he left. Thorin and Saeth are trussed up in weapons and armor. I'm exhausted and injured . . . and unarmed. They could kill me right now and there'd be nothing I could do about it. My fingers are clutching at the barn wall so tightly that splinters have dug under my nails, and I can hear my breathing shaking. It's only slightly louder than my heart.

Thorin moves first. He takes a step forward, and my breath catches. I draw myself up and brace against the wall.

But he drops to one knee. "Your Majesty." An instant later, Saeth and Quint do the same.

A relieved breath huffs out of my chest, and I almost sag against the side of the barn. I have to run a shaking hand over my face. "Rise," I say, and my voice is rough.

Violet looks from me to them and back. "Am I supposed to do that?" she whispers.

"No." I study her in the morning light. "You were gone so long. I thought something happened to—" My eyes fall on her bare feet, which are red and blistered, one toe stubbed and bloodied. I snap my gaze up. There are so many more important things to worry about, but I say, "I told you to buy boots, Violet."

Thorin and Saeth exchange a glance.

Quint looks like he's not entirely sure what to make of this conversation.

Violet doesn't even look chagrined. "Well, I was *going* to, but I wanted to give some extra coins to Toby. Then I kept thinking about how you said you weren't coming back, and I didn't want anyone to think the Fox was gone, so I kept leaving a few coins on the other doorsteps. Just here and there."

Of course she did.

Today, however, I can't be irritated. It reminds me of the way Maxon gave me his medicine. And Violet likely risked her life.

"Did you run all that way in bare feet?" I say.

"I didn't run the *whole* way. It took me a long time at the gate. And then I couldn't find the palace. It's not like I've ever been inside the Royal Sector. You could've told me it was in the *middle*."

I look at Quint. "Have a pair of boots sent."

He opens his mouth, then closes it. He draws a small book from inside his jacket and makes a note. "Of course, Your Majesty."

I look between him and Violet. "I said no guards."

She scowls. "I told him that, but he wouldn't listen." She huffs. "Gryff wouldn't listen either. It took *hours* to convince him to fetch Master Quint. I had to sing until I didn't think I'd have a voice left."

I have the sense that I can't follow this conversation. "You . . . you had to *sing*?"

"Yes. He wouldn't listen. He said your ring was a fake. So I sat down and sang every annoying song I know, and it's a *lot*, I tell you—"

"She sang until daybreak," Quint says. "Meanwhile, when you did not return, I had to alert Thorin. We were beginning to discuss a discreet search party when one of the day maids mentioned the girl singing at the palace steps." He takes a step forward, but then he seems to think better of it. He glances from my leg to my head, and his mouth forms a line. "Your Majesty," he says quietly. "Forgive me, but you're bleeding." He pauses. "We've brought a closed carriage."

"Good." I touch a hand to my ear, and I'm surprised when it comes away wet with fresh blood. "Who else knows of this?"

"No one yet," Quint says. "*Sullivan* is a person of interest. That's all."

I look at Thorin. "Who among the guards?"

"Just us." He hesitates and glances at Saeth again. "We all know how Huxley has an ear for gossip. We've been keeping close ranks."

Huxley has more than just an ear for gossip, but I don't say that.

I straighten from the wall, and Saeth steps forward to help me, but I wave him off. I still feel too unsteady, and I want to walk out of here on my own two feet.

"Violet," I say to her. "Can I trust you to keep this secret?"

As I say the question, I know the answer. Even if she promises, even if she swears, this is too big.

She shakes her head anyway, and I must look fierce, because she throws up her hands. "Well, I had to tell Toby." Her expression turns somber. "In case something happened to me. I needed someone to tell Ma."

As if on cue, a boy of about ten years old comes skidding into the barn. He's barefoot, too, and so quick that Thorin and Saeth both have weapons drawn before he even comes to a stop.

The boy cries out and flails backward, sitting down hard in the straw. But he doesn't look frightened. He looks *fascinated*. "I saw the carriage, Vi! Are those real palace guards?"

"Real enough, boy," says Saeth. "Is anyone else coming behind you?"

"No," he says. Toby's gaze skips past them, then looks to me and Quint. His eyes go even wider, and he scrambles to his feet. He bows to Quint, who's in a half-buttoned red brocade jacket. "Your Majesty."

"Ah . . . no," says Quint. But he glances at the boy's feet, then draws out his little notebook again and makes a note. He looks to me. "Your Majesty," he says pointedly. "Perhaps we should depart while it's still early."

Toby looks at me, and his face scrunches up. "Him? Really?"

I'm too tired for this. My night has been too full of fear and loss and uncertainty, and I have bigger worries than anything I'll find inside this barn. "No," I say. "Quint. You said you brought a carriage?"

I don't wait for an answer. I just start limping. Outside of the barn, there's a carriage and one of the guards' horses.

"Wait!" cries Violet. "Will I ever see you again?"

No. She won't. But I can't look into her desperate eyes and say that.

"I'm the king," I say wearily. "Everyone sees me." Before I climb into the carriage, I look at her. "You have my thanks, Violet. Truly."

She looks so troubled. "We need the Fox," she whispers.

I frown. "Forgive me. Please." I climb into the carriage. Quint climbs in behind me. The door slams.

"We need you!" she calls shrilly. She bangs on the door of the carriage. "We need the Fox!"

"Violet!" a woman calls from somewhere distant. "Violet, what are you doing?"

"It was the king, Miss Tucker!" the boy calls. "The king was in your barn!"

I freeze, staring across at Quint. His expression is somber, his eyes searching my face, but he says nothing.

"What is this?" the woman calls. "What is happening?"

"A man was hiding in your barn," calls Saeth. "He was impersonating the king. We've taken him into custody, miss."

"He wasn't impersonating him," calls the boy. "He *wasn't*—"

A whip cracks, and the carriage starts to rattle away.

We need the Fox.

The words hit me almost as hard as Maxon's death.

She ran on bare feet. She sang all night.

And now I'm riding away in a carriage, leaving her behind.

"Your Majesty," says Quint.

I blink, then look at him. "How did Corrick do this for so long?" I say. "How could he bear it?"

He frowns. "He had Tessa. He wasn't alone."

I swallow. I'm always alone.

Quint pulls a stoppered bottle of water from a trunk set under the seat, then pulls a handkerchief free. He wets an end, then holds it up. "May I?"

"I don't need tending, Quint."

"It's morning. I can do my best to keep you out of sight, but if you don't want to raise too many questions, you'll need to be somewhat presentable to walk into the palace." He glances at my leg, which is stretched across the space between us, because bending it hurts. "Presuming you can walk at all."

I glare at him, and while Quint is always respectfully deferential, he's not easily cowed. He lifts the handkerchief in response.

I scowl. "Fine." I take the handkerchief from him, but when I touch it to my neck, it comes away with more blood than I expect. I frown and take another swipe, dragging against my ear, and I hiss at the sudden pain.

"Honestly." Quint shifts across the carriage to sit beside me. "Allow me." He doesn't wait for an answer; he just plucks the cloth from my hand, adding more water from the bottle. Diluted drops of blood fall, disappearing in the velvet cushion. When he touches the handkerchief to my neck, I almost jump. Quint isn't rough, but he's not quite gentle either. My head aches, and the water stings where it finds broken skin, so I have half a mind to yank the handkerchief back out of his hand. I have to fight not to squirm like an errant schoolboy.

But maybe Quint can tell, because his movements slow, the handkerchief tracing lightly over the injury.

"How often did you do this for Corrick?" I say.

"Tending his wounds or fetching him from the Wilds?"

I don't like the way he phrases either of those options. "Both."

He shakes his head. "Neither, really. Corrick was rarely injured." He pauses. "Aside from the time your soldiers found him with the rebels, he never failed to return of his own accord." He pauses. "He never went on his nightly runs without a mask. He never even let Tessa know who he was."

I draw back and turn to face him. "Are you chastising me, Quint?"

"Never, Your Majesty." He rinses the handkerchief again, then lifts it. When I don't move, he raises his eyebrows.

I sigh and turn my head. I have to run a hand across my face. Corrick did this for years. Only a few weeks, and I nearly brought down the kingdom.

He's better at this than I am.

He's better at a lot of things than I am.

"Maybe you should be," I say. The water is cold, and I shiver.

"Hmm?"

"Chastising me," I add. "When I told you I wanted to do this, you didn't even try to talk me out of it."

"I'm honored to think I could have talked the king of Kandala out of anything at all." He pauses, and I wince as he passes the handkerchief over the worst of it. "This will need stitching, I'm afraid."

"The arrow nearly took me in the face."

"You were very lucky."

"Lucky." I should be worried about my consuls and my guards, but instead, I think of Maxon, lying dead in the middle of the woods. My voice has gone rough. To my horror, my chest tightens. I frown and push Quint's hand away. "Enough."

He recedes, wrapping up the cloth so it doesn't drip too badly, and I fix my gaze on the opposite wall of the carriage. The air between us is thick with silence, and that's not better. It leaves me with too much time to think.

Information on the king. On how he's tricking you.

Arella and Roydan have been having private meetings for weeks—but they've been reviewing shipping logs. I have absolutely no idea how that could be related to me tricking anyone.

And I still can't see Arella conspiring with Laurel Pepperleaf and Captain Huxley. He's a gossip, everyone knows that, but I've never thought he was disloyal. Laurel was at the dinner with Allisander, and Arella *hates* him and everything he stands for. I can't quite see Laurel and Arella working together either.

But the night patrol showed up, and everyone scattered.

Maxon helped me—and then he was killed for it.

My eyes burn and I blink it away.

"If I may," Quint begins.

"No," I say, and he shuts his mouth.

I don't like that. I glance up. His red hair is nearly brown in the dim light of the carriage, but his eyes are piercing. We've never been friends, so I have no idea how old he is, but he has to be older than I am. He was an apprentice when he first came to the palace, and he's held his position as Palace Master for years now, so he must be . . . twenty-four? Twenty-five? I only ever really kept him on because I know Corrick is so fond of him. Personally, I always found him a bit bothersome: he might be good at his job, but he prattles endlessly about everything, and he seems to enjoy doing so.

It's only in these recent weeks that I've discovered that Quint's mindless chatter is a front for someone who's sharp, attentive, and deeply loyal.

Brave, too. He saved my life when the palace was under attack. And cunning, if he secretly helped Corrick for so long.

"Was that your idea?" I finally say. "To give the impression that the guards were arresting me for 'impersonating' the king?"

"Yes," he says. "Violet didn't have much of a story, really. If she protests, I rather doubt anyone will listen. It's a lot easier to believe that a man tricked a few children into thinking he was royalty."

He's right, but Violet doesn't really deserve that. I can't believe she took the money for boots and used some of it to make people think the Fox was still making rounds. A new thread of guilt joins the first few that are already tugging at my heart. At least I can make sure she has warm feet for a while.

I think of the way Quint glanced at Toby's feet, too, how he added a note to his little book.

"Forgive me," I say. "What were you going to say to me?"

Quint blinks at that. "I was going to ask how you were injured." He pauses. "When we arrived at the barn, you did not seem relieved to see us."

"How did I seem?"

"With all due respect, Your Majesty—"

"Just tell me, Quint."

"Terrified."

"Ah." I run a hand across the back of my neck. Just the memory of . . . of *all* of it causes me to shudder. "Well." I try to draw my leg up, but my knee protests, and I wince and shift my weight. I give up and sigh. "I heard there was going to be a meeting. I wanted to see if I could learn what was said."

"What did you learn?"

That sending the King's Justice away has emboldened dissenters, just as we feared.

That sedition and treason still wait in the shadows. That the consuls are still working against me—and they have the support of the palace guards.

That my brother is gone, and I can trust no one.

That I am very much alone.

I can't say any of that. I'm the king. Even the barest utterance of uncertainty can sow discord and distrust.

I don't even know how much I can tell Quint.

I wish I had Corrick.

"Your Majesty . . . ," Quint begins, but he stops there, as if he expects me to cut him off again.

"Go ahead," I say. I fix my eyes on the sunlight that streams around the draperies.

"Corrick did not share everything with me in the beginning," he says. "In fact, it took him quite some time before he saw fit to share what he was doing, even though I had my suspicions." His voice is very quiet, very serious. "You trusted me enough to tell me that you hoped to help the people in the same way he once did. You trusted me enough to come to your aid this morning." He hesitates. "Surely you must know your guards will have some suspicions.

Corrick did not do this alone." Another hesitation. "There's no need for you to do it alone either."

That draws my gaze back to his. My thoughts keep spinning, and I know now is a time to issue warnings and orders and begin making plans to protect the palace—and the people. I draw a breath to tell him about the consul, about the guard captain.

Instead, I open my mouth, and I find myself saying, "A man died. He was—he tried—" I have to breathe past the lump in my throat that feels ever-present. "His name was Maxon. The night patrol shot him."

Quint doesn't flinch. He doesn't look away. "What happened?"

Corrick did not do this alone.

I don't know how to do it any other way.

But I draw a slow breath and tell Quint everything. At first, my words are tight and formal. A sterile recitation of events. I expect him to interject with questions or take notes, as if we were sitting in a meeting at the palace and advisers would need a written report later. But he's quiet and attentive, and as the carriage rolls along, I find myself sharing details I wouldn't otherwise. The food stall. The crowds. The honey and cheese on warm nut bread. Arella and Captain Huxley and their announcement—followed by the panic over the arrival of the night patrol.

Maxon's generosity—and his death.

"When you arrived with guards," I say, "I wasn't sure what to expect."

"I didn't mean to alarm you," he says, his tone full of contrition. "I apologize."

"No," I say. "You don't need to apologize."

"Will you discharge Captain Huxley?"

"I've considered it." I pause. "If I do, I worry that it may tip my hand too quickly. Anyone he's working with will better hide their activities." I think of how Thorin said they know about Huxley's ear for gossip, how they've closed ranks. I wonder how tight that circle is.

"Arella will surely deny all of it," Quint says. He *tsks*. "Do you have any idea how they planned to explain how you're *tricking* the people?"

"Tessa's medicine?" I guess. "But Lochlan already implied that the people were worried. They don't need Captain Huxley to reinforce it. What could the end goal be? To simply spur revolution? The crowd wasn't organized. They scattered when the night patrol arrived."

"It takes more than the promise of gossip to unite people," Quint says. "For as much as Corrick hates Lochlan, the people were willing to follow the rebel's lead when he offered a new path." He pauses. "Just as you allowed him to be a part of your negotiations—and sent him away on Captain Blakemore's ship."

That's all true—and there's something about that simple leadership that I envy.

"Tessa once said that we could be loved," I say to him. "She said that we hide the truest parts of ourselves. Do you agree with that, Quint?"

A line forms between his eyebrows, and he looks half-amused, half-sad. "Is this a trick question, Your Majesty?"

"No."

"Then . . . yes. I agree with every word."

When I say nothing, he rushes on. "We're riding in a carriage after your attempt to hide yourself among the people ended in peril." He pauses. "After Prince Corrick's attempts to do the same ended in revolution."

That's true enough, I suppose.

"I have another question," I say. "This one isn't a trick either."

Quint nods. "Yes, Your Majesty."

"Do you think I hide behind my brother's viciousness?"

He inhales as if he's going to offer platitudes, but I hold his eyes, and he goes very still.

That's answer enough. I speak into his silence. "So you think I'm a coward."

"What?" He looks a bit incredulous. "No. Certainly not."

His answer is quick, and I frown. "Why not?"

"You have to ask me *why*? I watched you face down the rebels in the square when they were shooting consuls and throwing fire at you. You were safe in the woods after they laid siege to the palace, and you took *one guard* to confront them all."

"In all truth," I say, a bit chagrined, "I expected to find more on the way."

He doesn't smile. "Corrick boarded that ship because he doesn't want to disappoint you. Before we learned of Violet's claims, I think Thorin was ready to walk every trail of the Wilds until he found you. Tessa stood by your side because she believes you truly want to better Kandala." He pauses. "Cowardice does not breed this kind of loyalty."

"Yet you believe I hide behind my brother."

"No. I believe you allow his actions to speak for you."

I almost flinch.

"Forgive me," he begins.

"Don't apologize," I say. "I'm glad you're being forthright with me."

And I am, I realize. I've spent months—no, *years*—guarding my thoughts and my actions, not allowing a shred of vulnerability to reveal itself. Not even in front of Corrick.

How did I seem?

Terrified.

I study him. When the palace was attacked, Quint took an arrow that was meant for me. "You stayed by my side, too, Quint."

"Yes, Your Majesty."

I run a hand over my face and sigh. "If only I could convince the people to be equally loyal."

"Well," says Quint, "perhaps you can."

"How?"

"You're not a coward," he says. "You're not afraid to walk among them." Quint's eyes don't leave mine. "Corrick is gone. Perhaps it's time to speak for yourself."

CHAPTER TWENTY-FIVE

Corrick

By midday on the third day, we've lost sight of land.

We haven't lost sight of those ships, though. Once the river dumped into the ocean, the other ships began to drift away, and now those two are the only to remain.

Captain Blakemore is suspicious. I've seen him in conversation with his lieutenant as they share a spyglass.

I'm suspicious, too. But it seems that we've grown so wary of each other that we know questions and demands won't yield a single word of truth—or a single word we'd believe, anyway.

Now that we're in the ocean, the water surrounding the ship has turned to a vivid blue that stretches on for miles, and the winds here are quieter than they were on the river. The storm seems to have moved off to the east, granting us starry skies at night, and brilliant sunlight by day. It's hard to believe that our ships often wreck on the way to Ostriary, because the seas here are so placid and calm that the ship hardly seems to sway.

On any other journey, I might be enjoying myself.

I'm not the only one who's grown irate. As the days have passed, the attitude among the crew has shifted. A weight seems to have settled over the *Dawn Chaser*, and I can't quite identify it. Tempers are shorter. Voices are sharper. Lochlan is still working with the crew—and of all of us, he seems the most at ease. I resent him for it. Even Rian has been keeping to his stateroom more than usual today, talking to Gwyn and Sablo, and I've seen them peer at the ships on the horizon more than once.

"They're growing uneasy," I say quietly to Rocco at dusk, when the others have disappeared belowdecks to get food.

"I can tell," he says. "That makes *me* uneasy."

Me too.

Members of the crew have begun to form a circle on the widest part of the deck with their dinner plates, which means I should retire to my own quarters. But then Captain Blakemore comes up the steps with Tessa by his side, and I stop short.

She looks as beautiful in a vest and trousers as she did in the elegant finery she wears in the palace. Maybe more so, because it reminds me of Tessa in the Wilds, sneaking through the darkness to deliver medicine. My heart kicks at my ribs like it wants to punish me, and I probably deserve it.

The calculating side of me specifically told her to talk to him, but right now, my heart wants me to go drag her away.

The captain sees me looking, and a derisive spark lights in his eye. He glances at Tessa, but his voice is loud enough for me to hear. "Come sit," he says. "Everyone's due for a bit of entertainment." His eyes shift back to me. "Care to play a game, Your Highness?"

No.

But I force a smile onto my face and say, "Of course."

They sit near the main mast, but I have no desire to torture myself further, so I choose a seat near Lieutenant Tagas and her little girl. Kilbourne is on deck as well, lingering to my left, but he doesn't sit.

"What's the game?" I say to Gwyn.

"Blade and Brawl," she says.

I cast a glance down at Anya. "Well, that sounds a lot more exciting than knucklebones," I say.

She makes a face at me, but her mother says, "It can be. It's mostly to keep the crew from getting too antsy. Nothing's worse than a bored sailor in the middle of the ocean."

Anya tears her bread in half and offers it to me. "Here, Corrick. You don't have any dinner."

It's so odd to hear a child say my real name, so I smile, charmed, and take the bread. She's wearing a short-sleeved dress, and those scars down her arms are very visible.

It was war.

But she's a child.

Maybe that's my own naiveté talking. I tear a small piece of the bread and give her back the rest.

I glance across the circle to find the captain watching me. When my eyes meet his, he looks away and says something to Tessa, something too quiet to hear. She nods, but she doesn't look up at me.

Usually, I'm good at figuring people out. With Captain Blakemore, I think what I hate the most is that I can't figure out if he's completely playing us both, or if he's astonishingly earnest about his desire to help everyone. If he is, then I'm an ass who owes him an apology.

But . . . I don't think he is. I want to know what he's hiding. I *need* to know what he's hiding.

Marchon, the navigator, rises from where he was sitting, and he draws a blade from his belt. The crew falls quiet.

"I'll explain the rules of Blade and Brawl for our newcomers," he says. "You'll spin the blade to find your opponent." He sets it spinning on the deck, and the blade glints in the fading light as it whirls. "Once it stops, you make a request, and they respond with a challenge. It can be anything: a race, a riddle, a wrestling match, anything. But it can't take longer than a few minutes so the game keeps going." The dagger comes to a stop, pointing straight at little Anya.

She squeals, sitting up straighter.

Marchon smiles. "Fine, Anya. I want those wooden dice you took off me last time."

She leaps to her feet. "Then I challenge you to slip between the sail and the beam."

He rolls his eyes. "Go ahead." As the little girl squeezes through the tiny gap that a grown man could never fit through, Marchon says, "She gets to keep the dice because I can't do that." Anya skips forward to spin the dagger, and it lands on Tor, who's taking a swig from a bottle someone passed around.

"Tor!" she cries. "Hmm. I want your spyglass."

Tor snorts and rolls his eyes. "All right. Whoever can touch the highest point on the mast gets it."

She scowls, but they step up to the mast and he obviously wins.

Gwyn leans close to me. "It's a bit of a slow start because Anya was first. But once the crew gets going, the asks get bigger—and so do the challenges."

"You can ask for anything?"

"Yeah, but you've got to be ready to battle for it. The other person picks the challenge, so they have the advantage."

Tor's spin slows and lands on Kilbourne, and a few whistles go up from the crew. The guard doesn't move. Tor glances from Kilbourne to me, and his gaze falters. "I . . . I can just spin again, Your Highness."

"No," I say. "The guards can play." I look up at Kilbourne. "If you'd like."

I watch Kilbourne size up Tor, and he grins. The guards are probably just as bored as the crew. "All right," he says easily. "What would you like?"

Tor looks back at Kilbourne, sizing him up in return, probably wondering what kind of challenge he'll face. Tor isn't a small man, but the guards are well-trained warriors, and they look it.

Tor says, "Well, I wouldn't mind that dagger you've got."

"Fine. If you can take it from me in less than a minute, it's yours."

Tor's eyebrows go up, and for an instant, I think he's going to ask a question or request a new challenge, but instead, he lets out a shout and charges at the guard.

Kilbourne sidesteps smoothly, but Tor recovers quickly, and he nearly tackles Kilbourne on his second attempt. The guard shoves him away, and Tor slams into the deck so hard that he cries out. The crew whistles and jeers.

Tor is breathing heavily, glaring up at Kilbourne.

The guard's smile widens. "You still have forty-five seconds," he says, and a laugh ripples through the crowd.

Tor goes after him again—and Kilbourne puts him down again. Then a fourth time.

After the fifth attempt, Tor has blood on his lip, and he's panting. Kilbourne says, "Ten seconds."

Tor makes a final run, and he's all but snarling from the effort, but Kilbourne sends him sprawling onto his belly.

"A valiant effort," Kilbourne says, and there's nothing mocking in his voice.

But Tor rolls over, and that dagger is clutched to his chest. "It sure was," he says, laughing and coughing at the same time.

Gasps and laughter come out of the crew.

Kilbourne swears and slaps the empty dagger hilt at his hip, then scowls ruefully down at the crewman. He laughs lightly. "I'll get that back."

"You'll have to wait your turn," Tor says, grinning. He limps his way back to his seat.

Beside me, Gwyn is laughing softly. "Tor was a bit of a pickpocket before he turned to the honest life of a sailor."

"So that was all misdirection," I say.

"Yes, but Tor looks like he's regretting it. He'll probably be asking your girl for a poultice later."

My girl. I feel those words like a fist to the gut.

She looks up at my guardsman. "Go ahead, Kilbourne. Spin the blade."

He spins, landing on a crewman—and loses, when the challenge is to tie a complicated knot. The game continues. Sometimes the asks are simple: an extra roll, an hour of covered duties, a bit of gossip. Sometimes they're bigger: a treasured book, a valued piece of jewelry, a night of companionship.

The challenges are varied, too. Some are physical, and enough blood is spilled that I hesitate to call the game *friendly*. Some are mental: riddles and questions.

I learn more about the crew during the game than I have in three days on the ship. I see who can fight and who can trick and who is quick to yield.

Across the deck, I watch Rian's keen eyes determining the same exact thing when the dagger points to my guards.

A bottle of liquor has been passed around during the game, and when it reaches Tessa, I see her hesitate. There's a bit of a lull in the conversation, so I can hear Rian when he says, "It's very sweet. But there's a bite."

Her eyes flick up and find mine across the deck.

She holds my gaze, turns up the bottle, and takes a long drink.

I know she means for it to be a dismissive gesture, but I find myself watching the movement of the bottle, the way her throat moves when she swallows, the way the wind tugs tendrils of hair free. The way a few drops cling to her lips.

Her eyes haven't left mine, and her eyes are full of fire. She mouths three words.

Mind your mettle.

I smile in spite of myself. *Mind yours.*

Then she turns and hands the bottle to Rian, and it's like she dumped an entire bucket of icy water over my head.

But then I hear a gasp from some of the crew, and I look up.

The dagger has stopped on me.

I've lost track of the game, so I have no idea who spun until Gwyn says, "I have half a mind to ask you for an hour of babysitting, Your Highness."

A bit of laughter erupts among the crew. It's funny, and I should laugh, too, but my thoughts are still tangled up in Tessa and Rian and the fact that I'm trapped on this boat.

"Go ahead," I say, and Anya beams with glee.

I like the lieutenant, and I don't want to upset her daughter, so I frown as if trying to think of a difficult challenge, then say, "Whoever can spell their name fastest wins."

When Gwyn wins, I sigh and tap Anya on the nose. "I suppose I'll be stuck with you for an entire *hour*."

"Tomorrow?" she says hopefully. "Will you teach me a game from Kandala?"

"Sure," I say, and I absently spin the blade. Someone passes the liquor my way, and I take a long drink without even thinking about it.

But when I lower the bottle, I find Tessa looking at me.

I feel too warm, and it's too quick for it to be the liquor. The bottle is still in my hand, but I watch that weapon spin and spin, until my heart seems to beat in time with the rotations.

Suddenly, I realize it's going to stop on her. As the blade slows, I can see it coming, and my breath nearly catches.

There are so very many things I want to ask for.

A night. An hour. A minute.

Forgiveness.

Tessa isn't watching the blade. She's watching me.

The blade stops, but I don't look down. She doesn't either.

Someone in the circle whistles, and then another. A bunch of shouts go up. I swallow and pass the bottle to the next person.

But then I realize what they're saying.

"He'll ask for the ship!"

"Nah, he'll ask for his girl back."

"Make him walk the rail, Captain!"

What? I frown and snap my gaze down.

The blade didn't stop on Tessa. It stopped on Captain Blakemore.

I'm frozen in place. My thoughts weren't ready to realign so quickly. Across the deck, the captain has gone absolutely still, too. The jeering from the crowd has become a dull roar in my ears.

"Go ahead," Rian says, and the crew quiets. He hates this, I can tell. "Tell me what you want."

There's been only one thing he's refused me since the moment I got on this ship. "You know what I want."

"Then ask for it, and we'll fight for it."

A dark cloud winds through my thoughts, cool and familiar. "You want to fight me?" I say darkly.

"You haven't asked for anything yet," he says.

"Fine," I say. "I want to see the inside of that locked room."

"Fine." Rian stands and begins unbuttoning his jacket.

All right, then. Adrenaline burns through my veins. I uncurl from the deck and unbutton my own.

Rocco had been by the railing, but, seeing this, he's at my side in an instant. "Your Highness."

I shove the jacket at him. "Hold this."

"I must advise that you—"

"Stand down," I say.

Tessa looks between the two of us. "Corrick," she says in a rush. "Rian—stop. You don't know— He can fight—"

"So can I," we say at the same time, and we both scowl at each other.

I have no idea which one of us she was truly warning.

Then Lochlan says, "The prince broke my wrist with his bare hands," and a little murmur goes through the crowd.

Rian looks at me steadily. "I'm hardly surprised."

Despite my order, both Rocco and Kilbourne have moved closer. Any levity is gone from the air now. The whole crew has gone silent.

"If you wanted to fight for it," I say, "we could have settled this yesterday."

"That's not my challenge." Rian nods at the main mast, then walks to where the ropes and rigging are connected to the crossbeams. "I'll race you to the top. Go."

Before I can even process the words, he's ten feet off the ground. *Well, damn.* I don't think. I just leap.

I've never done this, but I've watched his crew do it a dozen times now, and I'm no stranger to climbing. There are dozens of footholds, and this is easier than scaling the wall of the Royal Sector. Weeks ago, the rebels dislocated my shoulder when they took me prisoner, and I feel it give a twinge now, but I ignore the pain. I look up at the miles of chains and netting and try to find a path, but I cling to the outer edge and swing myself higher with each pull, hooking the ropes with my feet to gain more momentum. Harristan taught me to climb when I was a boy, and I can still remember his voice. *Just keep your eyes on the rope, Cory.*

I've always been a strong climber, swift and nimble on the ropes. When Tessa and I were making rounds as Wes and Tessa, she was brilliant with medicine—but I was twice as fast at getting over the wall. I'd take the harder runs because of it.

To my left, the captain is quick, using a combination of ropes and rungs, but I'm nearly even with him. In another ten feet, I'll be close to the first crossbeam and I'll have better leverage. When he glances down to check my progress, I enjoy the flare of surprise in his eyes when he finds me nearly even with him.

"You should've picked the fight," I say.

"You're on the outside edge, and it's a good way to fall."

I brace my foot against the ropes and half leap, half drag myself ever higher—ahead of him. "I'll take my chances."

He redoubles his speed. "Did you really break Lochlan's arm with your bare hands?"

"Yes."

"And you claim there's no basis for your *reputation*?"

"I never claimed that." We make it to the beam, and the wind is strong up here. My fingers grip tight to the rigging, and I fight a wave of vertigo. I have to keep my eyes on the ropes, because if I look out over the sea, I know it'll be disorienting.

I can't believe we're only halfway.

Rian puts a hand on the next section.

I let go of the ropes entirely, thrust my feet against the rigging, and *jump.*

For what seems like an eternity, I'm weightless, nothing around me but wind and sky. When my fingers close on the rope, a gust of wind catches the sail, and I nearly miss it. My feet miss the rigging entirely, but I haul myself upward with my hands, rope fibers tearing into my palms. That twinge in my shoulder turns into a needle of fire.

If I survive this, Harristan might kill me. Or Rocco might beat him to it. Down below, the shouts are incomprehensible.

There. My feet find the ropes, and I shove myself higher. The netting is narrower here as we near the top, with extra ropes and chains that make the climb more complicated. My breathing is ragged, my heart wild, but it's worth it, because I gain a lead. I scramble along the ropes as the boat tips and sways with the current.

"If we catch a gust of wind," Rian calls, "you're going to end up in the ocean."

"Save you a lot of trouble then, won't I?"

But then, like he summoned it, a gust of wind hits the sails so hard that I lose the rope between my feet, and for a single terrifying moment, I'm suspended by nothing more than my grip on the rigging. It's so sudden that I slip at least six inches. My palms burn, and I can't breathe.

I make the mistake of looking at the water, and the horizon spins. The people down below seem to be a mile away.

"It's there," Rian says. "Just there. Swing your feet up a foot and you'll find it."

His voice is a bit closer, and for a second, I can't comprehend what he's saying. My thoughts are too focused on survival, and that means gripping this rope forever.

But then I swing my foot higher and I find the rigging. My hands are so badly rope burned that it's a miracle they're not bleeding, but the pain hasn't set in like it has in my shoulder.

I stare across at Rian. I'm almost panting, my heartbeat a roar in my ears.

He doesn't move. "Take a moment. Get your bearings."

I don't know if he expects me to take a breath or count to three or acknowledge some kind of fresh start, but I have no interest in those options. We're ten feet from the top, and I know what I want. I break the eye contact and shove myself upward.

He swears and rushes to match my pace. We scrabble for the top of the mast at the same time.

But he taps it a second earlier.

For an instant, I almost can't process that I've lost. We're both a little red-faced and breathless, glaring across the inches of net-ting that separate us. Anger fills my gut, chasing breath out of my lungs, leaving me speechless.

His chest is heaving from the exertion. I expect to find vic-tory in his eyes, but there's only relief. That chases some of my anger away.

Whatever is in that room, he *really* doesn't want me to see it.

Then he says mockingly, "At least you got to keep your dagger."

"Can you not win honorably, Captain?"

"Honor!" he snaps. "What do you know of—"

He breaks off, staring out at the sea. I follow his gaze, and it's like I've forgotten how high we are. The horizon tilts and shifts, and I want to close my eyes, but then I notice that those ships have drawn even closer.

"As I said," Rian grinds out, "what do you know of honor?"

He doesn't wait for an answer. The rigging tugs and pulls at my fingers as he begins to climb down.

Fine. I can do the same.

The climb is a lot more dizzying on the way down. On the way up, I was singularly focused. I wanted to win. I *needed* to win.

When I'm less than ten feet away from the deck, the pain in my hands begins to match the ache in my shoulder, and I allow myself to drop, springing onto the boards. Rian does the same.

The silence between us is louder than the crew on the deck.

"Who won?" says little Anya.

"I did," says Rian. "Despite the prince attempting to take advantage."

"You chose the challenge, Captain. You chose it *expecting* to have an advantage. You can't act as though I cheated just because I kept going."

"I would have been *well* ahead of you. I only stopped to make sure you weren't going to fall."

"Corrick," says Tessa. Her voice is a quiet rush. "Let me look at your hands."

My eyes meet hers, and it's a mistake. In her gaze, I see her worry, her unease, her longing.

For a moment, I almost give in. But I know what a mistake it is to seem vulnerable. I jerk my eyes away and press my fingers into my palms. "My hands are fine."

"It's done," Rian says. "I won. I suggest you get over it, Your Highness." He drops to a crouch and spins the blade.

I want to kick him in the face. I settle for claiming my jacket from Rocco. "You fought so hard to keep that room hidden that it's making your claims of *safety* seem a bit suspect, Captain."

He straightens to face me, while that blade keeps spinning between our feet. "I'll keep my people safe the way I see fit," he says.

The people on the deck have gone silent again, likely transfixed by this battle of wills. There's a part of me that enjoyed the climb— but a larger part of me wonders if I would have enjoyed a good fight a bit more. But as I discussed with Rocco, we're outnumbered here. If I threw a punch, I'm not entirely sure my guards would be able to keep me safe.

But still, Rian is glaring back at me. He's waiting for it. He's *ready* for it.

Then the blade stops, and it's pointing right at Tessa.

CHAPTER TWENTY-SIX

Tessa

The blade has stopped spinning, but unease has pooled in my belly, as if nothing will release the pressure between Rian and Corrick until they come to blows. I've seen Corrick climb a rope a hundred times, but this felt too loaded, too tense, too dangerous. When his foot slipped, my heart stopped dead in my chest.

But now they're back on the deck, and no one looks happy.

Little Anya says, "Miss Tessa. It's your turn."

I blink and look over. She points down at the dagger. The point has stopped right at the toe of my boot.

Rian and Corrick are still locked in a death stare, but I put a hand on the captain's arm. "Rian," I say quietly. "Continue the game. Tell me what you want."

He finally tears his gaze away, turning to meet mine.

"Yes," says Corrick. "Tell her what you want, Captain."

We're all so close, and it feels as though the boat could sway and tip me into one of them. Rian's eyes are on mine now, and my breathing goes shallow. I have no idea what he could ask for, and the moment stretches between us. Butterflies spin in my gut. He's so mad at Corrick. He's so protective of his crew. He's protective of *me*. Somehow I feel like a pawn and a princess all at the same time, both eager and afraid.

He takes a step closer to me, and I hold my breath. I half expect him to ask for something just to aggravate Corrick. *A kiss. An hour alone. An embrace.*

But Rian's eyes hold mine, and he doesn't ask for any of those things. "I want to know the purpose of those ships that are following us. I want to know how to ensure they turn back."

It's the first time his voice has ever been harsh toward me, and it's my turn to freeze. "I don't know," I say. His expression doesn't change, and I rush on, "Truly, I don't know."

"Prince Corrick does," he says. "My terms were very clear. I told you I wouldn't lead warships back to Ostriary."

"And I didn't send warships to follow you," Corrick says. "They're not *mine*."

"I realize that you think I'm just a stupid sailor," says Rian. "But even on my worst day, I know how to use a spyglass. I can see how those ships are outfitted."

"Then allow *me* to use your spyglass, because I have no idea where those ships came from."

Rian stares back at him. The tension somehow grows thicker.

Marchon steps forward. "Here," he says. He's offering a spyglass to Corrick. "We're close enough. That's the flag of Kandala, yes?"

Corrick takes the spyglass and looks. He's gone completely still.

"Your ships have no purpose this far into the ocean," Rian says. "So try again."

"I didn't send them," Corrick says again. He lowers the spyglass. Some of the animosity has disappeared from his voice. "Truly."

"I might have believed you when we were still in the river, but now we're too far south of Sunkeep. In another day we'll be in dangerous territory, and those ships *cannot* follow us."

"Because you think they'll wreck?" says Corrick. "If you're so concerned, maybe we should just wait and see how they fare." He pauses. "If you're as honorable as you say, their presence should be of no concern."

The captain runs a hand across the back of his neck, clearly agitated. His jaw is set, his shoulders tight. Rocco has moved close again.

Actually, so has Kilbourne. Sablo and Marchon aren't far either. For the first time, I realize that the tension has spread beyond just a battle of wills.

"Rian," I say softly. "If the king sent ships, it was protection for Corrick. They're not hostile."

He glances at me, but his eyes return to the prince. "Then your brother has put me in a bad position, Your Highness. Since you like to speak of advantages, I would like to remind you that you and your people are outnumbered. Your ships will not fire on mine while you are on board. It's no secret where your vulnerabilities lie—"

Rocco moves so swiftly that I'm barely aware he's *there*, blocking me and Corrick from the captain, one weapon drawn. Kilbourne is just to our side.

Sablo and Marchon are there, too. Lochlan is on his feet, glancing between the two men, but Gwyn has dragged her daughter out of the fray. I can hear the little girl squealing in protest, but my eyes are locked on the conflict.

I expect Rian to tell everyone to back down, the way he has before, but he's not the one to speak up. To my surprise, Corrick is.

"Rocco. Kilbourne. Stand down."

His voice is quiet and steady, and they obey—barely. They each take one step back.

Sablo and Marchon haven't moved. If they drew a weapon, Corrick would never be able to move in time.

"Captain," says Corrick, "if you don't like fighting on your ship, I suggest you not issue threats you can't walk back."

"I didn't threaten you." He glances at those ships on the water. "Kandala is the aggressor here."

I glance at Corrick and think of what he said about the rebels, about the king—how they listened to *me* when it came down to trust. But I have no idea how to fix . . . *this.*

I go to take a step forward, to somehow convince Rian that those ships aren't warships, but before I can move, Corrick catches my wrist. He doesn't look at me, but there's an urgency in his grip. A plea that I don't fully understand.

I go still again.

"Rian." My voice is too soft, and I wet my lips. "They're not warships," I say. "They're *not.* I know you think he's a villain, but Kandala truly needs medicine. Corrick might have done horrible things, but they're not bringing a battle to Ostriary. There's no purpose. They barely avoided a revolution. They wouldn't start a war with another country. I swear it, Rian. I *swear it.*"

He says nothing.

"Please," I say quietly. "Please believe me."

"That much is true," says Lochlan, and Rian's eyes shift his way.

Lochlan shrugs. "I might've hoped for the prince to fall—but we really do need medicine. They can barely manage their own people, Captain. Even if they wanted to attack Ostriary, there's hardly an army to fight."

Rian runs a hand across the back of his neck again. He hasn't looked this agitated before. It reminds me of the moment I begged him to continue the game, and he turned harsh eyes my way.

Corrick's hand is still on my wrist, but he still hasn't looked at me. "I think our competition may have gotten the best of us this evening, Captain." His voice is so smooth, the way he used to cajole Consul Sallister into yielding—because every word sounds absolutely sincere. "I give you my word that I do not know the origin of those ships, but I understand your suspicion. Perhaps we should make an early night of it so you and your crew can determine a way to move forward. If you'd like to return us to Port Karenin, I'd fully understand."

Rian studies him, and a muscle twitches in his jaw. Sablo and Marchon stand at his side, ready for whatever order their captain gives.

Corrick flexes his hand and grimaces. "In truth, I'd appreciate the time to find some tweezers and a bit of salve, because I obviously don't have the hands of a sailor."

One of the crewmen snorts. I think it's Tor. A ripple of quiet laughter goes through the people on deck. Rian looks like he wants to roll his eyes, but he doesn't. "Fine. Return to your quarters." He glances at Sablo. "Stand down," he says. "Allow him to leave."

Corrick turns to me. "Miss Cade, do you have any salve left?"

There's so much tension on deck that I don't know how to

respond to the formality, so I hesitate, then nod. "Yes—yes, Your Highness. I have some in my quarters."

He gives me a nod in return. "Excellent. Let's head below." He offers me his arm.

So much tension clings to the air that I don't know which location carries less risk: down below with Corrick, or up here with Rian. But if I stand here deliberating, it's going to make everything worse, and I sense that the dynamics have changed. I hold my breath and take his arm, and we descend the staircase in silence.

I feel Captain Blakemore's eyes on me the whole way.

—✦—

At the bottom of the stairs, I'm surprised when both guards take up stations in the narrow hallway. More than that: Kilbourne raps at the door of the quarters the guards are sharing, then orders a sleepy-eyed Silas to stand at the top of the staircase and keep watch.

"I'll get the salve and leave it with Rocco," I say to Corrick.

"I'll wait," he says, and there's something in his tone that reminds me of the way he insisted that Mistress Woolfrey not make him a new drink.

He's unsettled. That says more than anything he said to Rian on deck.

I swallow and nod and slip into my quarters. When I return with a satchel of supplies, Corrick is there waiting. I offer him the bag, but he gives me a look, then opens the door to his own quarters.

"Come in, Miss Cade."

I step past him into the room. Only two lanterns are lit, so the room is dim, and his eyes are shadowed, only revealing blue irises when the lanterns flicker.

Now that I'm here, I'm not sure what to say.

I jerk my eyes away from his and set my bag on the table, fishing through it for my salve. "I'll take care of your hands and leave you in peace," I say quickly. "Just let me—"

"I don't care about my hands," Corrick says. "And I don't want you to leave." He pauses, his eyes holding mine intently. "If you don't want to be in my presence, I'll join the guards in the hallway. But I'd rather not allow you out of my sight."

I frown. "Why?"

"When the captain speaks of my vulnerabilities, it's very clear what that means."

A cold spike of fear pierces my chest and lodges there. I don't know how to respond. This is like that moment in the carriage, when Corrick was afraid of Lochlan using me against him.

That was different, I said.

Was it? How?

It reminds me of another moment, the first night I had dinner with Corrick, when Consul Sallister himself threatened to cut off the supply of Moonflower to the entire Royal Sector. Corrick was smooth and assured, then, too.

Who just yielded? I said to him.

He did, but it looks like I did, Corrick replied. *And that's what's most important.*

I think about that moment he grabbed my arm on deck. The way he told Rocco and Kilbourne to stand down. The way the crew laughed when they thought he couldn't handle a little rope burn, when I've seen Corrick grit his teeth and not make a sound when a literal needle was stitching his skin back together.

"You pretended to yield," I say softly.

"Yes," Corrick says. "I know what men are capable of when they feel they have no other choices, Tessa. He is very worried about those ships."

"I don't think he would hurt me," I say.

"I certainly won't let him."

His voice hides the promise of violence, and I shiver again. "Maybe this isn't about the ships at all. Maybe he's angry that you keep demanding to know what's in that room."

"I have a right to demand it. The captain is hiding something, and I haven't yet decided whether it's worth the risk to force his hand."

"Just like you hid the ships!"

"I didn't send those ships," he says. "And as much as it might pain you to accept this, Captain Blakemore may be in charge of this vessel, but he is not in charge of Kandala or Ostriary. He is a means to an end."

"It looks like you lied."

"If I'm responsible for every moment of suffering in Kandala since the assassination of my parents, then *lying* shouldn't come as much of a surprise."

I study him in the darkness. His voice is cool and smooth, the voice of the King's Justice, but I've known for a while how many masks he can wear. He's been so sharp and prickly since we climbed on board this ship that I've been judging him the same way.

If I'm responsible for every moment of suffering in Kandala.

With a start, I realize Corrick isn't just talking about Captain Blakemore's perception of him. He's talking about me. Lochlan. The people in that candy shop. Everyone.

Including himself.

I realign everything he's said since he got on board. I was way-laid by Lochlan's comments, and my doubts were reinforced by Rian's own thoughts about Corrick.

But the prince got on this ship because he wanted a better way.

I haven't yet decided whether it's worth the risk to force his hand.

So Corrick risked his life instead of picking a fight.

And when a fight seemed apparent, Corrick all but threw himself on his own sword.

It's exactly what he did when he was in the palace. He couldn't fight Allisander Sallister without risking everything, so he went out into the Wilds to help people in a different way.

All while allowing everyone to think he was the most vicious man in the country.

I move to the table and pick up the jar of salve. "Will you let me take a look at your hands?"

"I told you. My hands are fine."

I draw an exasperated breath and stride across the room to him. I let my bag drop to the floor and seize his wrist.

I half expect him to pull away from me, but he doesn't resist at all. In fact, he looks somewhat amused. "Your bedside manner has grown rather rough."

I gentle my grip. "I'm sorry. I thought—" I stop myself. "I don't know what I thought."

"You thought I'd fight you."

Yes.

But I can't say that, because it feels like we're talking about something else entirely, and my heart skips a beat. We're so close together. I can breathe in his scent, and it reminds me of when we'd stand together in the workshop, when it was just the two of us against the night.

I uncurl his fingers to find two of them already red and blistered, with a neat tear in the skin across his palm. The injury isn't terrible, but I'm sure it hurts.

"Come sit," I say. "Let me wrap it for the night."

He studies me, his eyes searching mine, but then he nods.

I pull a roll of muslin from my pack, along with some other herbs, and we drop into the seats. I open the jar of salve and dab some onto the worst of the wounds. His hand rests in mine, warm and steady, and he's so quiet that I can hear each inhale.

When I glance up, his eyes are right there, watching me.

"I can't believe you did this," I say quietly.

"You think I should've just let go? You're not the only one, I'm sure."

"No. I meant the climbing. The competition."

"I wanted an answer." He pauses. "You climbed the mast, too."

"Well, I wasn't racing. It was still terrifying." My heart jumps at the memory of the spinning sky, the rough water below. "Why was he acting like you cheated?"

"When I slipped," he says, "the captain stopped to tell me how to guide my feet back onto the ropes. In doing so, he lost his chance to take the lead."

I frown and shake my head. "I don't understand why he would help you if he's worried that you and Harristan are working against him. Do you think there's any chance that he's being earnest? That maybe he really is worried you're going to take advantage of *him*?"

"No. I think I'm the king's brother, and it wouldn't go well for him if I fell to my death."

"Hmm." I pat a final bit of salve into the injury, then begin to wrap his hand with muslin. "Maybe he sees you as a man trying to keep his brother on the throne through any means possible, while he's just trying to help everyone."

"I've told you before that I'd walk out of the palace if I could. Harristan probably would, too. And then what? We leave governing to Allisander? Or Baron Pepperleaf? Do you really think that would be better?"

No, I don't.

Just when I tie off a knot, he closes his fingers around mine, and I look up.

"I'm sorry," he says.

I hold his gaze, and I think of all the things he could be apologizing for, and I swallow.

Then he continues, "I'm sorry *I* can't be altruistic."

That wasn't even on my list. I frown. "Don't be silly."

His thumb brushes my wrist. "I know he caught your eye at dinner. I know he seems to be everything you want."

My heart thumps hard in my chest. "He's not everything I—"

"Yes," Corrick says. "He is. I know he is."

"How?" I whisper. "How do you know that?"

"Because he's the kind of man Weston Lark would be, if he were real."

"He's not—" My chest is tight, and I have to take a breath. "He's not Weston Lark."

"I'm not either, Tessa." He pauses, considering. "The other day, Rian compared my actions as King's Justice to locking someone in a room without food or water, then punishing them for trying to escape. I hate him, but I hate that he keeps making me think that he's *right*, that Harristan and I have solved nothing. That we've only created more problems."

I stare at him. "Corrick. You haven't locked anyone in a room."

"Tessa." He gives me a look.

"No! I mean—you *have*. But that's not his analogy. You didn't cause the illness. You didn't force people into this situation. The fever sickness *isn't your fault*."

He frowns and looks away.

"Do you understand that?" I say. "There are a lot of things that you could have done differently—but this part is not your fault. It's not." I swallow. "If the fevers locked people in a room to starve, you were the guard sneaking them food and water."

"So were you." He finally lets go of my hand, but it's only to reach up and touch a finger to my cheek, tracing the line of my jaw. I shiver.

He frowns and draws back. "Forgive me."

"No! You don't—I don't—it's—you're—"

A line forms between his brows as I stumble over my words, and I blow a breath out through my teeth. Corrick is terrible and wonderful and aggravating and inspiring, and somehow he manages all of it, all at once. He allows everyone to think the worst of him, and all the while, he sacrifices everything *he* wants for the betterment of others. I don't know if I want to punch him in the face or wrap my arms around him.

I make a frustrated sound and throw my arms around his neck. "I hate you so much."

He catches me, but lightly, his hands soft against my waist. "I've always told you that would work out for the best."

And then I realize that his hands haven't moved, that I might be attached to his neck like he's a life raft keeping me above water, but he's holding me like perhaps I've mistaken him for someone else.

I draw back a bit so I can see his eyes. I don't hate him at all. Not really. But I think of our argument at sunrise yesterday. Every word he spoke was true, but he was so biting, so cruel.

"You're still doing it," I say.

"Doing what?"

"Hiding who you are."

He ducks away, but I put a palm against his cheek, and he goes still.

"You are," I say. "You say you can't be altruistic—but I think you can. I think you *want* to be. Instead, you set everyone you meet as an adversary. You turn people into opponents before they have a chance to be an ally. Even the day I snuck into the palace and you had me chained in your quarters, you could have been kind, and you could have been gentle, and you could've *explained*."

His eyes close. His jaw is so tight.

I brush my thumb against his cheek, tracing the skin his mask once covered. "You said you never took the mask off in the Wilds because you couldn't take a chance that I might recognize you. But I don't think that's true. I think you were afraid for me to know who you were. I think the King's Justice is afraid to be vulnerable, even in front of me."

He flinches.

"Cory," I whisper, and his breath catches.

"You don't like who I am, Tessa."

"I don't like who you pretend to be." I swallow, and it hurts. "I love the man I think you are. But sometimes it takes me a little while to figure out which one is real, and which one is just another face you show others."

His eyes search mine, but he says nothing.

"Like when you came on board," I say. "That first night." My cheeks grow warm, but I force myself to keep going. "You were so careful in the palace, and then we were here, and I thought maybe—"

"I know what you thought." His voice is rough. "I stepped onto this ship, and I realized what I was leaving behind. What I was risking. And I was so relieved that we would be facing it together. It reminded me of the Wilds, and I . . . I found myself regretting all the times we could have been together, and I stopped you. Because you're right about everything. I know what Lochlan said, and I now realize how it seemed, and for that, I apologize. Truly."

"I'm sorry, too."

"Lord, Tessa. Never apologize to me. You always make me better."

"Is that really what you think?" He frowns, and I rush on, "In the candy shop, I thought you were going to kill that man."

"I didn't."

"No! I know you didn't." I can't meet his eyes now. "But I thought you were going to, and when you didn't, I was . . . I was so worried that the only reason you didn't kill him was because I was standing right there."

His lip quirks up, as if he's somewhat confounded but also amused. "I feel as though you're proving my point."

"No! I just—" I blow a breath through my teeth and stare at him. I know exactly what he means about vulnerability, because this is so hard to say while looking into his eyes. My voice is very small. "Sometimes . . . sometimes you are still very frightening."

He inhales, but I put a hand up. "Wait!" I say. "Please. The worst part is that . . . is that I know you *have* to be. I've seen that. I know the King's Justice can't be some benevolent figure either. I know what's at risk for you and Harristan. I do." I pause. "I just . . . I wish sometimes your illusions weren't *so* effective."

"No illusions now," he says.

It's the same thing he said to me once before, when he was covered in blood and shaking from what he'd had to do to two men who'd attempted to escape from the Hold.

But this is different. This *moment* is different. My heart flutters, but Corrick draws himself up, putting distance between us.

"When we were in Kandala," he says, "I should have made some declarations." He pauses, studying me. "I regret that I didn't, because now I worry that I'm too late."

"You're not too late," I say softly.

"I love you, Tessa," he says, and I inhale sharply, because I wasn't ready for him to come right out with it.

He touches a finger to my lips. "Let me finish."

I nod.

"I have always loved you," he says. "I love your brilliance and your courage. I love your faith in me, and your faith in my brother, and your faith in Kandala." His hand slides to my cheek, and his blue eyes soften, filling my vision. "I don't ever want to frighten you. I want to take actions that will make you proud." His jaw clenches, just for a moment. "But I will never be wholly altruistic. Even now, I want to go back on deck and make him regret even *insinuating* that he would use you against me—"

"Corrick."

"He can want to do what's right for Ostriary, Tessa—while *also* knowing that earning your trust is a way to manipulate me."

I clamp my mouth shut. I hate that all of this feels so calculated.

"I need you to realize that your life is bigger than you think," Corrick says. "I need you to realize that you are important to me, and to my brother, and to all of Kandala. Do you think just anyone could have snuck into the palace and convinced Harristan to try a new dosage? Tessa, when those men took us prisoner, I spent much of that walk thinking of every terrible thing I could do to them, just for causing you pain, because I know how much you've risked. How much you've *wanted* for the people of Kandala. Sometimes I look at Lochlan, and I remember, and I want to—"

My breath catches, my heart thumping in my chest, and he breaks off.

"Well." Corrick raises a rueful eyebrow. "My point is that I did none of it. You found a way to forgive them, and so I found a way to forgive them." He pauses, and his voice grows grave. "You said I see everyone as an adversary. But since the moment my parents died, that's all I've had. Adversaries. I've had to fight to hold Kandala together. I've had to fight to keep my brother safe. And now, if I have to, I'll fight to hold on to you."

I swallow and lift a hand to cover his, holding his bandaged palm to my cheek.

He brushes a thumb along my cheekbone. "If you'd allow me, I would say all that and more once we return to the Royal Sector. I would officially declare our courtship before the king. But only if you want the same, Tessa."

His eyes are so honest, dark blue in the dim candlelight. This reminds me of the moment we kissed in the workshop, the first time I saw him as Wes and Corrick all rolled into one man. It reminds me of the way I was sitting on the deck, and he brought me food, even though we were at odds. It reminds me of our first carriage ride together, when I was terrified of him, and he offered me a pouch full of silver and a dagger from his belt, and he told me how to find freedom.

Impulsively, I reach forward and put my arms around his neck again.

This time he catches me for real, his hands secure against my back. He smells so warm, so familiar. I press my face into his neck.

I missed you, I think.

Because I did.

I blink, and the world goes blurry. Tears sit on my lashes.

Corrick must feel the shift in my emotions, because he draws back. He *tsks* under his breath, then touches a thumb to my cheek, brushing a tear away.

"Do you still hate me?" he says softly.

"No," I whisper, like it's a secret. "I love you."

He leans closer. "What's that?" he teases. "I can't hear you."

"I said you're a huge pain in my—"

I break off with a squeal when he kisses me, then melt into his hands when he pulls me close.

"Will you stay here with me?" he says quietly, and I freeze. Before I can say anything else, he adds, "Things are so precarious with Captain Blakemore. If something were to happen, I don't want the guards to have to split their attention."

The room is so quiet, and so warm, and the boat rocks beneath us. He might be right to worry, and he might not.

But tonight, we're alone, darkness pressing against the window.

Tonight, like before, it's the two of us against the night.

"Will you?" he says, his thumb stroking over my lip.

I stare into his blue eyes and nod. "Yes."

CHAPTER TWENTY-SEVEN

Tessa

Eventually, we have to sleep, and I don't really know *when* he drags me to the bed, just that we're somehow *there*.

"I'll sleep on the floor," he says. "I want to hear if anyone gives the guards trouble."

"I'm pretty sure it's a crime to allow the King's Justice to sleep on the floor," I say, but my heart skips, because it sounds a bit coy.

I thought it would make him smile, but it doesn't. "I rather doubt it. Harristan left me to sleep in a *cell*, if you recall." He grabs a pillow and one of the blankets, then moves to the door, dousing one of the lanterns on his way.

For a moment, I don't think he's serious, but he unlaces his boots to kick them free, then unbuckles his jacket to toss it over the back of a chair. When his hands fall on the hem of his shirt, my breath catches, and he stops, his eyes glittering in the shadows.

I realize I'm staring at him, and my cheeks catch on fire. I flop back on the bed and drag a pillow over my face. "Sorry."

He laughs softly. "Don't be sorry."

"I've seen you shirtless before."

Fabric rustles. "Ah, yes. So you're immune."

"Completely." I slide the pillow down, peeking around the edge.

He's wrapped in the blanket already, lying on the cold, hard wood of the floorboards. His eyes are on me now, and I unlace my own boots to kick them free, then untie my vest.

"You're not getting a show either," I say.

"Good. Because I'm *not* immune."

The heat on my cheeks goes nowhere. I crawl under my own blankets and reach to lower the flame of the other lantern, leaving us with little more than moonlight and the rhythmic creaking of the ship.

But as I lie there in the silence, I think about everything he said. I've always risked my life to help others, but my choices have always been simple, because I've never had much to lose. If I were thrown into the Hold or killed while distributing medicine in the Wilds, the world would keep on spinning.

But Corrick always has so much more at risk. I've been judging him and Rian by the same standards—by the standards I would apply to myself—but now I wonder if that's been fair.

Corrick and Harristan have an entire country to lose. Their choices have threats and vulnerabilities built into each one.

For the first time, I wonder what Rian has to lose.

Across the room, Corrick shifts his weight, and I glance over.

"Corrick," I say softly.

"Tessa?"

"Come lie in the bed."

It's too dark to see him clearly from here, but I can sense the weight of his eyes. I wonder if he'll refuse. But then fabric rustles, and he uncurls in the darkness, approaching slowly, the faint moonlight revealing the shadows and lines of his body.

I shift over to make room. His bed is narrow, and not quite wide enough for two people, but he slips in beside me. Despite my shirt and trousers, I can feel his warmth, and somehow it makes me shiver.

"Are you cold?" he says. He doesn't wait for an answer; he just rises up on one elbow to arrange the blankets.

"No," I say quickly. "I'm not cold."

He's looking down at me, his eyes fixed on mine, affectionate yet predatory, gentle yet primal. Something inside me grips tight, stealing my breath.

Corrick lifts a hand as if to stroke my face, but I put a hand against his shoulder before he can touch me.

"Wait," I whisper, and he does. He holds there, one hand half lifted, the other braced against the bed to support his weight. It's doing impressive things to the musculature of his arms, especially when combined with the tiny remaining glow from the lantern.

But he waits, no impatience in his eyes.

I don't know what I wanted him to wait for. Maybe it's exactly this: reassurance that no matter what everyone else sees in him, his word is true.

A scar cuts across his bicep, and I trace a finger over the line. His skin is smooth and warm. "How did you get this one?"

His eyes don't leave mine. "The night patrol caught a smuggler in the Sorrowlands. It's a two-day journey to the Royal Sector. Somewhere along the way, he was able to fashion—and hide—a makeshift blade."

"You're lucky he didn't sever a tendon."

"I'm lucky he didn't stab me right in the heart. That was his goal."

I think of how quickly he dodged the attacker in the candy shop—but I don't want to think about *that* Corrick.

I run my fingers along another scar, this time on his abdomen, and his breath shudders a tiny bit. "What about this one?"

"Ah . . . big man out of Steel City. Took a blade off one of the Hold guards."

It looks like a puncture wound. "He stabbed you?"

He nods. "I was sixteen. I thought that one was going to do me in. It took ages to heal."

Sixteen. I fight to keep a frown off my face. Sometimes I forget how long he's been doing this, how young he was when he was forced to become someone terrible.

He has another deep scar on his lower back, I remember. I reach up to trace the jagged line to where it disappears under the waistband of his trousers, my fingers slipping under the edge of the fabric.

He hisses a breath, and his eyes close. "You're killing me, Tessa."

"Tell me about this one," I say.

"That one wasn't a smuggler." He smiles, a little fondly, a little sadly. "That was the result of boyish nonsense with Harristan."

"Climbing trees?" I say, and I'm only partly teasing.

"Racing horses in the snow. I was in the lead, but the horse slipped, and I came off. Harristan's horse nearly ran right over top of me. I broke two ribs, too. I thought Mother was going to kill us both." His tone sounds like it's dangerously close to turning too heavy, so he presses a hand to my cheek, his thumb tracing under my eye. "How about you? Any dangerous apothecary scars for me to discover?"

"Just one. Nothing exciting."

"Hmm." His finger keeps tracing the line of my face, but his blue eyes hold me captive. The boat rocks and sways, but I'm content to stay here and inhale his scent. I wait for him to try for more, because I'm here in his bed. I'm not sure I would *mind* if he tried for more.

But his hand keeps stroking my face, and ventures no farther. My eyes begin to drift closed.

"Are you afraid?" I whisper.

"No. I'm ready."

I look up at him. "Do you really think we're in danger tonight?"

He leans down and brushes a kiss against my forehead. "Let's just say that I'll be surprised if Blakemore lets us sleep till morning."

—✦—

We do sleep till morning.

Well, I do. I have no idea whether Corrick slept at all. When my eyes open, the room is almost fully dark, the remaining lantern burning through the last dregs of oil. The ship is tossing more violently this morning. I don't know what time it is, but it must be early, because there's barely any light in the porthole. We're tangled up in the blankets, his breath warm against the shell of my ear.

Locked in this room, feeling the heat of Corrick's body at my back, I could forget everything happening on the other side of the door.

The only reminder that keeps bringing things to the forefront of my mind is the brisk rocking of the ship.

"We made it to morning," I say.

"Yes, we did. Hopefully he's not waiting on the other side of that door to execute us."

His voice is full of sarcasm, but there's a note of truth hidden in there, too.

"What if the ships have drawn closer?" I say.

"If they have, I suspect Captain Blakemore will make good on his threat to return us to Port Karenin. We'll disembark and book passage back to the Royal Sector. But that's assuming those ships were sent by Harristan and that they mean us no harm."

"Do you think he sent them?"

"No. I truly don't." He goes still, his eyes fixed on mine. "Harristan would have no reason to send them. He's good for his word, Tessa."

"What did you see in the spyglass?"

"They do fly under the flag of Kandala. That means *someone* sent them—and it's someone with funding, because outfitting two brigantines as fast as we set sail would have been *very* costly. So that indicates one of the consuls."

"Allisander?"

He winces. "Maybe? I'm actually wondering if Laurel Pepperleaf begged her father to allow her to follow us. She wanted to come along."

"So she just . . . forced her way here?"

"Are you surprised?"

I sigh, thinking of how earnest the young woman seemed. "Well, maybe a little. But could you explain that to Rian?"

"I could, but he's too nervous about those ships—and I'd have no way to prove it. I'm not sure it would matter, anyway. I think there's more at play than just worries about us leading forces to Ostriary."

"Why else would he worry?"

"I think he's worried about whatever is hidden on board this ship." Corrick runs a hand through his hair. "If it *is* Laurel, she's doing it in defiance of Harristan, and we already have a rocky relationship with all the consuls. I'm worried about whoever else might be working against him. Whoever might be *helping* her." He draws a heavy breath. "I just want to get to Ostriary safely so we can negotiate for steel and Moonflower. I don't want to worry about threats to my brother. I don't want to worry about warships that might mean to interfere with this—"

He breaks off.

"What?" I say. "What happened?"

Corrick sits up in bed and runs a hand across his face. "Before we left, there were rumors about the guards. Rocco chose Kilbourne and Silas for this trip because he said Captain Huxley wasn't trustworthy. But Rocco also said that Harristan was suspicious of me for *months* before he discovered what you and I were doing." He looks at me. "Did my brother do the same thing to me that he did to Lochlan? Was he getting *me* out of the way?" Before I can even answer, he rakes a hand back through his hair. "But then . . . was Rocco a part of it? Why would he—"

"Corrick. Corrick, *stop*." I sit up, putting a hand on his wrist. "Harristan was *not* getting you out of the way."

"I wish I knew who sent those ships. Maybe my brother wasn't getting me out of the way, but it's not a secret that I'm alone in the middle of the ocean. Someone else could." He glances at me, then at the door. "I wish I knew what Rian was keeping in that room."

He sighs. "I'm reluctant to believe it's more weapons. He's too worried about those ships for him to have a full arsenal." He makes a scoffing sound. "There's a part of me that wants to take a hammer to the lock."

"If that's what it will take to satisfy you, then do it."

His eyes flare in surprise, and he smiles ruefully. "Weston Lark might have been able to get away with it, but I don't need our dear Captain Blakemore arriving in Ostriary with stories of how the king's brother can't be trusted."

I frown. He's right. I don't have any doubt that Rian would portray the prince exactly as he is, reputation and all.

"I could feel the tension on deck," Corrick continues. "Even if I wanted to break in, I have no doubt my every move is watched. On our first night, Rocco mentioned that it's easy to defend our rooms here—but it's also easy for them to note when we leave."

"What do you think he could be hiding?" I say.

"Barrels of gunpowder for the cannons?" he says. "Bricks of gold? His father's corpse? I truly have no idea." He sighs. "And with the other ships following us, I'm left to wonder if they know something I don't. Did Harristan discover something after we left? Are the ships a means to *rescue* me? But if they are . . . why would they keep their distance? Those are brigantines, with coal-fired engines to support the sails. They're too big to be nimble, but they *are* fast."

"Do you think they're a threat to you?" I say quietly.

"I don't want to think so," he says. "But if they're not a threat to me, then they're a threat to Rian and his crew—and we're on the boat. It's clear that their presence makes him very anxious."

And there's no way to figure out anything about those ships. Not from here.

I turn my thoughts back to the secret room. On what Corrick just said.

Weston Lark might have been able to get away with it.

But maybe not. Weston Lark may have been an outlaw, but he wasn't a thief. Not really. He knew where to find Moonflower petals by virtue of his position—or he'd buy them outright and bring them to our workshop.

I didn't have that luxury.

"What if you didn't smash it?" I say. My mouth has gone a bit dry, but my brain is as sharp as ever. "What if we could find out what's inside that room without leaving any evidence?"

"Captain Blakemore surely still has people watching me—"

"Not you," I say. "Me."

Corrick's eyes are intent and fixed on mine. "You."

"I may not be a good liar, and I'd make a terrible spy. But perhaps you've forgotten, Your Highness." I twist my fingers with his and smile. "Before I was an apothecary in service to the king, I was a rather good thief."

CHAPTER TWENTY-EIGHT

Harristan

We're stopped at the gate.

At first, this isn't a surprise. I don't have a pocket watch on me, but it's still early, and ever since explosives made it into the Royal Sector, the guards at the gate are more cautious about closed carriages.

Thorin and Saeth are palace guards, though, in livery that designates them as members of my personal guard. Our halt at the sector gates shouldn't take long. A pause, nothing more.

It's more.

As time ticks on, I look across the carriage at Quint, who's trying not to look worried, but I can see in his eyes that he's registered the delay, too.

I strain my ears to listen, but the voices are a bare rumble of unintelligible sound. The carriage windows are set with thick glass—meant to maintain privacy *inside*—and we have the wool curtains drawn closed so no one could see me. My heartbeat finds a rapid rhythm and refuses to settle.

I shift to the window, ignoring the throb in my leg when the wound pulls and aches. I slide a hand below the curtain and gently ease the latch to the side, then push with my fingertip to slide the glass as slowly as possible.

Quint is watching me with wide eyes, but he says nothing. It looks like he's holding his breath, listening just as hard as I am.

"—king's business," Thorin is saying, his voice muffled and distant because he must be on the other side of the carriage. "You have no right to demand a search of this vehicle."

My eyes lock on Quint's. If anyone sees me like this, the rumors would not be good.

And why are they demanding a search?

"We've been given orders directly from the palace," a man says sharply. "No one enters the sector without being searched."

"I didn't give those orders," I whisper to Quint. "Was this because I was missing?"

His expression is grave. "No. No one was aware you were missing." He takes a deep breath and flicks his gaze over my form, from my injured leg to the bloodstains that seem to be everywhere. "I should've thought to bring appropriate attire."

Outside the carriage, Thorin is snapping at the gate guard. "Our orders supersede yours. You will stand down and allow us to pass."

"You will allow us to search your carriage, or you will have to answer to Captain Huxley," says the gate guard. The door to the carriage rattles, and I freeze, drawing back against the wall as if I could disappear.

But then something slams against the door, and Saeth speaks.

"If you try to force your way into this carriage, you will find a fight you're not ready for."

I don't know what's happening. I don't know why we're being stopped, or why they're demanding to search this carriage.

I do know my guards shouldn't risk their lives because I'm scared of idle gossip.

I steel my spine and shift forward, intending to open the door, to put an end to this. I'll declare myself and we can be on our way.

But then the gate guard snorts and says, "What's wrong? Did you catch the king yourself? I'm not looking to snag your reward. I'm just following orders."

I stop with my hand on the latch.

The door rattles and Saeth snaps again. "I told you not to touch this door."

What reward? I mouth to Quint.

A line has appeared across his brow, and he shakes his head. *I don't know.*

"What reward?" Thorin demands.

"For the capture of the king," says the guardsman, as if it's obvious. "For what he's done."

For an instant, the air outside the carriage is absolutely silent, and those words hang in the air dangerously. I'm staring at Quint, and it's hard to breathe. I have no doubt my guards are outside this carriage, deliberating the best course of action.

The gate guard must figure it out at the same time, because I hear the click of a crossbow. "You *do* have the king! Larriant, call for the captain! Send for the night pa—"

Someone throws a punch, and something heavy collides with the carriage. The vehicle jolts and lurches forward, turning so quickly that I'm thrown back against the seat. The sudden movement jars my leg, and I cry out, just as the carriage begins to tilt to the side. Hooves pound against turf, but we're still turning, and I feel myself slam into the wall. We're going to tip over. We're going to *crash*. My stomach flip-flops.

But then Quint grabs my arm and hauls me away from the side, and the suddenness of our movement slams the wheels back into the ground. The carriage bounces *hard*, then fishtails on the path, then finally straightens out. Shouting erupts outside the carriage, and a few arrows strike the outer walls, but we're traveling fast.

We're both a bit sprawled on the floor, and I'm breathing like we've run a race, but I look at Quint. "Thank you," I say. "That's the second time you've saved my life."

He's breathing hard, too. "Crashing didn't seem like a good option, Your Majesty."

"We still might." The carriage is going too fast for the terrain, and we rock and sway every time we hit a rough spot.

I want to demand information, but Quint is just as trapped as I am. I don't even know if we're heading into the Royal Sector or away from it.

I ignore the pain in my leg to lever myself back to the window, then jerk the curtain to the side. A jagged crack splits the glass, but it still holds. Trees are flying past, alarmingly fast.

We're heading back into the Wilds.

I look at Quint. "I don't know where we're going," I say, and I choke on my breath. This is worse than waking up in Violet's barn, terrified of who might walk through the doorway. At least then I wasn't worried about the barn crashing down around me. "I don't even know who has us now."

What reward?

For the capture of the king. For what he's done.

My breathing threatens to go thin and reedy, stealing all my thoughts while my body strains for survival. I focus on slowing each breath, until I can *think*.

"I trust Thorin," Quint says.

"I do too. I just don't know if he's still driving this carriage." I cast a glance at the window and wonder if we should risk jumping out. Landing in a pile of broken bones doesn't seem like it would have much of an advantage.

I skip my eyes over his attire. I have no idea whether he can fight, but he's not armed. I'm not either. But most of the palace carriages are outfitted with hidden weapons from a time when we had frequent cause to travel outside the Royal Sector, when bandits and outlaws were a concern for the royal family.

I tug at the velvet casing beneath the rear seat, then thrust my hand inside.

Nothing but dust.

Quint is a quick study, and he's checking the opposite side before I even need to order him to do it.

He withdraws two daggers, both small, both coated in dust. I can see rust along the edge of one blade. Quint brushes them off against the floor of the carriage, and I cough.

"Forgive me," he says.

"For what?" I wheeze. "Give me one."

The weapon is hardly longer than the width of my hand, but I grip the hilt and brace myself against the wall opposite the door. No more arrows have struck the carriage, but branches whip the walls and trees fly past the narrow window. We're still traveling dangerously fast.

And then . . . we're not. The carriage slows.

I look at Quint. "We're going to leap out. Be ready to run."

He glances at my injured leg. "Can you run?"

No. Even leaping is going to be a challenge. But I don't say that. "Just be ready."

"I'm not leaving our injured king—"

"I'm *ordering* you."

The carriage slows further, but his eyes don't leave mine. "Then I suppose you'll have to have Corrick issue a decree of punishment, Your Majesty."

"Quint!"

The carriage stops. He tightens his grip on the dagger and finally drags his eyes away from mine, but he doesn't move.

Lord. I grit my teeth.

The door is flung open, and sunlight floods the gap, but I can't see much more than that because Quint launches himself forward. A man swears, and there's a scuffle, but by the time I make it to the doorway myself, Quint is in the dirt with a bloody nose. Thorin is standing over him, looking a bit bemused.

"Master Quint?" he says. "Exactly what was your plan?"

"In retrospect," Quint says, wincing, "it's unclear."

"Defending me," I say. I limp down from the carriage, then hold out a hand to Quint. I keep my eyes on Thorin. "We weren't sure who had the carriage. Where's Saeth?"

"Unharnessing the horses, Your Majesty. The road is too narrow to continue with the carriage, and it's too obvious a target."

I run a hand over the back of my neck. Sweat mixes with the dirt from last night, and I grimace. "And why am I a *target*?"

"We don't know," Thorin says. "If they'd summoned the night patrol, we might not have been able to get away. As it is, they're likely giving chase. We should not delay." He glances at my leg. "Can you walk, Your Majesty?"

"Yes, but not far." I tuck the dusty dagger under my belt and look up and around. We're deep in the woods, surrounded by trees, far off a worn path, but nothing seems familiar.

Still, four people and two horses won't take long to spot. Especially not beside a carriage.

"Thorin," I say. "Do you know the way to Tessa's old workshop from here?"

He hesitates, then looks around the way I just did. When his gaze returns to meet mine, he nods. "I do."

"Good." I look past him, to where Saeth is leading the two horses away from the abandoned carriage. Their harness leather has been abandoned in the dirt beside the shaft, leaving the animals bareback, in nothing but driving bridles, complete with long reins and blinders. They're already snatching at the reins, blowing anxiously, sweat-slick and confused by everything we've already done.

If we're confronted by the night patrol, these horses aren't going to get us far.

But standing here worrying about it won't solve the problem. If this is the best we have, it'll have to do.

I let out a long breath. "Thorin. Check the path ahead. We'll follow."

—+—

It's only been a matter of weeks, but the trail leading to the workshop is overgrown, and once we get inside, we discover that a thick layer of dust clings to everything. I run a finger along the work table, then stifle a cough as a plume of dust lifts into the air. It's clear no one has been here since the night the rebels attacked the palace.

It made for a good hiding place then, and it makes for a good one now.

A narrow cabinet is bolted into the wall near the cold hearth, and Quint is checking the drawers. I order Saeth to tether the horses and walk a perimeter, then call for Thorin to join us in the workshop.

When he does, I waste no time. "This is another act of insurrection," I say. "Though this one appears to be more insidious. Do you think Saeth could be involved with whoever is working against me?"

If he's surprised, it doesn't show. "No."

"Are you certain?"

"As certain as I can be. Saeth and I have served together for over five years now. We were chosen for your personal guard together." He pauses. "If he were working against you, he could have aided the guards at the gate and they could've taken the carriage. There were four of them."

I work that through in my head, trying to think of any reason why it would be more advantageous to allow me to escape, and I come up with nothing.

I run a hand across the back of my neck again, then take a long breath.

We can't stay here forever.

I need information.

I glance from Thorin to Quint and wonder how far rumor has spread. They've only been out of the palace for a few hours, but clearly Arella, Laurel, and Captain Huxley were able to take advantage of my notable absence. Quint might have been able to leave quietly, but if anyone came looking for me . . .

I sigh. My leg is throbbing again, and I can't seem to think past it. I can't remember the last time I had water, or anything to eat.

I drop into the chair gracelessly, and I must be a bit woozy, because I land clumsily, then bite back a yelp as my wound strikes the arm of the chair. I'm gritting my teeth so hard I can taste blood.

Or maybe I've bitten the inside of my cheek. A bloom of sweat breaks out on my forehead. I inhale slowly through my teeth because the alternative is to start swearing and never stop.

Quint steps away from the cabinet, takes one look at me, and glances at the guard. "See if there's fresh water in the rain barrel, Thorin. You and Saeth should strip your palace livery. Is there anything nearby? We'll need food, at the very least."

"Yes, Master Quint." The door hinges creak in protest, and then he's gone.

I close my eyes and let out that breath. The tiny workshop is suddenly very silent.

But then Quint speaks, and his voice is closer than I expect. "Your Majesty," he says quietly. "You're bleeding again."

My eyes blink open, and I look down. He's right. Along the tear in my trousers, fresh blood has soaked through.

"Tessa had more rolls of muslin in the cabinet," Quint says. "We should bind the wound." He hesitates. "If I may . . ."

I shift my weight and wince. "Go ahead."

As he wraps the bandage, he says nothing, and I grow very aware of his closeness. It's a weird kind of intimacy, and not altogether uncomfortable.

I once bound his wounds as well. Just like this, in this very workshop.

Now we're even, I think.

But Quint looks up, and his hands go still, and I realize I've said the words aloud.

He confirms it when he says, "What was that?"

I don't repeat it. "You ignored my order in the carriage."

He inhales like he's going to protest, but then must think better of it. "I'll await your judgment, Your Majesty. But I promised Corrick that I would look after you—"

"*Look after?* Quint, I'm not a child."

He tugs the bandage tight, and I hiss a breath through my teeth.

He meets my eyes, but he doesn't apologize. "I am well aware."

Then he knots off the bandage and straightens, moving away.

I feel off-balance, off-kilter, like too many people have confused me in succession. Before I can puzzle it out, Thorin returns with a bucket of water from the rain barrel. He's in his shirtsleeves now, but no less armed.

"Saeth is going to walk toward Artis," he says. "He's got a pocket full of coins, so he'll see if we can purchase some food. But I don't think we should stay here for long. They'll eventually discover the carriage. We've had days of rain. Our tracks won't be hard to follow."

"I don't know which consuls are working against me," I say. "If I try to find sanctuary with any of them, we might as well hand ourselves over right now."

Quint lights the tiny stove in the corner and pours water into the kettle, then sets it to boil. "We can't return to the Royal Sector, surely."

"If they're spreading word that there's a reward for capturing the king," Thorin adds, "we'll be hard-pressed to find sanctuary anywhere."

Because people will do anything for silver—or access to medicine. I know that better than anyone.

I study both of them. "Do you think this was a trick? Was

Captain Blakemore a ruse to separate me from Corrick, to remove the King's Justice before Consul Cherry and Captain Huxley took action?"

"Possibly," says Thorin.

His answer is quick, and I frown. A spike of fear enters my heart. I believed Captain Blakemore. I was inspired by his eagerness to help the people of Kandala. I admired the loyalty of his crew.

I encouraged Corrick to get on that ship.

But Quint says, "I don't think Captain Blakemore was a part of this. His documentation was solid. His story seemed sound. It would be an unnecessarily complicated plan if their goal was simply to separate you from Corrick—especially if they have the guards on their side." He pauses. "To me, it's more likely that whoever conspires against the Crown realized Corrick was gone, and the rebel leader was gone, so the time to overthrow the king was *now*."

"And here I am," I say bitterly, "trapped in a tiny workshop once again, while others attempt to take the throne." I scowl and try to ignore the throbbing pain in my leg. "Only this time, there's a bounty on my head, and the guards have been turned against me."

"Not all, Your Majesty," says Thorin.

Not all. I'm grateful for that, but I'm not sure what the four of us are going to do against the entire kingdom.

I think of young Violet, begging me to come back.

I think of Maxon. *You'd do the same, I'm sure.*

My throat tightens. The kettle whistles.

I don't know where to go.

Not to Allisander, obviously. I have no doubt that whatever Laurel Pepperleaf is doing is under his direction. Lissa Marpetta has been keeping to her sector since it was determined that she was also working with Allisander to distribute shoddy medicine. At one point I would have considered Arella Cherry an ally—but not now. Roydan Pelham is out for the same reason. Leander Craft died in the first attack.

So that leaves Jonas Beeching, the consul of Artis, and Jasper Gold, the consul of Mosswell.

To reach Jasper, we'd need to travel to the other side of the Royal Sector.

To reach Jonas, we'd need to cross the Queen's River.

Both options seem impossible.

And even if I could reach either of them, I have no idea whether they would help me. Consul Beeching asked for funds to build a bridge across the river, and his request was denied. I assume he's still smarting from the way Corrick refused him, because he *also* hasn't been present at court very often.

Then again, his lover was killed by rebels right in front of him. Perhaps his reasons for avoiding court are justified.

Still, the majority of the consuls are working to overthrow the throne. Trusting *any* of them is too big a risk.

Would the rebels help me? That feels like a dice roll that's weighted against me. Surely any of them would claim the reward being offered by the palace—and that's *if* I could convince any of them to believe I am who I say I am. I think of how Violet sang on the palace steps for hours, barefoot in ragged clothes, and no one was willing to listen to her. If I knocked on anyone's door and claimed to be the king, most people would likely laugh in my face. They knew Corrick and Tessa, but not me. Lochlan is gone, and he's the only rebel who knows me well enough to recognize me, even in a state of disarray.

My thoughts freeze on that thought.

Lochlan *isn't* the only one.

"Quint," I say. "Do you remember Tessa's friend Karri? The girl Lochlan kept by his side?"

"I do."

"Do you know where she lives?"

He frowns. "She lives in Artis, but I would need access to my papers for her specific address." He hesitates, thinking. Suddenly, his eyebrows go up. "But she worked for the same Mistress Solomon who employed Tessa. Perhaps we could find her there."

My heart is pounding again. This is also a risk. I don't know her well.

But Karri would recognize Quint. She'd be willing to listen.

She wanted to make things better. Just like Tessa.

"What do you recommend?" says Quint, pulling my thoughts back around.

"Take Thorin," I say. "See if you can find her."

"Your Majesty—"

"No," I snap. "And this time you will obey, or I will have Thorin drag you by force. Leave the horses so I have a means to escape, if necessary. But find Karri as quickly as possible. Stay out of sight."

"What shall we tell her?" says Thorin.

I shift my weight and wince. "Tell her that the king needs her help."

CHAPTER TWENTY-NINE

Tessa

Once we have a plan in mind, I want to execute it immediately. I meant what I said to Corrick: I'd make a terrible spy. I don't mind stealth and danger, but I'm not a good liar.

But Corrick steps out of the room to talk to Rocco, and when he returns, he tells me to wait.

"The crew is too anxious," he says. "Rocco believes he had someone watching our rooms all night. We need to find out if those ships have drawn closer. We need Blakemore to lower his guard again."

"How are we going to accomplish that?" I say.

While I button my vest, the prince glances at the porthole, which is just beginning to reveal the faint hint of a pink sky. "Why don't you go offer to climb the rigging with him."

There's enough of an edge to the suggestion that I study him.

"You were jealous," I say.

"I was."

"Are you still?"

His blue eyes are dark in the dim light from the lantern. "It's more than jealousy now."

I shiver at the warning in his voice. "Do you trust me?"

"Trusting *you* has never been a problem. I told Rocco to make sure one of the guards is nearby the entire time."

That's probably intended to make me feel better. It doesn't. I fasten the last button, then give my vest a tug to straighten it. I finger-comb my hair and rebraid it loosely.

I peer at Corrick as he buckles his own jacket into place. "Does it ever bother you that the guards see everything?"

A line appears between his eyebrows. "How do you mean?"

I gesture at the door. "They saw me come in here. They know I never came out."

"Tessa, I've had guards outside my door from the moment I first drew breath." He takes my face in his hands and kisses me softly. "Moments of true privacy are rare and precious."

I suppose there's something to that, but I can't keep the blush off my cheeks. "We . . . ah, we probably shouldn't go up together. If you want Captain Blakemore to trust me."

"I agree. Go ahead." He lets go of my face, and I turn for the door.

All three guards are still on duty: Rocco stationed between my room and Corrick's, Silas near the other end of the hallway, and Kilbourne at the bottom of the steps.

I wonder if they've all been on duty throughout the night.

"Tensions are high among the crew," Rocco says. "Kilbourne will accompany you if you go above."

Even though Corrick warned me, a ribbon of fear wraps around my spine. I thank Rocco, then turn for the steps.

When I reach the deck with Kilbourne at my back, the morning sky is darker than I expect, heavy with pink and purple clouds that obscure the sunrise. Wind blasts my cheeks, sending the sails and rigging to rattle. The water seemed so calm yesterday, but today, the ocean is choppy, small waves slapping the hull from all directions, making it hard to walk evenly.

Off to our east, those two brigantine ships have drawn closer. I can make out the flag of Kandala now.

That ribbon of fear around my spine seems to tighten.

A flash of motion catches my eye, followed by the smack of boots on the deck just to my left.

I jump a mile, but it's the captain. He must have jumped down from the rigging, because he's a little red-cheeked and windblown, his light eyes just as stormy as the sky.

"Rian," I say in surprise.

He gives me a nod. "Miss Cade." Without another word, he moves away.

Oh. Well then.

That tightness in my chest goes nowhere.

After a moment, I follow him. He's stopped near the railing, where the boom is tethered. Sea spray has collected on the deck, but he ignores it, unwinding the rope from the steel cleat. I watch his hands move, the motions tight and controlled.

I don't know if he's upset about the ships, or upset about Corrick, or upset about *me*—and not knowing is leaving me off-balance.

I try to be direct about it. "We're back to formality, Captain Blakemore?"

"We probably should have maintained formality from the very beginning. Watch yourself." He nods at the beam.

I step out of the way, but I follow him. "You're upset with me."

"I'm upset that Kandalan ships are drawing closer just as we're going to enter the most difficult part of the ocean." He follows the swinging beam, then grunts as he digs in his heels to stop at the next cleat, deftly whipping the rope around the steel bar. "It's hard enough to navigate this part. I don't want to do it while fighting off two well-armed brigantines."

"I don't have anything to do with those ships," I say.

He laughs under his breath, but not like anything is funny. He knots off the rope and then strides to the next.

I follow him again. "Don't do that," I say. "Don't treat me like—"

He whirls so quickly that my breath catches, and then the boat is hit by a swell of water, knocking me into his chest like the first night I boarded the *Dawn Chaser*.

He catches me by the arms, and I can feel the warmth and strength in his hands through the loose muslin of my shirt. But he's holding me a touch too tightly, and my heart skips.

"Don't treat you like what?" he says.

My mouth is dry, and I can't tell what's driving his temper, whether it's betrayal or anger. I don't really like either option.

"Captain," says Kilbourne. "Let her go."

In the space between heartbeats, I think Rian isn't going to obey. His grip is too tight, those storm clouds in his eyes too tumultuous.

But then he does. He releases my arms, then steps back, running a hand across his jaw. "You should return to your quarters, Miss Cade. Or Prince Corrick's quarters. Whichever you find most suitable."

Nothing even happened between me and Corrick, but my cheeks flame. I can't help it. "Why are you acting like I betrayed you?" I demand. "On the day you invited us on board, you knew—you knew—"

"I knew you were involved with a man who has a reputation for treachery and violence," he says. "I knew you were afraid to speak your mind. I knew—"

"I was not!"

He continues, heedless. "I knew you were determined to help the people of Kandala, risking your life to bring them medicine—which I find admirable. But I also know what it is to be tricked and manipulated, and—"

"I am not tricking and manipulating you!"

"I know," he says. "I'm talking about what Prince Corrick has done to *you*."

"He hasn't done anything to me. You don't know him at *all*."

"I don't need to know him. I know men *like* him. If he wanted to help his people, he could have boarded this ship with determination and valor. Instead, he views every interaction as a battle that waits for a victor. I hoped Kandala and Ostriary could find a new path to favorable trade, but now I'm worried that I'm delivering a prince who will sow discord and start another war just because I've poked at his pride."

"That is *not true*," I seethe.

"Oh, it's not?" Rian takes a step closer to me, and his voice drops. "He lost a battle to me last night," he says. "So it comes as no surprise that he sought to win another by cajoling you into his bed."

That's it. I'm swinging a fist before I fully think about what I'm doing.

Rian's hand shoots out and he catches my wrist. The motion is so quick that it steals my breath, especially since his grip is tight, and he doesn't let me go.

"He invited me to his quarters because he was worried you were *threatening* me."

"So he didn't have to cajole you. He just had to frighten you."

I jerk my hand out of his grip. My breathing is rapid. I wasn't sure what to expect from him, but it wasn't this.

"You know I'm right," he says roughly. "I expected better of you, Miss Cade."

He's not right. He's *not*.

But in so many ways, he *is*. So much of what he said echoes exactly what I said to Corrick in the shadows of his quarters.

Rian turns away. "Tell him that if those ships are coming for his capture, I'll hand him over, and gladly."

I'm barely listening to him. My heart is roaring in my ears. My breath is shuddering when I get to the steps, tears hot on my cheeks.

But then I realize that this is the perfect time.

It's early. Most of the crew is asleep. Rian thinks I'm running right back into Corrick's arms.

But I think of those ships, and I think of that room, and I think of how much we've risked already.

Instead of heading for our quarters, I turn the bend and head down the next set of steps.

Kilbourne moves to follow me, but I stop him. "You need to tell Corrick to go up on deck," I say to him in a rushed whisper.

"But, Miss Tessa—"

"Now," I say urgently. I swipe the tears off my cheeks. My chest is full of longing and betrayal and uncertainty, but now is the time for action. "Prince Corrick needs to go pick a fight with the captain. Right now." He inhales, and I add, "Quickly, Kilbourne! Stay in the hallway before anyone in the crew sees me."

Then I don't wait. I hold my breath and I skip down the steps.

CHAPTER THIRTY

Corrick

I stare at Kilbourne dubiously. "She wants me to pick a fight with Blakemore," I say. "Now."

"Yes, Your Highness."

I draw a long breath. I know why.

But it's too soon. We should wait. Last night was too tense, too close to real conflict for my comfort. She could be seen, and all of this would unravel around us.

There's no way for me to tell her all of that without going after her—and the only thing worse than *Tessa* getting caught breaking in would be her doing it with me at her side.

So I nod, leave my quarters, and head for the main deck. Rocco and Kilbourne both fall in behind me to follow.

They're both wearing more weapons than they were yesterday. I understand it, but I don't like it. The presence of more weapons rarely convinces anyone to let down their guard.

As we pass Lochlan's door, it swings open, and he strides out so brusquely that he almost walks right into Rocco. He quickly falls back, irritation plain on his face. He looks like he wants to slam the door on us all, but he's not sure he should dare.

Last night, when things went sour between me and the captain, Lochlan spoke up to defend Tessa—and me, in a way. Well, he spoke up to defend *Kandala*, at the very least. I might not shed a tear if he fell into the ocean, but I can appreciate that he spoke up when it was sorely needed.

And Tessa is right. We're never going to build trust between the palace and the populace if the King's Justice can't get along with one rebel.

"Going up to the main deck?" I say to him. "Join us."

He scowls. "Is that an order, Your Highness?"

He all but spits the words at me, and I see Kilbourne draw himself up. I put up a hand before he can slam the man into the wall again. "No," I say with every bit of courtly patience I can muster. "Join us, *if you please.*"

I watch the emotions play out on his face as he deliberates. He wants to refuse, but I've surprised him. I didn't mean for the words to sound like a challenge, but I can't really help it.

"Fine," he eventually grinds out.

But a moment later, we're ascending the steps together, and his movements are tight and forced. His shoulders are rigid, his fingers twisting together. His jaw is so tight that I can see his throat jerk as he swallows.

I'm no stranger to people being afraid of me. But that's usually in the Hold, where someone has been imprisoned for committing a crime.

Lochlan told Tessa that I only brought him on this journey with the intention of throwing him over the railing if I found a convenient moment. When she told me about it, I brushed off his words because it was so obviously untrue.

Until this moment, I didn't fully consider that *he* believed it.

The wind catches my hair and tugs at my jacket as we reach the top and step onto the deck. I expected Blakemore, but there's no one here. I glance over at Lochlan. "It really wasn't an order," I say to him.

He doesn't look at me. "You're the King's Justice," he says, as if that explains everything.

And maybe it does. I frown. "And I really didn't invite you along with the intent to kill you."

"That's reassuring," he says flatly.

I do have a limit. I round on him. "You took *me* prisoner and encouraged a mob to beat me to death, and then you took consuls and citizens hostage, killing them when you didn't get your way. Yet Harristan still invited you and the rest of the rebels to negotiate—"

"You put *me* on a stage," he says. "With a sack tied over my head, and a crossbow pointed at my back."

I've changed my mind. Now I do want to throw him over the railing.

Not really.

But maybe a little.

"You resorted to violence and death when you had no other choice," I say to him. "But somehow you mean to hold me to a different standard?"

"Yes," he says.

"Why?" I demand.

He scoffs and turns away.

I grab his sleeve and hold fast. "Tell me why."

He jerks free, his hands in fists like he longs to throw a punch. "Because your brother is the king!" he snaps—but then he breaks off. His eyes flick to the guards, as if he's worried they're going to get physical if he says much more.

"Go ahead," I say evenly. "Talk."

He stands rigidly, his hands still clenched tightly, but he says nothing.

"They won't hurt you if you remain civil," I say.

He inhales a tight breath and takes a step back, then looks away, out at the sea. For a moment, I think that's going to be it. The gulf between us is just too vast. He doesn't trust me, and I don't trust him, and no matter what we say in this moment, our past actions will overshadow every moment of our future.

It feels bleak and hopeless, and I want to sigh.

But then Lochlan speaks, his voice rough. "The king didn't just invite me to sit at that table. He invited Consul Sallister, despite everything *he* did." He pauses. "The Benefactors promised money and medicine. They knew we were desperate—and we believed they truly wanted to help. But in the end, they were no better than you were, *Weston Lark*. They had the power to make a difference, but instead, they just watched as the night patrol rounded up more of us for execution."

I flinch. I can't help it. My own voice is rough. "Lochlan. That's not why I was bringing medicine—"

"I know!" he snaps. "I *know*. You don't think I know? You don't think the *people* know? That night we held the sector, we laid down our weapons for Tessa. But it wasn't *just* for Tessa."

I stare at him.

"So we took a chance," he says. "We trusted that this was an opportunity for real change." He swears and looks away, but he must gather his mettle, because he takes a step closer to me. His voice is a low growl. "And then we had to sit across the table from a man who truly *was* a criminal, a man who faced *no* repercussions for his actions. None! Where's the sack over Sallister's head, Your Highness? Where's the stage? Where's the noose? Where's the crossbow? And you want to know why I'm holding *you* to a different standard?"

Somewhere on this ship, Tessa is picking a lock while I'm supposed to be causing a distraction. But just now, I'm frozen in place, considering the implications of Lochlan's words.

Because he's right. About all of it.

Before I can say anything, motion flickers above me, and then Rian lands on the deck beside us.

Of course. I should've looked up.

I wonder how much he heard. His eyes are shadowed and tense, and I'm fairly certain he heard *all* of it.

I expect him to chastise me, or mock me, or to be openly critical of my brother's rule, especially now that he has more ammunition.

His eyes meet mine, and a spark of his typical belligerence flares in his gaze, but this time, it's a bit darker, a bit angrier. "All that, and you still managed to lure Tessa into your quarters." He raises an eyebrow and gives me a once-over. "I trust you're well rested, Your Highness?"

No. I'm not.

Which is probably why I stride forward and throw a punch.

It's reckless and impolitic, and if we were only at odds over the appearance of *ships*, I never would've done it. But his comment is a barbed dig at Tessa, and I've reached a limit. The captain sees it coming in time to dodge a full strike, which is unfortunate, because it gives him an opening to drive a fist right into my midsection. It steals my breath, but I grab hold of his jacket, dragging him off-balance, then clip him in the jaw. I'm distantly aware of Lochlan swearing and getting out of the way, but this fight has been brewing for *days*, and it feels terrifyingly good to hit something. My hands still ache from the rope burns, but I don't care. I strike and grapple until the ship sways and we begin to fall. I don't even know which one of us goes down first, but I feel the collision with the wood planks of the deck a moment before the guards start dragging us apart.

We're both panting, but I feel a bit of grim satisfaction when I note that there's blood on his lip.

That satisfaction goes away when I swallow and taste my own blood.

Kilbourne lets me go almost instantly, but Rocco keeps Rian's arms pinned behind his back. The captain isn't struggling, but he's glaring at me. So is Lochlan.

I look at Rocco, who's waiting for an order. I remember the moment we stood in the Hold and I told him to break Sallister's arms.

I'm tempted to do the same to Captain Blakemore. It's the worst part of myself. The part that Tessa hates. The part that Lochlan fears.

I think Rian knows. I'm not sure if he expects the guards to hold him down while I beat the piss out of him on the deck, or if he thinks Rocco will do it on my order, but either way, I can see the expectation in his eyes. He's bracing himself.

"As I've said before," I say roughly, "contempt doesn't suit you. Any other clever remarks?"

"I'm sure I can come up with one or two."

I take a step forward, but he doesn't flinch. His eyes hold mine.

"Let him go," I say to Rocco, but I keep my eyes on the captain. I touch a hand to my face, and it comes away with spots of blood. "He was just defending himself."

Rocco obeys, and Rian blinks in surprise. To my right, Lochlan does the same.

The captain swipes the blood off his own lip. He regards me for a moment, and this time I brace *myself* for him to take up the fight again.

Instead, he says, "Those ships have drawn closer."

It's not what I expected him to say, but I cast my gaze to the horizon. He's right. They're much closer.

"If they're here at my brother's order," I say, "I'll have them take command of your ship, and you can cry all the way to Ostriary."

"They're within firing distance," he continues. "If they're *not* here at your brother's order, I'm handing you over."

"You're alone on the deck," I say. "I could have my guards kill you right now."

We can all feel the nervous energy in the air. Rian fixes his gaze on me. "If you kill me, you can't outrun two brigantines. They'll sink the ship or take you by force."

"Perhaps we'll have to take our chances," I say.

"We're nearing the most dangerous part of the ocean," he says. "Are you sure about that?"

I look at Rocco. "Advise."

"He's right about the brigantines. If they're not here by King Harristan's order, it's a risk."

"Can you continue sailing toward Ostriary?"

He hesitates. "I've never sailed past the southern point of Sun-keep. I can absolutely try, but I don't know what to expect in the next leg of the journey."

Rian's eyes flare as he realizes the implication of this, and then he swears. "So you brought a sailor anyway."

"I brought a guard with sailing experience," I say.

"He won't get through Chaos Isle. The current is too strong. There are rocks beneath the surface. If you don't know where they are, the *Dawn Chaser* will be destroyed."

"We'll see about that," I say. "What are your intentions if they *don't* demand my capture?"

"To sail straight through Chaos Isle and hope we lose them." He pauses, his gaze darkening. "You should let me go while I'm still willing to maintain civility on my ship."

I inhale to answer—but somewhere belowdecks, a woman screams.

CHAPTER THIRTY-ONE

Tessa

The lock is the easy part. It's only been a few weeks since I last picked a lock, but it's a simple padlock, and I have years of practice breaking into homes in the Royal Sector. The hallway was quiet and dark, with no one about this early. As I suspected, the captain is one of the few up and around, and if Kilbourne went to Corrick, the prince will keep him distracted while I find out what's so important about this small, locked room.

I don't know what I'll find, whether it's detailed records or secret weapons or barrels of gunpowder. I simply have no idea what Rian could be hiding in here that would be worth all this tension with the prince.

Somewhere deep inside, I'm terrified that I'm wrong, that this is a betrayal, that I'll reveal something horrible.

But I keep thinking of every moment I've looked into Rian's eyes. He's not horrible. He's not. If he's hiding something from Corrick, it's because he doesn't trust the prince.

I wish I'd brought a lantern. It's very dark down here. I might need to swipe whatever I find and sneak it back to my quarters. Hopefully it's something small.

Click. The lock gives. The door swings open. I smell seawater and mildew, and something surprisingly floral, but the room is a well of darkness. I can't see anything at all.

Without warning, a figure explodes through the doorway. It's too dark for me to see much, but I catch a glimpse of long, wild blond hair, wide dark eyes, and a filthy face. It's a woman—or a girl, I can't tell. She screams in rage.

Then she slams right into me with enough force to nearly knock me off my feet.

I cry out in surprise, then throw up a hand when she swings a fist at my face. Pain explodes behind my eyes, then in my forearm. I fall back involuntarily. Too much is happening all at once. It doesn't help that she's pummeling me like she wants to break every bone in my body. I'm lucky that she hits like a child, all weak strikes with bony knuckles.

"Stop!" I cry. She might be weak, but she's *quick*, and I can't seem to catch her wrists or hold her off. I'm thinking of the number of times Corrick said I should take some lessons from the weapons master, and the equal number of times I told him it could wait. "Stop—*stop it!*"

Finally, my thoughts catch up, and I swing a punch at her midsection. She's practically weightless, and I feel ribs when my fist connects. She grunts in pain, then slips to the side.

I all but throw myself to my feet in the shadowed hallway.

Again, she's quick. She leaps off the floor and tackles my back. Her fingernails dig into my arms, and I struggle to take a step forward.

"Corrick!" I shout, just as I feel her break the skin. "Guards! Help!"

The girl on my back hisses into my ear. "I'm going to kill you all."

Well, now I know why he kept that door locked.

I throw an elbow back and hear her grunt. It hardly dislodges her. I stagger forward, bearing her weight.

A light flares to life in front of me, and I gasp. A lantern.

I gasp in relief.

But it's not Corrick. It's not the guards.

It's Marchon, with Gwyn at his back. The flickering candlelight turns their faces into nightmarish caricatures.

Especially when Marchon plucks the girl off me, twisting her arms behind her back until she squeals in pain. Gwyn points a crossbow at me.

I'm frozen in place. I don't know what's happening.

I raise my hands. "Please," I gasp. My arms are stinging from where the girl clawed at me. "Please. I don't know—"

"How did she get out?" Gwyn demands.

Before I can even answer, Marchon swings the lantern. The padlock is visible on the ground.

Both their eyes shift back to me.

"She picked the lock," Marchon says. "Sablo!" he shouts.

The young woman—because it *is* a young woman, I can see now, rail thin in clothes that all but hang from her frame—tries to kick at Marchon, squirming in his grasp. "I'm going to kill *all* of you," she snaps. "Oren will set fire to this ship and then you'll—" She breaks off with a gasp when Marchon tightens his grip.

Oren. Oren Crane? I swallow and look at Gwyn. "What's going on?" I say. "Who is she?"

Her expression is full of sorrow and also resignation. She sighs, then gestures with the crossbow. "Walk, Tessa. Rian's going to have to decide what to do. Bring her along, Marchon."

The young woman grunts and struggles. "I'm going to slit Rian's throat with a—"

"Enough." Marchon clamps a hand over her mouth—then lets go with a yelp. "She bit me!"

The woman does one better. She punches him right in the throat.

Marchon chokes and drops her. She sprints away.

I want to do the same, but Gwyn steps closer with the crossbow. "Don't, Tessa."

"Who is she?" I say again. "Gwyn, *who is she?*"

The girl disappears into the darkness—but a moment later, there's a thump. The girl lets out a brief shriek, followed by a low sob of pain. Figures slide out of the shadows, and I recognize Sablo's large form, pinning her more effectively than Marchon did.

She's cursing a blue streak, and she spits at Gwyn when they come near.

Then she starts coughing. Her breathing turns to a wheeze, and her struggles against Sablo's grip seem to turn more panicked.

"Let her go!" I cry. "She can't breathe."

He glances at Gwyn, who shrugs, and he loosens his grip fractionally.

The girl catches her breath, then swings her head back like she wants to crack him in the face with her skull. Sablo jerks back, then tightens his grip.

"My father should have cut off more than your tongue," she says roughly. "I know what I'll start with when I get the chance."

My father. I can't put this together fast enough. "Your father is Oren Crane," I say.

"He is." She bares her teeth. "I hope he hangs Rian from the bow of his ship until the gulls peck every bit of flesh from his bones."

I look from her to Gwyn and back to Sablo and Marchon. "Rian is keeping Oren Crane's daughter prisoner?"

"You don't understand," says Gwyn. "Walk, Tessa."

I don't know if I can. I'm still too stunned. This is so much bigger than hidden weapons or secret letters or anything Corrick might have imagined. I just don't know *why*. It's so counter to everything I've learned about Rian in the last few days that I simply can't make any of it seem reasonable in my mind.

My thoughts aren't getting any clearer with that crossbow pointed at my chest.

Another voice speaks from the darkness. "Lower that weapon, Gwyn. We have your captain."

Corrick. I almost sag with relief.

Gwyn doesn't lower the weapon. If anything, she pulls closer to me, until I feel the point of the arrow against my skin. I feel every beat of my heart.

"Gwyn," I whisper. "Please. I don't understand."

More figures step through the shadows. Corrick, trailed by Rocco—who's all but shoving Rian ahead of him, a knife against the captain's neck.

I expect a moment of negotiation. A discussion. An argument. Because clearly Corrick is using Rian as leverage.

But Gwyn takes that crossbow off me and aims at Corrick. I hear the click and the snap an instant before I realize what it means.

Rocco is quicker than I am. He lets go of the captain in time to shove Corrick out of the way, but that bolt hits *something*, because I hear the impact, the grunt of pain in the shadows. I don't know who it struck.

Then Kilbourne is there, shoving me away from Marchon just before the sailor pulls a knife. Glass shatters, and the lantern goes dim, plunging us into near-total darkness. A body slams me into the wall, and I lose sense of which way is out. I want to run, but I don't know where to go.

"Corrick," I cry.

He doesn't answer.

My mouth goes dry. I hear the sound of a blade piercing flesh. Male voices are shouting, crossbows are firing, and over the top of it all, that woman is screaming in rage. I can't make sense of any of it. Panic keeps my heart racing at a rapid clip.

Out of nowhere, a fist connects with my shoulder, knocking me to the floorboards. A body lands on top of me, and I cry out. Just as quickly, I'm flipped onto my stomach, and my hands are jerked behind my back.

"Please," I say. The woman's shrieking is piercing my thoughts. "Please—I just wanted—"

"Enough," a man growls. I think it's Marchon.

Someone throws a punch, and the woman's screaming goes quiet.

All I hear is my breathing. Someone is binding my hands, and then I'm wrenched upright, onto my knees. My shoulder feels like it's being ripped out of its socket.

A match sparks in the darkness, and a new lantern flares to life.

The scene is worse than I was expecting.

Corrick is on his knees, bleeding from his temple, but he's slumped against the wall. At first I think he's just dazed, but then I realize his eyes are closed, and his hands are bound just like mine are. Blood is in a spray across the front of his jacket.

"Corrick," I whisper.

He doesn't move. My heart thumps. But I watch carefully, and his chest rises and falls with breath.

Beside him, the young woman is unconscious on the floor, limbs sprawled, but there's no blood.

Then my eyes shift left, and I recognize one of our guards. Sandy hair, a stocky build. Kilbourne.

Facedown, two bolts from the crossbow in his back. I wait, but his chest doesn't rise at all.

I didn't want to leave Sara. That's what he said on the dock. *I want to buy her a house.*

I've seen death a thousand times by now, but this is different. I have to stop a whimper from choking out of my throat.

Rocco is on the floor, too, but he's still alive. He's panting, bleeding from a wound in his side, and Sablo and Rian both have a crossbow pointed at him. There's blood on Sablo's face, and a fair amount on his clothes, too. Rian has a trail of blood running from a slice on his neck, soaking into his shirt and jacket. His eyes are dark and terrifying in the shadows.

Sablo looks at the captain, then draws a finger across his throat, an eyebrow raised. A question.

"No!" I shout. "Rian, no. Please. *Please.*" I can't get the words out fast enough, but they've already killed one guard. I can't watch them execute Rocco, too. I *can't.* "Please, Rian." My voice breaks. "Please. He's a good man."

"He's a sailor. Proof that Prince Corrick didn't honor our agreement."

"No." My voice breaks. "He's a guard. A loyal guard who's risked his life more than once. Please. Rian. Don't hurt him."

Rocco is glaring up at them both, but he speaks to me. "Don't beg for me, Miss Tessa. He knows what he's done. He knows what will happen when they catch up to him."

Rian looks at me. "You should have left the room alone, Tessa. What's been done here can't be undone."

"Please," I say. "Please just . . . just explain. I want to understand. Was this all a trick to hold the prince for ransom? Was this . . . was this for . . . ?" My voice trails off. I can't even understand it. Everything seems unnecessarily complicated.

Then my eyes fall on the unconscious woman again. I don't know where she fits in with *any* of this.

"Rian," says Gwyn. Her voice is quiet and resigned. "We shouldn't leave the guards alive."

"Please," I whisper.

Rian doesn't move. A muscle twitches in his jaw.

His crew is waiting.

I tug at the ropes binding my hands. "You don't want to do this," I say. "I know you don't. You won't let your crew fight. You don't want to kill him. I know there's a reason, if you'd just let me understand—"

"Tessa." His eyes flick to mine. "It's bigger than you and me."

I hold my breath, because those crossbows are still pointed.

After an eternal moment, Rian lowers his. "Bind him as well," he says. "Bring them all up to the main deck. Chain them to the masts. If the others survived, do the same with them, too."

The others. Lochlan and Silas. My heart clenches.

Tell Karri I loved her.

"Rian," I say. My chest is tight.

"It wasn't for ransom," he says to me. "Truly." He grabs hold of Corrick's arm and hauls him upright with enough force that the prince moans and his eyes flicker open.

Corrick sees who has him and tries to jerk away.

Rian gives him a good shake. "*Walk*," he snaps. Then he looks at me. "At least it wasn't *supposed* to be for ransom. But now . . ." He sighs. "Now, it's going to have to be."

CHAPTER THIRTY-TWO

Corrick

My thoughts are hazy as we approach the main deck, and I can't tell if we've ventured into rougher waters, or if I simply can't keep my balance. Rian keeps jerking me upright, and I do nothing to help him. Only some of that is deliberate. I don't know who hit me, but I'd bet good money it was Sablo, because his fist caught me in the face with enough force that I'm wondering if my jaw is broken. It wasn't long ago that I was standing on this deck, issuing threats to Captain Blakemore.

And now we're all trapped.

I didn't hear much from the girl from the locked room aside from enraged screams, but it's obvious she was a prisoner. Her limbs are frail, and she seems malnourished and pale.

Rian drags me to the main mast.

"I knew this was all a ruse," I say to him.

"It wasn't a ruse." He all but shoves me to the deck.

My head spins, but I glare up at him. "Of course not. This all feels very diplomatic, Captain Blakemore."

He ignores me. Sablo carries the unconscious girl to the next mast, then ties her to the wooden beam securely. Marchon tethers Rocco to the same one.

Gwyn ties Tessa two beams away, facing away from me.

That feels very deliberate. At least she's unharmed. I want to negotiate to keep her safe, but I don't want to give them more leverage over me than they already have.

I never should have let her do this.

Every time I swallow, I taste blood. There's an ache in my side that won't let up. I glare at Rian. "I should have had Rocco throw you over the railing."

"You still wouldn't have overtaken my crew. We had you outnumbered."

"On purpose."

"Well. Yes." He kneels beside me to tie my bound hands to the mast.

"Harristan will never negotiate with you," I say.

"He will if he wants his brother back."

"He's the king," I snap. "Why would he negotiate for anything with you? You're not in a position of power."

He gives a humorless laugh, then tugs at the ropes. "Oh, that's right. I'm just here to sail the ship." He draws back to meet my eyes. "King Harristan very specifically told me he expects you to return unharmed."

"He's not going to yield anything to a man who's little more than a pirate." Rian doesn't move, so I add, "Who's the other young woman? Why did you keep her locked in that room?"

"It's not important."

"You have me tied to a mast," I say. "You killed one of my guards. You've taken me hostage." Anger is building in my chest, and my head pounds. I have to take a steadying breath. "It feels rather important."

"You could have just stayed civil until we reached Ostriary. None of this had to happen."

"I feel like that's skirting the edge of the truth. Again, contempt does not suit you."

"It's not contempt. She has nothing to do with you. She has nothing to do with Kandala. I *told you* to stay away from that room— and you manipulated Tessa into breaking in on your behalf."

"If it makes you feel any better, she was breaking in to prove that you weren't working against us. So I suppose we *both* manipulated her."

He glowers but says nothing. He doesn't like that.

Good. I'm not done. I glance at the young woman bound near Rocco. "How did you hide her when my guards searched your ship?"

"Does it matter?"

Probably not, but I'm curious.

He shakes his head anyway. "Bella has nothing to do with any of you. I've approached you in good faith since the beginning."

"Good faith! You lectured me on the ethics of Kandalan laws, while you were starving a prisoner right here on board."

"I wasn't starving her!" he snaps—but he quickly regains his composure, and he straightens, looking down at me. "We could have helped both our people, Your Highness. But your pride got in the way, and you set me as your adversary the very instant you placed a foot on board the *Dawn Chaser.*"

"Both our people?" I repeat. "You really *have* allied yourself with Ostriary, haven't you?"

He says nothing.

I study him, trying to figure it out. My head aches and it hurts to think, but I say, "Did this new king promise you something if you made a deal with Kandala?" I say to him. "Why are you risking yourself?"

"No one promised me anything. I've promised *them*." He runs a hand back through his hair and sighs. A bruise has formed on his face from where I hit him. Good. I hope it hurts spectacularly.

"Why?" I demand. "You said yourself that you were a boy. Your father put you in this position. You owe them *nothing*."

His eyes snap to mine, but he snorts. "Just like your father put *you* in this position."

I stare right back at him. I remember the day we met, when I asked about his father.

Dead. The same as yours.

"What happened to him?" I say. "You said he died in their war. You'd think that would make you *more* loyal to Kandala. Not less."

He drops to a crouch and looks me right in the eye. "I'm not loyal to Kandala. I never was."

He says it so plainly that the words hit me like a blow.

Then he leaves me bound there and moves away.

There are too many variables here. I can't quite piece any of them together. I wanted access to that room because I was seeking proof that Rian was lying about something—and I guess I got it.

I just didn't expect it to be in the form of an unconscious girl who looks like she hasn't eaten in weeks.

But I can't do anything for her. I can hardly do anything for *us*.

I blink in the early sunlight and take stock of our situation.

It's not good.

I look over at the girl. Her wheezing is worse than Harristan when he has a coughing fit. Tessa seems unharmed, which is good, but Captain Blakemore isn't stupid. She's on the other end of the deck. I hope she has the good sense to be compliant. Despite everything, she has the best chance at being released.

Rocco is on his knees, bound to the mast between us. I don't know if he was struck by a bolt from a crossbow or if he took a blade, but he's a bit slumped, as if his bindings are all that's holding him upright. I'm concerned about the amount of blood on his livery.

No Silas. No Lochlan. I don't know what they've done with them—if anything.

I swallow again. My throat is thick.

I glance out at the water. One brigantine is closer, but I doubt they're close enough to see that we're held captive on deck, even with a spyglass. If they're here at my brother's order, I wouldn't mind the assistance, but it's not like Rian can't slit my throat if they start firing cannons. The only leverage I have is that he'll want me alive if he intends to use me against Harristan—but that clearly doesn't mean I'll be kept in comfort.

But if that ship is here for nefarious purposes, I don't want to face it with my hands lashed to a wooden beam.

Not that I have a choice. Knowing my luck, they'll fire on the *Dawn Chaser* and we'll all drown.

More of the crew have come up on deck now, and it's obvious they've heard what happened—but you'd think we weren't even here. They begin going about their morning duties, barely glancing at any of us. Rian has retired to his stateroom, but he's not far from the window. I can see him watching all of us. Gwyn isn't far either. She stands at the helm. Sablo and Marchon are at the other end.

The crew might be working, but the key players are stressed. I might be able to use that to my advantage.

Maybe? Possibly?

I don't know who I think I'm fooling.

I test my bonds. The ropes don't give an inch. I'm on my knees, but I'm tied too tightly to sit fully. My hands are already tingling, so I shift to try to slacken the pressure. It doesn't help.

Panic threatens to bubble up in my chest, but I force it back down. I've been bound before. I've been captured before. I survived that, I can survive this.

I don't know what will happen if we try to talk to each other, but it's not like things can get much worse.

"Rocco," I say.

He blinks and looks up, and it takes a second longer than it should. "Your Highness."

"You're injured."

"A blade caught me under my ribs. It's not too deep." His breathing seems shallow, contradicting his words.

"Do you know what happened to Silas?"

"They could have confined him to his quarters."

I hear what he's not saying. *Or he could be dead.*

Even if we somehow get free, there would be three of us against Rian's entire crew. Unarmed and injured.

If Silas survived, that only makes four.

"Lochlan was on deck with us," I say. "What happened to him?"

"I don't know." He pauses. "Possibly confined to his quarters as well."

"Your boy's down in the galley," calls one of the crewmen. Tor, I think. "Dabriel's got him shelling the crabs."

Down in the galley. Like he's one of the crew. I scowl.

I suppose I shouldn't be surprised.

Rocco winces, then shifts his weight. A bloom of sweat glistens on his forehead. I should ask if he's more injured than he's letting on—but I probably don't want the answer. It's no secret that he's hurt and in pain—but Gwyn was calling for Rian to shoot him. I'm sure he worries that being seen as a liability would not improve his position.

I draw a long breath and try to think of a plan.

I have nothing.

Instead, I think of my brother.

That's no better.

Harristan. I failed. I'm sorry.

I swallow thickly, and I try to freeze my thoughts before emotion gets the better of me while I'm bound here on the deck. We're definitely moving into more tumultuous waters, because the ship rocks and sways. I clench my eyes closed and tug at the ropes.

One of the crewmen pours a bucket of water across the deck, and it's like ice when it hits my knees. My eyes snap open, glaring, and I find Tor shoving filthy water across the deck with a broom.

He sees my look and shrugs. "Can't help it. Orders are orders."

Nearby, a woman moans, and I jerk my head around, worried it's Tessa.

No, it's the blond woman who's all but lying in a heap against the mast beside Rocco. Her hair is a wild mess of tangles, and her clothes are loose and ill fitting. Her skin is the color of wet sand, her eyes so dark they could be black. She's so thin that I can't tell how old she is. Not much older than Tessa, surely.

She uses her bindings to lever herself upright, then blinks at the sun. She cranes her neck around to see Rocco, then me, then the crew.

Tor gives her a grin. "Looking bright this morning, Bella."

She inhales deeply and coughs—then spits at him. "Make a meal of your own entrails, Tor."

He laughs and sweeps another bucketful of water away. "Always a lady."

She's wheezing a bit, but she looks at me. "Which one are you?"

I'm not sure if my titles would be a good thing or a bad thing to this woman, and I'm hopeful she'll give me more information than the captain is willing to share.

"My name is Corrick," I say.

"The prince." She sneers. "You're the one who's stupid enough to give him steel."

No, I'm the one who was stupid enough to get on this ship at all. "He has me tied to the mast," I say. "I don't think I'll be giving him much of anything." I pause. "Who are you?"

She evaluates me like she's also wondering how much to share. But she works her fingers against the bindings, then must realize secrets don't matter. "I'm Bella," she says. "Rian's keeping me for leverage."

"That makes two of us. Why are *you* leverage?"

"So my father doesn't blow this ship out of the water." She coughs again, then wheezes. She turns her head to yell at Gwyn. "But he *should*. I hope he does. I don't care if I drown. I'll scream it to him the whole—"

She breaks off coughing again, then wheezes, trying to catch her breath.

Her fractured breathing doesn't just remind me of Harristan's lingering illness. It sounds so much of the fever sickness—which Rian said wasn't prevalent in Ostriary. Did she catch it from us somehow? Or was he lying?

Or do they simply have so much Moonflower that no one ever gets sick? Has he been withholding medicine from her? Is that why she was locked in that room?

But then I realize what Bella said. "Why would your father blow him out of the water?" I say. I consider all the political ramifications here, and I straighten. "Is your father the king? Is that why he's holding you—"

She bursts out laughing, a sound bordering on hysteria. "My father is Oren Crane, and he *should* be king. If he were, Rian would've been dead a year ago." She sobers quickly, her eyes a little wild. She screams at the stateroom. "He should have slit your throat, Rian. He should've drowned your brat, Gwyn. He should've—"

Rian steps out on the deck. "That's enough, Bella."

"Or what?" she demands. "You'll lock me back in that room? You'll keep feeding me poison? Go ahead." Rian starts walking toward her, but she keeps going. "They already know who you are, you lying, conniving son of a—"

"I don't," I say quickly, worried Rian is going to shut her up and I'll learn nothing new. "Tell me."

She looks at me. "You don't know who he is?"

Rian is striding across the deck now.

"He said he was a spy sent by Kandala," I say in a rush. "He said he wanted to introduce me to the king of Ostriary with the goal of negotiating for steel. He was willing to liaise with the royal court—"

She bursts out laughing again. "*Liaise with the royal court.*" Her laughter ends with choked coughing. Rocco meets my eyes with concern.

"Bella," Rian says sharply.

I look from him to her. I'm still not fully sure what's happening here. "There's no royal court?"

"Oh no. There is." She spits at Rian's boots, then glares up at him, a trail of saliva clinging to her chin. "But you don't need a liaison. You could negotiate with the king right now."

My thoughts are spinning, but on that sentence, they go still. Even my heart seems to pause. The crew is paying attention now. Brooms have stopped. Chatter has gone silent.

I look up at Rian, backed by the sun. The wind tugs at his clothes and sparks color in his cheeks, but he's staring back at me implacably.

I'm not loyal to Kandala. I never was.

"Go ahead, Your Majesty," says Bella, choking on laughter again. "Why don't you introduce yourself?"

CHAPTER THIRTY-THREE

Harristan

I'm alone in the workshop for what feels like an hour, but is probably less than half. It's not until Quint and Thorin are gone that I wonder if I should have had them wait until Saeth returned.

I'm not sure what good that would've done, though. Right now, time is our enemy. I'm terrified the night patrol will come crashing through the woods at any moment, waiting to drag me back to face whoever is willing to stand against me.

Or worse, waiting to execute me right here.

I limp to the horses, who've calmed somewhat, sweat dried into streaks along their flanks. They're narrow driving horses, bred for harness instead of saddle, and I spare a moment to worry the animals aren't broke for riding at all. I suppose I'll find out in a moment. The bay gelding seems less flighty, so I adjust the bridle to remove the blinders, then use the dagger to cut the reins to riding length, knotting them together. I'm left with several feet of leather, which

I loop into a breastplate of sorts, tying it in place at the horse's withers. Bareback, it'll give me something to grip if I need it.

A branch breaks somewhere in the woods, and I freeze.

I wait an eternal moment, but nothing follows.

If the night patrol is close, I don't want Saeth to have to waste time prepping the other animal. I make quick work of the other bridle, then fashion another workable breastplate.

My leg aches something *fierce.*

I think of Corrick and my chest tightens.

That ship is a farce, Arella said. *It'll never reach Ostriary.*

Does she know? Or was she playing to the crowd? There's no way to be sure.

I take a slow breath and force my thoughts into order. I can't help my brother if I'm dead. I need to get on this horse so I'm not trapped.

I grit my teeth. I haven't made a bareback mount in years. I grab hold of the reins and the straps of leather, then stride forward to swing aboard.

The horse shies sideways. My injured leg gives out. I end up in the underbrush.

I swear with words I'd never use in the palace.

My second attempt ends the same way. Maybe I should just start walking.

My third attempt gets me on the animal's back. I'm so relieved about *that* that I nearly forget everything else I know about riding. The gelding has clearly had enough of this nonsense, because he jerks his head down, rounding his back to buck. I grab hold of the reins and get his head up. He sidesteps, pawing at the underbrush.

"Easy," I say, a bit breathless, hooking a hand under the strap in case I need it. His tail swishes, but he stands, chewing the bit in irritation.

"This is no treat for me either," I say, but I stroke a hand along the crest of his neck, and the horse sighs.

Another branch snaps, and I take up the reins again. Both horses whip their heads up this time, ears pricked. I nudge my heels into the gelding's ribs, ready to gallop—or fall—but Saeth appears between the trees, and I let out a sigh of relief. He looks startled to find me on a horse, but I don't wait for questions.

"I sent the others into Artis," I say. "We should follow. Did you find food?"

"Yes, Your Majesty."

"Good. You can't call me that now, Saeth."

He inhales, looking confounded for a moment, probably because he can't really call me *Harristan* either. When I was a boy, sneaking into the Wilds with Corrick, I used the name Sullivan, and I almost give it to Saeth. But my tongue stalls. For some reason, just now, that feels . . . special. A name to be shared between my brother and me.

Cory. Please be well. My chest threatens to tighten, and I shake off the sentimentality. I turn my thoughts to the present.

I think of Violet. I think of Maxon.

"Call me Fox," I say. I nod at the chestnut. "Mount up. We need to move."

—✦—

Saeth was able to find strips of dried beef that have been rolled in cinnamon and nutmeg, along with two peaches that are only a little bruised. I haven't eaten anything since the nut bread that Maxon prepared, so I want to inhale it all, but I offer half to Saeth.

He looks surprised by that, a frown line appearing between his eyebrows. "No. Thank you."

I hold out a peach and two strips of beef anyway. No matter how hungry I am, I can't afford weak guards. "Eat," I say. "We don't know when we'll be able to find more."

He obeys. We ride slowly and stay off main paths, crossing creeks and doubling back time and again so our tracks can't be followed. My trousers are still tacky with blood, especially since I reopened the wound trying to get on the horse. I wouldn't be recognized as the king, but an injury like this would definitely draw attention.

It's the guard at my side that's more worrisome, especially if rumor spreads that the king was traveling with two palace guards. In the dark, it might not be a concern, but in the bright light of day, Saeth is just too conspicuous. He left most of his livery at the workshop, but his trousers are the rich blue of his uniform, his polished black boots gleaming in the sunlight. Each weapon bears gold filigree, right down to the hilt of his daggers and the buckle of his belt.

I consider Quint, in his palace finery, and Thorin, who'd be attired similarly to Saeth. Maybe they didn't make it very far at all. Worry begins to crowd into my thoughts, and I force it away.

As we get closer to Artis, we begin to see people through the trees, families and workers going about their business.

"Stick to the shadows," I say.

"Yes, Your—"

I give Saeth a sharp look, and he breaks off, then gives me a nod. "Yes, Fox."

Eventually, we near an area where the Wilds begins to give way to the sprawling main city of Artis. The bulk of the sector is on the other side of the Queen's River, but there are enough people here to form a bustling city. Men and women come and go along the wall, children in tow, squalling infants strapped to the chests of women who are burdened with parcels or sacks. Larger carriages and wagons rattle along the road, too, and I carefully watch for any vehicles that might originate from the Royal Sector, but so far I haven't seen anyone.

After a while, distant hoofbeats pound the earth, and we pull farther into the dim light of the woods. A horn sounds, and people begin to clear the road.

I know those horns. The palace guard. *Anyone* in that contingent would recognize us.

I draw my horse to a halt and exchange a glance with Saeth. I'm split with indecision, whether I should dismount and attempt to stay out of sight behind the animal, or if I should stay right here with the means to run if I need it.

The horse tugs at the reins and paws at the ground, sidestepping agitatedly. "Shh," I murmur, keeping my eyes on the road.

I don't need to worry. A dozen guards gallop through without stopping.

I look at Saeth. "Did you recognize any of them?"

He nods. "Some of the outer guards. I didn't see the mark of your personal guard on any of them." He hesitates, then looks at me. "By now, Captain Huxley will know Thorin and I are with you. It's possible they've restricted the rest of your personal guard to the palace—if not the Hold."

I frown. I hadn't considered that.

Saeth adds, "It's also possible that Thorin and Master Quint have been captured, and those guards were summoned to bring them to the palace."

I hadn't considered that either.

"Advise," I say.

He takes a moment to consider, looking from the road to the town ahead, then back to me and my injured leg. "We could try following them—"

"Following them!"

"Yes. No one would expect the king to be *following* someone seeking him. Not out in the open." He glances at my leg again, then back at my face, which surely still bears streaks of blood. "No one knows you're injured either. If you could manage a faster pace, it wouldn't give anyone much time to see the state of your injuries anyway."

Or his weapons. "And what do we do once we're in Artis?"

"If Master Quint was heading for an apothecary shop, it would most likely be near the town square. The guards would have no reason to hide. If that was their destination, we'd see them in plenty of time to double back into the Wilds."

I don't waste time considering. "Let's go."

—◆—

It's a warm day, the sun beating down as soon as we step out from under the cover of the trees. The horses are eager to canter, but the gelding's lumbering gait gives me a jolt with every stride, made worse once we reach the cobblestone streets of Artis. My head will never stop aching at this rate, and my leg has turned into a stretch of pain from my waist down to my knee. I refuse to slow, because stopping feels like a guarantee of discovery.

Even still, I've begun to sweat through my clothes when we reach the main road leading into the town square. My breathing has grown thin and reedy, and I do my best to ignore it.

No sign of guards. But they must be around *somewhere*.

I don't spend much time outside the Royal Sector, so I don't quite have my bearings, but Saeth calls for a stop near the end of a row of buildings. I'm glad. One of my hands is hooked in the makeshift breastplate, and I have no idea how long that's been the case. My grip feels like the only thing holding me upright.

Saeth casts a glance around, but when his gaze settles on me, he does a double take. "Your M—*Fox*. You should not continue."

I must look worse than I feel. "I can," I say, and my voice is breathy and quiet, contradicting my words. "Proceed. Are we close?"

He looks around again, reassessing. He nods down the narrow alley between buildings. "If you take the horses down the back to wait in the shade, I'll go on foot to see if I can find what became of Master Quint and Thorin."

Sweat drips into my eyes, but I nod. He slips to the ground and hands me the reins, then hesitates. "I shouldn't leave you."

"You can't drag me down the street," I say, wheezing. "The alley is empty. Go."

He goes.

The alley is cool and dark, and I draw the horses to a stop under a stretch of awnings. The horses find a rain barrel before I do, plunging their muzzles into the water with abandon.

I'm so thirsty that I'm off the gelding's back before I have time to consider whether this is a bad idea, but then I'm cupping water in my own hands right alongside the horses.

When I try to get back on the gelding, he lashes his tail and snakes his neck at me, sidestepping away. I'm limping heavily anyway, and I have no desire to fall on the cobblestones.

From the end of the alley, someone yells, and my heart kicks.

The chestnut horse spooks, and both animals go trotting down the alley. I'm frozen against the wall, half-hidden by the rain barrel.

But no one comes down this way.

I can't chase the horses, so I don't try. I slide along the wall until I'm sitting, my injured leg stretched out in front of me.

Once again, I'm stuck and injured, debating what would be better: to sit here and wait for my fate, or to risk trying to escape.

I can hear every breath that fights its way into my lungs. Against my will, my eyes fall closed. The sweat was stinging anyway. Maybe this is all fruitless and I'll die in this dirty alley.

The crown is yours, Corrick.

But my brother isn't here.

A memory flickers in my thoughts, vivid like a dream. I was young, sick with fever, and my nurse had left my bedside. I was nine or ten. Maybe younger. Something cool touched my forehead, then my cheek. I opened my eyes to find my brother there, patting my face with the wet compress.

"Am I doing it right?" he whispered, just before squeezing a stream of water right into my eyes.

The memory is so potent that I can almost feel the cool water. "You're doing just fine, Cory," I murmur.

"He's coming around," a man says quietly, relief in his tone.

I inhale sharply, then cough. My eyes snap open.

Quint is on one knee in front of me, a wet handkerchief in his hand. Thorin and Saeth are behind him.

Beside them is Karri, Tessa's friend. Her fingers twist together, and she's biting at her lip. Her eyes are wide and alarmed.

I fight to get my good leg under me, then rise to my feet. My fingers clutch at the edge of the wall. I should offer her something for her assistance. She should not have to face her king like this, broken and bleeding and half-conscious in a dirty alley in the back streets of Artis.

But my head aches and my leg hurts and my brother is gone . . . and I have simply run out of options.

"I know there is a bounty on my head," I say roughly. "I know it would be easier to turn me in." She says nothing. Her fingers keep twisting together. I cough again, then press on. "It is very likely that you will not think I deserve it," I say. "But, Karri, I am prepared to beg for your help."

She hears those words and regards me, then glances between my guards, and then to Quint.

Finally, her eyes shift back to me. Her voice is soft, yet strong. "Did you send Lochlan away on that ship so Prince Corrick could kill him?"

"No," I say. "I swear it. It truly was meant as a measure of goodwill."

Her eyes hold mine, and there's a coolness there.

Fine. I take a long breath. "And . . . also a bit of insurance, so he wouldn't lead another rebellion while Corrick was away. It was a measure of protection for the kingdom. For *everyone.* Not just the elites."

She glances at the guards again, then back at Quint. "I believe you." Her fingers untwist, and she squares her shoulders. "And you don't need to beg me for help. Can you walk? That looks like it needs stitching." Her eyes shift to Thorin. "I live two blocks west of here. You'll have to help him. But I patch people up all the time. No one should think twice about it." She hesitates. "You'll have to stick to the alley. The palace guard have been searching the shops."

I nod, then grit my teeth. Relief is a powerful motivator. So is fear. I know that better than anyone, but I've never been on this side of it. "Lead the way."

—+—

Karri has a small apartment to herself above a cobbler and a butcher. There are only two rooms, but she has running water and a wood-burning stove, items that are clearly a point of pride, because she mentions them as Thorin helps me through the doorway—then blushes sheepishly and says, "Well. It's not very fine by your standards, I'm sure. But it was all I could afford on my own."

She's agreed to help me. It's better than a palace. "I'm grateful for your kindness," I say.

Thorin takes a spot by the door, and Saeth moves to the front window, where he pulls the curtain to the side. "Can I get to the roof from here?" he says. "I don't want to keep watch from the street."

Karri's eyes flare in surprise, but she nods. "There's a ladder from the window at the back of the bedroom." She looks at me, then glances at my leg. "I'll fetch my supplies, if you want to sit by the washbasin." Her brown cheeks redden further. "We'll have to remove that bandage. And I . . . ah, I'm going to need you to remove your trousers, Your Majesty."

As if this is the worst thing to happen to me today. I've reached a point where I no longer care. "Fine."

Quint helps me to a low chair, but I manage to work my way out of the trousers while Karri gathers her things. When she returns, I'm worried she might be too intimidated, but once she has her equipment in hand, she's more businesslike. The wound is crusted with dirt and sweat and several rounds of dried blood, but she soaks a rag and gently washes it clean.

It still stings, and I clench my teeth.

She glances up. "I'll stitch it, but I should dress it with an ointment first. There's a lot of dirt. It'll get infected."

I nod. "Whatever you think is best."

She winces. "It'll hurt."

"It already hurts, Karri."

"I know." She reaches up, touching my jaw before she catches herself. She grimaces. "I'm sorry, Your Majesty. Your ear likely needs stitching as well."

"Again, whatever you think is best."

She meets my eyes, then glances away and nods.

The room is very quiet as she fetches a few bottles of herbs, then mixes them with a fragrant cream. She takes a spoon and slathers it onto the wound with no warning at all, and I cry out, gripping tight to the chair.

Thorin appears beside us, but Quint puts up a hand to stop him. The guard waits for my order. I shake my head, gritting my teeth. "It's fine," I grate out.

Karri threads a needle. "May I ask how this happened?"

I huff a breath, because my thoughts are still fixated on the fiery pain from the ointment. "I was shot by the night patrol."

Her eyes meet mine. "Really?"

I nod, then swallow. "They didn't know I was the king." I pause. "I heard there was a meeting in the Wilds. I hoped to see who was working against me."

Her eyes skip down to my attire. "So because Prince Corrick was unavailable, you slipped into the Wilds yourself."

"More or less."

She puts the needle against my skin, and I brace myself, but she doesn't move further. "Do you want something to bite on?"

I have no idea. "I'm fine."

She gives me a look, then utters a little humorless laugh. "The two of you must have a will of steel."

"I don't know what that means."

"Prince Corrick pretended to be *asleep* when Tessa was stitching his face closed." Then she pushes the needle through my skin, and I give a jolt. It takes everything I have not to cry out again. Hearing that my brother did this while feigning *sleep* is enough to keep me silent. Both my hands clamp down on whatever is close.

Karri makes a loop with the thread, then slides the needle through for another pass. I hold my breath and grip tighter with my hand.

I look down at the length of the injury. This is going to take an hour. A day. A year. A lifetime. Sweat gathers in the small of my back, and I have to choke back a sound.

"You said the soldiers were searching the shops," Quint says, his voice calm at my side, as if I'm not a breath away from keening like a wounded animal. "Were they searching for the king?"

"And you," she says, her eyes flicking up for half a second. "Mistress Solomon—she owns the apothecary shop—she told me that the delivery boy said the king was guilty of poisoning the people."

"With the new medicine dosage?" I say. "Karri, I swear to you—" I hiss a breath as the needle goes through my skin again. My fingers clench tighter. "There's no poison. Tessa came up with the new elixir on her—"

"I know," Karri says, frowning. "That's what I told Mistress

Solomon. But she said I was a fool, and she's obviously talking about the poison that causes the fevers."

I have to repeat that in my head because it doesn't make sense. "What?"

"They're claiming that you've been poisoning the people to cause the fevers."

"How would the king poison all of Kandala?" says Quint.

"I don't know." She glances up. "But that's what she said." The needle slides through my skin again.

"Huxley told the people I was tricking them," I say to Quint. "Just before they fled." Another bite from the needle, and I force the words out. "Arella said she had proof."

"None she's shared with me," he says. "But Arella and Roydan have been meeting privately for weeks." He frowns and shakes his head. "To be honest, I have a hard time believing Consul Pelham would be involved in this."

That's true. The man is nearly eighty years old, and of all the consuls, he's always been fond of me and Corrick. He's the last one I would ever assume to be staging a coup against me.

But I saw Arella with my own eyes. I heard every word with my own ears.

"Done," Karri announces, and I look down. A dozen stitches hold my thigh together, but the wound is clean. I feel a little dazed, and I begin to unclench my fingers.

Only to realize I've been gripping Quint's hand.

I let go at once, then run a damp hand across my face. "Forgive me, Quint."

Karri glances between us, then wets a new cloth and reaches for my face. "I'm assuming you'll need fresh clothes. Lochlan stays here sometimes, so I have a few of his things. There's a shaving kit in the washroom." She hesitates. "If you like. Your Majesty."

"Thank you, Karri."

She cleans the blood from my face with care, and she's gentler than Quint was. "Are you hungry?"

"No."

"Well, I'm sure that'll change by midday. I'm not sure I have enough to feed all four of you for long, though." She hesitates. "May I ask what your intentions are?"

I've hardly been able to think past this moment, but that's not a suitable answer. "We'll hide here for the time being," I say. "It's not safe to be on the streets if the palace guard is searching for me. But I can't stay hidden for too long. Once rumor spreads, my absence will build an implication of guilt. I can't allow Captain Huxley and Consul Cherry to control the narrative."

I wish I knew what *proof* they claimed to have.

Karri shifts closer, putting her hand against my jaw to hold me in place. She's so close that the warmth of her breath touches my skin, and she smells like apples and honey. This should feel awkward, but she's so clinical that it's not. If anything, it reminds me of my childhood, when physicians and nurses would poke and prod as if I were a stuffed doll for their study.

"If you reveal yourself," she says, "how will you keep them from capturing you?"

"I'm not sure," I admit. "How did the Benefactors get the people to organize so quickly?"

"They promised money and medicine." She swipes with the rag. "Do you know how many people in the palace are working against you?"

"A lot, if they have control of the palace guard," I say. "Which means they control the night patrol. They might not have been able to spread word of my guilt very far yet—but it won't take long. When night falls, I may have Saeth and Thorin try to contact others, but it may not be worth the risk. I don't want to lose them, too."

"If the medicine isn't faulty," she says, "then why are they doing this?"

"I don't know," I say. "But I suspect Allisander is trying to force things back to the status quo. He never wanted to provide more medicine."

"So he can keep charging exorbitant prices that only the elites can afford."

"Yes."

"So more people will die."

"Yes. It's very likely the reason they chose to act now. If Corrick returns with a supply of Moonflower, we won't need Allisander."

That ship is a farce. It'll never reach Ostriary.

I force Arella's words out of my mind. There's no way they could know.

Unless they sent ships to follow.

The thought nearly steals my breath. There aren't many who could afford to do it, but Laurel's father is one of Allisander's richest landowners.

And there's nothing I could do about it.

"I need a way to reclaim the palace," I say. "But I'm not entirely sure how to do that if the consuls have turned the guards and soldiers against me."

"If I may," Quint says, "I don't believe they have *all* of them. Right now, they may be following orders simply because you aren't there to contradict them."

"You heard the guards at the gate," I say. "They have *enough* of them."

"I think your ear will manage without stitching," Karri says. "But I'll add some ointment."

"I can't trust the elites," I say, "and I'm worried the people would turn me in just to claim the reward."

Karri snorts and dabs some medicine onto her finger. "Forgive me, Your Majesty. But you think the people are going to trust Consul Sallister?"

"Well." I hesitate. "Maybe?"

"I think you might be surprised. You're taking up space in my kitchen."

"If I survive this, I'll ensure you're rewarded, Karri."

She smiles, but it flickers with sadness. "I'm not helping you for a reward. I'm doing it because it's the right thing to do." She pauses. "It's the same reason Lochlan was helping the rebels. We didn't want silver, Your Majesty. We wanted medicine."

"I know," I say. "I swear to you. I know."

She sits back. "I know you do. Even when Prince Corrick was terrifying, I could tell that you wanted to help the people. I could hear it in your voice when we held the Circle."

When they tried to take over the Royal Sector. The night they almost succeeded.

"Violet knew it, too," says Quint. "As I said, she sang all night."

I laugh without humor. "It's a shame Violet doesn't have an army."

"Who's Violet?" says Karri.

"A girl," I say. "She offered me shelter after I was shot, then risked herself to find Master Quint."

Karri's eyes go wide. "Did she know you were the king?"

"In the end I had to tell her. But before then, she called me Fox, because I would—"

"Wait." Karri drops her rag. "That was *you*?" she demands. "*You* were Fox? Did Tessa know?"

"No," I say quietly. "Not even Corrick knew."

She blows a breath out through her teeth. "So all that time we were bickering around the table, you were secretly going out and giving people silver."

I hesitate, then nod.

"Well," she says. "I'll see if I can gather the people in the commons tonight. You'll have to hide here for the time being." She glances at the window. "I'll need to get back soon, or Mistress Solomon will grow suspicious." Karri stands and begins arranging her things.

"Wait," I say. "Gather the people for what?"

She stops and looks at me. "To take the Royal Sector again." She smiles, and a dark light glints in her eyes. "Your Majesty, Violet might not have an army, but don't you remember? Lochlan does."

CHAPTER THIRTY-FOUR

Tessa

I'm such an idiot.

I spent so much time trying to convince Corrick that Rian was good, that this wasn't a trick or a trap.

And now Kilbourne is dead. Rocco might be close. We're all tied on the deck, sweating in the midday sun as those brigantines get closer. A half-starved woman is claiming Rian is the king of Ostriary—and he's not denying it.

I suppose I shouldn't be too surprised at myself. I spent years thinking Weston Lark was a friendly outlaw. Look at how that turned out.

A hand appears in my vision, holding a slice of fruit. It's so unexpected that I almost flinch.

"Eat," Rian says, and his voice is quiet. "I know you didn't have breakfast."

Wind whips at my hair, and I clamp my mouth shut and keep

my eyes on the deck. I remember Corrick feeding me berries, how it felt like a peace treaty.

This feels like an act of war.

"No," I say tightly. "*Your Majesty*."

He ignores my contempt. "Call me Rian."

"That's not even your name!"

"It is, actually. A nickname from childhood. The only true lie was *Blakemore*—but if you prefer it, I've grown accustomed to it. Call me what you like."

I snap my head up. "Oh, I'm *sure* you don't want me to do that. Was any of it true?" I demand. "Or did you make up the entire spy story, too?"

"All of that was true," he says.

I blink. "Wh-what?"

"All of it," he says. "The entire existence of Captain Blakemore and his journey from Kandala were all true. This ship, the documentation, the ring, the son who made the journey with his father—"

"None of this makes sense!"

"It makes total sense," Rian says. "Only . . . I'm not Blakemore's son. I just borrowed his identity."

I stare at him in disbelief. "You're diabolical."

"You're acting as if I'm the criminal here," Rian says. "When you're the one who broke into a room I was *quite clear* should remain untouched."

"You were holding that woman prisoner."

"I was keeping her *safe*."

"I feel like she would disagree."

"This is complicated."

"It's not complicated. You killed Kilbourne." Emotion tightens my throat when I say the words, and I try to swallow past it. It doesn't work, and I have to clench my eyes closed. I wait for Rian to say that it was the cost of battle, or to brush off the death as the ends justifying the means.

But he says, "I know, Tessa." His voice is soft and low, closer, like he's dropped to a crouch. "And I am sorry. Truly. He seemed to be a good man."

I don't want to hear sorrow in his voice, but I *do*. I hate him for it.

"His wife was going to have a baby," I say. I draw a shaky breath, remembering the gleam in Kilbourne's eyes when Rocco teased him about it. He was so excited to be a father. "Kilbourne only took this assignment because they wanted a bigger—"

"Miss Tessa."

Rocco's voice, rough and strained, makes me snap my eyes open. I'm bound facing away from him, but as I suspected, Rian is in a crouch in front of me.

"Don't give him that," Rocco says.

He's right. I clamp my mouth shut.

Rian is still offering the food. "He was a guard, Tessa. He died doing his job. The prince is alive."

"He died because you killed him."

For the first time, a thread of anger slips into his voice. "*No one* would have died if you'd followed one simple order."

I look away from him. "This is your fault. You're a liar and a fraud."

"I will not take blame for this. Did you ever consider asking me about that room yourself? I might have told you."

A chill grips my spine. That has to be a lie, too.

"Oh, but of course you wouldn't," Rian says, that anger in his tone growing stronger. "Because Prince Corrick convinced you that *I* wasn't to be trusted, even though every decision *he* makes is fraught with conflict and unnecessary risk. Just look at where you are right now."

He might as well slap me across the face.

"In truth," Rian says, "I lied about very little. Nothing more than was necessary."

"You lied about *everything!*"

"Eat the food, Tessa."

I don't want to take the food from his hand, and I can't quite make myself spit at him the way I heard Bella do.

I glare at him instead. "What are you going to do to us?"

"I'm going to keep you where I can see you until we're out of reach of those brigantines and we're past Oren Crane's stronghold. Then you're all free to go wherever you like, with the exception of Prince Corrick."

I feel the blood drain from my face. "You're going to kill him?"

"No. People only want to kill you when you're the king. When you're a prince, you're generally worth more alive. Trust me. I know the difference."

I want to declare that Harristan will never pay a ransom for Corrick's return, but he will. I know he will. He'd likely offer the entire kingdom for his brother.

Rian knows it, too. I can see it in his expression.

"So all this time, you were only after money," I say, seething. "Money and power. All that disdain, and you're no better than the consuls."

"No!" he snaps, irritation plain on his face. "Again, I lied about very little. Ostriary is desperate for steel. I have made promises that must be fulfilled. What peace I was able to achieve is *very* tenuous. If I returned empty-handed, I might have lost the faith of the people, and Oren would have swept in to claim everything."

"He'll do it anyway," Bella calls in a singsong voice before breaking into a fit of coughing. "I hope he hangs you from the bow. Upside down." A cough. "Naked. Painted with honey for the gulls."

Rian rolls his eyes. "Last chance," he says to me, holding up the slice of fruit.

"No."

"Suit yourself." He eats it himself and moves away.

Emotion threatens to overwhelm me again, and I have to take a deep breath. I probably should have taken the fruit. It makes no sense to lose my strength when I might need it later.

Then again, the ship is rocking in the strong current, the wind beating the sails so hard that the rigging rattles with every gust. The only thing worse than being tied with my hands behind my back would be the prospect of vomiting on myself in this position. Despite the fact that we're bound on the deck, the crew has been working tirelessly, moving sails and tying ropes and adjusting chains when Gwyn calls orders.

I make the mistake of looking out at the ocean just as a swell of seawater comes over the side, and for a brief second, I feel like I'm staring straight into the ocean, like the only thing keeping me in the boat is the rope binding my wrists.

Then the boat rights itself, and I'm staring at a wildly bobbing horizon.

One of those brigantines is definitely closer.

A whistle sounds from high overhead, and I crane my neck back.

Up at the top of the mast, Marchon clings to the narrowest part of the rigging, where Corrick nearly fell. I'm almost instantly dizzy, but he's got legs wrapped through the ropes, holding him in place.

"Cap!" he yells, and even in the wind, I can hear the urgency in his voice. "Get your spyglass."

The ocean swells again, and water splashes onto the deck. My breath catches.

"Is that normal?" I call to anyone nearby.

Tor looks over from where he's winding rope around a cleat. He laughs. "Oh, Chaos Isle gets a lot worse than that, miss."

Great.

Rian strides across the deck to fetch a spyglass from his quarters. He takes one quick look, then swears. "Brock!" he calls. "Roll those cannons. Tor! Be ready to man the bilge pump." The ocean swells again, and even Rian has to grab hold of the rigging. Several of the men shout as the ship tilts in the churning tide.

But a new worry has lodged in my thoughts. *Cannons.* "What's happening?" I demand, yanking at my bindings. "Why are you rolling cannons?"

"Because *they* are rolling cannons." He looks past me, to where Corrick must be tethered. "That ship doesn't seem overly friendly now, Your Highness."

"Maybe they know you're a lying bastard," Corrick calls back.

My heart skips to hear his voice sound so strong.

"If you let me go," Corrick says, "we could try to hail them. I can speak on your behalf."

Rian seems to consider this for a fraction of a second. "I could never trust you."

"You can trust that I don't want to drown with my hands tied to your mast."

"Please," I call. I think of the moment in the darkened hallway, when he was going to kill Rocco. Gwyn was urging him to do it, but then he didn't.

Because I asked.

Corrick was right: I do have the captain's ear. "Please, Rian," I beg. "Think of your crew."

He stares back at me, his stormy eyes full. "I always think of my crew." He sighs tightly, then unhooks his fingers from the rigging. He draws a dagger from his belt.

I don't know what that means, whether he's going to untie Corrick or something else.

I don't get the chance to ask. A loud crack echoes across the sea, just as Marchon leaps down to the deck. "Cannonball!" he shouts.

Just as the ball of black steel slams right into him, driving the man straight through the deck in an explosion of blood and splintered wood.

I'm staring, aghast, when Bella starts laughing hysterically.

"Oh, Rian," she says between bursts of laughter. "I think this is going to be even better than what my father would have planned."

CHAPTER THIRTY-FIVE

Corrick

Noise is everywhere at once, the crew shouting, people scream-ing, cannons booming. I watched Marchon get driven through the deck, torn apart by splintering wood, and the scent of blood and smoke in the air churns my stomach. It's the most horrific thing I've ever seen, and that's saying something.

"Rian!" I shout. "Rian, cut us loose!"

He doesn't answer. No one answers.

"Tessa!" I call.

Nothing. So many people are shouting conflicting orders that I can't hear my own thoughts. All the while, Bella is laughing hys-terically. The ship dips and sways, water splashing over the edge.

I swear I see one of the crewmen go over the railing.

Maybe these bindings aren't bad after all.

But then I see Lochlan come up from below, crawling along the deck. The ship is rocking so forcefully that he can't stay on his feet. Another cannonball comes screaming through the air, and men cry out—but this one smashes through the railing to land in the water below.

Lochlan keeps crawling across the deck. His jaw is tight, his face a mask of determination. His eyes look up and meet mine.

And then I realize he has a dagger in one hand.

My chest clenches tight. I'm lashed to the mast. A sitting duck.

I hold my breath. The ship pitches wildly in the current, but he stays low to the deck and keeps crawling.

"Rocco," I say. "Thank you for your service."

He looks over sharply, then follows my gaze to look at Lochlan, who's gained ground.

Another cannonball flies overhead, and for an instant, the shouting crew goes silent. Then it soars between the masts, narrowly missing the sails.

"Tessa," I shout, but there's no answer again. I have no idea whether she can hear me. I yell anyway. "I love you."

Lochlan has reached me, and he grabs hold of my shirt, dragging himself to his knees. The wind whips his hair around his face, and light glints on that dagger.

The entire ship is probably going to sink, but my life is going to end right here. I can see the hatred in his eyes.

But then he says, "Oh, stop being so dramatic," just before he jerks me forward and cuts my bindings.

—◁┼▷—

Together, Lochlan and I begin to cut the others free, with the exception of Bella. She's just too much of a wild card, and I know she'd rather see the ship sink. But there's something more dangerous about being *untied* with the ship this violent. I can't keep my feet, so I have to crawl like Lochlan did. When I get to Tessa, my heart nearly stops when I see blood on her temple—but she's breathing and dazed. Alive.

She grips tightly to my neck the instant her hands are free, and it reminds me of another night when I freed her of bindings and she grabbed me so desperately. Then, she wanted me to make everything all right. I couldn't.

I can't now either.

"They're attacking," she says. "We're going to sink."

"I'm hoping Rian is a better sailor than he is a king," I say, just as another cannonball tears through one of the sails and screams erupt from somewhere. Another blast sounds, and the ship shudders, and for an instant, I think she's right: we're about to be ripped apart.

But then I see a brief explosion on the closer brigantine. The *Dawn Chaser* has returned fire.

"Come on," I say to Tessa. "We're too exposed. Rocco!"

I struggle across the deck to get her into Rian's stateroom, where maps and markers are scattered across the floor from the battle.

I unwind Tessa's arms from around my neck. "Stay here," I say to her, just as Rocco makes it to the doorway. He's so pale, one hand clutching at his waist. "Help Rocco."

She opens her mouth to protest, and I add, "This time, *wait*."

Then I slam the door and try to determine where I can do more to help.

That ship keeps firing. So does this one. Many of the crew have gone below, but there are two men moving sails. I don't see Gwyn or Sablo *anywhere*. There's a part of me that's hoping Rian was the one who went overboard, but I see him at the stern, gripping tight to the wheel.

"Tell me what to do!" I shout at him from the steps.

I expect him to tell me to jump overboard, but he doesn't. Maybe he doesn't care who helps as long as his ship is at risk. "Take hold," he says. "Keep it straight. I need to help them."

I take hold.

It's like grabbing on to a bucking horse.

Rian grabs the wheel again before it can spin too much. "You have to keep it straight!" he snaps. "If you can't do it, get off the helm."

"I've got it," I say, breathless, digging in my feet.

He points directly ahead. "Nothing else matters if you can keep it straight. The current will fight you. This is where other Kandalan ships have wrecked. This is where *they'll* wreck, if we're lucky."

"Who? The brigantines?"

But he's gone, moving down to the main deck. Rian seems to have no trouble staying on his feet, and it seems almost preternatural when the ship tilts and sways. By some miracle, we haven't started to sink—and it's been a while since a cannon has fired.

Below me, Rian is shouting orders to the few men on deck, but I don't know what he's saying. They immediately move to opposite masts, unhooking chains and untying rigging. The ocean surges over and over again, water flowing over the sides. I grip tight to the wheel, not sure if I'm doing any good at all, but I do my best to dig my feet into the wet deck.

I take a chance and look up past the churning ocean to see the brigantines, and they're farther away than I expected, but they're rocking in the tumultuous sea just like we are. Somehow we're gaining ground.

And then, while I watch, one of the ships seems to shudder. All at once, it begins to break apart.

Then the other.

Within minutes, both ships are in pieces in the ocean, and we're sailing farther away.

I stare in shock.

But we're still rocking hard, water everywhere, the wind so fierce it's a never-ending scream in my ears. I feel a jolt in the wheel, and it almost steals my grip. The world seems to turn upside down, and the *Dawn Chaser* shudders just like those brigantines.

Somewhere over the wind, Rian shouts, "Hold that wheel!"

So I do. Water comes from all directions, and my hands are slick, my feet skidding on the deck. My teeth clench so hard that I taste blood.

Just when I'm worried I'm never going to be strong enough to keep a grip, Rian appears. His hair is soaked from the constant surge of seawater, the wind making it difficult for even him to walk.

"I usually have Sablo," he shouts. "We'll have to do it together."

I shift a bit sideways, to give him room. He reaches to grab hold just as a swell strikes the boat, tipping us dangerously sideways. The wind grabs him, and I see the panic in his eyes as his feet leave the deck. He's going to go over.

I reach out and snatch the edge of his jacket. For a terrifying moment, I don't think it'll be enough, that he'll rip free of my fingers and that will be the end of him.

But the ship rights itself and he slams into me.

"I told you to hold the wheel!" he snaps, right in my ear.

"You're so very welcome," I snap back.

But then the wheel tries to wrench free of my grip, and we both grab hold, side by side, riding out the stormy sea together.

Chapter Thirty-Six

Corrick

We don't pull free from Chaos Isle until darkness falls over the ship, and the sea suddenly grows calm, fog moving in over the water. The ship is eerily quiet. Casualties are many, including Silas, who must have gone overboard during the fray, leaving me with Rocco as my remaining guardsman. Bella is gone, too, no longer tied to the mast where we left her. I haven't seen Gwyn, and I'm afraid to ask after little Anya, but I hear from Lochlan that Rian's lieutenant is patching a hole in the galley with her daughter at her side. There's a gaping hole in the deck where Marchon died, and most of the railing is gone along the bow. Apparently there's another hole belowdecks, but nothing below the water line, which is why we haven't sunk. Most of the surviving crew have retired to catch a few hours of rest, and I've told Rocco to do the same, but there's no chance I'm sleeping anytime soon.

At midnight, Tessa has spent hours patching injuries and

stitching wounds, and I convince her to rest as well, but I head above to find Rian.

He's at the helm again, which shouldn't surprise me, but it does. I have no idea where things stand between us, but I haven't been tied to a mast again, which seems promising.

I stop at the top of the stairs that lead to the helm. "Permission to approach, Your Majesty?"

"Very funny," he says tersely. "What do you need?"

"I was hoping you might finally be honest with me."

"You mean after your countrymen killed my navigator?"

I flinch. I hadn't fully considered that regardless of who sent those ships, Kandalan forces really did attack his crew and kill his people.

But Kandala isn't the only country at fault here.

"Yes," I say. "After you hid your identity, lied about your motives, and *your* countrymen killed my guardsman."

He looks over. It's too dark to make out much of his expression, and I wish I'd brought a lantern.

"You should have stayed out of that room," he says.

I study him. He might be a strong sailor, but if any of his story is true, he hasn't been the king of Ostriary for long. I wonder how much of what's happened on board this ship could boil down to his inexperience. "And you should have approached Harristan as a king intending to establish a trade agreement with a neighboring monarch. Regardless of what you think of me, my brother is a reasonable man. He would have listened. He would have negotiated. My very presence here should be proof of that."

He glances over again, and says nothing.

"You brought me on board with the intent to begin negotiations between Kandala and Ostriary," I say.

He snorts a bit derisively. "And how do you think that's going?"

"I'm standing here, aren't I?"

I wait. Water slaps the hull down below.

Eventually, Rian sighs and runs a hand across his jaw. "You said I should have approached your brother as myself. I thought about it—but at first, we didn't know King Harristan was in power. What I said about King Lucas was true. There was bad blood between Ostriary and Kandala, stretching back decades. The old king may have been my father, but—" He scoffs. "The old king was a *lot* of people's father. I was raised as distant kin to royalty. Even when he died, I didn't want the throne. But everyone else *did*, and the islands started to turn on each other. I truly didn't speak many lies. I really did sail the waters looking for survivors. I just wanted to help. One of those men was Captain Blakemore, and I learned his story. I met his son. I helped him rebuild this ship, and we helped *more* people. I gradually formed a crew, and as we helped more and more people, they began begging *me* to defend them. Before long, I had people on every island swearing allegiance, begging me to make a claim for the throne. But Oren Crane still held the southern point, and everyone was tired of fighting. We were desperate for steel to rebuild. I promised the people that I would seek a new trade agreement with Kandala, but everything I knew from Captain Blakemore warned me to be cautious." His voice has grown a bit hollow, and he stops there.

"What happened?"

"Oren tried to stop us from passing. He attacked the ship. The real Captain Blakemore died in the battle." He hesitates. "Oren took his wife and son prisoner." Another hesitation. "But I took his daughter. Bella."

"As insurance. So you can get back."

"Yes."

I think about this for a while. "That still doesn't explain why you didn't just say who you were."

"Again, I thought about it. Truly, that was my plan. We docked in Port Karenin first, and that was easy. The *Dawn Chaser* could fly under the flag of Kandala, so no one gave us a passing glance." He pauses, then looks over. "And there, we learned of the fever sickness that seemed to be destroying your country—as well as the harsh penalties for theft and smuggling Moonflower, since you believe it's a cure."

"But you had Moonflower!" I say. "If you didn't know about it, how did you know to bring so much?"

"I didn't bring it as a cure," he says, looking at me like I'm crazy. "In Ostriary, we recognize Moonflower for what it is—a poison."

I roll that around in my head and say, "How is Moonflower a poison?"

"When you boil the stems," he says. "It causes the fever and the cough. That's how I've been able to keep Bella subdued. If you do it long enough, it can be permanently debilitating, but I only needed a few weeks. Making an elixir of the petals will generally reverse the effects."

I'm pressing my hands together over my mouth. I need Tessa. I need her knowledge.

But Rian is talking. I need to stay right here.

"Are you saying the people of Kandala are poisoned?" I say quickly. "How?"

"I don't know—but I admit to being curious when I learned that two full sectors are almost solely dedicated to growing Moonflower now—and there seems to be quite a wealthy trade to be had in selling petals to cure the 'sickness.' All Captain Blakemore knew was that the attempt on Harristan's life was thwarted when he was young, but it wasn't until later that—"

"*What attack on Harristan's life?*"

"Your Consul Montague tried to poison him to force your parents into demanding a higher price on steel—but Ostriary felt betrayed and refused to barter. Maybe Montague figured out a new way to make silver . . . or someone did."

Consul Montague—who later tried to assassinate my parents.

I run my hands through my hair.

Not only do I need Tessa, but I need Quint and Harristan, too.

I need to be back in the Royal Sector.

But now I'm on a boat in the middle of the ocean.

"All this time, you thought *we* were poisoning the people?" I say sharply. No wonder he hates me so much. Locking people in a room, indeed.

"I wasn't entirely sure," he says. "King Harristan was so invested in a new source of Moonflower that I didn't believe it was him. I suspected you for quite a while—but then you and Tessa were almost religious about ensuring your people took Moonflower tea once you climbed on board. But it's obviously someone in your inner circle."

I still can't make this make sense in my head. "For what purpose?"

Rian shrugs. "To prevent an uprising? It's clear one is brewing anyway." He pauses. "Once we docked in Artis and I learned of your reputation, it was clear to me that we could not begin as equals. Your country is overrun with sedition and sabotage."

I can't even argue the point. He's right.

"So now what?" I say.

"Now I'm going to do exactly what I said I'm going to do. We're going to dock in Ostriary. You will grant me a trade agreement—or I will hold you for ransom and demand one from Harristan."

"But—but I saved your *life*."

"I wouldn't have needed saving if those ships hadn't followed. As far as I'm concerned, that was an act of war."

I almost can't believe I'm hearing this. "So you're going to retaliate from your broken-down ship?"

"I don't need to retaliate. I need steel. *Again*, I have been mostly forthright from the beginning. I don't care about Kandala. I have no desire to go to war. Neither of our countries can sustain it. I need steel. You need to help your people. I will not get embroiled in your political scheming. Trade or not, but you have until we dock to make your decision. For now, we just need to get past Oren Crane." His expression is tense. "With a ship that's taken heavy damage, a hamstrung crew, and no Bella to trade for safe passage."

"When will we reach his territory?" I say.

"It's *my* territory," he snaps.

"Fine, when will we reach *your*—"

I break off when I hear a distant whistle, and then a flaming arrow comes sailing out of the darkness to strike the sail.

Rian swears. "Right now."

CHAPTER THIRTY-SEVEN

Tessa

I'm woken by shouts and screaming. I sit straight up in bed just as the boat shudders with the sound of an explosion.

We're under attack again.

I'm barefoot, in nothing more than my chemise and trousers, but I sprint for the door and find Rocco in the hallway. I stitched up the knife wound on his abdomen hours ago, but his coloring is a bit ashen instead of the warm brown I'm used to, and I'm worried he's lost too much blood.

Another explosion rocks the ship, and I put a hand against the wall to brace myself. We have bigger problems.

"Is there another brigantine?" I say.

"We need to get above," Rocco says.

I have to use hands and feet to climb the stairs because the water is so choppy. Rocco is right at my back. When we make it onto the deck, one of the smaller sails is on fire, red flames crawling along the edge to snake into the night sky. Brock is climbing the rigging with a bucket of water over one arm.

"Get that fire out!" Rian is shouting. "It's giving them a target!"

Brock tosses the water at the fire, but it only douses half. While I watch, another flaming arrow comes sailing through the air. Rocco pushes me out of the way as it embeds itself in the deck, just where I was standing.

He swears, grabs the arrow shaft, and yanks it free to toss over the railing.

Another arrow flies through the air, aiming right for the sail.

Worse. It catches Brock right in the middle of his back. He jerks, his hands slipping from the rigging, and drops to the deck below to land, motionless. The bucket hits the deck and rolls away.

More shouts come from below—and I become distantly aware of shouts coming from somewhere to our left. The *Dawn Chaser* shudders as one of the cannons fires, and a moment later, I hear the cannonball connect with a ship somewhere across the water.

"Corrick," I say to Rocco desperately. "Where's Corrick?"

But the guard is looking up at the sail. Some of the fire was doused, but it's smoldering at the edge. "That sail needs to come down. He's right. It's a target—but it'll catch the others."

And Brock was just shot down from climbing the rigging. Half the crew is missing or manning the cannons down below.

I remember Rian telling me about the rigging, about the fouled lines. I climbed the mast once. I can do it again.

"Give me your dagger," I say. "I'll cut it down."

"Miss Tessa—"

Another flaming arrow lands on the deck. Rian spots me and calls, "Tessa! You need to get below."

Rocco grabs this arrow and throws it into the water after the other.

I have half a mind to grab his dagger myself, but then Corrick is there beside me, wind whipping at his hair. "Tessa," he says. "Tessa, you need to get below."

I point. "The sail—the sail needs to come down—"

"I know. I'll go." He takes my face in his hands and kisses me. Then he looks to Rocco. "Get her below."

"Corrick!" I shout, but he's already moved away. Just like the night of the competition, his hands hook in the rigging, and suddenly, he's ten feet off the deck.

Beside that flaming sail, he's an easy target, just like Brock was. My breath catches in my throat.

There's no way I'm letting Rocco take me below.

He doesn't even try.

Another arrow comes sailing onto the ship, but this time it aims for Rian. He lets go of the wheel and dives out of the way. The flaming shaft drives into the deck at his feet, but he pulls it free and tosses it over the railing like Rocco did.

He sees me and points at Corrick. "Hold the beam!" he shouts at me. "When he cuts that loose, it'll swing."

Hold the beam. I stare at the complicated maze of sails and ropes and rigging in the darkness.

"This one," Rocco says, tugging me toward one of the beams. He's a bit breathless, and I'm reminded that he probably shouldn't be on the deck either. Sparks rain down around us, but I grab hold of the stretch of wood and grip tight, digging my feet into the deck.

"I told you to get her below," Corrick shouts down.

Rocco ignores him. "There, Miss Tessa. Put your feet against the mast."

Corrick must begin sawing at the ropes, because I feel the instant there's a bit of give in the beam. It jerks hard and nearly gets me off my feet. I whimper from the strain.

Rocco is stronger, by far, but his face has gone pale, his brown fingers white where they grip the wood.

Then, without warning, the beam stabilizes. I blink and look up.

Lochlan has a tight hold on the wood beside me. "Watch yourself," he says. "We don't want it to come down on top of us."

The warning is a moment too late, because suddenly canvas and ropes are falling. A hand grabs me around the waist and pulls me out of the way just as the beam swings wildly, knocking me in the shoulder.

Then I'm free, sprawled on the deck, a male arm around my waist. I look over, expecting Rocco.

Instead, it's Lochlan. His face is close, full of sweat and bruises, but his eyes lock on mine.

"Are you all right?" he says, and I'm so stunned that all I can do is nod.

I get to my knees just as Corrick drops back to the deck. It's been a few minutes since I've seen any flaming arrows, and I think maybe it's a good sign, until someone from down below shouts, "They're readying cannons."

"Who is it?" I gasp.

"Oren Crane," Lochlan says, as if that explains everything. He lets me go, then moves toward Corrick. He's pointing across the water. "Watch for cannon fire. We won't see the ball in the dark."

The *Dawn Chaser* bucks and shudders, and an explosion rocks below. *We've* fired.

A moment later, I hear the impact. The shouts from out on the water seem to indicate we've made a direct hit. The sudden cheering down below confirms it.

"We just need to get past them!" Rian calls down. "They can't follow now!"

I look across at Corrick, who's with Lochlan near the railing. His eyes meet mine, and I take a deep breath for the first time in what seems like hours.

Then a loud *crack* echoes across the water, and I see the blast of fire that lights up enough of the other ship that I can see that it is, in fact, sinking.

I remember Lochlan's words.

We won't see the ball in the dark.

The *Dawn Chaser* takes the impact. Wood explodes everywhere, and I'm knocked off my feet. This time Rocco catches me, pulling me down to the deck, covering me with his body as bits of wood and steel rain down. I can't breathe. I can't think. My heart is a wild roar in my ears, those sails snapping overhead, chains rattling.

It takes a second. A minute. An hour. An eternity. Eventually Rocco eases off me, and we sit up on the deck in the moonlight. I smell burned wood and smoldering sailcloth.

In front of me, there's a ten-foot gap in the deck. The entire railing is missing, and I can see clear through to the deck below. I'm looking into the guards' quarters.

My heart stops.

"Corrick," I whisper. The word is barely out of my mouth before I'm screaming it. "Corrick! Corrick! Corrick!" I stumble toward the railing, staring into the blackness of the water. I can't stop screaming his name, even when my voice turns harsh and ragged. He's in the water. I need to go after him.

Arms close around me from behind. "Miss Tessa. Miss Tessa. We're going too fast. He's not down there."

I remember the cannonball driving Marchon straight through the deck.

I imagine that happening to Corrick.

I imagine him drowning.

I choke on a sob, then fight Rocco's grip. "Corrick!" I scream. "Rian! Turn back! Turn back! You have to turn back!"

But he doesn't turn back.

Rocco doesn't let go.

Corrick is gone.

CHAPTER THIRTY-EIGHT

Harristan

It's well after midnight, and the forest is quiet, but I follow Karri along the pitch-black trails. Up ahead, there's a glow between the trees, and my heart skips in my chest. Quint is just beside me, the two guards at my back. We're all in heavy, hooded black cloaks, but they obscure my vision, and I almost wish we didn't have them.

But I can't afford to be recognized. Not yet.

When we draw close, a low hum of conversation is audible through the trees. I expected dozens of people. Maybe a hundred.

This looks like more than a thousand.

I nearly stop short. "We'll be seen," I say to Karri.

"No," she says. "We have runners to draw the night patrol. That's how they were able to attack so many Moonflower shipments."

My eyes widen, but I continue.

Karri steps up in front of the crowd, taking a torch from a man waiting there. We cling to the shadows between the trees. Thorin is to my left, Quint to my right, with Saeth following closely behind. My breathing is still loud in my chest, and every breath feels like a struggle.

I haven't taken a dose of Moonflower since Maxon gave me his.

A tiny flare of panic lodges in my heart, but I shove the fear away. People in the Wilds sometimes go for *weeks* without medicine. I can last a day or two.

Karri steps onto a wide stump and calls out to the people. Her voice carries well. "You know Lochlan is gone, on a ship with Prince Corrick—"

"The consuls said those ships have sunk!" a woman calls back. "That the king killed them both!"

"Those are lies," Karri says. "The consuls are trying to overthrow the king again, while Prince Corrick and Lochlan are away."

A murmur runs through the crowd. My heart keeps pounding. At my side, I can feel Thorin's tension. He and Saeth are two men. We have no horses. Few weapons. No matter what happens here, they can't hold off a thousand rebels who might want me dead.

But Karri raises her hands, and the people quiet. They like her. They respect her.

"The stakes are different this time," she calls. "We have another chance at rebellion."

"Because the King's Justice is gone?" calls a man. "You think the king won't have his army kill us all this time?"

"The king is gone!" someone else yells from farther back. "There's a bounty on his head!"

"Because he lied!" shouts a woman. "He lied about the Moonflower!"

Another murmur rolls through the crowd, more angry this time.

I inhale, preparing to step forward, but Quint reaches out and catches my wrist.

"Wait, Your Majesty," he says quietly. "Allow her to hold the crowd."

I glance down at his hand on my arm, but his eyes are on the people, on Karri.

"He didn't lie!" Karri calls. "The consuls have lied to you all. The king has been trying to protect his people."

"It's true!" calls a little voice. "The king was the Fox!"

Violet. She shouldn't be here. It's too dangerous.

A low snicker rolls through the crowd, but Karri doesn't laugh. "The king *was* the Fox. Just as Prince Corrick was Weston Lark."

Complete silence falls over the crowd.

Finally, a man yells, "If the king is trying to protect us from the consuls, why is he hiding?"

"*Now,*" Quint whispers, and he squeezes my wrist.

In that instant, time seems to freeze. I've stood before my people, countless times.

I've never done it without my brother at my side.

Corrick. Please be well.

But then I think of Quint's words from the carriage.

Perhaps it's time to speak for yourself.

I draw back the hood of my cloak and stride forward, limping, to join Karri. At first, no one recognizes me, which isn't a surprise. But then a few whispers start to run through the crowd.

Before they can turn into shouts, I say, "I'm not hiding. I'm here. With you. For you."

Silence falls again.

I stand in front of them all, my hood drawn back. Fully exposed.

Fully vulnerable. Torches and lanterns glow in the darkness, but so many faces stare back at me. They're wary. They're worried. They just want to be safe and well.

I want the same.

"You know what people like Consul Sallister will do if they're in power," I say. "You know what will happen if he is able to take the throne. We need to stop him."

"So what?" someone yells. "You think you're going to order us into battle against your own people?"

"No," I say, feeling the pound of my heart. "I think I'm going to lead you."

CHAPTER THIRTY-NINE

Tessa

I'm soaking wet and freezing on the deck of the ship. Fog is everywhere.

I feel nothing.

Corrick is gone.

I've lost him again.

Lochlan is gone.

I'm sorry, Karri.

A hand touches my shoulder. "Tessa."

Rian. I jerk away. I don't trust my voice. I choke on a sob.

"Please." My voice breaks. "Please go away."

He moves closer. "Tessa, I'm—"

"Keep your distance," Rocco says sharply. I didn't even realize he was nearby. I turn my head a fraction and see he's facing down Rian.

I think the captain is going to snap at the guardsman, but he doesn't. He straightens and takes a step back. "We'll reach Fairde before daybreak. We're in safer waters now. I thought you should know."

I don't care. I want to sink the ship myself. I say nothing.

"I told you to keep your distance," Rocco says again.

Rian inhales—but then he must think better of it, because he moves away.

"Thank you, Rocco," I whisper.

"Yes, Miss Tessa."

I swallow. We've both lost too much. "You don't . . . you don't have to guard me."

After a moment, he sits down beside me. After another moment, he takes my hand and gives it a squeeze. It's kind. Brotherly.

"There's no one left to guard," he says quietly.

I put my face in my hands. "Do you think we'll ever be able to get back?"

"I don't know."

There's something terrifyingly bleak about that.

We'll reach Fairde before daybreak. I thought you should know.

I draw a shuddering breath, then swipe the tears off my cheeks. I've been too naive for too long. Too trusting of too many people. All I ever wanted to do was help the people around me, and all it's ever led to is pain and suffering.

So I sit up straighter and I look at Rocco. "I don't know what to expect in Fairde," I say. "But we're all that's left, Rocco. We need to stick together. You and me."

"Yes, Miss Tessa."

I shake my head. "No Miss Tessa anymore. Just Tessa."

He nods. "Just Erik." He holds out a hand.

"Erik," I whisper. I clasp his hand. His almost dwarfs mine.

For an instance the fog breaks ahead, revealing a long stretch of glittering water. Beyond, I see a few scattered lights on the water, and my heart skips, expecting another attack. But they aren't more ships. They're fires or lanterns or something to indicate land.

And then, as I stare, the moonlight glistens on a large structure in the distance, a castle stretching into the sky.

I feel a band of steel wrapping around my spine, chasing away all the pain that feels too overwhelming. "I need you to help me with something," I say to Rocco—to *Erik*.

"Anything," he says.

"When we get to Ostriary," I say, "I want you to teach me to fight."

CHAPTER FORTY

Corrick

I wake up vomiting seawater.

It's unpleasant, but vastly preferable to getting kicked in the ribs, which is what happens next.

"I asked your name!" a man barks.

I can't breathe. I can't think, which is why I croak out, "What?"

"Your name."

I try to open my eyes, but everything is dark. I move my hands, and sand grits beneath my palms. I'm facedown, and I try to rise to my knees.

Someone kicks me back down again. "Your *name*."

I open my mouth to say *Corrick*, but I cough on a lungful of seawater that I spit all over my hands.

"I told you!" a man snaps, and it takes me a moment to place the voice. *Lochlan.* "He's just one of the prince's servants."

"Is that true?" A boot nudges me in the side.

My breathing is ragged. *One of the prince's servants?* I don't understand. I can't think.

"Come on, Wes," Lochlan says, and there's a bite of urgency to his tone. "Tell Mr. Crane your name."

Mr. Crane.

Come on, Wes.

I shove my hand into the sand and flip over. A dozen men and women stand over me. All are heavily armed. I can smell blood on the air, and I desperately hope it isn't mine.

One drops to a knee beside me and puts the tip of a dagger against my chin. He's the tallest man I've ever seen, with a line of jagged scars from his eyebrow to his neck. "Yes," he says. "Tell Mr. Crane your name."

I swallow thickly, but then my eyes land on Lochlan, at the edge of the circle.

"Come on, Wes. They're going to kill you if you don't talk soon."

I give a weak cough and look back up at the scarred man.

I must take too long, because he moves to kick me again. "Your! Name!"

I snap a hand out and grab his ankle, jerking hard, using his momentum to knock him to the ground. He goes down swearing. I expect someone else to grab me, but they laugh and whistle.

So I roll to my knees and grab his dagger out of his hand. I have it against his chest before he can roll away.

I spit seawater beside his face. "My name is Weston Lark," I say roughly. "What's yours?"

ACKNOWLEDGMENTS

Someday I'm going to write shorter acknowledgments, but today is not that day.

That said, this is my fifteenth published novel, so I am going to make use of the copy-and-paste function on my computer.

As always, I am so incredibly grateful to my husband, Michael. I am so thankful for every moment we have together, and look forward to every moment in the future. Thank you for being my best friend for all these years.

Mary Kate Castellani is my incredible editor at Bloomsbury, and I was really worried we wouldn't be able to pull this one off—but she kept saying to me, "It's fine! It'll be fine!" Even when I was sending sobbing emails about how it was impossible to write a single word at the end of 2021. But here we are. It's fine. Mary Kate, I have loved working with you on every single book. You're brilliant. [I totally copied that line from the last book, BUT IT'S SO TRUE.]

Suzie Townsend is my incredible agent, and I am so grateful for your day-to-day guidance, especially when I send you panicked emails at 5:30 a.m. I am so incredibly lucky to have you, Sophia, Kendra, and the entire team at New Leaf on my side. Thank you all so much for everything.

The team at Bloomsbury is beyond compare when it comes to their dedication to every book they work on, and I am so grateful for everything. Huge thanks to Kei Nakatsuka, Lily Yengle, Erica Barmash, Faye Bi, Phoebe Dyer, Beth Eller, Valentina Rice, Diane Aronson, Jeffrey Curry, Jeannette Levy, Donna Mark, Adrienne Vaughan, Rebecca McNally, Ellen Holgate, Pari Thompson, Emily Marples, Jet Purdie, and every single person at Bloomsbury who has a hand in making my books a success.

Huge thanks to the Cursebreaker Street Team! If you're a part of it, thank YOU. It means so much to me to know that there are *thousands* of you interested in my books, and I will never forget everything you've done to spread the word about my stories. Thank you all so very much.

Huge debts of gratitude go to my dear writing friends, Melody Wukitch, Dylan Roche, Gillian McDunn, Jodi Picoult, Jennifer Armentrout, Phil Stamper, Stephanie Garber, Isabel Ibañez, Ava Tusek, Bradley Spoon, and Amalie Howard, because I honestly don't know how I would get through the day without your support. I am so grateful to have you all in my life.

Several people read and offered insight into parts of this book while it was in progress, and I want to take a moment to specially thank Jodi Picoult, Gillian McDunn, Reba Gordon, Ava Tusek, and Heather Garcia.

Tremendous thanks to readers, bloggers, librarians, artists, and booksellers all over social media who take the time to post, review, tweet, share, and mention my books. I owe my career to people being so passionate about my characters that they can't help but talk about them. Thank you all.

And many thanks go to YOU! Yes, you. If you're holding this book in your hands, thank you. As always, I am honored that you took the time to invite my characters into your heart.

Finally, tremendous love and thanks to the Kemmerer boys. You surprise me every single day, and I am so very lucky to be your mom. Yes, I copied that paragraph from the last acknowledgments that I wrote (which was a copy of the one I wrote before that), but I still mean every word, and none of you are reading my books yet. So here's a bet. If any of you discover this paragraph before your eighteenth birthday, I owe you an ice cream.